DENNIS RILEY

FORTUNE'S CLOAK MERCY'S BLADE

FROM THE SECRET SCROLLS OF THE IMPERARE

FORTUNE'S CLOAK, MERCY'S BLADE

Written by Dennis Riley.

Darktalon Publishing, LLC

P.O. Box 7293

Amarillo, Texas

79114

ISBN 979-8-9885115-3-3

Cover art by MiblArt.

World map by BMR Williams.

City map by Moreno Paissan & Angela Gubert.

Developmental edits by Derrick Cummings.

www.authordennisriley.com

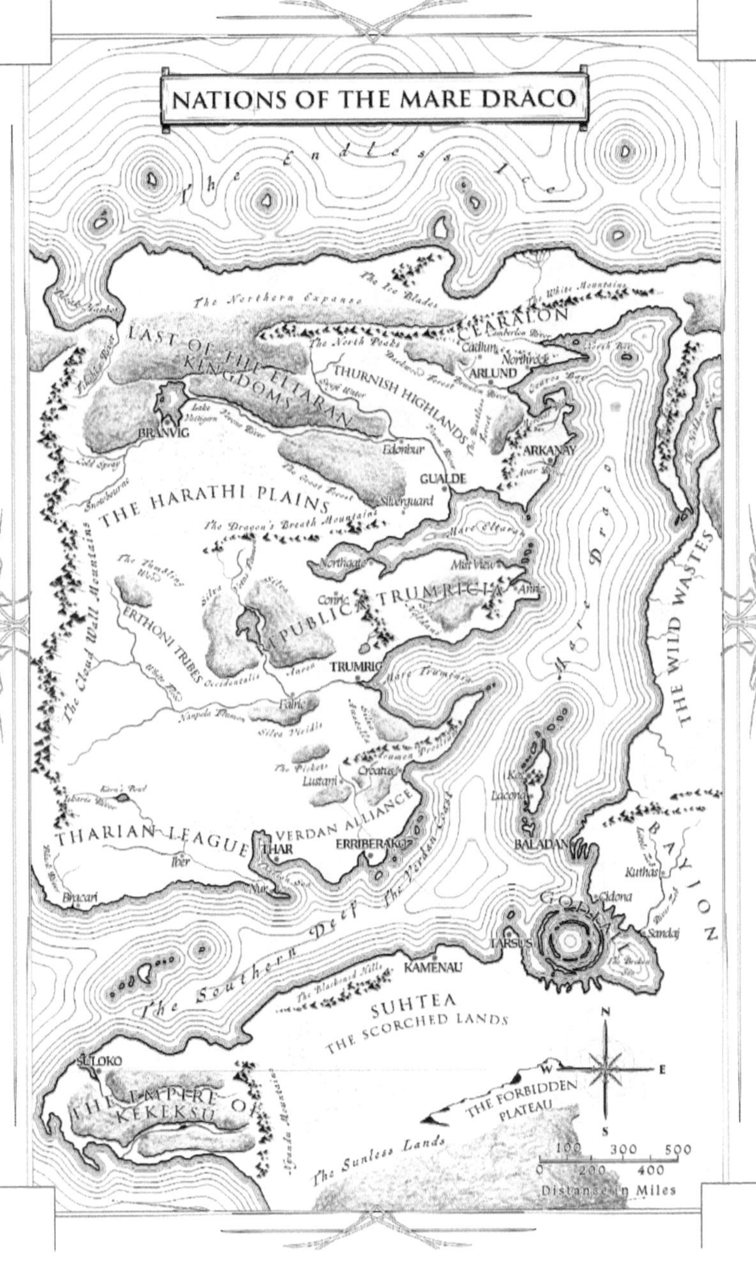

NATIONS OF THE MARE DRACO
The Endless Ice
The Northern Expanse
The Ice Blades
The White Mountains
CEARALON
LAST OF THE ELTARAN KINGDOMS
THURNISH HIGHLANDS
The North Peaks
Cadhun
Northrock
ARLUND
BRANVIG
Edonbur
ARKANAY
GUALDE
Silverguard
THE HARATHI PLAINS
The Dragon's Breath Mountains
Mare Eltaran
Northgate
Mist View
REPUBLIC OF TRUMRICIA
Annis
Corinc
ERTHONI TRIBES OCCIDENTALIS
TRUMRIG
Mare Trumrian
Falric
Silva Viridis
The Fishes
Lustani
Creatus
Kir
Laconia
BALADAN
THE WILD WASTES
BAYIOZ
Kuthas
Cidona
Sandaj
THARIAN LEAGUE
THAR
Iber
VERDAN ALLIANCE
ERRIBERAKO
The Verdan Coast
GOLD
TARSUS
Bracari
Nur
The Southern Deep
KAMENAU
The Blackhand Hills
SUHTEA
THE SCORCHED LANDS
SILOKO
THE EMPIRE OF KEKEKSU
THE FORBIDDEN PLATEAU
The Sunless Lands
N
W   E
S
100   300   500
0   200   400
Distance in Miles

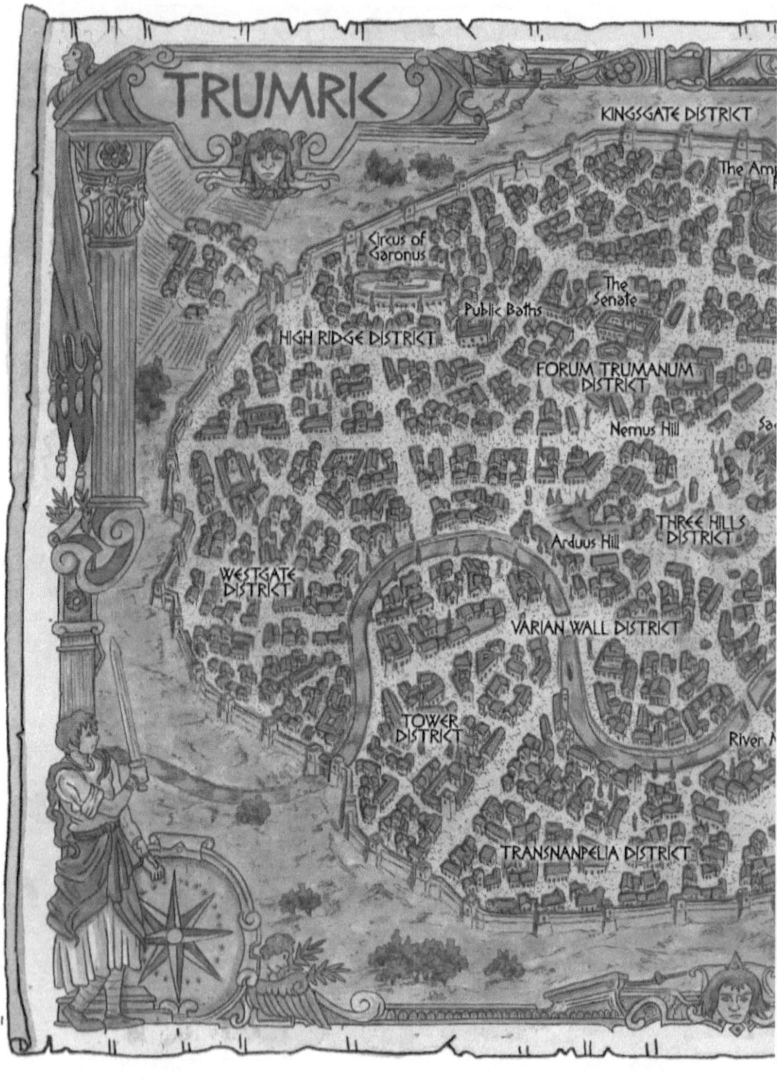

TRUMRIC
KINGSGATE DISTRICT
The Am
Circus of Garonus
Public Baths
The Senate
HIGH RIDGE DISTRICT
FORUM TRUMANUM DISTRICT
Nemus Hill
Sa
THREE HILLS DISTRICT
Arduus Hill
WESTGATE DISTRICT
VARIAN WALL DISTRICT
TOWER DISTRICT
River
TRANSNANPELIA DISTRICT

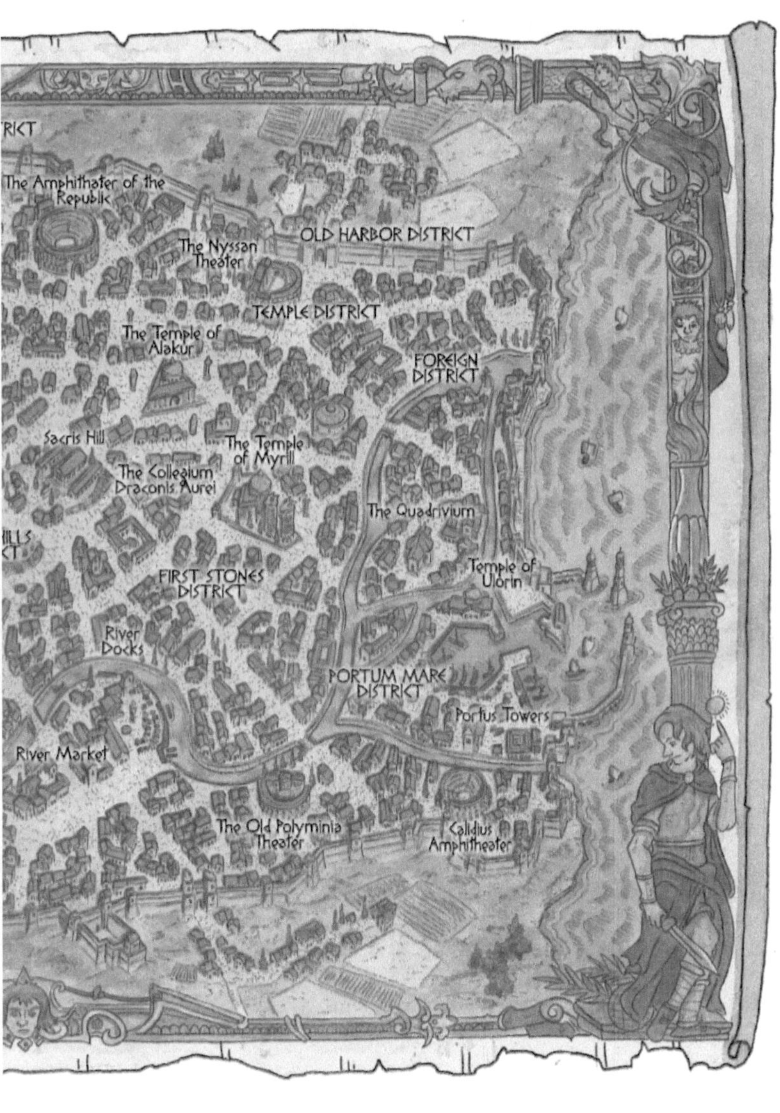

RICT
The Amphithater of the Republic
OLD HARBOR DISTRICT
The Nyssan Theater
TEMPLE DISTRICT
The Temple of Alakur
FOREIGN DISTRICT
Sacris Hill
The Temple of Myrill
The Collegium Draconis Aurei
The Quadrivium
HILLS CT
FIRST STONES DISTRICT
Temple of Ulorin
River Docks
PORTUM MARE DISTRICT
Portus Towers
River Market
The Old Polyminia Theater
Calidius Amphitheater

Table of Contents

Prologue

The Hound of Nyx stalked the streets of Mist View, a most reluctant murderer. Luciano Porteles, the most feared and notorious assassin in the Republic, had never turned his blade on a fellow member of the Dark Assembly. Until today.

Luciano strode past both patrician and plebeian, his thoughts ricocheting between his last assassination and the next. Killing Lepidus had been easy. The vice-addicted vicar had been at his remote villa on the shores of Bella Nostra Bay. Sneaking in had been no challenge; his guards were few, his only companions whores and slaves, and they had fled as soon as the assassin had flashed Aguja, his infamous needle-like dagger. Lepidus, a bloated, lethargic cow of a man, was incapable of defending himself. He was the kind of man Luciano despised: manipulative, lazy, and overindulgent. Once he realized his fate, he had fallen to his knees and begged for his life. Aguja put a swift end to his groveling.

Luciano approached the home of Tycho Gratianus, looking as stoic and stone-faced as a philosopher. No jackal's grin, no hyena's cackle. Like Lepidus, Gratianus was also a *vicar primi* of Mist View's Dark Assembly. But unlike Lepidus, Luciano respected Gratianus, considering him an ally, maybe even a friend. Gratianus had granted the assassin his first notable job, one which had catapulted him into renown within the Dark Assembly. Moreover, he had vouched for him when the business with

Ghostwalker had reached the boiling point. The vicar had earned Luciano's *pietas* over the years, and he returned it freely.

Luciano paused in the middle of the street, and a man carrying a large bundle bumped into him. The slave bowed low and apologized, but Luciano paid him no mind. His thoughts were elsewhere.

How had he gotten here? Sent to Mist View against his will to assassinate two members of the Dark Assembly, the very group which had earlier dispatched him to Trumric with a mission of their own: deal with Marius Secundus and retrieve the Eltaran scroll which had caused them so much trouble.

Luciano's hesitation brought with it an all too familiar response. Yellow tendrils of excruciating pain shot from the recesses of his mind and pierced the back of his eyeballs. He winced, gripping his fists so tightly his palms bled.

The agony subsided, leaving behind a dull throb at his temples. Although the pattern was familiar, he doubted he would ever grow accustomed to it. Cornelius Brocchus, the head of the Transnanpela Collegium, had imprisoned him and hired a Bayjoni Dominator to twist and torture his mind. The Dominator had wandered into the corners of his consciousness, revealing and manipulating long forgotten memories. The process had nearly driven him mad. And when the Dominator retreated, he left behind a mystical saffron spike with a singular purpose. Should Luciano entertain the idea of refusing—or even deferring—Brocchus' orders, the yellow spike would burrow into his brain, punishing him for his defiance.

Luciano stepped up to the doors of Gratianus' two story domus. A Dark Assembly heavy, well-armed and armored, greeted him with a welcoming handshake and a toothy grin.

A short time later, the guards escorted Luciano into Gratianus' famed trophy room. The assassin stepped inside, and the door closed behind him.

He had heard whispers about Gratianus' collection but had never seen it with his own eyes. The chamber was crowded with a dizzying assortment of ancient curiosities, exotic weapons, and monstrous beasts. Perched on a block of volcanic stone, a masterpiece of taxidermy gazed down at him with inky black eyes, its maw opened wide, revealing razor-like teeth. It was part woman, part bird of prey, all abomination. A harpy. He imagined the hellish screeches the thing must have made while alive. Luciano's gaze followed its smoky feathered wings as they stretched out and up, casting predatory shadows across the vaulted trophy room.

"Finally, the Dark Assembly's master assassin has returned."

Luciano looked for Gratianus, but the multitude of mounted beasts and elaborate showcases blocked his view.

"My fellow vicars didn't believe me, but I know you better than they do, Porteles. Your long absence may have raised doubts in some, but I've seen what you're capable of. I knew of your return, and I know why."

Does he know about Lepidus? How could he?

Luciano peered between the avian legs of the stuffed harpy. *Where is he?* A gold Suhtean statue atop an onyx pedestal caught his eye. He recognized the gleaming figure, a slender woman wearing an exotic headpiece, a large necklace, and little else. She held a staff in one hand and a hooked rod in the other. It was the first piece Luciano had ever acquired for the Dark Assembly. He had liberated it from a Suhtean merchant who had fallen fatally behind on his tributes. Luciano had slit his throat, then taken the statue as recompense. That had been years ago, and Luciano was surprised to see it now.

He kept this trophy, all this time? Why?

"You remember. She's beautiful, isn't she?" Gratianus said from somewhere deeper within the room. "When you brought her to me, that was when I knew you were the best. But more than that, you demonstrated your loyalty, Luciano. Just as you have now."

Loyalty. The word cut him deeper than any blade.

"The Eltaran scroll you recovered for us has more import than you know. It passed through many hands, including that wretch Secundus. But now that you're returning it to the Dark Assembly, we'll use it to buy more influence than we've ever held before."

Luciano followed the voice until he found Gratianus standing behind a wide desk, holding a wine cup in each hand. The ostentatious seat behind him was more throne than chair.

"The Eltarans will be very generous upon its return. Extraordinarily so. This scroll—whatever it may be—has great significance to them."

The vicar had dressed for a celebration: a toga befitting a senator, complete with a pomegranate sash draped over his shoulder and long, golden cords hanging around his neck.

Those cords. A slight, feral grin crept across Luciano's face. He had hoped an adequate weapon would present itself, as the guards had confiscated his precious Aguja, as well as his spatha and daggers. Now, one had: Gratianus' own impostrous adornments.

"Come. Let us share cups and celebrate your success." The vicar extended a cup towards Luciano. "Here, my Verdan friend, let us drink to your success. A success which others had doubted, but I had foretold."

Luciano accepted the cup. It held a clear, golden liquid smelling of almond, lemon blossoms, and cool stone. It was no Trumin vintage, but a wine from the vineyards of Lustani, in northern Verdith. The vicar smiled when he saw Luciano's surprise. He stared into his cup, lost himself in it, allowing his mind to dance through sunlight-filled vineyards. The golden light turned sickly yellow, and a stab of pain jolted him back to the trophy room.

"Lost taste for wine. Dulls senses. No disrespect, Gratianus." Luciano set the cup on the desk, near a piece of parchment. He couldn't read Trumin, but he recognized his own name written near the top.

Gratianus smiled again, picking up the document. "None taken, my friend. And yes, that's 'Luciano Porteles' written there." The vicar waved it in the air between them. "Do you know what this is, Luciano?"

The assassin shook his head.

"It's a Dark Assembly writ. A scriptum ad ascendum, to be precise." Gratianus placed his own cup on the desk, then opened his arms wide. "You are to ascend, Luciano. It's already been decided."

Scriptum ad ascendum. A writ of ascendance. After years of toil. And now it's too late.

Luciano screwed his eyes shut, searching for the will to act. He forced false hatred to fill his mind, hatred of this man before him with wide open arms. He summoned counterfeit anger, anger towards this man who had long been an ally. This man, who had stood with him against Ghostwalker. This man, who now offered him…

Wealth. Status. Respect.

Yellow pain raced up Luciano's spine. His eyes flashed open.

"What's wrong, my friend? This news surprises you? You've earned it." Gratianus smiled and moved a step closer, inviting him in. The master assassin had never seen a vicar look more vulnerable.

"You right, my friend. I earn it. Forgive me."

Luciano wanted nothing more than to walk away, but a putrid yellow light consumed him.

The heavy thunk of a closing door brought Luciano back to the trophy room. As the yellow haze retreated to the edge of his vision, he felt a great weight pulling his arms to the floor. He looked down. His white-knuckled hands still gripped the gold cord wrapped around Gratianus' neck. The vicar stared at Luciano with bulging eyes, frozen in a grotesque parody of surprise. He released the cords, and the body fell to the floor.

The door?

He turned.

The stuffed harpy obscured his view. Shaking out his aching arms, he took a few cautious steps to the side and spotted a figure near the entrance.

The stranger—man or woman, he could not tell—was tall and slender, with a soft face but an angular jaw. Underneath a black Trumin traveling cloak were hints of golden-hued skin and exotic clothing: pants, pleated garments, oversized jewelry, accents of shimmering rainbow feathers. These were not Trumin, nor any style he was familiar with. The stranger's long, frost-colored hair fell precisely down their chest, held together by a silver band. Thin lines of white and turquoise adorned their brow and cheeks. But none of these extraordinary things captured Luciano's attention as much as the stranger's red eyes, and the way their ears pushed through their white hair, their pointy tips adorned with gold piercings.

"What is Elt doing in Mist View?" Luciano asked. 'Elt' was a common slur used against the mysterious race spawned by the god Eltarus.

The stranger responded with a heavily accented voice, more male than female, but with a melodic lilt impossible for any human. "Is that Vicar Gratianus?"

"Who are you, Elt? Why here now?"

The figure lifted their chin, displaying an aloof smile. "Fine. I'll grant you an introduction." The stranger paused. "I am Raquin Velthar Usil, son of Aptrui Velthar Isil, wielder of Aracn Zanth, emissary of Talinoss, sent to speak with Vicar Gratianus of the Dark Assembly." He took another, longer pause, like an actor ready to receive his ovation. "Is that him on the floor?"

"I am Luciano Port—"

"I didn't ask," the stranger—Raquin—interrupted dryly. "I asked if that was the vicar."

"What business of yours, Elt?"

"As I said, I have come to speak with Vicar Gratianus. I have traveled many days for this audience. If that is indeed him, that is… inconvenient. And if it is you who has inconvenienced me, I shall most assuredly repay you in kind."

"You speak like senator."

"And you talk like a toothless slave." Raquin flared his nostrils and turned away from Luciano. "You smell like one too."

Hot anger pulsed through Luciano's body. Not the yellow tendrils of pain he was familiar with; no, this was red fury. He glanced around the room for a suitable weapon. The vicar's gold cords would be no help against this opponent. His eyes landed on a remarkable falcata displayed on a nearby wall. Falcata, clumsily translated by the Trumins as "elegant curve," was the proper Verdan word. Its curved blade and unique hilt, which encased the wielder's hand, gave the sword its unusual appearance.

When his eyes darted back to Raquin, he realized the Eltaran had followed his gaze.

Raquin, his eyes fixed on Luciano, flung his cloak aside with an exaggerated flourish. From underneath sprung an exotic collar of gold pauldrons, tipped with sea green and blood red feathers, supporting a waist length sky blue cape with gold trim. His tunic was embroidered with a hypnotizing array of colorful geometric patterns which ended above the knee in a series of feather-shaped pleats. Around his waist was a belt of white leather embellished with gold plates and radiant jewels. Tan trousers tucked into tall black leather boots completed the astounding look.

Raquin reached across his waist and drew a long, slender sword from its scabbard. The sword's pommel was a gold disc which reminded Luciano of a huge coin, and a pair of outstretched golden wings served as its hilt. Luciano had never encountered such a weapon: elegant, to the point of almost appearing ceremonial. *This must be the fool's prized 'Aracn Zanth.'* It was the sort of weapon that would be nightmarishly deadly in the right hands. Raquin stretched out his arm and pointed the sword at Luciano. With the slightest flick of his wrist, the blade became an indistinct blur of movement. Then the sword stilled and he once again pointed it at Luciano. He extended his free hand towards the Falcata and said, in a bored tone, "By all means."

Luciano made his way towards the sword, desperately formulating a strategy to defeat—or better yet, escape—his new opponent. "I know where to find scroll, Elt."

"I doubt that."

Luciano grabbed the falcata and slid his hand into the guarded hilt. "Doubt me. Bad move." There was no reaction from the Eltaran.

The weapon felt good in his hand. It felt like Verdith, like home. A stinging behind his eyes brought him back to Trumric. He turned the blade over a few times, admiring its craftsmanship, then noticed the sorcerous Verdan runes inscribed along the edge. He allowed himself a brief smile.

Luciano had taken his eyes off the Eltaran for just a moment. When he looked again, Raquin had moved. In that instant, Raquin closed the gap between them, yet Luciano had not heard a single footfall. The Elt stood within striking distance, staring at him with those unnerving red eyes.

Luciano held his falcata in a low guard while Raquin stood as motionless as one of the room's stuffed monstrosities, his weapon pointed at the floor with indifference.

"I know scroll to find. And who."

"Is that Trumin you're trying to force through those ill-formed lips?"

"Scroll not here. In Capital. In Trumric city." That provoked a reaction, and Luciano used his opportunity to lunge forward, swinging his new falcata in an upward arc, aimed for the Elt's throat. But rather than flesh, his blade struck the steel of Raquin's sword. Luciano stepped back and braced himself for the inevitable riposte, which never came.

What they say is true: faster reflexes than any man. If only I had Ghostwalker's spatha.

There was nothing but raw condescension in his adversary's eyes. He had seen only a blur before the jarring impact of Eltaran steel. Raquin was toying with him. Luciano moved in again, feigning the same move, then thrust the falcata forward. Raquin evaded the thrust, allowing Luciano's own momentum to pull him forward, forcing him off-balance. He caught himself and prepared to parry any counterattack. Still, nothing. This was no Imperaré thug, and certainly no seventeen-year-old street thief. This was a highly trained and experienced swordsman. How experienced? Decades? Centuries?

Remembering Darktalon—and the trouble he had caused him—boiled his blood. Through sheer stubbornness and blind luck, he had turned Luciano's well-planned assassination of Marius Secundus into a farce. But that vengeance would have to wait. He had no time for rage-induced distractions. If he wasn't at his best, this Eltaran would be his undoing. He fell into a defensive fighting stance and contemplated his next move. Raquin kept a subtle smirk on his face, his sword held casually at his side.

Luciano kicked a marble pedestal towards the Eltaran, sending a bowl of blue-tinted pearls scattering across the floor. Raquin avoided the stone block as well as the careening pearls, but the move had the desired effect: he leaped backward, landing on Gratianus' desk. Luciano next struck the harpy's leg, and the Verdan falcata sliced through it with ease. With nothing left to support its weight, the stuffed monstrosity fell forward, crashing onto the desk. Raquin disappeared under a shower of feathers.

He sprinted towards the scene, ready to finish the downed Eltaran, but when he arrived, he saw only feathers and splintered bones.

An inner voice, one trained over dozens of duels, told him to dodge. He twisted to the side and Raquin's blade skidded off his back, cutting through leather and flesh. The blow set him back on his heels, and Raquin pressed the attack, moving in with blinding speed. Fortunately, his wound was not deep, and Luciano fended off a flurry of slashes and thrusts, seeing nothing but the occasional blur of steel. When the blows subsided, his sword arm ached and blood trickled down his back.

Luciano shook off the pain and braced himself for another attack. But before it came, the door swung open and several guards, swords in hand, burst into the room. Their eyes bounced from Luciano to the Eltaran stranger, to the lifeless body of Gratianus, then back to the Eltaran.

Luciano pointed at Raquin and shouted, "He kill vicar! This Elt scum kill Vicar Gratianus!"

As the Dark Assembly guards charged the accused, Luciano slipped past the men and bolted through the door. Once out of the trophy room, he retrieved Aguja and his other daggers. He forsook his old spatha in favor of the falcata, tucking the new blade in his belt before disappearing into the streets of Mist View. Not long after, the Imperaré's master assassin was on the road to Trumric, his mind wracked by guilt but devoid of agonizing yellow tendrils.

THIEF OF THE IMPERARÉ

With every passing moment, the room became more trap than treasure vault. Ulric searched the backroom of Tubero's taberna for what seemed like the hundredth time. Nothing. No hidden strongbox, no secret stash of black wolf or shadow-dust tonics. The Portus Collegium's spymaster, Igdir, had said it would be under the trapdoor, hidden beneath an expensive Suhtean rug. He had also said the coin and tonics supplied by the rival Transnanpela Collegium would be there. The wily Bayjoni was right about the escape tunnel—could he be wrong about the coin and tonics?

If the tonic and coin were here, Ulric thought, *someone could walk in at any moment to drop off one or pick up the other.*

It was nearing the eleventh hour. Harbor Men and Portus Collegium soldiers would soon flood the taberna and neighboring brothel like the oncoming tide, with orders to shroud Tubero and his men. A prince of the Imperaré always met an insult with murder, and for Ulric's boss, Horatius Silo, there was no greater insult than cutting a deal with his hated rival, Cornelius Brocchus, the leader of the Transnanpela Collegium.

Ulric almost pitied Tubero. He had run the Street of Hidden Pleasures for years, dispensing drink, drugs, and debauchery. His reputation as a loyal and formidable ally of the Portus Collegium was unquestioned. Until now.

How stupid do you have to be to trust a snake like Brocchus? He doubted Tubero's men deserved what was coming.

When the knife work begins, Tubero will burst in here with bodyguards in tow, grab his stash from…somewhere, and flee down the tunnel. My orders say to steal the stash and disappear before the first blade is drawn. How can I do that if I can't find them?

"Sweet Neesis, glorious goddess of fortune," he whispered, "I could use a bit of luck. And quick."

Ulric looked over the room once more. A table with a cracked tortoiseshell veneer, and no hidden compartments to be found. On the table, among a ledger and a clutter of uninteresting scrolls, sat a vial of pale glass filled with faint luminescent crystals. Ice wind, a rare and expensive tonic. *Not part of the stash—it's mine now! What else?*

A stained reclining couch and footstool. *I can guess what Tubero uses it for.* Two unremarkable chairs and a colorful Suhtean rug, all illuminated by a single shuttered window too narrow to squeeze through. *And no place to hide if someone walks in.*

He began another search of Tubero's office. His movements were quick, quiet, and precise; he disturbed nothing, nor left anything out of place. He knew how to search a room, how to discover a man's hidden treasures. Arrius Ghostwalker, the greatest thief ever to tread the Shadow Ways, had taught him his craft.

Nothing. Again.

A sudden rage set him alight. He circled around the room, stifling a scream through gritted teeth. Unbidden, a shaking fist snapped into the air, ready to smash more cracks into the desktop veneer. He stood there shaking until his anger drained away into a nauseous pool of shame. He hoped Arrius hadn't witnessed his tantrum from the depths of the Underworld.

Ulric lowered his fist, then took a slow, deep breath. Ghostwalker had always said emotion had no place on the job. He knew the value of focus. So Ulric closed his eyes, seeking the beginnings of a Shadow Mind trance. It was part of the Shadow Ways, a secret discipline Ghostwalker had taught him; it took his mind to a place where will could forge thoughts into ironhard commands. The trance was remarkable for controlling pain and accelerating healing, and it also offered a strange tranquility. It was a deep trance that could last hours, taking the practitioner far from the waking world, but Ulric could only afford a moment to calm himself.

Footsteps in the hall, heading toward the door—fast.

Thanks to the calm of Shadow Mind, he assessed his options quick as lightning. The spaces beneath the table and couch were exposed. The small room offered no blind spots. No time to reach the trapdoor. No place to hide.

If he was caught, things would get bloody. Maybe he could escape down Tubero's own tunnel, but then he would fail the job and tarnish the legacy of Arrius Ghostwalker. And he would fail Silo, the man to whom he had sworn his allegiance under the auspices of Neesis Umbra.

The footsteps stopped outside the door. All was silent but for the drone of the hard-drinking crowd beyond. The bronze handle turned with a faint rattle, and the door moved inward.

Ulric's heart skipped a beat. The Shadow Mind trance snapped. He crossed the room and flattened himself against the wall, drawing a dagger from beneath his tunic and praying to Neesis Fortuna that he wouldn't have to use it. *Maybe they'll leave the door open, show me where they've hidden the goods, and leave. Are you listening, O' glorious goddess? Bless your most devoted worshiper with some of that wild luck.*

The door opened, filling the room with lavender perfume. Someone took two tentative steps inside, then turned to face the hall. A woman's hand shifted to the door's edge, and it was clear she intended to shut it.

Gods below! So much for luck. Is it madness and bold action you want, Neesis? Then let's go shadow dancing!

THE IKON OF MYRILL

Every day, the memory darkened, slipping further into a murky dream with each passing hour. Julia recalled her tearful flight toward the theater exit and the jolt of pain as she slammed through the cold iron gate, but instead of Trumric's dark streets, she had burst into sunlight and perfect bliss. She had been transported to the Empyrean realm—she was certain of it! She stood before Myrill Regina, Queen of the Gods. Myrill, Mother of Mercy, had taken her hand and spoken words of comfort. Words of portent. Words of doom.

What Myrill had said, Julia could not remember. Well, not exactly. When she tried, it was like watching a play through a dark shroud of mist, the stage all shifting shadows, the actors' lines distorted and unreal. No details of the Empyrean realm nor Myrill's wisdom remained. The memory of Julia's divine audience—her most precious of memories—had faded the moment she returned to the mortal world. She only knew the memory filled her with a rare peace, a celestial contentment. Words of comfort.

That had been over a month ago, after Julia fell in love with the outcast thief Marcus Octavius Ulric. Something in his wild nature had inspired her to confront Myrill's high priestess and excise the growing corruption within Her temple. Facing her own past sins, she at last accepted Myrill's blessing, becoming Her ikon, a conduit of Her divine power.

Now it was the Ides of Quintilis, high summer, and Julia and Ulric had both fallen under the influence of Horatius Silo, the leader of the Portus Collegium and a prince of the ruthless criminal organization known as the Imperaré.

Did I escape corrupt priests, she wondered, *to become the slave of criminals? How do I serve the Mother of Mercy while in the company of thieves and murderers? There must be a way out!*

Julia glanced back through the crowd toward the two Harbor Men who had been escorting her through the markets of the Portum Mare District. *Harbor Men! Harbor men escorting a servant of Myrill?* The thought was offensive. The Harbor Men were just another street gang, after all. One that brutally enforced order on the docks at the behest of the Portus Collegium—and ultimately the Imperaré. Under her breath she said, "*Hmph*! My bodyguards? More like my jailers."

"I wouldn't complain," said a breathy voice. "I think the big one's kind of cute; in an oafish sort of way."

"Uh, what?" Julia turned to find her friend Ide staring past her, admiring the taller of the two men. "Ide! How long have you been standing there?" She pulled her green palla low over her face and leaned in close, making the two of them look like a pair of conspirators. "Thank the gods you found me." Julia checked to see that the Harbor Men were out of earshot, then continued. "I need some pleasant company."

"Finding you is easy," Ide teased. "I just follow your *followers*."

"Careful, Ide. I don't have followers," Julia said sharply—though she regretted the harshness of her tone almost instantly. "To acknowledge such a thing would be an affront to the Temple of Myrill."

Ide slapped Julia's shoulder with the end of her own palla, which she wore draped over an ample figure. "Then explain it to them, instead of snapping at me," she said. She pointed to several men and women who followed Julia from the edge of the crowd. Each supplicant bore fig branches and holy symbols, carrying small bundles of offerings meant for the Ikon of Myrill. They watched Julia intently, their eyes curious and eager.

"Forgive me. I've been too absorbed in my own troubles."

More of Julia's followers joined the crowd. Penitents and seekers, the sick and the strays. The Harbor Men drew closer and Julia hurried north, toward the Portus Towers and home.

"Like I said, don't complain about bodyguards when you live in the Portum Mare. It's the only place worse than the Transnanpela District."

"Myrill's mercy!" Julia huffed. "Didn't you hear me? More like jailers, I think."

Ide raised her eyebrows—something she always did if she thought she was about to win an argument. "Are there locks on your doors?"

"No."

"Is any part of the city forbidden to you?"

"You already know the answer. None."

"So how are you two still at the Polyminius Theater? After Ulric nearly burned down the Night Market, I'd have thought the Transnanpela District would be the one place you're not welcome."

Julia lowered her voice beneath the thrum of the crowd, ensuring the Harbor Men couldn't hear her. "The princes of the Imperaré agreed to a truce. All to do with some grand scheme of theirs. I really don't understand it. Ulric could explain it better, but I don't think he's supposed to talk about it."

"Oh, it sounds like you're quite the prisoner. I can almost hear the chains rattling behind you."

Julia's dark eyes narrowed. "No. No chains. Not yet. But who knows—" she checked her growing anger and returned her voice to a whisper— "who knows what Silo will do next?"

"Seems to me he's protecting you. You and Ulric."

"But thugs don't follow *Ulric* everywhere."

"Oh, Julia. You've spent months among us 'lowborn plebes' and you still don't know how things work. The *Darktalon*—" she spoke the name with comical exaggeration— "doesn't need bodyguards. The Portus Collegium tattoo on his arm is Silo's protection."

"And Myrill Regina is mine!"

Several nearby supplicants intoned: "Myrill Regina, may You grant eternal safety, victory, and health to the Trumin people! Strength to Your Ikon!"

The two Harbor Men closed in. One of them shot Julia a worried look she understood as a suggestion to pick up the pace.

"I don't doubt it," Ide said, struggling to keep up with Julia. "When I asked why Myrill let my mother die from the pox, what did you tell me?" Ide stopped in front of Julia and waited. "Well?"

Julia grew tired of Ide's game, and not, she told herself, because she was losing the argument. "I told you that even the gods can be distracted. They do not always see our suffering. Nor are we always worthy of their mercy. And I told you how sorry I was."

"Then it seems even the great Persius Julia could use an extra bit of worldly protection."

Julia sighed loud enough to attract looks from several passersby. "Were you taught rhetoric by Mother Joveta, by any chance?"

"Are you admitting I won?" asked Ide.

"Ha! I concede nothing. You lack the facts needed to make an informed argument."

"Still keeping secrets?"

"Of course," Julia replied.

A girl's entitled to a few, she thought. *Like the fact that I'm the daughter of Gnaeus Trumerus Julius, the Ravager of Gualdé, the Conqueror of the East and twice consul of Trumric. Or the fact if Ulric's friends knew, half of them would ransom me back to my father. Fools, them! He wouldn't give a fig for my corpse. At least, I used to think so. You can't hear the chains, but they rattle all the same!*

Julia adjusted the bundle she had been carrying and hurried down the street. "Come on. I want to get home—" she glanced back at the growing train of supplicants following her— "and out of the sun."

"Bodyguards or jailers," Ide said, wiping the sweat from her brow, "the least they could do is carry your bag. What is it? Leaves and powders, as usual?"

"I'll not trust my herbs with a couple of thieves."

They continued north toward the river, emerging from the shadow of the Calidius Amphitheater into the heat of the forum vinarium, a small market specializing in wine and other spirits. Despite the late hour, the square bustled with shoppers, no doubt thanks to the presence of a popina selling food and drinks on every corner. The thought made Julia thirsty.

"Let's grab a drink," she suggested. "I have a few coins left."

"Oh, Julia! I need a cool drink! Let's head to the Blue Cup."

"I prefer Atella's. It's closer and—"

"Julia? Persius Julia?"

The voice cut through the forum with an orator's power. A toga-clad man emerged from the crowd, tall, broad shouldered, with a prominent nose under a scarred brow. The scars gave him a sinister aspect, but he wore the toga well, despite its cut being a few years out of fashion. *Really, Julia?* she chided herself. *That's the sort of thing you still notice? Myrill, forgive me!*

"I missed you at the Polyminius Theater," he said. "Such good fortune I found you here." As he drew closer, he quickened his pace and slipped a hand beneath the folds of his toga.

Ide snatched at Julia's tunic, almost pulling her off her feet. Julia gasped and tried to regain her footing. "What are you—"

The Two Harbor Men appeared as if conjured by a magus. The one she knew as Strabo seized the man's wrist in a stone-like grip, eliciting a yelp of pain. His taller partner, Corvus, charged a second man rushing from the crowd and sent him sprawling with one swift blow.

"Step back!" Strabo commanded. "If that's a blade in your hand, we're gonna break a lotta things. Starting with this wrist."

"Unhand me, you thug! I have important friends, senators and magi among them!"

Julia tore herself free of Ide, then squeezed herself between Strabo and the toga clad man. "Let him go! I know this man. He's no assassin. He's…" she struggled to recall his name, having only met him briefly the past month, "Memmius Drusus, an advocate."

Strabo yanked the man's hand from beneath his toga, revealing no dagger, only a small cloth pouch. Nearby, Corvus stood guard over the other man, a slender youth with the ruddy complexion of the northern Gualdean tribes.

"Master Drusus! Are you in danger?" At least that's what Julia thought she heard; the slave's words were slurred and muted through cupped hands, held over a bruised and bloodied face.

"No. A simple misunderstanding." To Strabo he said, "See? I'm unarmed."

"I see that. Now." Strabo released the man's wrist and stepped back. Corvus, his demeanor transformed, helped the slave to his feet and they both approached. A curious crowd gathered.

"It pleases me to know I can still look dangerous. I earned my scars marching with Maculla against the Harathi, but that was a long time ago."

"Memmius Drusus, can you forgive me?" Julia asked.

"There's nothing to forgive. The fault is mine. I never realized you'd become so famous you needed bodyguards."

"Neither did I," Julia replied.

"Famous?" Strabo spat the word. "It's not like she's some chariot racer or champion gladiator."

"How rude!" Ide turned to Corvus and placed a gentle hand on one massive bicep. "You're not rude, are you?"

In response, the giant Harbor Man shrugged. "Maybe."

Drusus looked over the gathering crowd. They whispered Julia's name, called her a healer, praised her as Goddess-blessed, and said she was a true Ikon of Myrill. "Perhaps you *are* becoming famous. I sought you at the theater to give you this." He opened the pouch, revealing a small sum of silver denarii. "My wife insisted. We could never pay you enough for saving our son."

"Give her my thanks, but I couldn't accept this. *I* did nothing. I only facilitate Myrill's will."

"No, Julia, you must accept this gift so we may honor both you and Mother Myrill. And if I return home with the money, my wife will be furious. Please, take it. You have no idea what it's like being married to a Harathi woman."

Julia laughed politely and took the pouch. "Give her my thanks. And may Alakur and Myrill bless your family and watch over young Drusus."

"Thank you. Now, I've delayed you long enough. I'll be on my way." Memmius Drusus, with his slave close behind, pushed through the surrounding crowd and was gone.

"He's right," Strabo said. He looked west to gauge the time. "It's almost the eleventh hour. We need to get moving."

"Why the sudden haste?" Julia asked.

Strabo stepped closer and said, "Lots of reasons."

Then the crowd closed in.

A man draped in a fashionable toga rushed toward Julia, demanding she bless his latest business venture. He waved a well-manicured, coin-filled fist near her once before Corvus tossed him aside with shouts of "Clear the street!"

A young mother knelt before Julia, her eyes red-rimmed and despairing. She thrust her feverish child toward Julia and begged for healing. The babe wailed pitifully. Julia reached out, but Strabo dragged the woman back into the crowd as another man, an old, homeless stray, clawed at her tunic with weak, sore-covered hands. He claimed he'd be dead within days without Myrill's mercy. Ide pushed the old man away, but a fellow stray rushed to his defense and Ide fell into a shouting match with the two. Julia became the center of a maelstrom of grasping hands and desperate voices, each demanding absolution, a blessing, a healing touch.

Julia's heart thudded in her chest like the hooves of horses fleeing before a wildfire. She spun around, looking for a way out, but there was none. The air became thick and smothering. She tried to speak to one supplicant, but her voice came in weak gasps and was drowned out by the cries of the mob. How could she help them all? She shrank further into the center of the storm and prayed for guidance.

Strabo and Corvus stood at Julia's side, pushing back against the crowd while Ide traded insults with the two strays. Julia felt the fire engulf her. *I did this. This is why the priests loathe my freedom, why they gather the favored of Myrill at the temple. But Myrill told me…* Julia ignored the chaos and tried to remember the words of the goddess. Something about Her daughter's shadow cloak! *I must stay close to Ulric. He'll lead us… somewhere. But where?*

One stray pulled a small club from beneath his tunic. Julia tried to warn Ide, but her voice was nothing but wind. The club smashed into the side of Ide's head and she disappeared into the mob.

Julia released a soundless scream. She tried to reach Ide, but a sharp tug snapped her back. A hand clutched her palla, twisting her around. Out of the corner of her eye, she glimpsed a dark-haired young man behind her, his eyes distant and hollow.

"Ulric?"

"My love is dead. Should I join her?"

He spoke with the voice of utter despair.

"Who?" Julia turned around, but he was gone.

Her blood ran cold. His words held an echo of future memory. Words of portent.

Julia screamed. And screamed. Until the scream turned into words.

"Be still!"

Julia spoke with the voice of the goddess. Myrill's dawning light burst through her caramel skin, filling the forum with a golden glow, and all was silent but for the distant sounds of the capital. Myrill's presence brought a deep contentment, a divine peace, and all fear was forgotten. Julia walked into the mob. They fell back like a field of rushes before a sudden wind.

Ide lay cradled on Corvus' lap. The side of her face was bloody and bruised, but she softly mumbled curses at the two strays, one of which lay unmoving nearby.

"Myrill's mercy is a gift given freely to the worthy—not a commodity to be fought over and bartered in the market!" As she spoke, she searched the crowd for the dark-haired man with the hopeless eyes, but he was not among them. "We must comport ourselves as honest and loyal Trumins, worthy of our great republic. And if we are worthy, if we have honored Her temple and held Her mercy in our hearts, then we will receive Her blessing."

Shamed by their earlier behavior, the people cried out for forgiveness, and many scurried away into the surrounding streets. Julia led those that remained in prayer while Strabo impatiently stalked the edge of the crowd.

For some, the simplest invocation could channel Myrill's divine power. A quick prayer, and a child's fever was gone. A few words, and an old stray who honored Myrill's holy days was cured of his afflictions. A soft touch, and a loyal friend's bashed head was healed. Her mercy was limitless for the innocent and the faithful.

For others, no prayer could summon Her divine power. The wicked or impious had to endure ill fortune without divine aid. They made do with a salve or physic from Julia's bag and good advice born from the teachings of Myrill's temple, a treatment not unlike that of any Kreslan trained doctor.

A short time later, the last of the supplicants left. Julia, to the great relief of Strabo, was ready to return home, so she hoisted her bundle of herbs and prepared to leave the forum vinarium. Ide came alongside, her gait wobbly despite Myrill's blessing. She noted Corvus hovering over her with a lustful look she had seen before. Julia shook her head and smiled. *Never change, Ide.*

"It's never a dull day with you and the goddess," Ide exclaimed. "But I've had enough."

"Oh, my dear Ide! Thank you." Julia opened her arms, inviting a goodbye hug. "Be safe."

Julia turned to Corvus. "Would you escort Ide home? Keep her safe for me?"

The giant Harbor Man broke into a wide grin. "Yes." He took Ide gently by the arm and added, "Very safe."

Julia took a step, but Strabo stopped her with a hand on her shoulder. "No," he said, "you're going the wrong way."

"The Portus Towers are still across the river, are they not?" Julia asked with as much sarcasm as she could muster.

"The Vinarium ferry won't be safe. We head west: cross the river on the Calidius ferry."

Julia cast a knowing glance at Ide, who remained to watch the latest drama unfold. Now Ide would see her jailers in action.

Then she looked at Strabo as if he had sprouted the ears and tail of an ass. Despite his feigned concern, she sensed a pent-up anger launching itself at the bars of its cage like a wild animal. He was desperate to command, not serve, but he had seen her power and feared her.

Strabo took a hesitant step to the west. "This way. We need to hurry."

Julia didn't move.

"Come on, Julia," Corvus pleaded. "You don't want to get Strabo in trouble, do you?" The good-natured Corvus sounded pitiful. Even Ide looked tired of her stubbornness.

Julia expelled an exasperated sigh and headed west with Strabo. Over her shoulder she called, "Goodbye Ide! My chains are pulling this way."

Shadow Dancing

Ulric slipped out from behind the door of Tubero's office and stood behind the woman. She peered into the hall, then shut the door. The woman was tall, with a wild mane of brunette hair and a voluptuous figure wrapped tight in an obscenely short red tunic. He knew she was up to no good from the way she had nervously checked the hall, but he wasn't foolish enough to think that would make them allies.

The woman turned to face the room and Ulric turned with her, mimicking her movements in perfect synchronicity. As her weight shifted, he did the same. As she stepped forward, he stepped with her. His feet, legs, every limb moved to the rhythm of her body, as if tethered by invisible strings. With his breathing shallow and controlled, his clothing and gear rigged for silence, and his steps but a whisper, he became the woman's second shadow. Ghostwalker had called it Shadow Dancing, and it was an advanced technique, one Ulric admittedly had not mastered. Maybe if he impressed Neesis with his daring, the goddess would grant him a bit of luck?

The woman approached the table and Ulric followed, never more than a handbreadth behind. She stared down at the cluttered tabletop with a posture of disdain.

"What a mess. No wonder he's run us aground." After a moment, she said, "There you are."

The woman took a quick step back, closing the narrow gap between them until her shoulder brushed his tunic. The touch sent Ulric's stomach twisting into an icy knot. He fell back, struggling to match her movements as she circled around the table, a trickle of sweat dripping between his shoulder blades. He thanked Neesis she hadn't noticed.

The woman leaned over the ledger and began flipping through its pages, mumbling to herself all the while.

"I know you've been shorting me. I know it… I know it… I know it."

Oh, Sweet Neesis! She's here to balance the books, not steal anything.

The woman slammed the ledger shut. "Caught you, Tubero. You thieving bastard!"

She straightened and Ulric moved closer, an unseen second shadow. The woman stepped away from the table, then paused.

Go on. Time to go!

The woman reached beneath the clutter and retrieved the vial of ice wind. "Ah, what's this?" She stepped into the light streaming through the shutters and raised the vial high overhead. The fine, powdered crystal glowed with a pearly luminescence and flashes of pale blue light. She held it there, admiring it. "Keeping the best for yourself, I see."

Fine! I was going to split that with Corvus, but if it gets you out of here, take it.

The woman gasped, and the vial slipped from her fingers.

Ulric's blood ran cold as ice wind powder. Out of the corner of his eye, he saw what she had seen, what had caused her shock of terror: there were two shadows caught in the window's light.

The vial shattered into a cloud of billowing powder as she turned to face her shadow. The woman, a pale beauty with full lips and fierce eyes, gasped and prepared to scream. Instead of air, she sucked in a lungful of sparkling ice wind powder. Instead of an ear-piercing wail, she released a soft moan. Then her knees buckled and Ulric, who had held his breath, lowered her onto the desktop.

With his dagger at her throat, he waited for the euphoria of the ice wind to fade.

"Who… who are you?" she asked. The woman trembled, her once fierce eyes now wide with fear. "Where'd you come from? You a magus?"

"No magus. A thief. Ulric Darktalon. And I can walk through walls," he lied. "What's your name?"

"Diantha."

"Well, Diantha, I'd bet all of Tubero's stash you're not supposed to be here any more than I am."

"A deal, then?" she asked. Her voice held no hint of her previous fear. Her eyes flashed with their earlier fierceness, then became soft, seductive, deceptive. She arched her back, slowly pushing her breasts against him. "I could be very agreeable."

Oh, you trembled when you thought I was a magus, but now you're trying to scheme me? Why is magic so feared in this city? I can be frightening, can't I? He pressed his dagger against her throat and donned a mask of cruelty. "Save it for your clients. I already bed the most beautiful actress in Trumric."

"Please… please don't kill me," Diantha sobbed, loud enough to sound pathetic but quiet enough to avoid drawing attention.

"A performance worthy of the Polyminius Theater. You should audition." Ulric smiled—and he thought it was a very charming smile.

"Bastard!"

"*Shh*! We're agreeable conspirators, remember? Here's the deal: tell me where Tubero hides his stash, and you walk out of here."

"In here. Somewhere."

Ulric pulled her to her feet and held her close. "Where? It's a corner room with little furniture and no hidden compartments." He pressed the dagger's point against her throat. "Where, exactly?"

Genuine fear returned. "I don't know. If the boys need more, Tubero comes here—alone—then comes out with more."

"Maybe he moved it? When was he here last?" Ulric tried to keep the desperation out of his voice.

"This afternoon. Sometime after the ninth hour," Diantha said. "You have to believe me. I won't tell them you were here. I won't—"

"Not enough time…" Ulric said.

"Huh?"

"That's not enough time." Nothing made sense. The job was hopeless. "Not enough to move everything. Not without leaving... something. Where in the Nine Hells... Shroud work begins soon."

Tears streamed down Diantha's face, a face stripped of all masks and contorted by terror. Ulric's panicked mutterings had convinced her she would die under his blade.

Ulric found what it took to be frightening, and it left him feeling ill.

He almost succumbed to despair and hopelessness: the madness of Mantius. One half of the Infernal Twins, Mantius served in Arakru's underworld court, a god of madness and death. While Mantius, like all gods, needed to be appeased, Ulric was devoted to Neesis, the goddess of luck, lust, and an altogether different sort of madness, one born of ecstasy and inspiration. Ulric knew Her by three names: Neesis Fortuna, Neesis Amoris, and Neesis Insania. He also knew Her secret name, Neesis Umbra—the patron and protector of all thieves.

As Neesis Amoris, goddess of lust, She was also the patron and protector of another far more popular profession.

"Diantha, I'd never hurt you. In fact, I'm going to save your life." Ulric guided the confused woman to the far corner of the room, extended a sandaled foot, and flipped over the corner of the rug, revealing a wooden trapdoor with a single inset iron ring. "Soon men are going to arrive with orders to shroud Tubero and his men, both here and at your brothel. They won't hurt your girls or your boys, but *you*? Best not find out." He opened the trapdoor.

A musty, earthy smell rose out of the darkness. She hesitated. "No time to fetch a lamp. Just feel along the wall. It's a straight run; not far."

"How do you know those killers will come?" Diantha asked.

"They're my friends."

Diantha nodded silently, then descended into the tunnel and disappeared into the darkness.

Ulric returned to Tubero's desk and once more cast his gaze across the room. The Portus Collegium would attack at any moment. Should he leap into the tunnel and follow Diantha to safety? No, he couldn't abandon the job. He had stood in Silo's office at the top of Portus Towers and received his orders from the Imperaré prince himself. Failure would risk breaking the sacramentum and losing Neesis Umbra's protection. For a thief, no disaster was greater.

Ulric exhaled, forcing himself to stop worrying about failure, Silo, and the imminent attack. Instead, he concentrated on the moment, on every little sensation. Almost immediately, he felt a rush of excitement. The gloom of the office faded and the distant sounds and smells of the taberna filled the small room. It was what Ghostwalker had called the Thieves' Glimmer. It was an essential tool of the Shadow Ways, sharpening senses and heightening awareness.

He began to take a deep breath but stopped himself, remembering the vial of ice wind. The cloud of white powder filled the room, drifting and rising through the air on unseen currents. Sunlight streaming through the shuttered window set the crystals ablaze, each twinkling like a precious gemstone. Yet at the center of the interior wall, only visible at the edge of his vision, there was an impossible place where the crystals were absent.

When he looked at the spot, everything was as it should be: air filled with sunlight and shining crystals. When he looked away, forcing himself to see the spot out of the corner of his eye, he saw a space of clear air. He twisted his head this way and that, pushing his eyes into their corners until they ached. The strange space of clear air had a shape: it resembled a cabinet, the width of a man and half as tall.

It was Tubero's stash, masked by a fabrication!

Every muscle relaxed, the tension evaporating as if he had taken a caldarium dip at the High Ridge bathhouse. A wide grin stretched across his face as he moved closer, careful to keep the shimmering cabinet shape "focused" at the edge of his vision. He'd found the fabrication. Now all he had to do was break it.

It was an expensive and complex illusion. If he couldn't see the cabinet, provide his mind with proof it was really there, then his other senses refused to acknowledge its existence. That was how he had walked past the spot again and again, convinced he had checked the wall.

When he was close enough, Ulric thrust his hands into the void.

I see you. I know you're right… here!

With a loud thwack, his knuckles struck hard wood and bronze. Where before there was empty air, a cabinet now stood, broad and squat on four stubby legs. He yanked the knobs to no avail.

It's locked. Of course. Sweet Neesis! As if the fabrication wasn't enough…

Ulric reached for his lock picks just as a commotion began outside the taberna. He ignored the shouts and focused on the lock. Fortunately, a straight bar and dragon-tail pick made quick work of it. Inside there was a small iron strongbox and shelves full of tiny bags and vials of blue lotus, shadow-dust, black wolf, and more.

"O' Glorious Goddess, how did I ever doubt you?"

The unmistakable sounds of battle entered the building. Odds were Tubero and his bodyguards were heading toward the office. He needed more time! Ulric raced to the door, grabbed an iron spike from his gear, wedged it under the threshold, then returned to the cabinet. He pulled a sturdy linen sack from his belt, dropped to his knees, and shoved every last vial and bag inside.

A sudden thump made Ulric jolt to his feet. The hall filled with angry, confused shouting, and a second blow shook the door. He grabbed the strongbox and tucked it under one arm, tossing the bag of tonics over his shoulder. The clash of steel erupted in the hall, followed by the sharp crack of splintering wood as the door buckled. Ulric leaped into the comforting darkness of the tunnel, dragging the Suhtean behind him.

Eltaran Stone

Traffic on the Street of Hidden Pleasures scurried past Julia with all the dignity of soldiers fleeing a rout. Strabo marched down the street without pause, dragging Julia close behind. His sharp gaze and Harbor Man tattoos sliced an easy path through the panicked horde.

"Why lead us toward danger?" Julia asked.

Strabo ignored her. Instead, he drew a dagger and quickened his pace. "Best keep moving."

The street meandered wildly, cutting this way and that, all sharp turns and narrow spaces lined with tonic dens, brothels, deep alcoves, and blind alleys. The sea breeze sweeping the rest of the Portum Mare District was not welcome here, leaving a pall of strange herbs and human filth. Julia struggled to breathe the thick air.

The last passerby fled, leaving her alone with her dubious guardian. Julia walked on, heedless to whatever dangers had frightened the hardened patrons of the Street of Hidden Pleasures. Curious stares followed her, hidden behind half-opened shop doors and shuttered windows. If they knew what lurked ahead, they offered no warning. Why should it matter? Earlier, in the forum, Myrill had spoken. The goddess was near, Her power close at hand. Julia should fear nothing. Yet she recalled the stranger with hollow eyes and shivered despite the stifling heat.

The street took a jagged turn, and Julia stepped into the aftermath of a battle.

Harbor Men, identified by their wicked knives and nautical tattoos, milled about the street, bloodied but triumphant. They had smashed open the doors of a nearby taberna and torn its sign (*TUBERO'S* written in bold, blue letters) from its post. Slaves, with the stiff look of men given no choice in an unpleasant task, dragged bodies from the taberna and tossed them onto an old pushcart. The corpses left a trail of red muck smeared across the dirty cobblestone.

"By Alakur's Light! More pointless butchery?" Julia asked.

Strabo ignored her, instead calling to the lead Harbor Man. "Looks like they got the red sword right up the ass."

"Ha! Damn right!" The Harbor Man swaggered over and thumped Strabo on the back. "We hit 'em like a thunderbolt. Ya should have seen them traitors running about, begging and weeping like women."

"What of the big man himself? And the dust?" Strabo asked, slipping Julia a strange, eager glance.

"We got him making a run for the goods, but the tonics were already gone." The Harbor Man grinned. "Just like the boss planned."

"Eh, the gods grant us the bad with the good." Strabo said, sounding disappointed. "Anyone make the lists?"

"Yeah, poor Medios. Must've offended Neesis."

"Damn. I liked that Kreslan bastard."

The Harbor Man nodded toward Julia. "Gotta few needs tending."

"Of course," Julia said, adding an unconvincing smile. "That's why I'm here, after all." She looked pointedly at Strabo.

"Orders."

"You only had to ask," Julia said.

"Really? Cause it's been nothing but trouble since you came to the Towers. You act more like a foreign princess than one of our girls."

Julia said nothing. Perhaps it was true, after all.

"Plain unruly, you are."

Finally, she said, "Then I suggest you stop trying to rule me."

The Harbor Man led them into the front room of the taberna. The dark interior was spacious and smelled of spilt blood and stale wine, like the cavernous lair of some drunken beast. Several gang members sat around the only table left standing, nursing their wounds and drinking the spoils of victory. They greeted Julia with smiles and praise for Myrill.

Julia dropped her bundle of herbs in the middle of the table, scattering their cups and jugs. Ever since joining Ulric at Portus Towers, she had been called upon to tend the collegium wounded, and she had a well-rehearsed speech for such occasions. "I've warned you before. Myrill's mercy isn't for street brawlers and killers," she said, arranging her little scalpels and sutures across the table. "The Goddess reserves her divine power for wounds nobly earned, either in defense of the innocent or in defense of our blessed Republic."

The table gave a collective groan; they had heard it all before. A young man, cradling one arm wrapped in a dirty bandage, said, "Well, I say gutting Tubero is a kick in the balls to ole Brocchus. And that's good for the Republic!"

The table banged their cups and shouted their agreement.

Julia softened her dark eyes and smiled at the man. "Celsus, isn't it?" The Harbor Man's rough demeanor changed. *Ah, too easy*, she thought. "I have no love for that wicked man, but we'll have to plead your case with generous offerings to Myrill's shrine on the Via Delubrarum."

Celsus stared sheepishly at the table. "Yeah, I know where it is. It's just that Neesis demands a hefty share, you know."

"Oh, I know," she replied. "Now give me your arm. This might hurt."

Julia began examining the men's wounds. They were mostly light cuts, but a few were deep lacerations requiring more than dirty bandages. She sent one of the men deeper into the taberna to look for vinegar and clean linen.

A few moments later, Julia was startled by a loud thump on the ceiling, followed by the hollow sound of muffled voices. Strabo stiffened and reached for his dagger.

The lead Harbor Man, who had been lining wine bottles along the bar, raised his hand in a signal to stop. "Relax. That'd be our host, Tubero. Silo's having a chat."

"The prince himself?" Strabo glanced at the ceiling and gave a low whistle. "Oh, he must have angered the gods!"

There was another, louder thump. Then a scream.

"Myrill's mercy!" Julia threw her scalpel onto the table. This senseless cruelty had to stop. She would put an end to it, even if she had to confront Silo himself. "No more!"

"No more what? What did I miss?"

"Ulric!" Julia ran to embrace him, trying to avoid the colorful rug slung over his shoulder. He turned to the side and pulled her close.

"What are you doing here?" he asked.

Julia nodded toward the wounded men. "What else?"

"Sweet Neesis. I'll speak to Gwynedd."

Julia wouldn't let Ulric shift the blame to Gwynedd, Silo's taciturn second in command. Not this time. She cupped his face and looked straight into his pale blue eyes. "Not Gwynedd. Silo. Silo gave the order." Then she kissed him, a long, lingering kiss. She made a show of it, knowing it made some men jealous—men she didn't like. Men like Strabo.

"Silo," Ulric said after a moment. "Right."

"Why do you smell of lavender perfume?"

"What in the Nine Hells?" Strabo exclaimed. "No one ordered a rug, boy."

Ulric ignored the jab. "The tunnel in the back stretches near half a mile into Transnanpela territory. How could I double back through those streets carrying Tubero's stash?" With a flourish, he unrolled the rug, sending a small iron strongbox and linen sack tumbling onto the floor. "Tell Silo I have his treasure!" To Julia, he grinned and added, "We keep the rug. It's Bayjoni; fresh off a boat from Baladan."

"I can't be bribed," Julia said. "You didn't answer my question."

"Neesis' sweet tits! You two are full of yourselves." Strabo leered at the sack at Ulric's feet. "Is that the dust?"

Ulric placed a protective foot on the sack. "Don't even…"

"You saying I can't be trusted? Say it. Go on, say it! See what happens next."

"Humph!" Julia was in no mood to play the peacemaker. "If Ulric won't say it, I will."

Before Strabo could reply, all eyes turned to the rear of the taberna. Silo strode in, wiping down the blade of his sword with a bloody cloth, silencing the room with his presence. He was lean and tall, nearly as tall as the giant Corvus, with iron-gray hair and a hard body tempered by years of commanding both back alleys and battlefields. Julia didn't know what to make of him. Silo was quick with a smile, an encouraging word, or a generous reward for the men who performed well, but she feared it was all an act. She always felt the violence roiling beneath the mask. And worst of all, Silo and Ulric fought about everything—but somehow, Ulric still admired him.

"You'll say what, Julia?" Silo asked with a smile. He slid his gladius into its scabbard with a soft thunk. His eyes sparkled with what may have looked like good-natured mischief, but there was a glimmer of disapproval in the man's stare. She decided Strabo wasn't worth the trouble, so she said nothing.

"I've got Tubero's stash!" Ulric gathered the strongbox and sack and offered them to Silo. "All the coin. All the tonics. Just as you wanted."

"Excellent work! I knew you'd get it, Ulric. No other thief in the Portum Collegium could've handled this job. Hells, no other thief in the city!" Silo motioned toward the lead Harbor Man. "Set it on the bar."

Two men, Imperaré soldiers by their red scarves, dragged a third man into the room. The man's tunic was torn and bloodstained, and they had beaten his face into the color and shape of a rotting cabbage. Julia had never seen someone look so defeated. The soldiers came to a halt, and Tubero fell to his knees, clutching his bandaged right hand, an odd lump of blood-soaked linen. Julia realized his fingers were missing.

"Myrill, have mercy! Why?" She started forward, but Ulric stopped her with a slight shake of his head.

Silo rested his hand on the pommel of his sword. "It's a taste of Silo's mercy."

The Harbor Men laughed and jeered, Strabo loudest of all. Tubero looked up through swollen, half-closed eyes that fell upon Julia.

"Mercy! Mercy, revered priestess!" he cried. He lunged and crawled toward her until one soldier kicked him flat onto his stomach. He looked up from the floor, sobbing, his good hand grasping at Julia's feet. "Myrill, Mother of Mercy, save me. Don't let them take me, priestess. Grant me sanctuary or swift mercy. Please?"

Julia's heart sank, heavy with pity and guilt. "I cannot grant you sanctuary. I'm no priestess, just one of her humble servants."

Silo and the others listened to Tubero beg for his life with sadistic glee, filling her with disgust. Did he deserve mercy? Was he any more wicked than the men of the Portus Collegium? He was a hard man, no doubt, but so were many she had befriended since her exile. Did any man deserve the torture that awaited Tubero?

"No? But I've heard of you," he said, scrabbling to his knees. "A woman with the voice of the goddess. A true ikon!"

"Enough of that!" Silo struck Tubero with the back of his hand, sending him sprawling onto the floor. The two Imperaré soldiers picked up Tubero, holding the defeated man between them. Silo headed for the exit. "We'll finish this back at the Towers."

The needless cruelty had to stop. Julia stepped in the way.

"Mercy." She had had enough of crude men and their endless killing. "You've taken his livelihood, his fortune, and his dignity. You took his fingers. You need take no more."

"Julia, he sided with Brocchus." Ulric spread his hands in a gesture meant to calm her, which failed. "You know, the man who tried to kill us both?"

I know what he's done, and to whom. Hearing Ulric explain the obvious only inflamed her righteous anger. *The question is, who do I serve? Myrill Regina? Or Silo and his thieves and murderers?*

"Out of the way, Julia," Silo commanded. "Ulric's right. Tubero is as much your enemy as he is mine."

The whole room tensed. There was a palpable sense of fear, a shared dread of what might happen next. Everyone knew death was the penalty for assaulting a sanctified priest of Trumric, and although she had only been an acolyte, the tradition had inculcated in the Trumin people a deep respect for the divinely blessed. And many of them had seen her wield the goddess' power. No one would act against her.

"Myrill, Mother and Healer of all Alakur's children, to Your mercy do I appeal."

A rush of divine vitality surged into Julia, and her skin shimmered with the faintest glow of dawning light. She would channel that light into a blazing sun to blind the cruel and spur fresh growth from wooden floors to bind the wicked. Then Myrill's mercy would grant Tubero the strength to flee and disappear into the city. And to the hells with Silo; let Arakru himself welcome him to the Underworld!

"Ulric! Control your whore!" It was Strabo, his voice dripping with disdain.

Instead, Ulric launched himself at the older Harbor Man, who doubled him over with a swift blow to the stomach and sent him tumbling into the bar. Ulric rose and threw himself at Strabo once again, as both spat curses at one another. The Harbor Men cheered.

Julia ignored the chaos and readied to unleash Myrill's power.

Nothing happened. Her light faded. Julia's eyes locked with Tubero's, who had been watching, searching for a seed of hope, but there was nothing she could do. All hope withered.

Tubero gave Julia an almost imperceptible nod, as if to say he forgave her. Her, who deserved no forgiveness!

She rushed toward Tubero and fell beside the doomed man. With his guards distracted by the brawl, Julia slipped one of her scalpels into Tubero's good hand.

Julia whispered, "Myrill offers mercy where man has none."

"Praise Myrill. Praise the gods. Thank you!" An instant later, Tubero collapsed, the scalpel buried deep in his heart.

Julia took hold of his hand. His touch was wet and slick with blood.

"Do not blame yourself." His voice was weak, and every word came with great effort. "I was unworthy… of Her power. You'll need it… for what's coming. Stay close to the thief."

"What's coming? What do you mean? How do you know about Ulric?"

The air grew fetid and chill, the noisy chaos of the taberna mute and distant. She could barely hear Silo, even though he was shouting, commanding her to use her magic to save Tubero.

"I'm close now," Tubero said. He looked through Julia as if he could see beyond her, beyond the room, beyond the living. "I stand at the threshold… of the Underworld. I see… I see…" He coughed, and bright flecks of red spittle sprayed from his mouth. His chest and lungs were filling with blood.

"What do you see?" Julia asked. A dark mist obscured her vision.

"I see the dead!"

It wasn't Tubero who spoke, but the dark-haired, hollow-eyed young man whom she had glimpsed earlier in the forum vinarium. It was Ulric, battered, bloodied, and defeated by some terrible foe. A familiar-looking dagger pierced his heart: Aguja, the slender blade of the assassin Luciano Portelos.

Julia screamed and tried to tear herself away, but Ulric held her in an iron grip. She looked around, desperate to find the real Ulric, but there was only a maelstrom of black mist.

"You're hurting me. Let go!"

"There's something else! Something beyond death. Beyond our world. It's waiting for us, Julia."

Julia whispered the triarchy of universal power. "Gods Above, Gods Below and… Gods Beyond. Is that what you mean?"

"You'll know soon. When you're entombed in godless Eltaran stone, felled before a dark gate by a thief's blade."

She had heard those words before, spoken by a goddess. Julia shuddered as the memory of those words returned. Words of doom.

The mists cleared, and Julia was back in the taberna. Tubero was dead.

A Bit of Tax Collecting

Ulric peered from the royal door of the Polyminius theater house, watching the last of the audience disappear through the exits. His performance as Icarius, the foolish young soldier in love with a foreign princess in *The Captive Ransom,* was a success; everyone had laughed and stomped at all the right times. The old Polyminius had only been half full, but Leufroy, the always optimistic theater manager, assured him it was a good crowd.

It was the last day of the Ulorinalia, the festival of the sea god Ulorin. Piso had reminded everyone that only an outstanding performance could end the summer drought, but Julia said no rain would come until Myrill and Ulorin reconciled. Something about a dispute over pirates and dryads, she had explained. Ulric had enjoyed everyone's look of confusion.

"Ulric!" Julia bounced across the stage, beaming with excitement. "I've invited everyone to Capito's Corner for celebratory drinks. Everyone's coming! Even Severa!"

Julia's smile pleased him more than any successful performance. After the raid on the Street of Hidden Pleasures, she had become quiet and withdrawn. Ulric suspected that something more than Tubero's death weighed on her, but when pressed, she revealed nothing.

Of course not, he thought. *Why make it easy?* They tried not to argue. She spent more time with Ide; he spent more time dicing. They had both been grateful for the distraction *The Captive Ransom* rehearsals had provided.

"Severa consorting with us lowly bit players?" He flashed a comically skeptical smile. "This, I have to see."

"But you were Icarius, and I, Princess Cytheris. We're proper actors now!"

"Gods Below!" His smile left as he threw up his hands in frustration. "I can't. It's my turn tonight."

Julia rolled her eyes. "Again?"

"Ugh! Silo didn't exaggerate when he said this job was long, boring, and—"

"And no money in it. I've heard," said Julia.

"What's this? Ulric's not coming?" Severa approached the couple, still looking regal as the queen of Xanthus. She stood before them as if she was holding court. "A pity. I'm planning to broach the subject of fabricators once more. Only after Leufroy has too much wine, of course." She had long tried to convince Leufroy to add magical illusions to enhance their productions. The practice was fashionable among the wealthier theaters, but he rejected the idea out of a professed devotion to tradition. Everyone knew it was really a matter of money.

"You have my support," Ulric said. "I'd tell him myself, but I must be in the First Stones District before sundown."

"Working through the night? Careful, Julia." Severa brushed her fingers through Ulric's hair as she spoke. "Don't let this one out of your sight. Some woman might snatch him away."

The shutters on the front of the shop were well-secured, and the second-story windows were too narrow for entry. Fortunately, the back door was not barred, only protected by the simplest of locks. Ulric slipped inside without a sound, then paused to let his eyes adjust to the gloom. Somewhere above him, a floorboard creaked. He ascended the stairs, careful to avoid the loose fourth step. On the upper floor by the window, a man sat hunched on a stool, peering through half-closed shutters. Ulric drew his dagger as he crept forward.

"Torched again!" the man cried.

Ulric slammed his dagger back into its sheath. "Sweet Neesis! How, Decius?"

The man spun around, a look of triumph in his eyes. "When the back door opens, I can feel a change in the air."

"That's damn impressive," Ulric admitted. "But come on, the average mark would never notice."

"We don't steal from average marks."

Gratius Decius was his senior by several years and a well-respected Portus Collegium enforcer. Ulric didn't dare ask what he had done to earn such shit duty from Silo. He slid off the stool and stood, the top of his head rising only as high as Ulric's nose. His body was thick, compact, bristling with muscle and covered in scars. Ulric had a list of men in the city he did not wish to cross, and Decius was near the top.

"Speaking of marks, has Rat-Face done anything interesting?" Ulric asked.

"After the fifth hour, he hit the streets and bought three bottles of pricey ink from a shop called Royal Codex. He kept his head down and spoke little. I saw nothing suspicious—or interesting."

Ulric looked through the shutters and across the wide avenue of the Via Fontum. The Collegium Draconis Aurei was a vast complex of marble halls, golden basilicas, temples, and towers protected by high walls and gates of shimmering adamant. Above it all, the eyes of the draconic towers observed the city with an arrogant disregard. Ulric thought the walls and gates were needless; the legions of magi that lived and studied at the collegium would be deterrent enough.

"Decius, has anyone ever done a shadow walk inside the collegium?"

"Are you mad? Rob the collegium? Are all provincials cursed by Neesis Insania?"

"Don't worry, I wouldn't dare. I just wondered if anyone had."

"You're a godsdamned fool! Don't let the bosses think you're even dreaming about it." He moved to the stairs and began his descent.

Ulric couldn't let it go. "So… somebody tried, and it didn't go well?"

Decius paused at the top of the stairs. "Over two generations ago. No one remembers their names or can agree on what they were after. They were caught and crucified in front of those very gates. They lingered for months until they were no more than screaming corpses."

"Months? Impossible," Ulric protested.

"Any horror is possible with magic. The priests of Eltarus demanded the Imperaré be punished for their blasphemy. Several princes fell in the reprisals and many collegiums were destroyed."

"Gods Below!"

"That's why you can't sneak up on me, Ulric. I'd never let my guard down so close to those damned gates."

Ulric's fellow spy left, and he began his lone watch on the collegium gates. A sudden chill ran through him, a nagging prick of fear. He hurried to the window and narrowed the shutters. How much of Decius' story had been true, and how much did he invent to frighten the ignorant provincial? He leaned forward and peeked through the shutters, trying not to imagine crucified thieves screaming for death.

Before the gates stood four temple guards, resplendent in their mail, motionless as painted statues. Great plumed helms obscured their eyes, but they faced unerringly forward, no doubt glowering at the dwindling traffic on the Via Fontum.

Ulric shrank back from the window. After a lifetime of thieving, the mere sight of those guards put him on edge. A shadow walk inside the collegium was a bad idea, he had to concede.

His orders were simple: observe, follow, and report. The problem was the mark rarely left the collegium, and if he did, it was always some inconsequential errand. It was Silo's punishment for his recklessness at the Night Market, but Ulric felt he'd been punished enough.

Why is Silo letting this drag on? My talents are being wasted, and for what? Brocchus backed down as we knew he would; there was no war between the princes. I did my part dealing with Tubero's betrayal. Why am I being punished for success? Why?

The mark, whom the watchers had nicknamed Rat-Face, was a mere discipulus, a student bound to a recluse dragon magi. He was only important because his master possessed the Eltaran scroll the Imperaré desired. The streets sizzled with the whisper: the Eltarans were offering a king's ransom for its return. Some said the Elts would pay twenty, while others said as much as a ridiculous one hundred talents of gold.

Ulric returned to the shutters with a puzzled look. The job had never made any sense. *If Silo wants the scroll, we should plan a shadow walk—fear of magi be damned. Watching these gates day after day doesn't help. That reclusive magus is never coming out. Unless… Unless the scroll leads somewhere.*

The mark emerged from a small wicket door set within the broad, adamant gates. He hoisted a satchel over his shoulder, clutched its strap to his narrow chest, and sprinted down the street.

Ulric had never seen the satchel, and he had never seen Rat-Face run. He sprang from the stool, leaped down the entire length of stairs, and burst out the back door. Somehow, he knew the satchel was what he'd been waiting for.

The mark known as Rat-Face was oblivious to any danger, but he still blundered toward safety. Ulric was running out of time, so he gave the signal. Corvus, acting as decoy, crossed the street and headed toward the mark while Ulric quickened his pace behind their victim. He gave a last glance at the lookout, whose posture signaled no warning, and moved in.

It was a simple pickpocket job, or "tax collecting" as the gangs of Trumric called it. The mark was a tall, gangly youth, with a long face topped by a mess of reddish-brown hair. His ears stood out like the handles of a wine jug, which—combined with his awkward gait—gave him a tragically comic appearance. His clumsy attempts to navigate the crowd on Lantern Street only made matters worse.

The mark was moments away from safety when the decoy ran into him, almost knocking him to the ground.

"By Eltarus' Lamp!" the mark shouted.

"Watch it, you rat-faced bastard!" Corvus yelled.

"Y-You ran into me!" the mark sputtered. "And my name is Flaccus. Sextus Pinarius—"

Corvus moved closer, towering over the mark. "Your... name... is... Rat-Face."

Flaccus tried to stand his ground, but soon took a nervous step back. He glanced around the crowded street. Everyone did their best to ignore him. He never even noticed his leather satchel being opened.

"Forgive my clumsiness. Now, if you please, I'm already quite late. Official business of the Collegium Draconis Aurei, you understand." He tried to continue down the street, but the decoy stepped into his path.

"What? Is that how you say you're sorry? Throwing the collegium in my face? Saying you're better than me, Rat-Face?" Corvus grabbed Flaccus' blue tunic in one beefy hand. "These fancy clothes give you the right to go knocking citizens about, is that it?"

Flaccus tried to cry for help, but only a faint squeak emerged.

He never noticed his coin purse and scroll case being collected from his satchel.

"Ha! You even squeak like a rat." Corvus watched Ulric move on and disappear into the crowd, then broke into a surprisingly charming grin. He let go of Flaccus' tunic and gave him a friendly thump on the shoulder. "Forgive me, citizen. I was in the wrong."

Flaccus recoiled as if he had received a death blow. Corvus walked on as if nothing had happened.

Ulric watched the mark from the safety of a shadowed alcove. Flaccus stood dumbfounded, jostled by the crowd. He looked over his shoulder but saw no sign of the strange brute. He shook his head and let out a sound somewhere between a chuckle and a question.

Gods Below! Were you not in a terrible hurry a moment ago? You're supposed to be leading me somewhere interesting. "Official collegium business," is it?

As if on cue, Flaccus spun around, failing to hoist his satchel higher on his shoulder. He ran down Lantern Street in a panic, stumbling to a halt before the notorious taberna called the

Quadrivium. Taking a moment to catch his breath, he approached the doors, then stopped to take an inventory of his satchel.

For the first time that night, Ulric saw real fear on the mark's face. Flaccus looked about in a panic, then plunged into the Quadrivium. Ulric moved to follow, but Corvus' beefy hand fell on his shoulder.

"Not running off with our cut, are you?"

The lookout, a dusky young Bayjoni, cut through the crowd. "What's next? Trouble?"

"No trouble, Igdir," Ulric said with a grin. He pushed Corvus' hand aside. "Corvus and I were about to divide the spoils." He looked back at the doors of the taberna. What official collegium business could Flaccus be conducting there? He had an idea, but the mystery would have to wait until greed was satisfied.

In a nearby alley, Ulric tossed Flaccus' coin purse to his accomplices. Corvus, a good two heads taller than Igdir, snatched it out of the air.

"The coin is for the both of you," Ulric declared. "My thanks for coming along on such short notice."

Corvus weighed the purse and peeked inside. "Neesis' sweet tits! You're feeling generous."

Igdir held up a hand to collect his share. "You seem very pleased with yourself, Darktalon. I thought you were in a sour mood after all those nights following that rat-faced magus' pet."

"I was. But something interesting is finally happening."

"Yeah… but weren't you supposed to just follow him?" Igdir asked.

"What use are eyes to a thief if he can't see opportunity?"

Corvus looked up from counting his coins. "What? If this job gets me on Silo's bad side, I'll bounce your head off every hull in the harbor."

"No need to worry. The whole point of following Rat-Face was to act when the time was right," Ulric lied.

Satisfied, the two thieves returned to dividing their coin and arguing over whether to use their cut on women or a pile of shadow-dust.

It was the middle of summer, and the night was warm and humid. Ulric leaned against the wall and took a moment to enjoy the cool breeze created by the narrow alley. While he relaxed, Corvus and Igdir chose sex over tonics, then fell into arguing over which brothel to visit.

Ulric mouthed a quick prayer to Neesis and retrieved the scroll case. He removed the cap and pulled out a roll of papyrus, then unfurled the scroll, holding it up for a better look. A faint light from Lantern Street trespassed across the edge of the alleyway; more than enough for a thief trained in the Shadow Ways.

It was a map. Ulric pushed himself off the wall and leaned into the scroll like a starving stray pouncing on a fine meal. The papyrus was old and the writing had faded, but he could make out the city of Trumric on the coast, bisected by the great Nanpela river. To the northwest, there was a vast forest labeled Silva Aurea. Within that wild expanse, several landmarks were notated with the singular purpose of leading to a place labeled "Tmia Culscva."

Those words were unknown to Ulric; the letters were Trumin, but the words were strange. He unfurled the scroll further and discovered more illegible writing and strange diagrams. He glanced back to the map's destination and attempted a pronunciation. "Ta-mi-uh Kuls-kwa."

Igdir looked over. "Huh? What's that?"

"Something… interesting."

Near those mysterious words, in dark, unfaded ink, someone had scrawled "Eltaran gate-stone here—Guarded? Trapped?" Ulric's blood quickened—not at the hint of hidden treasures, but at the mention of Elts. Growing up in the city of Mist View, he had never seen an Elt, nor met anyone who had. The rare vagabond or traveler would claim to have had brief but terrifying encounters with the elusive Children of Eltarus, but the practical citizens of Mist View knew all travelers were liars and the gods cursed all vagabonds with madness.

Ulric did not believe in tales of Elts. After arriving in the capital, he had expressed this perfectly reasonable skepticism, and was met with an assortment of odd looks, sidelong glances, and even outright laughter from Silo. He discovered quickly that his views on Elts marked him as a fool, and worse, an ignorant provincial.

When he demanded someone show him an Eltaran, no one could. They could only say they knew someone who had once seen an Eltaran from afar during this or that religious festival. Julia claimed a delegation had been in the city years prior, during General Maculla's triumph. Everyone took it for granted an

Eltaran delegation visited the Senate every year and assumed there were still Eltaran settlements in the vast wilderness north of the Republic. There were even whispers that the head of the ancient academy of magics, the Collegium Draconis Aurei, was a secretive, centuries old Eltaran. Ulric began to suspect he was playing the role of the mark in a very long con, or as criminals of the city called it, an "honest scheme."

"What do you know about Elts?"

Corvus and Igdir stopped arguing and looked at Ulric as if he had grown horns. Finally, Igdir replied, "Untrustworthy bastards. The gods kicked 'em out of heaven. Or something like that."

Corvus made crude motions with his hips. "All I know is there's no sweeter ass than Elt ass!"

Igdir laughed and mumbled in his own strange language, saying Corvus was as sharp as a pile of camel dung. Ulric, who knew all the best Bayjoni insults, laughed too.

"What are you talking about?" Igdir asked Corvus, once again speaking in Trumin.

"Just another reason we should all go to Nymph's Grove first and not Silana's. They have an Eltaran whore there who'll make you forget Trumrician girls."

"Really?" Ulric was certain they would not find the answer to the Eltaran question at a local brothel.

"You idiot! She's a poor Kanchean girl that's had her ears clipped!" Igdir threw up his hands. "And I was wondering who was stupid enough to stumble into that scheme."

"Watch your mouth, you little Bayjoni turd! I'm not stupid."

The two bickered a short while before deciding to visit the Kanchean "Elt" at Nymph's Grove. Igdir told his friend to go on ahead and loitered in the alley. Ulric looked up from the map and made sure they were alone.

He rolled up the scroll and asked, "What do you have for me? Some real news, I hope."

"It's not been easy," Igdir said. It sounded like the beginning of an excuse. "Brocchus' men are tight-lipped and our friend with the Vintners wants more coin."

"Always more coin and fewer answers." Ulric sighed and secured the map inside its case. "Where's Luciano? Does anyone know?"

"The whisper on the docks is he's still in Mist View."

"You told me as much last ides! I'm not handing over a single copper iss for that!" In a flash, Ulric crossed the alley and pressed Igdir against the wall. "Don't scheme me, Igdir."

The Bayjoni threw up his hands. "Easy, easy, for Neesis' sake! I said that's the whisper. Our vintner friend says different."

Ulric backed off. "Let's hear it."

"Luciano shrouded his old bosses. Two vicars, dead."

"Names?" Ulric asked.

"Don't know. So much for fucking loyalty, am I right?"

"The bastard never had any. Where's he now?"

Igdir shook his head. "No idea."

"Can we trust your friend?"

"Honestly… no. He's been known to lie to keep the coin flowing. But he's told the truth. Occasionally."

Ulric cursed under his breath and handed over a handful of denarii. "If it turns out he's running a scheme—we bleed him. Understand?"

"Of course." Igdir pocketed the money and exited the alley.

So Luciano had betrayed and murdered his old associates. How was that surprising? Did his fate even matter compared to the mystery of the map? Still, he had made a vow to Neesis Fortuna. He had promised to send the assassin to the underworld in exchange for the goddess's help. Neesis had gifted him with her divine luck, yet Luciano still lived. An unfulfilled vow made to the goddess of luck made him nervous.

His mind turned back to the map. The Eltaran scroll was fought over because it was a map, and a map only had value because of where it led. And it led to something called a gate-stone. Or did it? He knew papyrus and ink could lie as well as any man, but at least the map's destination was a real place to investigate.

What if he could present Silo not with a bit of old papyrus, but a gate-stone?

How did it go? Arrius always started with a "Listen up, Darktalon!" Then it was, "Having eyes, but not seeing opportunity; having ears, but not hearing danger; having a mind, but deceiving one's self… these are things every thief should fear."

The unlikely events that placed the Eltaran scroll into his hands could only be the wild luck of Neesis Fortuna. It was an opportunity not to be squandered, and only the boldest thieves pleased the goddess whom many called Neesis Insania. It was time to do something crazy.

To discover what lay hidden at Tmia Culscva, Ulric would need friends, allies, people he could trust. Since none were available, he'd recruit help from those who had every reason to distrust him.

Herald of the Conflagration

A wall of cool, fragrant air greeted Ulric as he stepped inside the Quadrivium. Rumor said the expensive enchantments of a freelance ice magus kept the taberna comfortable, despite the thick crowds and summer heat. He paused at the threshold, enjoying the unnatural chill and the smell of warm bread, strong herbs, and wine.

Rows of magical Eltaran lamps hanging from the high ceiling and mounds of candles on every table ensured the interior was well-lit. People drank resolutely, laughed loudly, threw dice carelessly, and argued… cautiously. Ulric scanned the raucous patrons on the main floor. He didn't spot his mark, the collegium discipulus Pinarius Flaccus, but he noted the grim stare he received from the taberna's owner.

He shrank back, trying to disappear into the crowd. Silo was going to be furious; he had lifted the scroll case from Flaccus when his orders were only to observe. He shuddered to think what would happen if he started trouble in the Quadrivium the very same night.

Gwynedd, Silo's loyal primus, had told him the history of the taberna. Many years ago, the crime lords of the city had seen the advantage of providing a place where the wealthy and powerful could solicit their services without fear, and they decided that the Quadrivium was as good a place as any. At first, this meant secretive visits by Republic clerks, collegium agents, and the trusted slaves of wealthy patricians. When the Imperaré began using the taberna as a meeting place to settle disputes among the criminal gangs and resident collegia, the building became something of a local landmark. As the Quadrivium's reputation grew, some bolder among the wealthy and powerful would disguise themselves for a personal visit. After a time, the thrill of safely consorting with plebeians, foreigners, thieves, and murderers became fashionable.

The forbidding look from the proprietor was a reminder that while Ulric was in the Quadrivium, there would be no tax collecting, no back-alley parley, and no honest schemes—and Myrill have mercy on anyone caught performing knife or shroud work.

If I wanted so many damned rules, I'd have conned my way into a temple! But this is an honest scheme where honesty will be key. So I'm not really breaking any rules.

Ulric left the chaos of the ground floor and climbed the stairs to the second tier. It was a broad gallery that projected from the side and back walls of the taberna, overlooking the floor below. On the far wall, a small bar kept the most common wines and foods close at hand. Here, the patrons were subdued, their steady conversations creating an indecipherable drone. In shadowy alcoves along the walls, furtive groups conducted their business in hasty whispers.

Ulric joined a small crowd moving toward the bar. He spotted the back of Flaccus' head immediately; he couldn't miss those ridiculous ears. Across from him sat a woman draped in the unmistakable blue and gold robes of the Collegium Draconis Aurei.

All right, all right, no need to piss myself. I knew this scheme would lead straight into the jaws of our reclusive dragon magus. I have a role to play, and if I stick to the script, I'll recruit a merry little band of players. Unless… What if she knows the spells that can unmask any lie? It'd be over quick… and end bloody. But only a few know the trick, so I've been told, and they guard the secret jealously because of all the coin it brings. So, it's another throw of the dice, and for once, the odds are in my favor. Besides, I didn't lift the Eltaran map to have Neesis watch me slink away at the first sign of trouble.

As Ulric weaved his way through the gallery, he couldn't help but take a closer look at the magus. She must have been beautiful once, but time had turned her skin pallid, streaked her dark hair with gray, and sullied her once bright eyes with lines of ambition. All to be expected after a long life at the collegium, he guessed. What did her beauty the greater disservice was the exasperation and rage battling across her face.

Ha! I see the missing map has already come up. This should be a good bit of fun!

Ulric moved past their table without fear, confident Flaccus had never seen him. He loitered at the rear of the gallery, pretending to flirt with the dark-haired, sullen-eyed girl behind the bar.

"Proceed without the scroll? How do you propose we do that, hm?" The magus' voice dripped with condescension.

Flaccus sunk into his chair. "I… I don't know."

The magus' only response was a burning stare.

"You've seen the map. Maybe you remember enough," Flaccus said. "Maybe we could find our way without it?"

The magus erupted in a short, angry laugh. "You half-wit! You jar-eared clunk! Even if we found it, how would we ever enter without the cipher?"

So that's what all the strange writing and weird diagrams are? Some sort of cipher? I'd never have sorted that out!

"Did you pay any attention during the planning of our little expedition, hm?"

"I… of course… I…"

"That was a rhetorical question, you slack-headed moron!" Exasperation sallied forth once more. "Why the administration has punished me with such a discipulus I know not. Perhaps a rival has placed you for the sole purpose of ruining my career. Is that it, hm?" She gave an exaggerated sigh. "I'd return you to the rank of precator and be rid of you, but the collegium doesn't want your family to suffer any more embarrassment."

Flaccus had sunk so far into his chair he had disappeared, but he sat bolt upright at the mention of his family. "My father has nothing to do with this." He slammed his balled fists on the table. "Besides, I wouldn't have been carrying the map if you hadn't left it at the library!"

That's the spirit, Rat-Face! Give some back to the old bitch! I talked back plenty to Ghostwalker. Still have the scars to prove it!

"And," he continued, "I wouldn't have been robbed if you'd keep your dealings in the respectable parts of the city! Instead, we sit here surrounded by thieves, drunks, and whores. What business could an honorable Trumrician woman have at the Quadrivium… hm?" He emphasized the last part with a thrust of his sharp chin.

Ha, ha! Blood drawn! Well struck, Rat-Face.

Rage vanquished all competing emotions and consumed the magus like a wildfire. Whatever courage Flaccus possessed turned to ash in mere proximity to her fury.

Sweet Neesis!

She struggled to spit out every word. "You would impugn the honor of a magus? Mock your betters? Imply I'm a whore?"

"I didn't call…" Flaccus squeaked. He fell back into his chair.

"I didn't say you did! I said you implied it, you ill-born imbecile!" she shouted, loud enough to attract the attention of every nearby table. "I've been too soft, too kind. That's now clear."

Flaccus panicked. "Forgive me, please! I was wrong to speak so disrespectfully."

"Yes, too kind, for too long. What you need is a return to discipline. Maybe then you'll develop the character needed to advance."

The magus thrust her right hand forward. She contorted her fingers into something resembling a claw or an accusation, then spoke a single word. Ulric heard it, but just barely.

A searing wave of heat passed over his body, reigniting the unwelcome memories of Aquila's hot irons. He staggered and grabbed the bar for support, trying to recall the precise sound of the word, but it hurt to think of it.

Although Ulric wasn't the target of the spell, the mere sound of the word brought pain. For Flaccus, there must have been incessant and debilitating agony.

A spasm wracked Flaccus' body and his legs kicked as if he ran through a nightmare, pushing his chair away from the table with a loud screech. His skin reddened, sweat streamed down his face, and a shuddering moan escaped his lips. He forced his trembling hands to grasp the edge of the table, then let out a short, high-pitched scream. He hunched over the table and sobbed. The macabre display drew the attention of the whole of the upper floor.

"Not here! Please! I'm sorry!" Flaccus struggled through every word. "Not… in front of… everyone."

"Oh, but why ever not?" she asked in a sweetly mocking tone. "You'd insult me in front of them, would you not? And, as you said, they're only 'thieves, drunks, and whores,' so what do you care what they think of you?"

This elicited a round of jeers and laughter from the rough crowd. Ulric didn't think it was possible for Flaccus to look any more miserable, but he did.

It's not my fault he doesn't know when to shut up! Not my fault. But Myrill's mercy, I've seen enough of collegium discipline. Now is the time to strike. Ulric stepped away from the bar, reciting a quick prayer as he marched toward the dragon magus. *Neesis! Look to the shadows! Another one of your unruly brood of unfathered children is about to risk it all. A single throw in the dark will determine my fate. Bestow upon me your blessing, your divine luck!*

Ulric emerged from the shadows and, without a word, sat in an empty chair between Flaccus and the magus. He placed the missing scroll case on the table. He looked straight at Flaccus and said, "This belongs to you."

The magus snatched up the case, releasing Flaccus from his torment. He slumped back into his chair, exhausted, wiping his tears away with trembling hands. In a weak and cracking voice, he asked, "Who are you? And how did you find the map?"

The magus, who was doing her best to authenticate the contents of the case without sharing them with the gallery, glanced over the scroll. "Two surprisingly intelligent questions. Let's hear his lies first. Then we'll reason the truth."

"Who am I? I'm Ulric Darktalon: professional thief, part-time actor, and full-time liar. Except for tonight. Tonight I am that rare species of Trumrician—an honest man." There were looks of confusion from one side of the table and skepticism from the other. "Who do I have the pleasure of speaking with?"

"I'm Sextus Pinarius Flaccus, a discipulus of the Collegium Draconis Aurei."

Ulric nodded and turned to the magus, who secured the map and hid the case within her robes. She said nothing for an uncomfortably long time. Ulric thought she stared at him like an augur might examine a portentous set of entrails. He wondered what she saw. A young man not much older than Flaccus with an athletic body, pale skin, and night-black hair. Did she think he was handsome? Could he charm or flatter her? What did she make of his expensive tunic, fine leather belt, and well-made shoes? What of the silver and bronze rings and arm bracelets he adorned himself with, or the silver chain supporting two small wooden cubes inlaid with silver, the tesserae of Neesis? What did a priestess of Eltarus, God of Magic, think of a follower of Neesis Fortuna, Goddess of Luck?

"I am Magus Vipsania Tertia of the Collegium Draconis Aurei, priestess of Eltarus—may His lamp shine eternal—and Herald of the Conflagration. Now, for the second question."

The Conflagration? Ulric felt the searing agony of Aquila's hot irons once again; recalled the smell of his own burning flesh. He saw Gwynedd's scars; again heard his warning. *Fear the fire magi most, for they become like Ukorus, the God of Earth and Fire: obsessive, secretive, and ill-tempered.*

"How did I find the map? That's not the right question at all. Because I stole it."

An Honest Scheme

Ulric took a moment to relish the look of utter confusion on Flaccus' face.

"You stole it? How?" Flaccus asked.

"Oh, hide your astonishment," Magus Vipsania said. "As if it requires skill to take anything from you." She looked at Ulric, and he was certain her eyes flashed with blue flame. "As for you, honest thief, I'd rather burn the truth out of you, but since we're in the Quadrivium, I'll play along."

"It's a high-stakes game, Magus Vipsania. One we can both win."

"Ha, pish posh. Tell me why you stole the map, only to return it."

"It was sheer luck! I saw someone dashing through the streets clutching a satchel as if he'd just robbed the state treasury. I couldn't pass up an opportunity like that: I had to see what was inside."

"And what did you find?" Vipsania asked.

"A map, a cipher, and maybe the answer to a mystery that's been gnawing at me."

"And what sort of mystery interests an ignorant thief, hm?"

"What happened to the Elts, of course! Where have they gone? Why did they go? Where I grew up, most people don't even believe they exist."

"Ignorant provincials!" Flaccus gleefully exclaimed. "You can't be that stupid, can you?"

"Shut up," Vipsania commanded. "You no longer have the privilege of commenting on other people's ignorance."

But Ulric thought he deserved an answer. "Honestly, Flaccus, I was that stupid. The philosopher tells us that education is the constant discovery of our own ignorance. Since arriving in the capital, I've discovered quite a lot."

"Oh, I have the pleasure of being lied to by an honest *and* educated thief?" Magus Vipsania said. "Tell me which philosopher said that, and I'll keep playing your game. And if you want to sound educated, stop using slurs like 'Elt.'" She crossed her arms and waited.

Oh, no! What did Ghostwalker say about showing off? This is a magus, not some pretentious freedman! Forgive me, Ghostwalker, but I should have paid more attention when you were droning on about the philosophers. Think! It started with a… D?

Vipsania glowered at Ulric, looking very self-satisfied.

"Diodorus of Kos!" Ulric said, with all the confidence he could fake.

A faint smile crept across Vipsania's face. "Very well. The game continues. If you recognized the map's value, why return it?"

"Oh, I had a coin purse," Flaccus prompted, but they ignored him.

"Because I can't solve this mystery on my own," Ulric said. "And you'll need my help."

"Your help?"

"We need no one else," Flaccus said, sounding panicked.

"The map mentions traps, guards, and who knows what other dangers."

"Guards, I'll burn," Vipsania said with a sadistic spark in her eyes. "As for traps, I think I can handle a few mechanical inconveniences."

"If you go after this gate-stone, whatever that is, what better ally than one of the best thieves in Trumric?"

Vipsania cocked an eyebrow. "I commend your humility. I was certain you were about to say, 'the best thief in the Republic.'"

Ulric gave his most charming smile. "See, honesty, education, *and* humility: these are a few of the fine qualities I can bring to your expedition." Magus Vipsania laughed, an honest, cheerful laugh. Ulric's hopes rose. "But there's another reason I should go. You bought the map from Marius Secundus after he commissioned Arrius Ghostwalker to steal it from two senatorial couriers traveling through Mist View. The job cost Ghostwalker his life."

"So?" Vipsania looked bored.

"Arrius was my mentor. His death drove me to Trumric, and this business with the map has nearly killed me twice already." Ulric grasped the tesserae hanging around his neck. "And now, luck—praise Neesis Fortuna!—has led me back to the map. I have to see where it leads. The Goddess demands it."

"Add presumption to your list of qualities, thief. You were foolish to appeal to one of the gods below. Or to think me sentimental. Or that I have no allies." Vipsania looked past him toward the stairs and stood, anticipation blossoming on her face, evoking the lost beauty of her youth. It faded quickly, replaced by her usual sour expression. "Your services will not be needed."

Ulric wanted to continue the game, but he had to see what inspired Vipsania's brief transformation, so he stood and followed her gaze. Flaccus, realizing he was the only one left sitting, leaped to his feet, knocking over his chair with a clatter.

A man bounded up to the gallery, sliced through the crowd loitering at the top of the stairs, then marched straight toward their table. He was tall, with the sort of body that could only be forged by years on the battlefield or the arena. His skin was dark and scarred, his hair and beard close-cropped with a light dusting of gray. He wore an expensive red tunic trimmed in gold and a belt adorned with bronze plates. A bejeweled Bayjoni cavalry saber hung at his side. Mercenary or gladiator, Ulric thought he looked prosperous and formidable.

In a booming voice, he called out, "Vipsania Tertia! It's been too long. You look as beautiful as ever!"

Vipsania's sour expression did not change. "It has been a long time, Kehindé; enough time to turn you into a liar."

Kehindé laughed. "My lovely Vipsania, I forgot how much you dislike flattery, no matter how sincere." He moved to embrace her, but she sat down, leaving him and everyone else standing awkwardly. Kehindé grabbed a nearby chair and swung a long leg over it, sitting between Vipsania and Ulric. "Your letters were guarded; your purpose left vague. We came, of course. How could we refuse?"

Vipsania cast her eyes over the gallery. "Where is Rexinda? I can't wait to see how she's grown."

"Rexinda grew fast and wild, like a weed!" he said proudly. "With its share of thorns. She'll join us soon. She's below, making arrangements with our host." He looked across the table, seeming to notice Ulric and Flaccus for the first time. His eyes focused on the blue collegium tunic. "You must be Vipsania's student... Flaccus?"

"Uh, yes! Sextus Pinarius Flaccus. Forgive my surprise, but I didn't know Magus Vipsania had hired common mercenaries."

Vipsania shot Flaccus a look that could kill, and Ulric was certain it could have if she willed it. He watched everyone intently, looking for subtleties he could exploit. Flaccus had become more anxious since Kehindé arrived, and he wanted to know why.

Kehindé waved off the insult. "Forgive the boy. It's no insult to be called a mercenary. But we are *uncommon* mercenaries, young Flaccus." He turned to Ulric and asked, "And who is this? Another student?"

"A *common* thief," Vipsania said. "He was just leaving—"

"A thief?" Kehindé interrupted. "Good! We'll need one if we're stealing from Eltarans."

It was time to continue the game. "I told Magus Vipsania the very same thing." Ulric extended his hand in greeting. "Marcus Octavius Ulric, known as Darktalon on the streets of Mist View and the capital. I am a thief, Kehindé—an *uncommon* one."

Kehindé took Ulric's hand in a crushing grip. "Kehindé of Suloko."

"We're not stealing anything, Kehindé," Vipsania corrected, sounding annoyed. "We'll be studying artifacts of historical and magical significance."

"Would the Eltarans want you to have it?" Ulric asked.

"You are not part of this conversation," Vipsania said with a glare. "In fact, it's time for you to go."

"Would they?" Kehindé asked mischievously. When she didn't reply, he turned to Ulric and said, "Seems we're stealing from the Eltarans."

"Are we? Good! I've never fought an Elt before."

The voice belonged to a young woman with long, sun-bleached blonde hair, streaked with northern style braids that gave her a fierce, barbarous appearance. She wore a bright shirt of feathered armor over a dark tunic; its rows of tapered bronze plates resembled the breast of a golden eagle. An apron of leather strips, each weighted with bronze caps, covered her thighs but left her well-tanned legs exposed. A gladius hung from one side of a metal studded belt, a broad-bladed dagger on the other. Seeing such a beautiful woman outfitted like a Trumrician soldier was strange, yet provocative.

Vipsania leaped from her chair. "Rexinda! I didn't recognize you. When I left Kos, you barely came up to my waist." She stepped forward with open arms. "Come, embrace me."

Rexinda gave her a warm hug, despite her obvious embarrassment. "Dearest Theia Vipsania," she said, using the Kreslan word for aunt, "I feared I'd never see you again."

Vipsania returned to her chair. "I'm grateful to Eltarus you were both able to come."

"It was fate." Kehindé leaned back in his chair and stretched his long legs under the table. "Kresla rebels no more. The Harath frontier is secure. Bayjon keeps to itself, while the Verdans are quietly plotting their next mischief. If you hadn't summoned us, we'd be out of work!"

Rexinda grabbed a nearby chair, ignoring the meek protests of the table's occupants, and sat between Kehindé and Ulric. She glanced at Ulric, her eyes lingering a little too long. He couldn't resist giving her a wink. She rolled her eyes and looked to Flaccus, who had been staring at her lasciviously since her arrival. Were there no young women at the collegium? Was Flaccus even aware of how he looked?

Kehindé started to make introductions, but Rexinda interrupted him. "Who are you?" she asked Flaccus.

"I'm Sextus Pinarius Flaccus, a discipulus of the Collegium Draconis Aurei!" he announced. It seemed as though he couldn't decide between a smile or a dignified expression. The result was an awkward grimace.

"I do not like the way you look at me. You will not look at me that way, or I will take your eyes."

"Oh, do stop embarrassing me, Flaccus!" Vipsania sighed, then spoke to Rexinda. "My apologies. Ignore him; he's harmless."

"If he's harmless, why do you keep running him down?" Kehindé asked.

Vipsania shot Kehindé a sidelong glance.

Flaccus stared down at the floor and whispered, "Sorry."

Rexinda motioned toward Ulric. "And this one?"

"Ulric. An uncommon thief," Kehindé replied.

"An unwelcome thief!" The magus' anger was rekindled. "One who has stolen from me—"

"I returned the item in question," Ulric interjected.

"—and refuses to leave. He must be removed before we proceed."

Rexinda bolted to her feet. "Let me do it!" She placed a hand over the hilt of her gladius and smiled down at Ulric.

"Careful, Rexinda. Remember what I said about the rules here," Kehindé warned.

"He's right: this is the Quadrivium," Ulric said. "We can't go starting brawls, Rexi."

Kehindé laughed, though it didn't seem to be because Ulric had said anything amusing. Rexinda lashed out with a swift kick directed toward Ulric's chin. His eyes followed the line of her sandaled foot, past her shapely calf, and lingered on her tanned thigh for a moment too long. At the last instant, he pushed his chair back, avoiding the kick and hitting the floor with a thud. He rolled out of the fall and sprang to his feet just as Rexinda slammed into him, driving him toward the gallery railing. Ulric didn't want to believe she'd push him off the gallery but, Neesis forgive him, he wouldn't take the chance. He swept her feet out from under her and they both fell. By the time they hit the floor,

Rexinda's broad infantry dagger was at his throat, and Ulric's own blade was pressed against her armpit.

"You don't like being called Rexi?" Ulric asked, voice dipped in both amusement and sarcasm.

"My name is Rexinda Hamunds-Daughter."

Ulric could feel Rexinda's cold iron at his throat, but the closeness of her body and the intensity in her green eyes was far more distracting. "I'm Marcus Octavius Ulric. You can call me Darktalon."

"But that's a silly name."

Ulric tried to think of something clever to say, but Kehindé hauled Rexinda away like she was a sack of goose feathers. Ulric stood and sheathed his dagger as two Imperaré enforcers appeared at his side, demanding to know who started the brawl.

"There was no real brawl," Ulric said. "It was an audition. They wanted to know if I could handle myself, and Rex*inda* was willing to spar." It was a ridiculous lie, but sometimes the more ridiculous, the better.

The enforcers asked if it was true, and Rexinda didn't hesitate. "*Darktalon* speaks the truth. Our apologies to the management."

The men were skeptical, but a small bribe from Vipsania eased their doubts. Kehindé then bought the entire gallery a round of drinks to apologize for the disturbance.

Vipsania turned to Ulric with a growl. "Not only do you waste my time, thief, but now you've cost me money. Pray to Neesis we never meet outside the Quadrivium."

Kehindé acted surprised. "I thought it was agreed—we need the thief."

"I agreed to no such thing, and you know it!"

"Time has made you even more stubborn, Vipsania." Kehindé paused. "We'll vote on the matter; like we used to with Hamund and Rubea."

"Don't be absurd. You know he can't be trusted. He wants to join us for some dark purpose of his own—thievery and betrayal, most likely."

"If that's his fate, I'll kill him myself." Kehindé turned to Ulric. "Does that sound agreeable?"

"Fair enough," Ulric replied. "Uh, do I get a vote?"

"No," Vipsania and Kehindé said in unison.

"Also," Vipsania added, "in the event of a tie, my will prevails."

"The matter before us: Ulric—in or out?"

Kehindé, as Ulric expected, voted "In." Vipsania was an unsurprising "Out." Rexinda looked at Ulric with the faint hint of a smile and said "In".

Everyone's eyes settled on Flaccus. If he voted "Out," then all of Ulric's efforts would amount to nothing. His hopes sank. Why would Flaccus vote "In?" Ulric had stolen from him, humiliated him, and caused him to suffer horrible pain. And he seemed smitten with Rexinda, however hopelessly. What man invites a rival? And didn't the discipulus have every reason to please his mistress, Magus Vipsania?

Flaccus gazed at Ulric with eyes that held both an invitation and a warning.

"In!"

Close to the Thief

The actors of the Polyminius Theater Troupe were well into their third hour of celebration at Capito's Corner. They had all come; the theater manager Leufroy, the troupe's leading man Piso, the beautiful and scandalous Severa, the two youths, Cordus and Ebbo, and many others. There was even a select handful of the troupe's more adventurous benefactors, those willing to brave the rougher streets of the Transnanpela District. Ulric had promised to come, albeit later, after he had finished the unprofitable job for Silo.

Julia pressed a clay cup to her mouth, allowing the cool wine to brush her lips but swallowing nothing. She had already downed two cups that evening, yet the wine had not produced its desired effect. No amount of wine would erase Tubero's words from her mind. The dying man's warning clung to her like a funeral shroud.

...felled... before a dark gate... by a thief's blade...

Piso's deep laugh brought her back to the moment. Cordus and Ebbo, unlike her, continued gulping down bottle after bottle of Capito's cheapest wine, having seemingly bottomless stomachs.

Julia doubted Lefroy's coin purse was equally unending, though she noticed the theater manager made no attempt to curtail the young men's revelry. The Polyminius Theater Troupe certainly made for a raucous crew. Still, Julia had certainly seen the narrow taberna more crowded, more boisterous. Had Capito made room for her and her friends to celebrate? How sweet of him.

Someone's fingers twirled her black curls, interrupting her thoughts, and she whipped around to face her tormentor. Her face broke into a smile.

"You made it!"

"Of course," Ulric said. "How often does the miserly Leufroy offer to wine and dine us?" He looked over at Capito, whose belly rested on the counter as he wiped a bowl clean. "I'll take some bread and cheese… and two cups of wine." Gesturing at Cordus and Ebbo, he continued, "And not that piss those street rats are guzzling! Something suitable for a Bayjoni princess and her consort." He winked at Julia.

One of Capito's sons soon returned with a tray laden with food and set it in front of Ulric, who squeezed into a chair in between Cordus and Julia, much to the half-drunk actor's dismay. Ebbo giggled and elbowed his friend in the ribs, which Cordus returned with a shoulder shove, nearly sending Ebbo tumbling off his chair. The two began arguing and tussling.

Ulric shook his head, then put his hand on Julia's shoulder. "Can we talk? Alone?"

"I don't want to leave yet. Everyone's having such a good time. It would be rude."

"Well, let's at least make our way to the back, where it's more private. I have something to tell you. Plus…" Ulric extended his hand toward her cheek with a lascivious smile. "I've missed you."

"Uh oh. I've heard those exact words before. You have bad news."

"No, not bad. Just news, that's all. Just news."

"Uh huh," she said with a doubtful smirk. "Come on, my love." Grabbing Ulric by the hand, she said, "Let's go hear this news."

Ulric grabbed their tray and the two of them pushed their way past the fighting duo, as well as a handful of Capito's regulars. Severa was attending the troupe's most generous benefactor in the way that only Severa could; bosom and leg on display, coupled with soft eye contact and the suggestive caresses of fingertips on the man's arm. As they squeezed past her, Severa's hand came to rest on Ulric's hip.

Julia swatted it away when she felt it had lingered there a little too long.

At the end of the bar, Leufroy and Piso were deliberating the nuances of senatorial politics. Piso ignored them both but Leufroy, lifting his cup, gave Julia a warm smile and Ulric a nod.

They sat at a table near the back of the taberna. The boy arrived with two cups of wine. Ulric gave one cup to Julia and raised his own high into the air. "To a successful performance. And more importantly, to Trumric's most stunning actress."

Julia eyed him over the rim of her cup, barely lifting it.

Ulric snapped his fingers at the boy and pointed at his cup, then Julia's. The boy nodded once, then disappeared behind a curtain. Ulric set his cup down and motioned for Julia to do the same. "Wait. Let's do this right. My princess deserves no less."

"Princess" was what Ulric called her when he was trying to bed her or apologize to her. She suspected the latter. She set her cup down on the table, tilted her head, pursed her lips, and waited.

The boy emerged from the back room and dropped a piece of burnt bread into each cup. Once again, Ulric raised his wine, clearing his throat.

"As I was saying... to my beautiful Bayjoni princess, Trumric's finest actress. Drink! Drink and may you live forever, as you live in my heart!"

Julia waited before touching cups with him. Whatever news he was about to share, she knew it wasn't of the good sort, and she wanted to watch him squirm for a few moments.

When their cups finally met, Ulric took a long gulp.

"I'm waiting," she said.

Ulric guzzled the rest of his drink, then set it down, gripping it with both hands. "I got a new job."

"Oh really? A new job? And what exactly is this new job?"

Ulric's next words stumbled out of his mouth like drunks out of a taberna. "I'm going to... uh, was hired to go..." He mouthed an incoherent sound. "Out of the city... with some people... exploring people... explorers!" He fidgeted with the empty cup. "Out of the city and... beyond. Far beyond."

...beyond...

Julia lost her breath at the utterance of that word. "Beyond?" Her voice cracked. "What do you mean 'beyond?'"

"Well, you know... north and west, pretty far. Really far, actually. Northwest. Up the Via Borealis. Far as it goes, I suspect."

...stay close to the thief...

"Fine. When do we leave?"

"You can't come with me."

"I can't go with you?" Her voice was raised now, and she was sure Ulric had noticed. "Really? I can't?"

He thought for a moment, then finally said, "I mean, I think it would be better—safer—for you to stay in the city."

"Am I not capable of deciding what is safest for me?"

"Julia—"

"Don't you dare say "princess" right now. We are way past that."

"Julia. Look. It was hard enough for me to…" Ulric pressed his lips together. "To persuade these people I was the man for the job. There's no way she… they… are going to let you come along as well. No way."

Julia cocked an eyebrow. "She? Did you say 'she?' Who is 'she?' And how exactly did you persuade her?"

"She's nobody, Julia. You've got it all wrong."

"Uh huh." Julia crossed her arms and glared at Ulric.

"It's not like that. She's nobody. Just some dragon magus."

"A dragon magus?!" Julia imagined a green-eyed, blonde-haired, fair-skinned beauty, in a low-cut silk robe trimmed in gold. "Now I'm definitely coming along!"

Ulric's cheeks heated, his eyes darting around the narrow room.

But Julia didn't care if others took notice. The added pressure of their gaze would only help her. Nonetheless, she lowered her voice before speaking again. "Have you forgotten? Myrill is the goddess of mercy, healing, and nature. I can fare better than you in the wilderness."

"Julia…"

She could feel Ulric's defenses failing. "You don't understand. I must go with you. The Goddess compels me. Mother Myrill told me to stay close to you. That's what She said to me. I have to, my love. I have to."

Ulric raised an emphatic hand.

But before he could respond, Julia added one last argument. "And, my love, what a bold move it would be as well."

Ulric's mouth wrinkled into a pursed grin as he shook his head. He reached for Julia's hand. She smiled, and they locked eyes.

"Fine," he said. "I can't believe I'm saying this, but fine. I'll figure it out."

"You always do," she said. "Now, where exactly are we going? You said she's exploring. Exploring what?"

"I don't know where exactly. Somewhere within the Silva Aurea, I think. What we're exploring is an Eltaran ruin."

"Silva Aurea? Eltaran?"

…entombed in godless Eltaran stone…

"I know, I know. The magus is after something called a gate-stone, whatever that is. I only know it must be valuable because all the Imperaré are after it too. Even though Silo would never approve of what I'm doing, I mean to steal it for him, however I can, whatever it takes. It's the only reason I'm joining their expedition. Are you okay with that?"

Julia fumbled for words. "You're going to steal an Eltaran relic? From a dragon magus? Oh, Ulric, what have you gotten yourself into? This isn't just another Porta Mare burglary Silo assigns you. Do you have any idea how mad you sound?"

"Boldly mad," Ulric replied with a grin. "I need you to hear me: I'm going to steal the gate-stone." He gripped her hand tightly. "And with you at my side, my mad plan can't help but succeed."

For a moment, she said nothing. Did nothing. Then she leaned across the table and kissed Ulric on the lips. He eagerly returned her passion.

Their moment was interrupted by approaching footsteps. Julia opened her eyes to see a hand reach for the loaf of bread on their table. The man, whose long, stringy hair blocked most of his face, tore off a hunk of bread and stuffed it in his mouth.

Julia stared at the man who, still chewing, grabbed her cup of wine. He washed down the last of his bread, then set the empty cup back on the table, wiping his mouth with the back of his hand. After cleaning his teeth with his tongue, he said, "Boy, still follow around this Bayjoni whore, eh?"

Without looking up, Ulric took another drink. "I thought I smelled something. What's wrong, Luciano, doesn't Brocchus bathe you?"

Luciano clenched his teeth. "Maybe I pay your whore to bathe me. I think she like that. Maybe I like it too, eh, boy?"

Ulric moved his hand toward Ghostwalker's spatha, returning Luciano's glare.

"Heh. Boy, know just like I know: you not use that now." A smile.

The smile surprised Julia. She didn't think this murderer was capable of it. She didn't like it; it made her nervous. Scared her.

"Truce, eh, Darktalon? I come back to town and hear news. Truce, no war. Everyone happy. No more fight. You not disobey you boss, eh?"

Ulric did not release his grip on the sword. He clenched his teeth, glaring at Luciano. "What do you want?"

"I follow you here to tell you something, Darktalon."

"And what is that, Luciano?"

"You know what they say on streets about you, boy? Not just I say. All the whisper in city. Everyone talk about you." He paused, as if waiting for a reaction. Ulric gave none. "They say you are coward. So do I."

"Is that what they say about me? So they've moved on from 'brash fool,' have they? Well… I'm sure you've heard your names, haven't you, Luciano?" Ulric didn't wait for a response. "Betrayer; murder, and friend-slayer."

Luciano bristled, his hands tightening into balls. Ulric looked as if he might stand up, so Julia reached for his free hand.

Luciano must have noticed, because he sucked air in through his teeth and bit down on his lip, looking like a snarling animal. "You could have killed me, boy. You had easy chance. But you gave you balls to this girl." He laughed that familiar, hyena-like laugh. "She has your balls, boy. You should have killed me when you could, but you too scared of your Bayjoni girl." Another cackle. "You more afraid of her than me, I think, eh?"

Julia gripped Ulric's hand so tightly his fingertips turned bone white. He glanced at her, and when their eyes met, she shook her head subtly.

Then Luciano turned his attention to her. "And you… I find out you not just Silo's new physic, you also people's new priestess. Pretty little Bayjoni priestess. You think what you did was show me mercy? Right, girl?"

"Mother Myrill granted you mercy, though you certainly didn't deserve it."

"No, girl. Not goddess. It was you. Darktalon should have kill me that day. You make him not. You understand this, girl? You! You show me no mercy that day. You damn me." The Verdan put his hands on the table and leaned in close to Julia. "You damn me, you little bitch. And one day… when Darktalon not nearby… I plunge Aguja in your heart and watch her drain your life."

Ulric stood, maintaining his grip on his spatha. Luciano placed his hand on the golden hilt of his new falcata, smiling once again. Each of them took a step closer to the other, their feet practically touching. Neither unsheathed. Yet.

Julia's heart raced. Mother Myrill, not this, not now. She reached for Ulric's arm, but he recoiled in response.

His chest heaved and his eyes narrowed, while his jaw clenched in sync to some unheard war drum. She had seen Ulric this way only once before—the evening the Night Market burned. And that had nearly ended in death. She feared she could not prevent it this time.

"Porteles!" A baritone voice rang out from the taberna's entrance. Three large men—rough men—stood just inside the doorway. Julia cringed at their elaborate tattoos, portraying violent rituals conducted upon bloody altars from beyond.

...beyond...

"You're to come with us, Porteles. Brocchus' orders."

Luciano's eyes remained locked with Ulric's, neither man budging. But Luciano's face hinted at something else. A grimace had replaced the smile; he looked like a man burying pain.

"Porteles! Let's go, Hound! Brocchus' orders. The prince wants a word."

Luciano released his grip from his sword and brought his hand down hard on Ulric's shoulder. He patted it harshly as he spoke. "Truce, eh, Darktalon? Yes. Truce." He squeezed down hard, whispering, "For now. Heh."

Ulric smirked and gripped Luciano's shoulder, squeezing it mockingly. "That's right, Luciano. But we both know all truces are temporary." Each man maintained his hold on the other's shoulder. Neither said anything further, but their eyes betrayed a boiling tension.

Julia grabbed Ulric's sword arm with both her hands before he could make any further 'bold' moves.

The Hound of Nyx slowly backed away, knocking Cordus and Ebbo's drinks off their table before walking out the door with the Shrine Alley thugs.

...stay close to the thief...

The Ikon of Myrill wrapped her arms tightly around Ulric Darktalon and pressed her head against his chest. His heart beat frantically, and every muscle felt tense. She squeezed him tightly, gazing up at him. "Stay close to me, my love. Please don't leave me. Just stay close." When he met her gaze, his face softened.

Julia exhaled, holding back tears she would not share with him. Not tonight.

Arena of Lies

Ulric entered the arena, eager for the day's performance. A yellow tunic, sandals, and the tesserae of Neesis dangling from a chain of silver was his only costume. His only prop was a spatha-shaped wooden sword, not unlike the one he carried when portraying the Xanthian soldier, Icarius. His role would be a familiar one—that of the foolish thief. Ulric raised the sword and adopted a plunging guard: arm forward and high, blade angled down, defending his head and torso.

Silo approached within three sword lengths. The Imperaré prince stood tall and imperious, with iron gray hair that belied his age and a sleeveless tunic that accentuated a lean body of hard muscle. Ulric thanked Neesis that they only carried wooden swords. He adjusted his stance, pushing his sandaled feet through cool sand. It was only the first hour of the day and the sun wouldn't crest the arena enclosure for some time.

Trumric had its famous Amphitheater of the Republic, of course, but within the Portum Mare District there was the older Calidius Amphitheater. Ulric had no idea what Gaius Calidius Pansa had done to have an arena named after him. Neither did the locals, apparently, since everyone called it the Harbor Arena because of its closeness to the sea. The Portus Collegium used it as a training ground thanks to a longstanding agreement between Silo and the Arena Master.

Silo assumed a prow guard: torso forward, arm out, blade held at the ready. "Have you been practicing your guards and strikes? Your footwork?"

Ulric made a quick survey of his form, then made several minor adjustments. "Of course."

And it was the truth. If he didn't improve, he'd be dead. The Republic's most feared assassin, Luciano Portelos, had defeated him not once, but twice. Each time Neesis Fortuna had saved him from death, but now Luciano was eager for a third duel, and She was a fickle goddess.

A faint smile crept across Silo's thin lips. "We'll see," he said, then lunged forward.

Practice weapons couldn't kill—well, not without a good bit of effort—but they still hurt like the Nine Hells. The thrust from a hardwood point could feel like the impact of a hammer, a slash from the wooden edge like the slap of hot irons. Ulric swept the blade aside and countered, a move Silo blocked with ease. He then launched a series of attacks that drove Ulric back across the sands until Ulric rallied and pressed his own offensive, eager to show off all he'd learned. The arena echoed with the thunk and crack of wood.

Silo looked unimpressed. "Your form is adequate. Footwork is good. Don't try fancy when simple will do. Fancy gets you killed."

You sound just like Ghostwalker. He always said: economy of thought, economy of motion.

Silo then began a fresh round of drills, emphasizing the guards and strikes best suited to the spatha's longer blade.

Ulric risked a glance across the arena. Nearby, Gwynedd—Silo's favored primus—sparred with the master thief Decius. The Portus Collegium primus fit the scene, the very image of a foreign captive forced into gladiatorial combat; a towering frame, wild red hair, long mustachios, and naked but for the strange, checkered pants worn by the tribes of Cearalon. He silently matched his paired axes against Decius' twin swords and endless taunts. Further afield, Collegium soldiers, along with a few elite Harbor Men like Strabo, trained in pairs or small groups. Some grappled, some fought with daggers, and some even fought with swords and shields. Julia and a couple of other women gossiped near the wall, ready to tend to any injuries.

Even though Ulric trained in a near-empty arena, it felt unreal to be fighting on the sands of one of Trumric's great amphitheaters. He had always loved the arena. He had no spare coin growing up on the streets of Mist View, but gladiatorial games were free. There was always another patrician trying to buy their way into elected office by hosting days of lavish games. He had watched in fascination as men, and sometimes even women, fought and died, their fates determined by strength and luck, as if the gods Cathus Bellicus and Neesis Fortuna lay entwined, gifting death and glory as they raced toward a bloody climax. To Ulric, it had seemed little different from life with the Low Street gang. Though quicker, he guessed.

After apprenticing with Arrius Ghostwalker, Ulric had no time for gladiatorial games. Even if his training hadn't consumed everything, Arrius never cared for the arena. He hated pointless bloodshed. *Just like Julia*, he thought. *He would have liked her, no doubt.*

Arrius may have disdained violence, but bloodshed lurked in every dark corner of Mist View. Ulric had seen Ghostwalker wield his spatha with unnatural speed and grace, dispatching threats with surprising ease. It was his advice of "economy of thought, economy of motion," pushed beyond human limits. When Ulric had begged to learn the technique, Arrius told him he wasn't ready for the deepest secrets of the Shadow Ways. Arrius said he would teach him when the time was right, if he didn't discover it on his own.

So Ghostwalker thought I could discover it on my own. How? What did he mean, exactly? The secret must hide in the fundamentals of the Shadow Ways. Maybe it's simply a new way of interpreting the old disciplines. Or combining them?

As Ulric struggled to block Silo's latest attacks, he let the rush of a Thieves' Glimmer overtake him. Suddenly, the smack of wooden blades became sharper, the smell of sweat more pungent, and the morning uncomfortably bright. Blinking against the light, he went on the attack.

While maintaining the Thieves' Glimmer, he slipped into a Shadow Mind trance. For a moment, all his fears abated, and time seemed to slow. He deflected Silo's counterattack before he realized what he'd done. Had he found the key to Ghostwalker's prowess?

Then Silo and the arena became a jumble of chaotic sensations. The Thieves' Glimmer, a discipline of the waking, luminous mind, slipped away. Shadow Mind, a deep trance of the unconscious, hidden mind, shattered. *How do I reconcile two opposites?*

A sudden white-hot shock of pain, then Ulric's hand was clutching his sword arm where a nasty welt was already rising.

"What did I say about keeping it simple?" Silo lowered his weapon and appraised the situation. "If this was real, your arm would be useless. And you'd soon be dead."

Ulric tossed his spatha in the air and caught it in his left hand. "I fight just as well with my other hand. Simple is for fools!"

Silo threw up his arms and spun around, looking at the empty stands, laughing all the while. It was a cheerful laugh that set the arena on edge.

"Simple is for the novice, the discipulus, the ignorant but wise. A fool flips the sword to the other hand and learns nothing."

The arena grew quiet as each fighter bent their gaze toward Ulric. Men he respected looked at him with curious mockery. He wanted to disappear, to flee the arena, but Silo's icy blue eyes kept him transfixed.

Ulric made a small, half-hearted flourish with the training sword in his left hand. "It was just a joke."

"Why bother with training if you won't listen to my council? If you won't obey my orders?"

Silo lunged and forced Ulric to defend himself, left-handed, from a dizzying series of attacks.

"Your pride complicates everything! And you're too arrogant to follow orders!"

Ulric was a passable left-handed swordsman, as he had claimed, but Silo no longer held back. Instead, he unleashed his full skill upon him. The wooden point of his sword struck Ulric's chest like a battering ram, driving him to the ground. Ulric lay sprawled across the sands, massaging the massive bruise on his chest. Julia rushed toward him, but he stopped her with a barely perceptible shake of his head.

Through pained breaths, he rose to his feet and said, "I'll endeavor… to take training… more seriously. I swear it."

"And what of your duties to the collegium? To its praeses, your prince? Do you take those seriously?" Before Ulric could reply, Silo asked, "What were you doing in the Quadrivium last night?"

There was no denying the meeting with Magus Vipsania. The whole affair had been public and memorable. Silo pressed the attack once more, driving Ulric back on his heels. He'd have to improvise and speak the truth; or as close to it as he dared. It was a dangerous move, and always one of last resort.

"I created an opportunity!" Ulric shouted over the incessant crack of hardwood. "One that will bring glory to the Portus Collegium and its prince!"

"You young idiot."

Silo's voice was flat and calm. There was a slight tone of disappointment that Ulric had never heard before that hurt worse than any blow.

"You've made me look the fool," Silo said, then disarmed him with one swift move. Ulric let out a sharp intake of breath, sudden eye-watering pain emanating from the stinging slap of Silo's wooden spatha.

"Your scheming undermines the very balance of power."

The sword struck again, opening a bloody welt on Ulric's thigh.

"Your careless actions strike at the heart of our truce."

A sharp thrust to the gut and Ulric doubled over, gasping for breath.

"Your pretense and abundant self-regard threaten the very plans of the Imperaré!"

Silo sent three more jabs into Ulric's gut. He fell to his hands and knees. If the sword was real, his intestines would be splayed across the ground. Instead, he only heaved the remains of his breakfast into a colorful puddle in the sand.

He tried to say something in his defense, but there was no breath for speech. Using the flat of the blade, Silo rained down blow after blow across his back.

"Must I beat discipline into you like a common slave?"

The pain was tolerable, but the humiliation gnawed like cold fangs into his heart. He feared the memory would linger, scratching and biting at his spirit, until... until he brought Silo the gate-stone!

To regain his dignity, he would have to finish the job: gain Magus Vipsania's trust, accompany her to the Eltaran ruins, steal the gate-stone, and deliver it to the prince of the Portus Collegium, Horatius Silo.

After leaving the Quadrivium the night before, Ulric had raced back to Portus Towers, desperate to speak to Silo before the whisper on the streets reached his ears. He had found the Imperaré prince in his shop playing the congenial fence, as sometimes amused him. Ulric confessed everything. Silo had been furious at first, but, like any good thief, he saw an opportunity and took it. He could also hear danger, so he and Ulric wrought a plan to inure himself and the Portus Collegium from accusations of treachery. All Ulric had to do was play the part of the outcast thief, a role with which he was intimately familiar. And, because Silo insisted no one outside the two of them could know of their scheme, not even Julia, he would once again become the damned liar.

At the moment, Ulric thought Silo performed the part of the vengeful Imperaré prince with a bit too much zeal.

"Mercy! Mercy, Silo!" Julia ran between Ulric and Silo and fell to her knees, one arm thrown protectively over Ulric and the other raised to ward off any blows. "For Myrill's sake, no more!" Her fist bristled with golden light.

Silo stayed his hand and stood shaking with rage. Everyone in the arena was silent. It seemed as if they were holding their breath before a deep plunge, preparing themselves for what may come.

Silo tossed his training sword into the sand. "Gwynedd! Decius!"

Primus and the thief ran over and nearly stood at attention, as if they were legionary soldiers. "Take these two back to the Towers. Confine them to their rooms. I'll decide what to do with them later."

"They'd be more secure in—" A glare from Silo cut Gwynedd short.

"Dis and Death! Are *you* disobeying orders now?"

The giant Northman stiffened, making him appear even taller. "No, chief!"

Silo turned his back on Gwynedd and addressed the arena. "What's everyone staring at? Back to training!"

Julia helped Ulric get to his feet. "Can you walk?"

"It's not as bad as it looks. I've been worse, as you well know."

"Wounded worse? True," Julia conceded. "In worse trouble? I'm not sure."

Going Shadowed

Despite the rolling carts and morning chatter rising from the streets behind the loft of the Polyminius theater, Ulric struggled to wake. Julia nudged him, but the early hour and the warmth of her body convinced him to stay in bed. However, they had to meet Magus Vipsania beyond the High Gate before the second hour. With a groan, he dragged his bruised and sore body out of their makeshift bed and forced himself to dress, watching Julia do the same. She caught his gaze and feigned covering herself up, then gave him a knowing wink.

Their escape from Portus Towers the previous night had been easy. Gwynedd and Decius had marched the two of them straight from the Calidius Arena to their rooms on the fourth floor of the aging insula. As expected, Gwynedd searched their rooms, confiscating Ulric's weapons and thieves' kit, plus anything that could be fashioned into a makeshift rope—except everything he found had been replicas and fabrications provided by Silo. Ghostwalker's spatha, Ulric's thieves' kit, and a generous supply of rope had remained hidden. They waited for the third watch of the night before slipping over the balcony and descending quietly to the street. A harrowing climb for Julia, but child's play for Ulric Darktalon.

Then it was a furtive trek across the night-drenched city, ending in an easy climb up the old stone pine to the safety of the theater loft.

They said little as they gathered their things and stuffed their packs. An hour before daybreak, they crept down the stairs, where several actors had already gathered on the stage. As Ulric and Julia passed, the actors whispered among themselves and Severa treated them to an approving look. Cordus and Ebbo eyed Ulric jealously. The rest of the actors stifled giggles, hands over their mouths like children. Ulric and Julia clasped each other's hands as they exited the Polyminius theater, leaving the glares and whispers behind.

They crossed the Nanpela River and made their way northwest as the sun crept over Nemus Hill, casting long shadows across the city. Shadows were always a welcome ally, but they were shrinking fast. Although he had serious reservations about leaving the safety of the city walls, at the moment he was more worried about being spotted by an overzealous Imperaré gang. He was certain the whisper was already on the street: capture Silo's renegade. Each time a pair of eyes moved in their direction, he bristled and picked up the pace. After a while, Julia grabbed his arm in frustration.

"What are you doing? You're like an over-wound harp string."

Ulric pulled them into an alley filled with broken crates and rotting barrels.

He lowered his voice. "No doubt the whisper's already on the street. They'll be looking for us. We need to get to the High Gate. Get on the road, join up with Magus Vipsania. The Imperaré won't extend their reach past the city walls."

Ulric felt a momentary queasiness. Would they? He wasn't sure. If he wasn't certain, it wasn't a lie.

"Fine, let's go. But can you stop dragging me around like a child? I know we're being hunted."

Ulric furrowed his brow. He released his grip on her wrist, then Julia interlocked her fingers in his.

"Better. Now… lead on, my love."

As they neared the High Gate, the Via Borealis widened into a broad square, its worn cobblestones betraying the frequency of travelers in and out of the city. Julia tugged on Ulric's arm, pulling him toward a street vendor hawking earrings, combs, and a myriad of colorful ribbons and bows.

Ulric sighed as Julia began perusing the wares. "There's no time for shopping."

"I'll be quick. If we're followed into the wilderness, I know a trick that takes only a bit of ribbon and supple twigs of fig and oak. And Myrill's blessing, of course."

"Uh, sure." Ulric produced a bronze coin from his pocket and flipped it to the vendor with an awkward smile. "Get all the ribbon you need. Fast."

The hairs on his neck stood up. He focused his senses and wove his glance through the crowd. Three men, High Ridge thugs by the looks of them, were watching them. One spoke to the others while pointing in their direction. He eased the cowl of his traveling cloak back; as he did, he willed the noise of the crowd to fade, focusing only on the men's conversation. Though unable to decipher every word, two caught his attention: "Let's follow."

Ulric laced his fingers in Julia's and clenched.

"Ouch! Careful."

"We need to go. Now."

Julia understood. She grabbed a handful of green and violet ribbons, and they hurried toward the gate.

Ulric glanced over his shoulder. The men were out of sight, but certainly not gone. He quickened their pace, mustering a smile for Julia as he did.

So these High Ridge amateurs think they have me tethered? I could fade easy, even with Julia in tow. But... they haven't made a move. They must be hoping I'll lead them to the Eltaran scroll. I could lead them into the blades of Rexinda and that Kekeksuan mercenary instead; they'd make short work of them. Then I could leverage their sympathy. How could they turn Julia away if they knew she'd be targeted for revenge?

It was an excellent scheme. He squeezed Julia's hand with pride.

The scene at the gate was split in two. On one side, the line was lengthy and slow, full of travelers seeking entrance into the city. Here, a handful of soldiers herded the people like cattle, while several clerks questioned the occasional traveler, even pulling some aside to search their packs or wagons.

On the other side, the outgoing traffic was sparse and facilitated by a mere two centurions. The line out of the city was moving briskly. *Thank the goddess! Soon we'll be leading those High Ridge fools into sharp steel.*

As they passed through the High Gate, the older of the two guards kept his bored look, but Ulric noticed the younger one undressing Julia with his eyes. Neither guard tried to stop them, their attention fixed on the procession of travelers and merchants lined up outside the gates for over half a mile.

Ulric's mind wandered back to that blustery winter's morning when he had been in a similar line, eager but exhausted, still reeling from the loss of Ghostwalker, but ready to conquer Trumric one coin purse at a time.

They were well past the walls of the city and passing the end of the traveler's line when Julia's voice brought Ulric back to the present.

"Hey, you with me?"

"Huh? Oh… of course. Just planning. Strategizing. That sort of thing."

Ulric stopped and looked back toward Trumric. First, there were the walls separating himself from the streets he had grown to call home. As his eyes moved across the city, he saw the immense hippodrome, the Curia Garonus, the great senate-house, and the city's architectural masterpiece, the Amphitheater of the Republic. Towering above them all were the draconic towers of the Collegium Draconis Aurei, ever present, ever watchful.

The Via Borealis was broad, and the traffic grew sparser the farther they traveled. Ulric felt vulnerable on the broad road.

"It's open out here. No cover at all."

Julia pointed toward the gray sky. "Not afraid of a little rain, are you?"

"No. Not the rain."

"What then?" Julia asked.

"Exposure."

"What a strange notion. If anything, we're free. Free of the smell, free of the filth, free of the crowds. And free of Silo and the Imperaré, if just for a time. We've broken through the walls!"

Not free of the Imperaré. Those High Ridge thugs are still on our tail.

"I guess most people see the walls that way," he said. "Confining, entrapping, engulfing. I find them... comforting. I always have."

"I understand. At least, I think I do. But remember, Myrill is the goddess of nature. Her power will only grow stronger as we journey into the wilderness." Julia was quiet for some time, then said, "There are shrines up the road, not too far. Let us make an offering to Myrill."

Ulric nodded, and they walked on.

Up ahead, several travelers congregated along the sides of the road. As Julia predicted, shrines of various designs were everywhere: some were well taken care of, others neglected. A few were simple, even crude, while others were beautiful and ornate. He nervously watched the road as Julia approached a granite rock taller than she was and wider around than she could wrap her arms. A large grotto had been carved into the stone, and offerings littered the ground before it. Within the grotto, a carving of a crowned woman stood, her outstretched arms serving as the perch for several sacred birds. Each bird waited their turn to eat the seed held in the palms of the woman's upturned hands. Behind the carving stood a fig tree with oversized fruit draped on its branches.

Julia knelt before the shrine, plucked several fig leaves out of the lining of her cloak, and laid them at the goddess' feet. She closed her eyes, and Ulric knew he should do the same, but found himself unable to remove his gaze from Julia and her tangled brunette curls. When she had finished her prayer, she rose to her feet and turned to face Ulric with a comforting smile.

"We have Myrill's blessing. She will watch over us during our journey. Now, let's be on our way."

Ulric glanced back to see if the High Ridge men were still tethering them. They were. But he knew the real danger was ahead, not behind.

Just before the second hour, Ulric spotted a sign boasting a taberna ahead: "Stop at the *Occasio Ultima*, your last chance for food and drink."

"That's our stop."

Julia was about to speak when a single raindrop splashed on her nose, startling her. Ulric chuckled as she flicked it off with a fingertip. Ahead, streaks of gray cascaded from nearby clouds.

"Look!" Julia cried. "Myrill and Ulorin must have reconciled!"

"Great," Ulric replied with false enthusiasm. "Now I know who to thank for our inevitable soaking."

They both quickened their pace, the shelter of the Occasio Ultima beckoning them.

The sparse drops became a steady sprinkle, and Ulric's cloak grew wet and heavy. He spotted the taberna, a single-story building fronted by a large patio which was covered by a blue awning. There were a few other small structures nearby, a home and stables. A grove of trees surrounded the Occasio Ultima, providing a bit of cover from the rain. Travelers crowded the patio, taking refuge under the awning, while raindrops concussed rhythmically upon it like liquid fingertips on a tight leather drum.

Ulric spotted Kehindé's dark, tree-like frame near the center of the patio. He sat erect, alert, towering over the other seated patrons. As Ulric and Julia drew closer, the warrior tapped someone on the shoulder and pointed in their direction. The head turned, and a familiar igneous face stared at him from under a gold-trimmed cowl. Magus Vipsania gazed at Ulric, then Julia, and back to Ulric, her face combusting into a familiar scowl. Meanwhile, the rain gained momentum.

Ulric looked around, rehearsing his prepared line of defense in his head. He noticed a group of men, maybe seven or eight, armed, sitting at a table beyond the awning, unconcerned with the falling rain.

Hired muscle? Mercenaries? No, wait… those are Imperaré heavies; I see the scarlet now. And they're not the men who have been following us. These are no High Ridge lowlifes. These are top men. Brocchus'?

Ulric slowed but didn't stop. He scanned the patio and the surrounding grove. Julia appeared unaware of Vipsania's fiery stare or the Imperaré heavies. Four male slaves flanked the magus, three young and strong looking men plus another, much older man. Flaccus sat nearby, awkwardly fiddling with an empty bowl and spoon. Rexinda met Ulric's gaze warmly, and Ulric hoped Julia didn't notice. Kehindé rose to his feet. Was this gesture a welcome for him? Or a warning for the Imperaré heavies? Ulric couldn't decide.

Julia stepped under the awning and praised the gods, shaking the wetness from her dark curls.

"Who is this?" Vipsania squeezed the words out between her teeth.

Ulric smiled and ignored her question. "Magus Vipsania, how pleasant to see you again."

"Who," Vipsania spat, "is she? And why…" she paused, allowing her anger to seep in, "is she here?"

Ulric was ready for this moment. He had prepared his lines. But he needed the help of the High Ridge thugs. Where were they? They were critical players in this scene.

"Vipsania, let me introduce my friend, Persius Julia. Julia, this is Magus Vipsania Tertia of the Collegium Draconis Aurei." Ulric's eyes continued to dart in all directions; searching for the High Ridge men, monitoring the heavies, appraising the looks of Vipsania's companions, and seeking a way out of the cauldron.

Vipsania addressed Julia for the first time. "And why are you here?"

Ulric feared Julia would respond—despite his earlier warning—so he kicked her foot. A gentle baritone voice broke the uncomfortable silence which followed.

"*Salve*, and blessings this morning, Persius Julia. I am Kehindé."

The three High Ridge men who had been tethering them left the road and filtered into the crowd. They moved with the type of walk that screamed trouble. The type of walk meant to intimidate. He was unsure if Kehindé had seen them, and certain that Magus Vipsania had not.

Here we go.

"Vipsania, if you give me a moment, I can explain Julia's presence. Perhaps if we—"

"Away with your rhetoric and manipulation, thief. Spit it out."

While delivering his well-rehearsed speech to the magus, he kept his eyes on the High Ridge thugs. More men followed—other gang members?—slipping into the crowded patio and surrounding Vipsania's table. The Imperaré men watched, some scowling, others smiling.

As if on cue, one of the High Ridge men headed straight for Vipsania's table with purpose in his stride and murder in his eyes.

Knife Work

Ulric recognized the approaching man as the leader of the High and Mighty, a gang who ran their corner of High Ridge District with less honor than the Harbor Men and fewer wits than the Gutter-Fish. They were all hard fists and quick knives.

The leader drew closer, gathering three gang members in his wake. Kehindé's eyes tracked them as they shoved their way through the crowd, heedless of who they offended. Ulric dropped his pack, grasped the hilt of his gladius, and gave Kehindé a look that signaled trouble. The High and Mighty leader was a scraggly-faced mess with a sparse beard and jagged teeth. He didn't impress Ulric, but the broad knife at his belt and the dozen or more unfriendly blades hidden in the crowd did.

Kehindé's voice boomed across the patio. "Let's stop squabbling and see what these fools want."

Everyone turned to the scraggly-faced man and his three companions. Vipsania said nothing, only looked them over like a poor meal she would return to the cook. The crowd on the patio grew quiet, the only sound the constant drumbeat of the rain.

"Well, who are you?" Vipsania asked.

The man licked his lips. In a raspy voice he said, "Who I am isn't important."

"Of that I'm certain."

The man's face reddened. "What's important is the scroll! Hand it over and things won't get bloody."

"The scroll?" She seemed more irritated than surprised. "Have you ruffians been hired by one of my rivals? Well, they should have hired more of you!"

Flaccus scanned the patio, fidgeting worse than usual. Rexinda gave the men a dismissive look and turned back to the table.

Ulric enjoyed the gang leader's growing frustration. He couldn't seem to understand why his threats weren't being taken seriously. He ran his tongue over uneven teeth and licked his lips again. "You're already surrounded! I have a dozen men hidden in the crowd." He put a hand on his knife. "Enough blades to slash you to pieces."

Vipsania glanced over the crowd. "I see no one of consequence."

The rain fell harder, and the staccato beat on the awning quickened.

"Listen, you thick-headed, magus whore—"

"You have your answer." Kehindé's calm tone held more power than any shout. "You get nothing. Walk away and live. Or, if you insult the magus again, die."

"Battle 'n blood! Why wait?" Rexinda cried.

Rexinda spun out of her chair, sweeping her sword upward in a graceful arc. The blade tore a red line along the scraggly faced man's tunic before slashing his neck and tearing through his jaw. He hit the ground in a spray of bright blood. Kehindé was at Vipsania's side, Bayjoni saber on point, before Ulric's spatha could clear its sheath. The older slave stayed close, while the younger men fled into the crowd. Flaccus let loose a startled screech and leaped to his feet, a look of sheer terror on his face. He uttered a single word and balls of red-hot flame engulfed his fists. Ulric wondered why his robe sleeves didn't catch fire.

One of the dying man's companions raised a gladius and charged Rexinda. Kehindé intercepted the sword and drew his saber up and over, forcing the gladius down and entrapping the blade under his own shoulder. He stepped forward, placing the saber's edge against the man's wrist, and twisted. The man screamed and dropped the sword. Kehindé kicked him square in the chest and sent him flying. He crashed into a nearby table in a tumble of limbs, chairs, and clattering soup bowls. The other two men drew their swords and retreated. Kehindé stood at the ready, now armed with saber and gladius.

Julia leaned close to Ulric and whispered, "We know some of these men! Do we fight?"

Screams and oaths rippled through the crowd. Some travelers ran into the taberna, while others fled into the rain. Like the tide draining from a treacherous shore, the retreating crowd revealed hidden dangers: a dozen or more killers brandishing grim looks and sharp blades. The High and Mighty were first on their feet, followed by the Imperaré heavies. The shower became a downpour, and the incessant crash of rain drowned out the scraggly leader's pathetic mewling. He lay on the crimson cobblestones at Rexinda's feet, grasping at his ruined throat and jaw, slowly kicking his feet along the ground, perhaps trying to flee from his killer. He went nowhere.

The circle of knives tightened. Kehindé spat out a series of orders. "Rexinda, stay close to Vipsania; don't let them draw you away. Ulric, let's see if you're any good with that sword. Support Flaccus and try not to get burnt. Julia, get under the table."

Incensed, Julia protested, "I could be more help than you know! Myrill—"

Rexinda joined Vipsania, brushing Julia aside. "Oh, under the table, little girl! You'll just get in my way."

Ulric moved to Flaccus' side, wary of the flames curling around his hands. "You should listen to Julia! I've seen her stop a dozen men in their tracks—" he gave her a wink "—and not just with her beauty!"

"Oh, this is becoming absurd." Vipsania stood and smoothed out her blue and gold robes. "Kehindé, I'd like to avoid further bloodshed this close to the city."

"Understood, but we may not have a choice. They'll not lay a hand on you nor insult you again."

Vipsania stretched out her hand and a long rod of ebony wood, embossed and capped in gold, appeared. Ulric had no idea where it came from. He looked closer and saw the gold was molten, flowing across the wood to trace arcane symbols in bright streams. The headpiece was sculpted in the visage of a dragon, with white-hot glowing eyes. Wispy blue smoke curled from its tiny nostrils. Magus Vipsania Tertia walked past Kehindé and stood in the middle of the patio, glaring contemptuously at the men and their blades. Lightning flashed in the distance. She waited for the thunder to rumble past before she spoke.

"You would dare assault a Dragon Magus and priestess of Eltarus in view of the collegium towers? Who set you on such a treacherous path? Who sent you to your doom with promises of coin you'd never collect, hm?"

The men were silent, but the circle of knives hesitated.

"Whoever they are, they will pay dearly. I will not be robbed or detained by such rabble. Who among you holds an honorable rank in the republic? Who here have the gods touched? No?"

A few of the High and Mighty at the edges of the patio slipped into the storm and disappeared.

"If any of you have walked in dragon's fire or traded riddles with the god of magic, I'll hand over the scroll! If not, get out of my sight or you'll know what it means to face a Herald of the Conflagration!"

The High and Mighty faltered and fled into the storm. The Imperaré men remained, but the rashness of the gang leader ruined whatever plans they may have had, so they retreated to the road. Strabo was with them, the Harbor Man who sometimes escorted Julia through the city.

"This doesn't end here!"

Ulric thought he would have kept quiet in Strabo's place, but realized he was lying to himself. Did he ever shut up? As Strabo passed, he saw an opportunity in the man's frustration. He smirked and made a rude gesture. Strabo took the bait.

"And you, Ulric! Traitor! You're a dead man!"

Once the men trudged into the rain, people began returning to the patio. Vipsania, her fiery rod now vanished, dropped into her chair with an exhausted sigh and ordered one of her terrified young slaves to bring a cup of honey-water. She proclaimed she would begin her journey once she drained her cup, storm be damned.

Julia squeezed Ulric's hand and gave him a sly look before turning to Vipsania. "I'll ask Myrill to end the rain so we may walk in Alakur's Light."

Lightning flashed, closer than before, and a crackling boom shook the patio a moment later.

Vipsania looked at Julia curiously, as if she was seeing her for the first time. "I doubt the Gods will alter the weather just to keep us dry." She gave Julia a flat smile, then returned to her drink.

Flaccus' mouth dropped open. He asked if it was possible, while Rexinda rolled her eyes and began cleaning her sword. Kehindé laughed and said he wasn't so proud that he'd reject help from the gods.

Julia handed Ulric her traveling cloak. "Wait here."

She walked into the storm, hands and face raised to the heavens. The rain came down in thick sheets, drenching her before her third step.

Ulric couldn't look away. Her beauty seized him once again. It wasn't only the way her tunic fell in heavy cascades of wet cloth down her narrow back, clinging to the curve of her hips. There was something more. Something about the way she moved through the rain, as if the storm was of no consequence. No, that wasn't it. She moved with divine grace; she became part of the storm, part of all storms everywhere. She knelt in the grove surrounding the Occasio Ultima and prayed.

Kehindé left to speak to the taberna's owner about the disposal of the scraggly-faced man, whose body remained where it fell. Rexinda slammed her gladius into its wooden scabbard with a loud thunk and followed.

Vipsania sipped her honey-water in silence. Flaccus must have sensed the tension, because he excused himself to study the lightning for signs and omens.

Ulric was left alone to face Vipsania, whose eyes smoldered over the rim of her cup. She finished a sip and placed it on the table softly, precisely.

"So… associates of yours?" She indicated the dead man.

Ulric used all his actor's training to overpower the sound of the pounding rain. "I knew a couple of the Imperaré men. The dead man I knew by reputation: he led one of the gangs that run the back streets of the High Ridge District."

"And you're going to tell me it's a coincidence they assaulted me after meeting you at the Quadrivium, hm?"

"Of course not."

"No?"

"Visitors to the Quadrivium are free to conduct business unmolested by the Imperaré, but there are no guarantees once they hit the street." Ulric stared pointedly at Vipsania. "Especially when they've been so indiscreet."

"What indiscretion? The only poor judgment I've shown was allowing you to worm your way into our company!" Lightning flashed, followed by a deafening peal of thunder.

"No, Magus Vipsania. I was lurking near the bar, and even I heard the words 'map' and 'expedition'. Then your cruel treatment of Flaccus brought the eyes of the entire gallery down upon you. I handed Flaccus a nondescript scroll case, but you were the one who exposed the map in full view of all those greedy eyes."

Vipsania sprung from her chair, knocking her carefully placed cup onto the cobblestones. A nearby slave quickly retrieved it but remained on his knees, frozen in fear. "Watch your tone, thief! Don't you dare lecture me!"

"Although I must admit my part in the spectacle when your charming niece tried to knife me. Really, when you think about it, it's only thanks to Neesis' luck any of us made it home alive that night!"

"Enough! I'll burn the impudence out of you." Magus Vipsania thrust her hand forward, the fingers contorted in an ugly but familiar configuration.

You know I'm right—well, as right as any lie can be—so what's left but to lash out? The Imperaré was here because you've been tethered since the Concilium—and that's no coincidence.

Ulric braced himself for the inevitable wave of agony.

Unwelcome Allies

Cornelius Brocchus stood behind his desk, hands gripping the top of his throne-like chair in his best impersonation of a praetor planning his next great conquest. As always, the prince was opulently dressed, draped in an abundance of gold, scarlet, and the finest white linen. His conspicuously peaked wool hat sat on the corner of his otherwise empty desk rather than adorning his pasty bald head. Another figure, cloaked and hooded, sat facing Brocchus.

Luciano froze as he stepped in. Fear bloomed. The Dominator? Nyx and Neesis! What now?

"Ah, so glad you made it, Porteles, and just in time." The prince gestured towards the figure. "I would introduce you to our honored guest, but I believe you've already met."

The man stood and removed his hood, revealing long white hair accented with colorful feathers, as well as familiar bronzed skin and crimson eyes, subtly painted at the corners. "Well met, Luciano Porteles. It is I, Raquin Velthar Usil. It pleases me that the road from Mist View to Trumric has kept you safe." The Eltaran wore a wide grin as he extended his hand in an exaggerated greeting.

Luciano said nothing, making no attempt to accept the handshake.

Raquin kept his hand out until Brocchus spoke again. "I have a job. One that requires a singular talent. Your talent."

Luciano glared at the Imperaré prince but remained silent.

Three slaves filed into the room, covering Brocchus' desk. One brought a variety of fruits and vegetables: pears, figs, radishes, spiced potatoes, and more. Another laid down a loaf of bread and a wheel of cheese. A third brought a decanter of wine and a pitcher of water, placing cups on the table beside each. Brocchus poured himself a cup of wine and carefully tore a bit of bread from the white loaf. He took a drink, waved a dismissive hand at the slaves, then returned his attention to Luciano.

"Come. Sit." He gestured to the empty chair next to Raquin.

The Verdan assassin didn't move.

"Porteles, sit. I insist." He gleefully emphasized that last word.

Luciano's legs moved as if they had a will of their own. A moment later he was sitting next to an Elt he detested, across from a man he despised.

"I have men." Brocchus paused, staring intently at Luciano. "Loyal men, men that can make someone disappear, if I ask. Perhaps not as—" his eyes searched the ceiling for the right word "—*elegantly* as you can. Yet make them disappear nonetheless." He dipped his bread in his wine, then popped it into his mouth. "But finding someone?" he said, still chewing on the morsel. "Tracking someone? Into the wilderness? Well, that's not something my men are—" again, searching "—*accustomed* to doing."

Still the glare.

Brocchus took a thirsty gulp. "We, the princes, we know about… the magus. Vipsania Tertia is her name." The prince sneered. "Another reason this job suits you. A man from Verdith should know how to deal with magi, yes, Porteles?" The portly prince sliced off a small wedge of cheese and placed it on his tongue, savoring the flavor before washing it down with another drink of wine. "The magi's companions should be easier. She has an apprentice—a lackey, really—of no concern. But she also travels with a Kekeksuan warrior. Dangerous. Battle-seasoned. Experienced. There's also a young woman, perhaps the Kekeksuan's hireling? Slave?" The Imperaré prince took another sip of wine, trying to hide a grin behind his cup. "Lover?" He waved his hand in the air dismissively and continued. "Regardless, she is quick to anger and good with a sword, for a woman."

Brocchus' glutinous display filled Luciano with disgust. He wanted to stuff the remaining food down the man's throat until his eyes bulged, but yellow shackles of pain stayed his hand. Luciano decided Brocchus wasn't worth the discomfort. He was a buffoon, and he was nowhere near finished; he loved the sound of his own voice too much.

"They left the city this morning heading north on the Via Borealis. And we know why. The magus is making her move on a much sought-after item. A relic. An Eltaran relic, to be precise. Which brings me to our guest here." Brocchus poured a cup of wine and offered it to Raquin, who gracefully accepted it.

Luciano rolled his eyes. He couldn't help but think Raquin's humility was all an act, and a poorly performed one at that.

"Thank you, Cornelius Brocchus," Raquin said. "On behalf of The Wise-Ruling Zalthu Perperna Superbus, the Eltaran Kingdom is happy to enlist the aid of the Imperaré in our endeavor to reacquire that which is ours. This map is of great significance to us."

Brocchus bowed to Raquin, lifting his cup as he did so, then took another drink. "Your job, Luciano, is to track this dragon magus and her companions. Deal with them however you must, but bring that map. And of course, our Eltaran friend here will accompany you."

"I look forward to the journey," said Raquin, "and more so my return to Trumric, where I can meet with the Imperaré and discuss the details of the map's rightful return."

Luciano gripped the arms of his chair and took a deep breath. *I'll murder this fucking Elt in his sleep*, he thought. *Even Elts bleed. Maybe Aguja wants a taste.*

Brocchus glanced at Raquin. "Yes. I am sure…" Brocchus looked uncomfortable, and Luciano relished the moment. "I am sure the Imperaré will be quite interested in that. The magus and her lackies were last seen at the Occasio Ultima, a small roadside taberna outside the city walls, around the second hour this morning. Raquin here tells us they're headed for some Eltaran ruins in the Silva Aurea… or perhaps the Crag Mountains." The prince bit into a hunk of lamb, tearing it from the bone with his front teeth.

Luciano studied Brocchus, but the prince did not return his gaze. He waited for him to continue pontificating, but after several moments, Luciano finally spoke. "When I leave?"

"You leave with our Eltaran friend here, and the others—"

"Others?" Luciano blurted out.

"Yes. The other princes demand representation. Seven princes. Three men each of their choosing. So twenty-one men in total. You, Petrus, and Strabo will represent the Transnanpela Collegium. Expect eighteen more to come along. Considering your experience at wilderness tracking, you, will lead them." Brocchus gestured to Raquin. "And of course our Eltaran friend here will go as well. So… twenty-two."

Raquin bowed, and Luciano detected a greedy smile.

"I work better alone," Luciano said.

"That is debatable, my Verdan friend. Besides, the Concilium insists. There's much at stake here, and all the princes have a vested interest in the outcome of this mission. It will take them some time to gather their men, so the soonest you can leave will be tomorrow morning. That means you will have some catching up to do. You'll need to make haste once you're out of the city." Brocchus turned his attention back to the plate of food, playfully nudging figs and radishes with his fingertips.

Luciano cocked an eyebrow at the prince, but held his tongue.

"Once you're well into the wilderness, attack the expedition. Do whatever it takes, but retrieve the map." Brocchus made eye contact with both of them. "The Imperaré would never sanction the murder of a dragon magus. But that journey is arduous and fraught with danger. The magus herself must know that. Such expeditions can be… unpredictably dangerous. Can they not?"

"The Aurea Silva holds many perils for mortals," Raquin said with a wicked smile.

"There's something else, Luciano."

The assassin shifted his weight, letting out a heavy sigh, convinced worse news was coming.

Whatever it was, Brocchus insisted on another dramatic pause. Finally, he said, "We have word that someone you know is with the magus." Another pause. And a cold smile.

Luciano was running out of patience for Brocchus' oration. Still he waited for the prince's next word.

"Darktalon."

That one word was all it took to awaken Luciano from his Brocchus-induced malaise. A gleam overtook his eyes, and he glanced at Raquin, who wore an expression of disinterest.

"That's it. I suggest you make your preparations for the journey. The other men will meet you tomorrow at dawn in front of the Occasio Ultima." Bowing awkwardly to Raquin, he added, "And you, my Eltaran friend… Please let me know if you need anything at all. I look forward to seeing you again upon your return from this most auspicious expedition."

Raquin returned the bow with an exuberant one of his own. Then, with a flourish of his colorful cape, he left the room, never giving Luciano another look.

Luciano thought the feathers adorning the Elt's shoulders and hair made him look like a prancing Bayjoni peacock. He was not looking forward to working with such a peacock. As he made for the office door, Brocchus spoke again.

"Wait. Not yet, Porteles."

Luciano stopped, cracking his knuckles with his thumbs.

"Close the door."

Brocchus motioned Luciano back to his chair, then sat at his desk, pushing the trays of food aside. His eyes moved toward the door. "Our Eltaran friend was an unexpected and unwelcome development. However, my intentions remain the same."

Something in Brocchus' tone pricked at Luciano's predatory instinct. He smelled blood.

"This Eltaran cannot be trusted. He wants the map for himself, so he can take it back to whatever shithole remnant of an Eltaran nation there is and present it to his king. That cannot happen. The map will be mine. Bring it back to me. And then—" the portly prince licked his lips. "—and then I will sell it to the Eltaran king and become the richest man in the city."

"The Eltaran prick never allow that."

"Ahhh, that is where your singular talent comes in, Porteles. After you have dealt with the magus… deal with him."

"Imperaré not worry about pissing off Eltaran King?"

"You let me worry about the Imperaré," Brocchus replied coldly. "As for the Eltaran King and his emissary… well, as I said, such expeditions can be unpredictably dangerous."

Luciano's mind raced. The chance to kill this Eltaran bastard that had mocked and dismissed him so casually? The opportunity to rid himself of Ghostwalker's last remnant, Darktalon, once and for all? He noted that neither thought brought with it a yellow spike of pain. Brocchus had forced him to assassinate two former colleagues, without pay nor pride, but to kill these two… This mission suddenly became much more gratifying. However, he made every effort to hide his pleasure from Brocchus. When the loathsome prince finally dismissed him, Luciano reemerged onto the dark streets of Trumric wearing a predatory grin. He knew he would sleep well that night. The dreaded Hound of Nyx would be dreaming of murder.

Caught in the Light

In the grove beside the Occasio Ultima, Julia chanted to the rhythm of pounding rain. She ignored the downpour's cool embrace, its hard caress along her back; all thought was bent toward prayer. Myrill would end the storm. Not because she asked, but because it was Myrill's will. The goddess needed her near Ulric, and that meant traveling with Magus Vipsania, a woman who embodied the fire magi's reputation for stubbornness and arrogance. If Vipsania required a miracle, then Julia had faith Myrill would provide. Whether Magus Vipsania would then lead her to revelation or doom, she did not know.

The rain stopped.

A jolt of excitement ended Julia's prayer. She opened her eyes. The storm still raged, falling in thick curtains of rain an arm's length away. She reached out and pushed her hand into the rain, letting the heavy drops pelt her fingers. Julia laughed with delight. *What a wonder*, she thought, *to be standing at the edge of a thunderstorm!*

A flash and a crack of thunder, and then the rain retreated in a rapidly expanding halo. The clouds opened, and slender beams of sunlight—Alakur's Light—broke through to illuminate the grove. In the distance, rain still fell, and lightning and thunder still flashed and rumbled. Julia stood at the center of a hole in the storm, twice as wide as the Calidius Amphitheater.

She lifted her face toward the sun, relishing the stinging heat, and felt her clothes drying faster than should have been possible.

She praised Alakur Brightest and Greatest and his queen, Mother Myrill, then returned to the taberna.

Runoff from the storm fell from the roof and awning of the Occasio Ultima, splashing into deep puddles. Meanwhile, a murmur rose through the crowd as everyone marveled at the storm's unexpected end. Ulric and Magus Vipsania stood at opposite sides of their table in the middle of what looked like another argument.

The magus unclenched her fingers. She tried to hide it, but she was as astonished by the storm's end as any other traveler.

"Why are you two glaring at each other when we have such a long journey ahead of us?" Julia asked.

Ulric leaned over and whispered, "You hit your mark perfectly. I was about to be scorched." He wrapped her traveling cloak about her, taking a moment to run a hand along her back and through her dark curls, sending a flutter through her belly. "Your hair's damp. But that's it? How?"

"Praise the gods."

Flaccus ran up to the table and breathlessly informed everyone the storm was over.

Vipsania shot him an irritated look. "We can all see that, thank you very much."

"Persius Julia!" Kehindé called as he emerged from the taberna. "You asked, and the gods answered." A broad smile stretched across the handsome Kekeksuan's face. "We should be friends!" He stood next to Vipsania and said, "I tossed a few coins to the owner; the shroud-men will collect the body. He wasn't even upset. Said a bit of notoriety would be good for business."

Rexinda returned from the taberna and hoisted her pack and shield, then tossed her blonde braids over her shoulder. To no one in particular, she said, "Storms begin, storms end. What's the point?"

Julia felt her eyes narrow and mouth twist at Rexinda's impiety. She glared at her for a moment, then chided herself for letting the blonde distract her.

In tones imitating High Priestess Gemella, the only other woman Julia knew to be as pompous as the magus, she said, "Now that Queen-Mother Myrill has blessed our endeavor, we may begin the journey in Alakur's Light."

Ulric suppressed a smile.

"Yes, you seem quite pleased with yourself, child," Vipsania said in her own pompous tones. "I am a priestess of Eltarus; I recognize the hand of the gods when I see it. So my question to you is simply: Why are you not at the Temple of Myrill but in the company of this lowborn thief? Hmm?"

Ulric stared at everyone with exaggerated shock. "Lowborn?"

Julia took Ulric's hand. "I am where Myrill wants me to be."

Vipsania summoned all her authority, which was considerable. "A young girl blessed as you should serve the temple—and the republic. Not run wild on the streets! Yet you claim to know Myrill's will? Such hubris!"

Julia stepped forward and fell to her knees. "No, Magus Vipsania, not hubris, but service and humility. I entered the Temple of Myrill in the year of Marcellus and Cotta's consulship and... I was expelled earlier this spring."

"Expelled! How shameful."

Rexinda sneered and began to speak, but a stern look from Kehindé silenced her.

Julia lowered her head. "Yes, shameful." She met Vipsania's harsh gaze. "But... despite my shame, the goddess showed mercy. Myrill speaks to me." Julia rose to her feet. "Myrill answers my prayers and channels Her divine power through me. All that happened has been Her will; that is how I know I am where I should be. Myrill wants me to accompany you to the Silva Aurea."

As the magus considered Julia's words, the fierce lines of her face cooled. Then Rexinda, her green eyes glittering with mischief, spoke. "Does Eltarus have a say in the matter, Theia Vipsania?"

Her defiance reignited. "Yes, what if Eltarus and I prefer you remain behind, hm?"

Before Julia could remind Vipsania that Myrill was queen, second in authority only to Alakur himself, Ulric spoke.

"Magus Vipsania, you can't leave Julia behind now. She was part of the bloodshed Rexinda started. After the death of the High Ridge man, she won't be safe. The gangs will be prowling for blood. And the Imperaré? They will have questions... and they don't ask nicely. We share a duty to protect her."

It was an excellent argument. Ulric appealed to their sense of duty, as well as their natural sympathy for a young woman in distress. *How fortunate we couldn't escape the men pursuing us in the High Ridge District,* she thought. Did Ulric purposely lead them into danger and death?

"Ulric's right," said Kehindé. "How could we leave a young girl to face such dangers?"

"Uh, should we offend Myrill before journeying into the wilderness?" asked Flaccus. He then gave Julia a welcoming, if awkward, smile.

"That does sound foolish," Rexinda conceded.

Vipsania's only response was a noncommittal grunt.

Kehindé hoisted his pack onto his shoulders and grinned. "We could take a vote?"

"Fine!" Vipsania shouted. She stood and straightened her robes. "Let's be off!"

THE FOLLY OF THE GATES I

Taken from the Forbidden Histories by Achle Nesvah

We are the Children of Eltarus, God of Magic and Revelation, may His lamp shine eternal.

When Eltarus breathed life into his Children, He shared with us the essence of magic. Gifted with these secrets, we became the rightful lords of the world, which until then, had been the domain of Men. A just and wise king named Cemthsta ruled over our ancient homeland of Eltareah, nestled between the great Nanmere Lake and the majestic Cloud Wall Mountains. And so it was that good king Cemthsta ruled the Children of Eltarus for countless years, maintaining peace and prosperity throughout the land. We are Eltarans, the Children of Eltarus, and Cemthsta was our king.

Over time, Men grew jealous of our power. They beseeched Alakur, Bright and Greatest of the Gods Above, that He might command His brother to share the secret of magic. Alakur refused. However, the always mischievous Eltarus gifted Men the secret of magic, and Alakur, ever the guardian of order in the Empyrean Realm, punished his brother for his insolence. And so it was that Eltarus spent an age in the Dragon's Breath Mountains chained above the fires of the Great Chasm as penance for his disobedience.

Yet the wine had been poured and could not be returned to the bottle. Consequently Men, who had been subjugated by the Eltarans for centuries, now wielded the power of magic. Their dominion grew, and they waged war upon the Children of Eltarus.

As the centuries marched on, and Men continued their relentless conquests, we Children of Eltarus grew weary of war, and sought an escape from this realm. We chose as our new home, Empyrea, home of our creator, Eltarus, and the Gods Above. We Children of Eltarus considered this both our birthright and our destiny.

We called upon our arcane knowledge, and began the construction of elaborate Gates which would transport our people to Heaven. Cemthsta proclaimed these Gates would be our crowning achievement, the most incredible monuments ever built, marvels of magic and mechanics alike. Marvels that would carry us home. So for years on end, the Children of Eltarus toiled, building our Gates while the victories of Men multiplied, bringing bloodshed and sorrow to our lands.

The Utility of Thieves

Magus Vipsania's expedition traveled on the Via Borealis as dark clouds raced all around them, the dark shapes galloping low over the countryside like mad charioteers. In the distance, lightning flashed and thunder rumbled, a roaring crowd to cheer on the storm. The air was cool and heavy with the bracing smell of rain, yet, thanks to Julia's prayer, the sun shone and not a single raindrop fell where they walked.

Ulric was in awe. He had seen the skies over Mist View do many strange things, but never anything like this. As they walked, he did his best to keep from gawking at the hole in the storm, trying to act as if Julia performed such miracles routinely.

The road was broad, unwaveringly straight, and bordered by an endless colonnade of tall narrow pines. It cut north through a land filled with farms, orchards, and the country estates of the Trumrician wealthy. Magus Vipsania and Kehindé led the way, quietly discussing their plans when not reminiscing about their youth in the Kreslan Isles. Rexinda marched a respectful distance behind, always drawing closer when the names "Hamund" or "Rubea" were mentioned. Flaccus walked several paces behind Rexinda, either gawking at the storm or doing his best not to get caught staring at her legs. Next, Ulric walked hand in hand with Julia. Finally, Vipsania's four slaves brought up the rear, laboring to keep up under the burden of their heavy packs.

Julia softly sang the liturgies of Myrill while Ulric marveled at the endless number of stones that paved the Via Borealis. He counted the typical amount on a ten pace stretch of road, hoping to divine the total number of paving stones since leaving the gates of Trumric, but the numbers got all muddled. Frustrated, his thoughts drifted to the distant lightning, then back to the road and the rainwater rushing along the ditches.

Flaccus meandered to the side of the road and gazed into a glistening field of red poppies and sparse, stunted cork trees. It was obvious he was feigning interest in an empty field. As Ulric and Julia passed, he turned a little too soon, a fake look of surprise on his face.

"Oh, uh… Darktalon!"

Ulric nodded. "Flaccus."

Somehow, the simplicity of the greeting ruined whatever Flaccus had planned. He walked silently alongside Ulric, occasionally looking over as if he wanted to speak. Ulric ignored him. If Flaccus wanted something, he preferred he take it.

Finally, Julia broke the stalemate. She looked past Ulric and gave Flaccus a welcoming smile. "Shouldn't you introduce us?"

"Didn't I?"

"No. We were too busy with all the accusations and ambushes."

Ulric adopted a voice befitting the stage of the Polyminius theater. "Julia, let me introduce you to Sextus Pinarius Flaccus, a discipulus of the Collegium Draconis Aurei. Pinarius Flaccus, meet Persius Julia, Trumric's most beautiful actress."

"Oh, don't listen to him," she said, cringing with embarrassment. "He's been known to exaggerate."

"He did call himself a full-time liar," Flaccus said, then froze—now it was his turn to cringe. "Oh, but he's not lying now, of course! You are beautiful! And an actress! You must be blessed by Nyssa as well as Myrill."

"Blessed by Nyssa?" Ulric repeated. "See, Flaccus, you can almost be charming when you try."

Flaccus looked away, out into the storm. "Sorry."

Julia slapped Ulric's arm. "Don't tease him!" To Flaccus, she said, "It was kind of you to say. Thank you."

Flaccus tore his eyes away from the distant lightning. "The storm! A true miracle. Even the highest-ranking storm magi would struggle to accomplish such a feat."

"I accomplished nothing," Julia corrected. "I merely prayed to Myrill and She answered. All praise belongs to Her. The gods *are* magic, so anything is possible so long as they will it."

"And that's why Magus Vipsania doesn't like you. She says—"

"And who exactly likes Vipsania?" Ulric asked.

"Uh… no one, really," Flaccus conceded. "Anyway, she says those favored by the gods are unpredictable, and therefore dangerous."

Julia's dark eyes widened. "How could anyone be threatened by Myrill's will?"

Flaccus only unleashed a stammering, disjointed defense of Vipsania's position. Julia was having none of it.

"The real danger is the magi and wild maleficae! Ask any priest, they'll tell you. Many hold the view that Eltarus should never have given the secret of magic to men."

"What a stupid idea born of… ignorance and jealousy!" Flaccus said, his face flush with anger. "Everyone seems to forget the collegium *is* the Temple of Eltarus. His gift has been nothing but a benefit to the Trumin people."

"Oh, is that why His fellow gods chained him over a fiery chasm in the Dragon's Breath Mountains?"

Caught in the middle, Ulric held up his hands, palms flat and out to his side. "Maybe I shouldn't have introduced you two?"

After a moment of silence, Julia spoke. "Forgive me, Flaccus. I loved arguing with my superiors at the temple. It seems I missed it more than I realized."

Ulric cocked his head. "We don't argue enough? You should have told me. I'd have been happy to help."

Julia scrunched up her face and stuck out her tongue. "It's an educated debate I miss, not quarrels over dicing and drinking."

Flaccus looked down, watching his feet splash along the paving stones. "Sorry. I shouldn't have brought up the magus. She doesn't like anyone."

Julia gazed ahead. "She seems to like Kehindé and that blonde well enough."

Ulric almost reminded her the blonde had a name, but caught himself at the last moment. Julia glanced at him just as he masked his half-open mouth with a smile.

Magus Vipsania, Kehindé, and Rexinda had stopped in the middle of the road. They murmured amongst themselves, occasionally peering southward along the Via Borealis. Ulric glanced back and saw the pale line of the road cutting through lazily rolling hills and well-tended fields, then disappearing into a dark wall of rushing clouds and rain.

Were they deciding they didn't need him and Julia after all?

The three of them walked into earshot as Magus Vipsania spat, "Let's be rid of them."

Ulric tensed and squeezed Julia's hand, prepared to once again defend their worth, but there was no need. Vipsania was speaking of two lone travelers who had been behind them since leaving the Occasio Ultima. Were they part of the rabble that had assaulted her earlier that morning? The mere thought of anyone daring to defy her warning clearly filled her with rage. It was an affront to her dignity, she said, and she insisted Kehindé deal with them.

Flaccus kept looking over his shoulder, but there was only an empty road and the distant storm. Had they already left the road for another destination? "Are they simply travelers who don't fear a little rain?" he asked.

"This storm's more than a little rain," Rexinda corrected. "And they're hidden behind a rise in the land, as we are." She turned to Kehindé with a predatory gleam in her eyes and suggested, "We lie in ambush alongside the road. The others continue north. We kill them, then catch up."

"A good plan," Kehindé replied, laughing. "But I'll talk to them first."

Rexinda placed a hand on one out thrust hip, gripping her sword with the other. "My way's quicker!" she complained with an exaggerated pout. Her display didn't go unnoticed; Flaccus leered, Julia expelled a disapproving sigh, and Ulric looked away, pretending to search for the two travelers.

"Quicker is not always best," Kehindé said gravely. "Ulric and I will remain behind."

Ulric spun around. "Uh, what?"

"Darktalon?" Rexinda exclaimed. "We don't even know if he can fight."

"He fought you well enough last night."

Julia gave Ulric an inquisitive look. "Oh, did you?"

"Oh, he did," Rexinda said playfully. "I was straddling him on the floor of the Quadrivium in no time, with my dagger at his throat." She gazed at Ulric lasciviously. "I think he was letting me win."

"That's *not* what happened!" Ulric protested.

"Enough!" Kehindé said, pointing at Rexinda. "Your foolishness has already spilled blood today."

Rexinda looked at Vipsania for help, but she only said, "Listen to Kehindé, child. And obey."

Kehindé kept his eyes on the road. "Why are you here, Ulric?"

"It was your idea to lie under these bushes... in the mud... getting soaked. I wanted to hide in one of the olive trees."

Kehindé had insisted they conceal themselves in a hastily dug hunter's blind, choosing a spot on the side of the road bordering an expansive olive grove. Magus Vipsania and the others had continued on the Via Borealis, marching in a tight formation in hopes of concealing the two's absence. As Julia walked north, she took clear skies and sunshine with her. By the time two dark silhouettes had crested the southern ridge, the sky was slate gray and heavy with rain. Ulric and Kehindé lay side by side on their stomachs, silent and well hidden under a tangle of bushes. Ulric had tried to ignore the rain soaking through his cloak, but his discomfort had only increased his longing for the safety of the olive trees. He thought better of grumbling when he looked at Kehindé, who betrayed nothing but stoic resolve. Annoyed, he tried to concentrate on the things he was enjoying: the lulling sound of the raindrops on the foliage above, and the warm, earthy smell of the soil beneath.

"Why are you here?" Kehindé repeated.

It was a question he had answered before. A question he feared. He knew lies didn't always hold up to repetition, no matter how good the liar. He gave Kehindé a concise version of what he had told Vipsania at the Quadrivium: fortune, opportunity, and Eltarans. By the time he finished, the dark clump had resolved itself into two travelers.

"You're not beginning to doubt the utility of thieves, are you?" Ulric asked.

"No. Thieves are most welcome, if they steal from our enemies."

"I wished Vipsania shared your outlook."

"Ah, but she does," Kehindé said. Ulric's expression made his doubts clear, but Kehindé persisted. "Rexinda's father, Hamund, was an ex-soldier and an accomplished thief. Years ago, back in Kos, he and Vipsania were comrades, along with Rexinda's mother Rubea and myself."

"And what do Hamund and Rubea think of their daughter cutting a bloody path across the republic?" It was the perfect question to change the subject and learn more about Rexinda. Ulric couldn't deny his interest in Rexinda, a realization that came with an inevitable pang of guilt.

Kehindé's stern face broke into a wistful smile. "Hamund would have been proud. Rubea? Furious with worry."

"Would have?"

"Rubea died when Rexinda was very young. Hamund fell years later during the Kreslan uprising."

"Sounds like a typical childhood: horrible."

"The elders of Suloko believe our fates were set long ago when the gods told our stories around the Eternal Fire of Creation. They teach that life is a struggle which must be endured. When misfortune falls, they say, 'this story was told long ago.'"

It was a rote reply. Ulric had seen enough to doubt his conviction.

"These elders must be in high demand during the festival season. I think I'll stick with the goddess of love, luck, and madness—thank you!"

"Well…" Kehindé grinned. "I don't see why we can't steal a little joy along the way."

Conversation ceased as the travelers drew near. The only sounds were the slow drip and drizzle of rain, the frail echoes of distant thunder, and rainwater flowing through the ditches. The two men walked in silence, hunched under rain heavy cloaks, small packs slung over their shoulders. They had pulled their hoods down tight, revealing only black shroud faces. Their pace was steady and purposeful despite the miserable weather. One man was tall and lean, the other even taller but much thicker. As the men passed, Ulric saw the outline of a small rectangular shield on the thick man's back and the tip of a wooden scabbard poking out beneath the hem of the other man's cloak.

Kehindé whispered, "I'll speak. You keep your eyes open."

They crept out of the hunter's blind and moved silently toward the road. Kehindé's ability to move quietly, despite his size, was impressive. Ulric hopped over the ditch, while Kehindé took one long stride across it. They tethered their quarry for several paces, then Kehindé walked with the flat, splashing footfalls of a common traveler.

The lean man spun around, tossing his cloak aside as he drew a slender spatha. High, sharp cheekbones and a prominent nose poked past the black shroud of his hood. The heavier man stopped and turned, giving his companion a placating gesture with the down-turned palm of his hand.

Kehindé called out, "Salve, travelers!"

The heavy man pulled his hood back, revealing a broad, scarred nose in the center of a round, friendly face. "Salve, citizens. You must forgive my overcautious companion." He indicated the lean man's sword with a quick flourish. "I've heard him remark, on numerous occasions, that the threat of banditry looms over every road and path." He spoke in a deep, soothing bass, all the while gesticulating like an undisciplined orator. His movements parted his cloak, revealing two long curved daggers on either side of his expansive waist. He pointed a thick finger to the heavens and proclaimed, "It is a maxim he lives by."

"It's true," was all the lean man said. His sword stayed on guard.

"Surely the roads are safe, this close to the capital?" Kehindé suggested.

"Ah, but with so many murders occurring every day *within* the capital, we'd be very foolish to assume any correlation between safety and proximity, would we not?"

"Very foolish," the lean man repeated.

Under his breath, Ulric said, "Can't argue against that. He's very educated for a murderous thug."

"Remind you of anyone?" Kehindé muttered. To the men, he said, "I am Kehindé of Suloko. He is Octavius Ulric. We're no bandits, but we do need to know who we share the road with."

"I am Sentius Aculeo, and this is my companion, Kriton. Was it simple curiosity that drove you to sneak up on us in such an alarming manner?"

"No. It was the command of my employer, Magus Vipsania Tertia. Recent events have led her to expect danger on every road and path."

Ulric pointed to the sky and grinned. "It's her new maxim!" He saw annoyance briefly slip past Aculeo's friendly mask.

"Ah, you two must be bodyguards?" Aculeo asked.

"Of a sort," Kehindé said.

"And what of your…" Aculeo searched the air before him for the proper word. "*Amusing* associate?"

Before Ulric could reply, Kehindé said, "An out of work actor."

Aculeo's face brightened and he became even more animated. "Then we share more than just a road! We too are out-of-work entertainers! Well, retired states it more accurately. We didn't honor the beautiful Nyssa with song and soliloquy in the sacred theater. No, our gods were Cathus, Morbus, and Dis. Our stage, the bloody sand of the republic's most famous arenas!"

"Such a voice!" Ulric exclaimed. "You missed your true calling; any man who loves the sound of his own voice as much as you should have been an actor."

Aculeo's face darkened as annoyance turned to contempt.

"And what drove two ex-gladiators into the storm today?" Kehindé asked with a hint of impatience.

"The same as you: a job. We are fugitivarii, slave-catchers. We saw your handiwork this morning—solid, professional work, I must say. And we heard the magus' warning, but there is no time to waste when on the hunt for runaways, as I'm sure you understand. So we waited for the magus to leave before beginning our own journey. It was exactly this sort of misunderstanding we hoped to avoid." He sighed theatrically. "Alas, here we are." He produced a small scroll case. "The writ from our employer, if you care to inspect it."

Kriton sheathed his sword and took a few steps back. Kehindé approached, taking the scroll case and opening the writ.

Kriton glared from beneath sharp brows. "You read Trumin, Keksu?"

Ulric tensed at the slur for Kekeksuans, placing a hand on the hilt of his sword.

Kehindé simply returned the writ and asked, "A Harath man and Kreslan girl?"

Aculeo secured the writ and pulled his cloak tight. "Yes. We think they are heading northeast toward the Crag Mountains. If you see them…"

"We'll remain vigilant."

"If we're done here, I'm sure you'll want to catch up with the rest of your party." Aculeo stepped aside and swept his arm northward.

Kehindé started walking but turned back after a few paces. "Don't stray too close to the magus. For such a woman, bodyguards are a mere formality, more status symbol than necessity. Stray too close to the flame and you will burn."

Aculeo feigned shock. "I assure you, Kehindé of Suloko, I would never cross a magus."

Kehindé and Ulric marched at the double. The storm was over; the late afternoon sun tore the sky into strips of ragged clouds, and the entire world seemed to glisten with Alakur's light. Despite the growing warmth, Ulric's clothes weren't drying nearly fast enough for his liking.

"Well done, Ulric."

"What?"

"You followed my orders," Kehindé said. "You stayed quiet and you let me speak. Well… almost. It must have been terrible for you."

Ulric laughed. "If I spoke, there was a design in my disobedience. I wanted to draw that fat fool out from behind his wall of horseshit."

"I also asked you to keep your eyes open. What did you see?"

Ulric considered the question for a moment. "I didn't recognize them. Didn't see any gang ink, but the Imperaré often use ex-gladiators for knife work. Could they be innocent slave-catchers? Possible. I think the real tell was how accommodating Aculeo was. What sort of ex-gladiators tolerate being interrogated on the road? I'm sure they thought the odds were in their favor, so why not bluster and threaten? Instead, there was barely a protest. Just some dirty looks and a single insult from that Kriton bastard."

"Hmph." It was a short, dismissive grunt. "I saw them inside the taberna, but I doubt they were allied with the men who attacked us."

"Agreed." Ulric stopped and took a deep breath. The others were in sight further up the road. Julia turned and beckoned them forward. "The question is: how many people are after this gate-stone?"

"I don't know. But I pray you're not one of them, Ulric Darktalon. I'm starting to like you, so it would be a pity to kill you."

A Midnight Skirmish

Ulric couldn't sleep. Normally, he could fall asleep anywhere, day or night. Growing up on the chaotic streets of Mist View, he had learned to steal his rest wherever and whenever he could. After a long march on the hard stones of a Trumrician road, he should be deep in slumber, like Julia. She was close, all warm shadows and moonlit curves.

He wanted her. Maybe then he could sleep. If only they had their own room at the hospitia instead of being exiled to the stable loft, a space they shared with Vipsania's slaves. He doubted the blanket they had hung from the rafters provided enough privacy to overcome her modesty.

Ulric rolled over in frustration and gazed out of the loft into the night sky. The rains had long passed, leaving only a black wall of clouds on the northern horizon. Nyx, the Goddess Beyond Night, had conquered two-thirds of the moon. A defiantly radiant crescent resting in a bed of stars was all that remained of Seranon's light. Even the moon looked sleepy, he thought, but he couldn't find rest.

To occupy his mind, he looked over to the hospitia and began planning ways to rob its many guests. The building, a large villa near the Via Borealis called the House of Spineta, sat on a broad hill overlooking the town of Corvaro. Its layout was similar to the home of the ill-fated Marius Secundus and the location of Ulric's own disastrous shadow walk, but on a much grander scale. The walled courtyard at the front of the villa was immense, able to hold a whole caravan of wagons. The main building had a second and, even rarer, a third story. At dusk, dozens of lanterns inside the courtyard and along the walls filled themselves with soft, golden light—Eltaran light. All those magical lanterns spelled trouble for a shadow walk job.

He imagined it had been the country residence of a fading patrician family, long ago sold off to pay their mounting debts. It now served as an official relay station, so by law, it had to provide accommodations for government officials and members of the courier service. Somehow Magus Vipsania, as a high-ranking member of the Collegium Draconis Aurei, had parlayed her status into two luxurious rooms: one for herself and Rexinda, the other for Kehindé and Flaccus. He knew they were luxurious because he had a brief glimpse of their soft beds and extravagant furniture before Vipsania had banished him and Julia to the stables.

Why couldn't he sleep? It wasn't the hard and uneven planks of the floor; he had slept in far worse. It wasn't the pervasive smells of horses, old leather, and unwashed travelers; a steady night breeze carried away the worst. It wasn't even Renier's incessant snoring, though he wondered if Vipsania would miss the old slave. No, it was Kehindé's question: "Why are you here?"

He thought he knew the answer: steal the gate-stone for Silo and glory. It was the sort of job that would make his reputation. The sort of job that had made Arrius Ghostwalker a legend. And if he learned something of the Eltaran mystery along the way, all the better.

The night he'd burst out of the safe house and tethered Flaccus, there had been no plan. There had been no *time* to plan; his instincts drove him, and those instincts had been right. Flaccus had led him to the map and then to the Quadrivium and Magus Vipsania. By the time he sat across from the magus, the details of his scheme were as thin as the parchment the map was written on. He knew stealing the gate-stone from a dragon magus was going to be dangerous enough—and then Kehindé and Rexinda arrived. Fortunately, Silo, himself a devout follower of Neesis, recognized the opportunity and endorsed his mad plan. Next, Julia insisted on coming along, further complicating their scheme. How had he thought she would ever agree to stay behind?

The answer's easy, Darktalon: you weren't thinking at all, were you, boy?

It was Ulric's own thought, spoken in an echo of Ghostwalker's voice. Or was it Silo's? He wasn't sure. *This scheme is getting all turned around,* he thought. *I'm starting to feel like I'm the mark. By the Nine Gates, it's Vipsania! I know I can scheme her. She's smart, true; she's a magus. Hells, she's brilliant in ways I could never understand, but her ambitions are constantly calling to her, dragging her ever forward to a narrowing spot on the horizon. She's blind at the edges, and that's where I lurk. People like her are easy to scheme.*

Then there was Kehindé. Ulric feared he saw the things Vipsania couldn't. He was every scheme's nemesis: an honest man.

And what of those two gladiators? Was Ulric the only one running a scheme? Trying to steal the gate-stone was seeming more and more impossible. Yes, he'd been a fool! But it was too late; he had to try. *After today, the Imperaré thinks I'm a traitor. The only way to prove otherwise and honor the Sacramentum is to bring Silo the gate-stone. If I don't, I break my vow and Neesis will abandon me.*

Ulric sat up, careful not to wake Julia. He watched her sleep for a moment, resisting the urge to reach for her dark curls. Why was she here?

She says Myrill demands she stays close; that the goddess wants her to travel to Tmia Culscva. Why?

He slipped away and sat at the edge of the loft, dangling his legs over the side. A fragrant breeze swept aside the stable smells in favor of cool, moist air, as the sound of droning insects and the warble of a single nightjar fought to be heard over Renier's snoring.

Ulric's doubts drifted away with the wind, and sleep crept up on the edges of his mind. His head drooped. His chin hit his chest. He struggled to keep his eyes open, but—

Someone was sneaking toward the hospitia.

Ulric's eyes snapped open. He slid off the edge of the loft and fell to the ground, landing softly on the turf, still wet and spongy from the rain. Then he crouched in the deep black beneath the stable wall and waited. To any other pair of eyes, the hillside east of the villa was a dark nothing. For Ulric, the faint light of a nearly conquered moon was enough. He spotted movement again, a dark lump slinking toward the villa. He focused his eyes and a tall, cloaked figure came into view.

Ulric's blood ran hot. Could it be the ex-gladiator Kriton? Was Aculeo hidden nearby? He knew they couldn't be trusted!

He bolted out of the blackness, rushing low and swift across the wet grass, moving in a curving path that would take him behind the ex-gladiator. As he drew near, he slowed, matching the cadence of his quarry.

Something was wrong. They crept toward the hospitia and into the pale golden light of its Eltaran lamps. The figure knelt, examining the muddy path they had both been skirting. Ulric gripped the dagger hidden beneath his tunic. The cloaked figure leaned forward, exposing tanned, shapely legs and bare feet.

"Rexinda?"

Rexinda spun around, her hand seizing the hilt of a gladius. Underneath her cloak, she wore a simple white tunic; nothing more, except for a hastily strapped on belt and scabbard. A small bronze sword, about the length of a finger, hung from a leather cord around her neck. It was the Red Sword of Cathus, Alakur's first son, Herald of Justice and God of War.

In unison, they both asked, "What are you doing—?"

Ulric eased his hand out of his tunic. "Creeping around outside the villa? That's my line."

"A line? You mean, a shield wall? What are you saying?"

"Not a formation. Dialogue."

Rexinda tilted her head, mouth slightly agape. He tried again.

"You know, words… in a play."

"Make sense, Darktalon." She released her gladius and threw back her hood, releasing a tangle of blonde hair. She eyed Ulric warily. "What are you doing out here?"

"I'm only here because of you!"

"Battle 'n blood!" she exclaimed with mock surprise. "A midnight skirmish?" She moved closer, her green eyes glittering seductively in the moonlight. "Hoping to penetrate my defenses?"

Had she mistaken his intentions? Ulric knew he should retreat, but he took a step forward instead. "I saw someone lurking. I had no idea it was you. Simple as that."

"Someone was sneaking along here." She pointed to the well-worn footpath at their feet. It extended from the hospitia to the road that connected Corvaro to the Via Borealis. "How do I know it wasn't you?"

Ulric looked over the path. There were several crisscrossing tracks in the mud: wagon wheels, bare feet, sandaled feet, and booted feet. He looked down and smiled, raising one leg and extending a bare foot toward Rexinda. It was wet and grass-stained, but otherwise clean.

"See? I've never walked that path."

Rexinda pretended to consider his foot as he stood there, looking absurd in his unbelted tunic. Finally, she said, "So you weren't sneaking about—this time."

He put his foot down and glanced sidelong toward the sky. "Well, I did sneak up on you, didn't I?"

"Any closer," she said, with no hint of humor in her voice or posture, "and by Cathus' Red Blade, you'd be dead."

Eager to move on, Ulric knelt over the muddy tracks and asked, "Who do you think was out here?"

Rexinda looked toward the town. "Same as you."

Ulric stood and peered into the valley. Earlier, when they had reached the House of Spineta, the town had blazed with torch and lamplight. He recalled eyeing those bright streets greedily, imagining the drinking, gambling, and easy marks waiting for him in the black between those glittering lines. Now only a collection of scattered lights remained visible.

He had turned to Julia with a mischievous grin and said, "You know, I've actually never visited Corvaro; I've only seen the name on a map." He held out his arm and suggested, "Let's explore!"

Julia's dark eyes had flashed with excitement, but before she could take his arm, they overheard Vipsania barking at Flaccus, "No, you may not: the town is forbidden!"

Vipsania must have felt their eyes upon her, for she turned and announced, "The town is forbidden—*to everyone!* We've already had enough trouble for today."

Julia frowned and whispered, "Oh, I'm going to be bored!" Then she sighed and added, "At least our rooms should be nice."

While Vipsania arranged for their lodging, Kehindé and Ulric had loitered outside, watching for Aculeo and Kriton. Kehindé stood before the courtyard gates like an ebony colossus, menacing, unmoving, and ever watchful. Ulric stood beside him, doing his best to look like an Imperaré thug. As expected, the two slave-catchers left the Via Borealis and headed east toward

Corvaro, ignoring the path that would bring them up the hill to the hospitia's gates. As they walked past, Ulric had noticed Kriton glaring at them from beneath his hood.

Now, Ulric turned back to Rexinda. "The two slave-catchers?"

"Yes! We should have ambushed them on the road—" she slapped her hand down hard onto the hilt of her sword "—and killed them like Theia Vipsania wanted."

"Kehindé didn't want to strike without cause."

"Cathus' crooked cock! You believe their lies?"

Ulric adopted a disapproving tone. "Does 'Aunt' Vipsania know you curse like a drunken soldier?"

Rexinda fluttered her eyes and smiled innocently, the transformation was startling and complete. Then she said, "Fuck, no!"

Ulric couldn't help but laugh. "And, no, I didn't buy any of their horseshit. Neither did Kehindé."

Rexinda stood a little taller. "Of course he didn't!" She seemed offended at the mere suggestion of Kehindé being fooled.

"Well, he had his reasons…"

Reasons Ulric began to doubt.

"To do what? Let them spy on us? Slit our throats in the night? If I had been there…" A sly smile flickered across her face. "Let's go into town! We'll hunt them down and get the truth."

Ulric took a step back, unsure if Rexinda was serious. "Ah, you make it sound so easy. What if they don't want to talk?"

"If they fight or flee, we have cause," she said, casually dismissing his concerns along with the men's lives.

He feared she was serious.

"And what of dear Vipsania? The town's forbidden."

Rexinda took an eager step forward. "If we're victorious, she'll forgive us. Well, me at least." she added with a smirk.

Ulric crossed his arms. "Not much incentive for me, then, is it?"

"I was joking. If we kill them, all will be forgiven. Remember, she wants them dead."

"Somehow, I doubt *I'll* be forgiven." His eyes darted to the stable loft.

"Afraid your little priestess won't approve?"

"What?" He knew he'd been caught. "You can't expect Julia to be pleased if I run off with another woman in the middle of the night, can you?"

"Cathus curse a coward! I heard Trumrician men were the conquerors and lawgivers of the world." She looked him up and down as if he was suddenly something distasteful. "I didn't know they were so servile to their women."

Ulric's pride and patriotism were both under attack. "Trumrician men rule from the Cloud Wall Mountains to the Kreslan Isles. We bow to no one."

"Are you sure? I can stand guard here while you crawl back to your, priestess and beg for your manhood."

"Oh, my manhood is just fine, thank you. Julia can attest to that. Uh… not because she has it." He shifted awkwardly and said, "What I mean is: I do what I want when I want."

"Do you?" She grabbed his hand and gave him a disarming smile. "Then we march into town!" She pulled him along the path toward Corvaro.

"Are you serious?" He pulled his hand free. "You want to sneak into town and hunt down two ex-gladiators?"

"Yes!"

Ulric held up the Tesserae dangling from the silver chain around his neck. "What a mad idea! Maybe you should wear the Tesserae of Neesis instead of the Red Sword of Cathus?"

"Are you afraid?" she taunted. "I never saw them up close. They must have looked *so* fearsome."

"Ha! I'm not the least bit afraid. Did you see the fat one? He's well past his prime."

"Ha! Gladiators? Their training is all for show. It's not real combat."

Ulric wasn't so sure. He had attended a few gladiatorial games in the arenas of Mist View. Good gladiators were expensive to train and brought their schools coin and prestige. There was little incentive to throw away lives needlessly. Arrius had explained the tricks employed to protect their investment: acting, stagecraft, hidden bladders full of pig's blood, that sort of thing. Yet some games demanded real blood, and there had been no doubt about the skill on display.

Could they defeat Aculeo and Kriton? Win Magus Vipsania's favor? Ulric began to think it was possible.

Eager for the battle to begin, Rexinda started down the hill, beckoning him to follow. Her mood was palpable, overwhelming.

"We fight—together," she declared, her blonde hair reflecting the far-off glow of the Eltaran lamps. Her eyes shone with moonlight and bloodlust.

He nodded; a slight movement at first, then more vigorously. "Together!"

Rexinda smiled. Savage, murderous, seductive. "For Cathus! For honor!"

"It's a mad plan, you know? And all the better for it. If our cause is just—"

"It is!"

"—then we'll have both Cathus and Neesis at our side."

"Victory is certain!" she cried.

"Guaranteed! Still, I'm not marching into Corvaro barefoot and nearly naked."

After a furtive visit to the stables, Ulric was outfitted for a midnight raid. Now he wore sandals and a proper tunic beneath a cloak of mottled blacks and grays. Ghostwalker's spatha hung at his side, and he had tucked a variety of daggers and throwing knives into his belt. Rexinda, too, had resupplied, returning from the hospitia in dark pants and a tunic of coarse brown wool. Her leather boots, arm bracers, short sword, and hand axe completed the image of a Gualdean barbarian.

They marched toward Corvaro, ready to hunt down the ex-gladiators, but first they would have to find them. Such a large town would have several hospitia where the self-proclaimed slave catchers could have taken a room, assuming they weren't staying with friends or an associate of their employers.

Rexinda preferred a frontal assault. She simply wanted to barge into each hospitia until they found the two men.

Ulric thought the idea gloriously insane, but impractical. They needed to be back at the House of Spineta long before dawn, and crashing through the doors of every hospitia would take too long—and likely get them killed. Still, by the time they approached Corvaro's gates, Ulric hadn't thought of a better idea.

The gates were shut, of course. They had been since sundown. Ulric guessed it was now well into the sixth hour of the night. He wore a thief's cloak and the marks of the Imperaré, while Rexinda was dressed like a northern savage. They both carried nothing but weapons. No guardsman would let them pass into Corvaro.

"Can you climb?" he asked.

"Kehindé and I were at the siege of Tylisus. Fuck yeah, I can climb."

Ulric and Rexinda conquered the walls of Corvaro quicker and quieter than the walls of the ill-fated Tylisus. When they rejoined the main road not fifty paces from the gate, the guardsmen were none the wiser.

"There's a hospitia nearby, surely?" Rexinda asked.

"No," said Ulric, "but I see a taberna." He pointed ahead toward the warm glow of lamplight and drunken voices. "Let's go!"

Ulric crossed the rain slicked street, bounding over puddles and filth.

Rexinda followed and asked, with more than a little skepticism, "You think the gladiators are there?" She eyed the taberna's bright purple sign suspiciously. It read: *Vinum et Voluptas*. Wine and Pleasure. "Still drinking at this late hour?"

"No. Maybe? What I do know is Aculeo—the fat one—loves the sound of his own voice so much he'd stop at the first taberna he saw. His throat thirsted for an audience even more than a drink."

With a wolfish grin, Rexinda said, "The hunt begins."

The ex-gladiators were not drinking in the taberna, but they had been there earlier. Just as Ulric had guessed, Aculeo couldn't resist the allure of a captive audience. While his companion Kriton had drank in silence, Aculeo had regaled the crowd with stories of their exploits in arenas all over the Republic. Somewhere between tales of bloody games and amusing slave hunts, Aculeo had let slip they were staying at a place called the King's Tower. According to the taberna's aged owner, it was the last remnant of the town's defenses from a time when Corvaro had its own kings. When he began recounting, with surprising detail and bitterness, how the walls were toppled by a newly formed Trumin republic, Ulric had to keep Rexinda from throttling the old man into silence. Neither of them were in the mood for history.

The King's Tower sat atop a hill in the northern part of Corvaro. It had a square base roughly fifteen feet wide and stood over three times that in height. Its well-weathered walls had long ago lost most of its lime mortar, giving it a sad patchwork appearance in the faint moonlight. Near the summit, a wooden platform encircled the tower beneath a peaked roof of slate gray tiles. There were a few narrow windows on each wall and a sturdy-looking door far above ground level. When it had been a military watchtower, Ulric guessed the door would have only been accessible by a retractable ladder, but now there was a flight of steps and a railed landing.

Rexinda wanted to flog whoever had added the stairs and ruined the tower's military efficiency, but she conceded it had a good view of the Via Borealis and the road east. They both agreed the location was ideal for spying.

Ulric crept up the hill and ascended the offending stairs, carefully testing each step before placing his full weight upon the beam. Halfway up the stairs, he felt the warm embrace of a Thieves' Glimmer. His heart beat faster and his breath quickened. His eyes pierced shadow, revealing the hidden things where only darkness had lurked before, and a host of previously secret sounds burst through the veil of midnight silence. He made a quick, hidden motion, tracing a "∞" in the air. It was a lemnis, a sign for luck. He felt he was going to need it.

Once on the landing he moved toward the door, a formidable piece of iron-bound hardwood perfectly fit within its frame with no visible lock or handle. He had just reached out to measure the gap between wood and stone when the booming sound of cracking wood broke the silence.

Ulric's breath caught in his throat. He recoiled from the door, then cursed himself a fool. The sound had only been the normal creaking and popping of wooden steps, made thunderous by fear and his heightened senses. As he watched Rexinda climb the remaining stairs, he tried to mask his annoyance at every new groan and crack.

It's not my fault, he thought, *that she walks with the exaggerated posture of the amateur sneak.*

Rexinda topped the stairs and shot Ulric a murderous look. "What?" she hissed. "The stairs are old."

"This door isn't." He ran his hands across the surface and down the edges of the door. There was no hint of light beneath the threshold. "There's no lock to pick…"

"It was a guard tower. It's barred from the inside. You're the thief. Can't you deal with it?"

"If I had the right tools, I could lift the bar. But the blades I have are too thick to slide through."

"Red Swords!" Rexinda slumped against the tower wall and twisted the hilt of her gladius until her knuckles glistened white under the moonlight. Ulric guessed she was imagining the hilt was his neck. "Now what, thief?"

Ulric pressed his ear to the cool wood. At first, there was nothing. Then he heard muffled echoes, followed by indistinct mumblings and the soft thump of footsteps from somewhere higher up the tower. The footsteps sounded unhurried, unconcerned, unaware.

He stepped back and gazed toward the top of King's Tower. "The gladiators are awake. But they don't know we're here. Yet."

"Good," Rexinda said. She stood and followed Ulric's gaze. "Only cowards murder someone in their sleep."

"Right." Ulric tried not to think of the dozen or more people he'd rather murder in their sleep than face in a straight fight. Still staring toward the sky, he said, "I bet the door leading out onto that walkway will be easier to sneak into."

Ulric and Rexinda's climb began easily enough thanks to the poor maintenance of the tower walls. Handholds were plentiful in the gaps between the rough stonework, exposed by years of missing mortar. Still, Ulric's legs and shoulders already ached from the long march from Trumric, and he doubted Rexinda felt much better. By the time the support struts of the watchtower platform loomed overhead, they were both quietly cursing their decision.

Ulric blinked. Sweat stung his eyes and dripped down his brow. He risked a glance below. The wooden landing looked ridiculously small. *A hard landing,* he thought with grim humor. He tried to wipe the sweat from his eyes, but he only left a warm, rusty smelling smear across his face.

Sweet Neesis. My fingers are bleeding.

He found the next gap in the wall and dug his bloody fingers into the rough stone. With a groan, he pulled himself within reach of the nearest support strut: a thick wooden beam, angled to support the walkway that encircled the uppermost level of the tower. He stretched for the beam and kicked away from the wall. An instant later, he hung under the platform, his arms clutching the strut, his feet dangling in the open air.

Ulric twisted his body toward Rexinda, a triumphant grin on his face.

Rexinda clung to the wall a full body length below, her blonde hair darkened and matted with sweat. She looked as bloody and exhausted as Ulric, but worse, she looked scared. She hid it well, but he could see it. He knew from bitter experience when a fellow thief had lost confidence in a climb.

"You should have stayed below," he said. Hand over hand, he slowly made his way toward the edge of the platform.

"What are you saying? That I can't climb? I can climb as well as any city-bred thief!" Rexinda insisted, her anger growing with every word. Still, she climbed no further.

"I thought you had breached the walls of Tylisus. A campfire boast, I guess."

"You soft-limbed catamite!" Rexinda climbed toward Ulric with newfound confidence. "You son of a whore!" Eventually, she scrambled up the nearest wooden strut and extended a tanned leg toward Ulric. "If I could reach you, I'd kick you off this tower."

With a wry smile, Ulric said, "But you need my help with the gladiators."

"Wrong." Rexinda swung her body toward the edge of the platform and said, "You need *my* help with the gladiators."

Looking back, she added, "Oh, and I'm not stupid. I know what you were—"

Voices from above cut her short. Ulric's own retort caught in his throat and, in a panic, he clamped his mouth shut and froze. With a look, Rexinda asked: *have they heard us?* As if in response, a crackling flash of light burst from the top of the tower, then faded into a pale blue glow.

Ulric focused his glimmer-enhanced hearing on the tower's uppermost level. Aculeo grumbled, "You keep damn peculiar hours, magus."

"They don't know we're here," Ulric whispered. "There's something else going on. Let's go."

They pulled themselves over the railing and fell onto the platform as quietly as possible. They laid there longer than was wise given the nearness of their enemies, but their limbs were fire and the wood cool and damp after the long rain.

Ulric heard an unfamiliar voice. It had to be this magus Aculeo had spoken to. It sounded both present and powerful, yet distant and hollow. "I have little time to myself, here at the Collegium," said the voice. "Besides, I do my best thinking late at night. It must be Nyx's dark embrace: it fires the imagination."

The voice, despite its oddity, had a likeable, lyrical quality.

"Yes!" said Aculeo, sounding a bit too enthusiastic. "One should never ignore divine inspiration."

A noncommittal grunt followed. It had to be Kriton.

"Well, enough about the peculiarities of my schedule. Let us speak of yours."

As the magus spoke, strange shadows danced in the blue light streaming from the open door. A tingling sensation rushed over Ulric and the hair on the back of his neck rose, followed by the hair on his arms and legs. The very air seemed to pop and crackle. He couldn't help but smile as Rexinda's loose blonde strands formed a pale halo about her head.

Ulric had to get closer: he had to see this magus for himself. Rolling onto his belly, he crawled to one side of the door. Rexinda joined him on the opposite side, then drew her gladius. He shook his head and extended his hand in warning. She shot Ulric an impatient scowl but relaxed her posture. They both listened, and Ulric snuck a peek past the threshold.

Sweet Neesis! I hate magic!

Aculeo and Kriton stood at the center of the tower, speaking to a man composed of shifting, shimmering, crackling lightning. It was as if Alakur had taken one of His thunderbolts and fashioned it into a man.

Ulric slumped back against the wall and tried to catch his breath. There'd be no fighting a magus, let alone one who could turn himself into a living thunderbolt! The best they could do now was to listen and learn what they could, then quietly disappear.

"I warned you to keep your distance," said the magus. A palpable sizzle of anger filled the air. "Only a fool underestimates Magus Vipsania Tertia!"

"It wasn't her," grunted an uncharacteristically verbose Kriton. "It was some damned Keksu."

"Yes. A Kekeksuan warrior. Called himself Kehindé," said Aculeo. "Had a boy with him. One of your local criminal types. What do they call them? Ah, yes… Imperaré."

"Don't try to shift blame, Aculeo. I'm not as easily misdirected as some bloodthirsty arena."

"Unfair! We planned for Vipsania and her discipulus. Now she's leading a veritable caravan."

"A damned caravan," echoed Kriton.

"Explain that, Nero!" Aculeo asked.

"Who knew she had friends?" replied a bemused Nero.

Nero? It had to be Modius Nero. The results of Luciano's interrogation had been reported to the Concilium. Silo had eventually shared the details relevant to Ulric's past, so he knew the storm magus had originally commissioned the theft of the Eltaran scroll. Then the broker, Marius Secundus, instead sold the scroll to Magus Vipsania Tertia to punish Nero for his affair with his wife. In turn, Nero conspired to have Secundus' former allies in the Dark Assembly assassinate him; the assassin being none other than Luciano Portelos. And thanks to Luciano's own petty scheming, Ulric had found himself suspected of the murder, tortured and imprisoned by his widow, and awaiting interrogation by none other than Modius Nero.

That night, he had escaped before meeting the storm magus. He dared not meet him now.

Ulric took another look. Aculeo wore an expensive tunic with leather boots, and still bore the long daggers he had noticed earlier. Kriton was still draped in his dark traveling cloak, but he had thrown back his hood, revealing a prominent nose and deeply inset eyes. Modius Nero hovered between the two ex-gladiators, a tall, slender figure of crackling light suspended above a small mechanism of crystal and brass. He recalled how Nero had said, "Here at the Collegium." Could he still be at the Collegium Draconis Aurei? If so, then the gladiators were speaking to an image, a sort of fabrication.

"The plan doesn't change," said the image of Nero. "Let dear Vipsania take the risks, then you bring the gate-stone."

At that, Rexinda impatiently readied her sword and hefted her axe.

"As you say," said Kriton, with a finality that signaled he was done speaking.

"One last thing, Aculeo. The Imperaré boy… Did you catch his name?"

"Hmm. Octavius… something. Something foreign-sounding. Northern, I think."

"Foreign-sounding?" Nero mocked. "Is that all you remember?"

Rexinda whispered, "I want to see this Nero for myself." She leaned forward to peek past the threshold, causing the planks beneath her to groan and pop. Nero shot a glance toward the open door and both Rexinda and Ulric jerked back out of sight.

"Never mind. How do you like the tower?" Nero asked. "Do you feel secure? Free from prying eyes?"

"Oh, we value our privacy, I assure you," Aculeo said.

The sudden change of subject was too obvious. It was time to go. Ulric risked one last look. Inside, Aculeo spoke to the image of Modius Nero. Kriton was gone.

Ulric turned back toward Rexinda.

Kriton stood behind her, shrouded in blue shadow, perfectly silent, poised to plunge his sword into her back. His glimmer-enhanced hearing had heard nothing.

Ulric's eyes went wide. Groping for the hilt of his spatha, he tried to shout a warning, but before a sound could escape his lips, Rexinda launched herself forward. She evaded Kriton's descending blade but crashed into Ulric, sending them both rolling in a chaotic tumble of limbs. There were brief flashes of an advancing, smirking Kriton, then a sharp pain as one of Rexinda's boots connected with his skull.

Rexinda sprung up into a low crouch, axe and gladius waving like eager cobras. "You'd spy on us? Steal from Magus Vipsania? By Cathus, I'll have your balls!" She sprung at Kriton, axe swinging and sword thrusting, her beautiful face twisted with murderous intent. This wasn't the flirtatious young woman who had playfully tried to throw him off the Quadrivium gallery—It was the mercenary Rexinda Hamunds-Daughter, veteran of half a dozen wars.

Ulric scrambled out of her way and leaped to his feet, only to have the platform pitch and roll like a storm-tossed ship. Head throbbing and stomach turning, he fell on his back with a thud. He lay there, surrounded by the clamor and clash of steel as

Kriton repelled Rexinda's onslaught, no matter how savage or skillful her attacks.

He feared to think the ex-gladiators were that good. After all, he reminded himself, the ambushers had been ambushed. And they were both exhausted from the climb. And now Rexinda had nearly kicked in his skull. Fine excuses, all, but excuses didn't win fights. He could hear the voice of Ghostwalker: "Listen up, Darktalon. Excuses are like paying good coin for old problems. All you buy are the same old failures." Arrius was right, and he knew Silo would agree, even if the Imperaré prince would put it less eloquently.

Rexinda needed his help. There was no time for the healing trance of Shadow Mind. He could try to discover Ghostwalker's secret fighting technique once again, but he'd need every advantage. No. Even though there had been a promising moment in the Calidius Arena, the attempt had ended in disaster. All Ulric could do was pick himself up and try to ignore the pounding in his head. He pulled Ghostwalker's spatha from its ebony scabbard, and the Eltaran runes flared with a brilliant white light before fading into a dull blue glow.

Ulric raised the sword and adopted a plunging guard, arm forward and high, blade angled down. He didn't hesitate to lunge at Kriton's back—he'd never known a fair fight.

"I think not, young Octavius!"

Aculeo's massive bulk hit him like a charging bull, emptying the air from his lungs in a single breath. It felt like exhaling hot gravel. For a moment, as he soared across the platform, he marveled at the damned luck of it all. When he crashed into the railing with a loud crack, he prayed to Neesis it wasn't his ribs. Worse, the impact sent his sword flying from his hand. He watched helplessly as Ghostwalker's spatha skittered across the wooden planks and disappeared over the edge.

He didn't bother to look below. "Damn me through the Ninth Gate!" he exclaimed, drawing his pugio and a throwing knife. Turning to Aculeo, he said, "I prefer daggers anyway."

Kriton disengaged from Rexinda and shot his partner a questioning look.

Rexinda fell back on her haunches and tried to catch her breath, keeping her wild eyes fixed on Kriton while dark rivulets of blood oozed from several minor cuts crisscrossing her arms and legs. Had the ex-gladiator been toying with her?

"Damn the pair of you," said Aculeo. He didn't sound angry, only resigned to a great burden. "You've likely cost us a considerable sum."

"Considerable," repeated Kriton.

"How much?" asked Ulric. "What is Modius Nero paying you to do, exactly?"

Aculeo rested his hands on the pommels of the exceedingly long curved daggers strapped at his broad waist. "Are you a fan of the arena, young Octavius?"

Ulric hesitated. He'd expected Aculeo would dodge his questions about Modius Nero, but he had no idea what the ex-gladiator was aiming at. "Of course."

"Then you know that few matches end in death."

"Most don't."

With a sly smirk, Aculeo said, "Sometimes, a gladiator even survives a deadly battle."

"I've heard the tricks: pig's blood in hidden bladders, minor fabrications, that sort of thing."

"Ah! As an actor, a fellow entertainer, you can appreciate the showmanship needed to create the perfect performance. But do you know why?"

"Because gladiators are all slaves and fucking cowards?" Rexinda suggested.

"Charming." Aculeo rolled his eyes and continued. "No. It's because a gladiator is worth money. More than the average mercenary—much more. Their school has put considerable time and coin into their training long before the first match. Unneeded death does their owners no good."

"Then there's *sine missione*," Kriton said with a dark gleam in his eyes.

Aculeo shifted his weight, letting his hands slip onto the hilt of his daggers. "Yes. A battle without mercy. A fight to the bitter end."

"And what sort of battle is this?" Ulric asked, trying to focus past the throbbing in his head.

"That is the question," answered Aculeo. "If we show mercy, our plans are ruined, and we'll very likely have an angry dragon magus to contend with. Most inconvenient."

"But..." prompted Kriton.

"Perhaps it's better if the two of you disappeared into the night." As Aculeo spoke, he waved his hand in a broad theatrical gesture like a vanishing fabricator. "Never to be seen again!"

"Kill us and Magus Vipsania will pursue a most fiery revenge," Ulric warned. "She's quite fond of the girl."

Rexinda's only reply was a slow spin of her gladius and a nervous rotation of her grip around the handle of her axe.

"So you say. I think your fates will remain a mystery."

"But it was Magus Vipsania who sent us," lied Ulric. "If we don't report by the eleventh hour, she'll know."

"A well-delivered line, young Octavius, but from a poor script." Aculeo unsheathed his daggers. The long blades were practically short swords, curved and wickedly sharp on the inside edge. "No, the two of you came on some foolish impulse of your own. You are alone."

In perfect unison, the two men attacked. Kriton drove Rexinda back onto her heels, battering aside both gladius and axe. Aculeo moved with surprising speed. Like scythes eager for a bloody harvest, his daggers sliced through the air and came within a hand's breadth of opening Ulric's throat.

Ice-cold panic gripped Ulric. Heart racing, head pounding, he backpedaled furiously as the tower swayed against the night sky. Wounded and armed with his meager daggers, he was no match for the ex-gladiator. He couldn't imagine the wild luck that could lead to victory. There was only *sine missione*: merciless death.

Aculeo hooked the back of Ulric's forearm in the curve of his dagger and yanked down hard, opening a deep wound. Others may have lost an arm, but Ulric was born fast and trained to be faster. He slipped his arm free, rolled out of range of Aculeo's next strike, and readied his throwing knife.

As he prepared to throw, the pain of the deep cut on his forearm finally hit him and his head began to spin. The knife launched with little power and struck far too low, barely sinking into Aculeo's massive belly and eliciting nothing more than an inconvenienced grunt from the big man.

Blast me through the Nine Gates! I'm going to die here. With Rexinda. I hope Julia doesn't get the wrong idea.

Further down the platform, Rexinda screamed a quick series of expletives and went silent.

Sweet Neesis! No!

Desperate to know Rexinda's fate, Ulric tried to rise, but a swift kick from the ex-gladiator sent him sprawling.

Aculeo pulled the knife free and tossed it aside, ignoring the spreading bloodstain on his tunic. He stalked closer. Behind him, Ulric saw Kriton had Rexinda trapped. Somehow he had taken her axe and used it to pin her sword arm beneath the beard of the blade, while his own sword rested ominously across her neck.

"The battle is over, young Octavius. You've lost." Aculeo hefted his daggers and readied the final blow. "A pity no one saw your final performance. Perhaps a cheering crowd would have demanded mercy? Alas, no one is watching."

"The gods are always watching!"

Julia's warning echoed across the night as she stepped from the watchtower. With Ghostwalker's spatha at her side, she raised a bloody hand to the heavens and cried, "Mother Myrill, bless us with Alakur's dawning light! Illuminate the wickedness of the night!"

Julia's caramel skin began to glow, becoming translucent, radiant, potent. Then she cast aside her traveling cloak and the top of King's Tower became brighter than the morning star, as dazzling as the dawning sun. Her light was warm and golden, like the kiss of the first spring day after a long, bleak winter. Bathed in Julia's divine radiance, Ulric's fears, doubts, and pain burnt away. An instant later, her light faded, leaving the top of the tower once again shrouded in pale blue shadow.

For the two ex-gladiators, the light had been blazing, blinding agony. Aculeo swayed to and fro, watering eyes screwed shut, wildly brandishing his daggers. Kriton released Rexinda, then dropped her axe and staggered across the platform, one hand covering his eyes, the other holding his sword out on point.

"Come on," Julia called, beckoning Ulric and Rexinda to flee into the tower. "Before they recover. Hurry!"

Ulric climbed to his feet with newfound vigor, clutching his wounded arm, where warm blood oozed through his fingers in viscous crimson.

"Not until the battle is done, priestess." With a shout of, "*sine missione!*" Rexinda lunged at Kriton and drove her gladius into the base of the ex-gladiator's neck, nearly severing his head.

"Kriton! Kriton!" Aculeo spun about, daggers cutting the night air. "Dis and Morbus take the lot of you!"

Rexinda yanked her sword free of Kriton's corpse, then said, "You're next, fat man."

"Please, Rexinda," Julia pleaded, "no more bloodshed."

"Didn't you hear, Julia? This match is *sine missione*. No mercy."

Aculeo backpedaled away from Rexinda's voice. Ulric had to hurry out of his way to avoid another wicked cut.

"I think the crowd would grant mercy for some answers," suggested Ulric. "What do you say, Aculeo?"

"No deals! He dies!" Rexinda grabbed her axe and headed for Aculeo.

"I'll talk… I'll talk!" Aculeo lurched away from Rexinda until he slammed into the platform railing. "Just put your bitch on a leash. Then I'll—"

With the sound of splintering wood and a surprised gasp, Aculeo fell through the broken railing and vanished over the edge. A moment later, there was a terrible flat, pulpy sound as the big man crashed into the wooden stairs far below. Ulric and Rexinda rushed to the edge to survey the carnage.

"So much for answers." Ulric sighed.

"They would have all been lies," Rexinda replied.

Julia stepped between them and said, "I found this below," and handed Ulric his spatha.

He admired the sword for a moment, then sheathed the blade. "Praise Neesis and Myrill! And praise Julia, Her Ikon."

Julia replied with a look of stern disapproval, "I can't wait to hear why you needed to be saved." Turning to Rexinda, she asked, "And what do you say?"

Rexinda glanced at the remains of Kriton and Aculeo. "I'll never underestimate gladiators again."

The Nature of Men and Elts

The sun was rising fast in the eastern sky, casting ever shrinking shadows over the Occasio Ultima. Luciano emerged from the popina, crossed a patio filled with travelers rushing to finish their morning meal, and approached a giant of a man nearly as thick as the tree he leaned against.

"What now?" The man, dressed in a simple brown tunic but adorned in expensive bronze bracers and silver chains, had spoken before Luciano had even made eye contact. He was not accustomed to the giant's abruptness, but it was growing on him. The man, called Petrus, was taller than Luciano and much broader in the shoulders. Luciano had found him severely lacking wits, but intelligence was not a trait common among Imperaré enforcers. His first choice could easily have been Decius, one of Silo's men, whom Luciano had concluded was level-headed and street smart. Nonetheless, Petrus had ingratiated himself to Luciano with his bloody-minded simplicity, bravado, and impressive size. Those traits were enough for Luciano to make him his right-hand man. Besides, that kind of muscle might be useful if that bothersome Elt caused any trouble along the way.

"Owner says they were here," Luciano said. "Yesterday morning. Magus, big Keksu warrior, blonde bitch, others. Seems like our prey, eh, Petrus?" Luciano looked impatiently down the Via Borealis. "All this we already know."

Raquin strode between the two, interrupting their conversation. Fortunately, the Elt looked nondescript in a common black traveling cloak and hood—the Occasio Ultima needed no more notoriety. Hopefully his white hair and red eyes remained hidden under the hood. As he casually ate an apple, he leaned on the opposite side of Petrus' tree, never saying a word nor looking at either man.

Luciano sucked his teeth. "This not concern you, Elt."

Raquin took a bite from the apple, crunching it loudly as he gazed at Luciano with indifference.

"I never knew Elts not have manners. Always thought they civilized enough to not interrupt. Guess I am wrong, eh?"

Raquin shifted his weight and tossed the apple into the air before taking another bite. "I spoke to the owner as well. He knew far more than he ever told you. But then again, you didn't think to reward the man for his knowledge. Or perhaps you couldn't afford it? Which one, I wonder? Ignorance or poverty?"

Before Luciano could reply, Raquin cut him off again. "I offered motivation in the form of Trumrician coin. I learned that their expedition consists of six members. Plus four slaves. They had a rather one-sided argument with a group of sword-carrying thugs; 'high and mighty men,' I believe he called them. The owner was paid generously by the Kekeksuan for the mess and the disposal of bodies." Raquin finished the apple with two large bites, examining it in his hand as he continued. "He was quite eager to impart this information. No doubt such news will bring his little popina some welcome notoriety." When he finished speaking, he tossed the apple core at Luciano's feet.

Luciano unsheathed his new falcata and paused. Petrus' eyes widened, his eyes darting back and forth between the assassin and the Elt. Slowly, his hand went to the hilt of his own sword.

Luciano stabbed the apple core on the ground and lifted it up to eye level. Plucking it off the end of the blade, he said, "I also talk to man more. I also give man motivation to say more." He held the apple core in one hand as he slowly twisted his blade in the air with the other. "He was… What was that Trumin word you used? Eager. Man was *eager* to tell me more. Owner tell me two others were there. Man call them mercenaries, not thugs. Armed better than Imperaré thugs. Armored better. Ask questions about magus and others. Head north after meal." He flared his nostrils. "I know how motivate men too," he said, then flicked the apple core at Raquin.

Luciano saw only a blur. When his vision settled, Raquin held a small, curved knife near his face, tipped with the impaled apple core.

Petrus cleared his throat and maintained his grip on his gladius. "The men. Getting restless. Hungry, too. You let 'em eat, Dominus?"

"Call me that again and I cut you throat, Petrus."

The giant stammered, "Sure, sure… uh—"

"Luciano."

"Yeah, yeah, of course, Luciano. You got it, Luciano. So…"

Luciano, falcata in one hand, placed the other on Petrus' shoulder, guiding his lieutenant a few steps from the tree. The assassin's eyes narrowed at the group of men scattered by the road. Some stood restlessly, while others lounged idly by the roadside. They had grumbled when he told them to stay clear of the Occasio Ultima; he didn't trust them to stay out of trouble. In fact, he didn't trust most of them to carry out the simplest of orders. The three men Brocchus had given him were reliable, if unimaginative, including Petrus. Another eighteen men had been drawn from the other six collegiums of the Imperaré, and he had found only a handful of those to be worth their salt. Was it the usual politics and old rivalries that drove the princes to horde their best men? Or did they want Brocchus to fail? Luciano to fail?

If the Concilium had wisdom, they'd have sent only Luciano. And tell that Elt to go to the Nine Hells. But what committee ever had wisdom? Not the vicars of the Dark Assembly; not the princes of the Imperaré. Still, twenty-one against six is good odds, even if one of the six is a dragon magus.

"No. Tell men we… No. No mind, I tell them myself."

Luciano cocked his head and walked toward the men. Petrus marched at his side. Though he felt Raquin's presence as well, he ignored him. As he neared the Imperaré men, some of them started to rise and dust themselves off.

"We leave. Now," Luciano commanded. "Go north on Via Borealis. Ilus, you scout."

Ilus, small and skinny as a ferret—and as furry as one—immediately darted north, taking to the high grass flanking the road.

"Rest of you, follow Petrus and me."

The rest of the men began filing in behind the giant.

As he watched Ilus disappear into the grass, Luciano heard a voice grumbling behind him.

"Don't know why we can't get some fucking food in our bellies first."

Luciano whirled around. He scanned the men from left to right, then right to left, spotting one's darting eyes. The glares of the others betrayed him. Luciano walked up to the man, a Night Legion gang member with matted orange hair and a boy's excuse for a beard. The man stood his ground, but Luciano smelled his false bravado as powerfully as the liquor on his breath—and he smelled the fear. Luciano's nostrils flared as he gritted his teeth, glaring at the fool. When the man gulped, he released a chuckle and walked away. He almost didn't hear the Night Legion man curse him under his breath. Almost.

"Asshole."

Luciano's movements were lightning quick.

The men saw only the result: two daggers, each striking the shoulder of the two men flanking the orange-haired fool. They both cried out in surprise, then pulled the daggers free. Their wounds were bloody, but shallow. When the initial shock and pain subsided, neither of the men looked at Luciano. Instead, their eyes—wild with anger—went to the man in the middle. They grabbed the Night Legion man, bloody daggers in hand, and hesitated. They looked back at Luciano.

"I gave you daggers. Use them."

Luciano watched as the Night Legion man's pleas for mercy were cut short. He returned to Petrus and greeted the giant with a hyena-like laugh. "When they finish, march north. Double speed." Then, staring at Raquin, he repeated, "I know how to motivate men, too."

The sun blazed overhead while the men marched at the double, suffering in silence. After a couple of hours passing by patrician manors and wine orchards, they arrived at a crossroads. The sign pointing north read "Via Borealis," while the other, "Via Lucesci," beckoned east.

Pausing, Luciano ordered Petrus to take the men ahead and wait for his orders. The giant gave him a puzzled look, but when Luciano waved him down the road, he led the men onward as he was told. When the last man passed, leaving Luciano alone with Raquin at the crossroads, Luciano stood in the intersection, staring down the Via Lucesci and into the horizon. He moved his gaze to the southeast and squeezed his eyes shut. He pictured his homeland, the nation of Verdith. Rocky coasts and high cliffs, rolling hills and mountain pastures, orchards of grapes and fields of barley…

Raquin cleared his throat.

Luciano gritted his teeth and peered at his side. The ever-looming presence of the Elt was becoming more and more of a nuisance. *Brocchus should have sent me alone*, he thought again.

He closed his eyes. Aqua blue waves crashing against white stone cliffs, salty sea breeze, the Spires of Ebidos piercing the sky.

A life devoid of that damned Darktalon, of Cornelius Brocchus, of servitude. But the moment he entertained the idea of abandoning his mission, a familiar yellow spike of pain pierced his mind. He could feel it slithering, creeping from his temples deeper into his brain.

When he opened his eyes, Raquin was staring at him with that Elt indifference. "Lost?" was all he said. Luciano spied the sarcasm in his voice, as well as the smirk hiding behind his placid face.

Luciano massaged his forehead, trying to ease the pain behind his eyes. "No, but you do give me headache, Elt."

"Do I? Well, for that I do apologize."

"Apology mean nothing, Elt." Luciano, still looking eastward, pressed his fingers and thumb against his temples, trying to mask Raquin's voice with the sounds of the Verdan kithara. The pain grew from discomfort to torment, yet Luciano held on to the fading memory of his grandmother's lute.

"Ah. You are lost," Raquin said. "Lost in a vision."

Despite the pain, the scene reminded Luciano of peace. Of freedom. And with that notion came a sudden explosion of yellow suffering. Luciano fell to his knees, baring his teeth, cradling his head in his hands.

"And the vision brings pain."

Luciano opened his eyes wide as he took in deep, laborious breaths.

"Perhaps a vision of..." The Elt studied Luciano a moment longer. "...home?"

The comment struck dangerously close to the truth, which infuriated Luciano.

"Strange," said Raquin. "Why not take the road east? You obviously have no true allegiance to Brocchus. Why not leave all of this behind?"

Luciano shot Raquin a warning look, then picked himself up off the ground. "We go." He cleared the visage of Verdith from his mind and marched down the Via Borealis. The yellow torment subsided, though the torture of the Elt's presence continued for some time afterward.

That afternoon, the ferret Ilus returned with news of the town ahead. "Corvaro. Small, but they cater to travelers. Places for food, drink, supplies. There's a hospitia that sits on a hill overlooking the town. No sign of the magus, though."

Flanked by Petrus and Raquin, Luciano led his men into the quiet town of Corvaro, where the citizenry gave them curious glances and a wide berth. The day had grown hotter and hotter as the afternoon waned, which reminded Luciano of the men's earlier grumbling. Just inside the gate stood a two-story building sporting a bright purple sign: *Vinum et Voluptas*—Wine and Pleasure. Luciano wasn't sure whether it was a lupinar disguised as a popina or a popina disguised as a lupinar, but it didn't matter. He beckoned to Petrus and pointed to the sign. "Tell men: one hour. Enjoy. Then back in street here." He grabbed the taller man by the forearm, squeezing for emphasis. "One hour, Petrus. You understand?"

"Yes, Luciano," the giant replied, saluting awkwardly.

Luciano rolled his eyes, then turned his attention to Raquin. "Elts enjoy wine? Women?"

"Wine? Yes. But not the grape-flavored horse urine Trumins make. As for women…" The Eltaran rubbed his hands together. "I've lain with many. Most of them Eltaran, though I admit to having shared my bed with a handful of human females. However, they were all thoroughly washed and perfumed. I doubt enough perfume exists to mask the stench of the women in there, nor enough wine to sufficiently…"

Luciano had lost interest in the Eltaran's answer as soon as it had begun. He walked into Vinum et Voluptas before the blowhard even finished his answer.

Friendly conversations with several wine-soaked locals bore fruit. Though no one had seen a dragon magus or a mountainous dark-skinned Keksu, there was plenty of talk about another pair. Well-armed men, who had spent the previous evening drinking and entertaining the patrons with stories of the gladiatorial arenas. Their tales of glory and bloodshed bought them plenty of wine and attention, but they left for King's Tower before either had gotten too drunk, unlike most of the patrons. A handful of the popina's regulars also described a second pair arriving late that night: a blonde Gualdean woman and a dark-haired man carrying an impressive spatha. They were quite interested in the ex-gladiators and left without downing a sip. The owner of the establishment, a loquacious and gregarious man, provided another morsel: news of a skirmish the previous evening at the King's Tower, at the north end of town.

Luciano tossed the owner a pair of denarii and marched out, eager to follow his new lead. Much to his dismay, Raquin waited for him in the middle of the road.

"Where does our investigation take us next?"

Luciano paid him no heed, striding past him toward the tower.

"I take it then, you have no interest in what I learned: a bright light filled the northern sky last night."

Luciano stopped.

Raquin casually walked up to the Verdan, and the two of them began marching towards King's Tower, shoulder to shoulder.

Luciano, his eyes fixed straight ahead, asked, "What you find out, Elt?"

"Several accounts from the people of Corvaro report an unnatural light, very bright—bright enough to illuminate the northern sky—emanating from that tower." Raquin gestured toward the north, nodding with condescension at Luciano. "One rather pious woman even characterized it as 'divine light.'"

Luciano glanced at Raquin, then narrowed his eyes toward the tower. He could guess the source of that divine light.

After a few moments of merciful silence, the Eltaran spoke again. "That pain, earlier. It must be excruciating." He paused, waiting for a reply which did not come. "Perhaps you are ill? Or... cursed?" Still no response. "Tell me of your homeland. Brocchus calls you 'the Verdan.' I know little of that land, Verdith. Fine wines. Powerful sorcerers. You must miss it, your home."

Luciano kept walking, ignoring the Eltaran's inquiry, recalling the tendrils of pain that accompanied his last recollections of home.

Raquin continued, "I've been told the people there are more cultured than the Trumins, who presume greatness over them."

Trumins don't know the meaning of culture.

"Seems unjust. No, more than that. Cruel. Cruel that the Fates have so adorned Trumric with the golden laurel crown, while granting Verdith only the leather sandals of a vassal, bowing at the feet of the Trumin Republic."

Luciano realized the futility of ignoring the long-winded Elt, so he switched tactics. "Why Elts so interested in map?"

The question worked better than he had hoped; at first, Raquin didn't respond, but silence did not last for long.

"The map…" Luciano noticed Raquin's cadence was much slower now.

The Elt chooses his words carefully. For once.

"It leads to…"

Yes?

"Something which will change the world forever…"

The Eltaran's voice drifted off, and Luciano realized he was no longer at his side. He looked back and saw Raquin's eyes were like coins, staring into the distance.

Now he is lost in his own vision. We have no time for this.

"We go, Elt. No time to waste."

Raquin's expression did not change.

"Raquin!"

The Eltaran blinked as if waking from a dream, then glanced at Luciano.

"We go."

Raquin resumed his place next to Luciano, and the two continued down the road in silence.

As they walked through Corvaro, the King's Tower loomed closer and closer. Raquin snapped his arm in front of Luciano and they both came to a halt. "You see that?" he said, pointing ahead.

Luciano squinted at the old tower, still a way off down the road. He saw nothing new.

"One man, standing at the doorway," said Raquin. "Another, near the top of the tower, probably watching us approach. We're not the only ones interested in last night."

"Armed?"

"No."

Luciano smiled a jackal's smile.

By the time they reached the tower, both strangers stood atop a flight of stairs that hugged the tower's exterior. They blocked the front door, which stood wide open. Luciano and Raquin faced the two men—common laborers, judging by their clothes. Both wore grim expressions, and one held tightly onto a weather-worn club.

Luciano took a step forward. The armed man lifted his club to waist level. The other fool shuffled his feet nervously.

Luciano glared at the armed man and slowly pulled out his new falcata, pointing its tip at the man's own weapon. He glanced at the club, then met the man's gaze once again.

The man gulped. His eyes darted from Luciano to Raquin, then to his partner, whose frightened look offered no support. The man lowered the club.

Luciano took a step forward, allowing his blade to caress the trembling man's club.

"What happen here?"

The man cowered in the shadow of the Verdan.

"There was a skirmish, Dominus. Last night. A sword fight. Blood and death."

"Who?"

"Two dead. Mercenaries, by the looks of 'em. Brutus and I already cleared 'em out. One fell from the top. Crashed through the stairs. Broke his neck. The other…" The man gulped and slid his free hand across his neck. "The other, poor bastard, had his head nearly cut off."

"And the others?" Luciano asked.

"Don't know, Dominus. Musta fled."

Luciano tightened his grip on his falcata.

"Who owns tower?"

"Lucius Pansa. That's who Brutus and I work for. He sent us to clean up the place. Make repairs. Remove any bodies."

Luciano sheathed his blade and pushed his way past the two men.

Raquin followed. "Excuse us." He smiled at each man as he slipped past them. "Excuse us, please."

Both men recoiled when they saw the golden skin and red eyes beneath the stranger's dark hood.

The ensuing investigation of the tower yielded a bevy of clues. The wooden planks of the door, warped and misshapen by some unnatural force. And something else upstairs. Shattered pieces of rune-encrusted metal and glass, remnants of some strange, arcane device. But the last bit of information was the most enlightening. No trace of Darktalon... or the Gualdean woman. They had won. And escaped.

A subsequent visit to Lucius Pansa' home resulted in more: the tower's current tenant? A man named Modius Nero, an influential dragon magus. And the two casualties of the battle? Ex-gladiators in Nero's employ.

So... two magi seek the map's treasure? I hate magi.

When the pair returned to Vinum et Voluptas, most of the men were waiting on the road. Moments later, Petrus emerged from the curtained doorway, gripping the last two Imperaré men by their belts, and dumped them on the road.

"That all of them?" asked Luciano.

"That's the last of them!" Petrus responded proudly.

"We go." Luciano pointed to a manor-like building atop a hill overlooking the town. "House of Spineta."

As they approached the hospitia doors, a sinewy, leather-skinned man standing next to the main gate took a measured step in their direction, his hand on the hilt of his gladius.

"Salve, travelers," said the guard. He craned his neck, looking past Luciano and Petrus. His forearm pulsed as the knuckles around his blade turned white.

Petrus started forward until Luciano's palm stopped him.

"Salve," Luciano calmly replied.

"Afraid we don't have the room for all your men. Perhaps you'll find something a little further down the road."

"You owner. Where is he?"

The guard's nostrils flared. "I ain't got no owner, Verdan. I'm a freeman. Now move along."

"Not *you* owner, fool. Hospitia owner."

At the word "fool," the guard took a step closer, prompting Petrus to push past Luciano's hand and impose himself between the two.

The man, though taller than Luciano, still had to lift his head to meet eyes with Petrus. Looking at him, but speaking at Luciano, he said, "He ain't got the time for the likes of you, Verdan. I said… move along."

Luciano's hand squeezed between the two, again resting his palm on Petrus' chest.

"No trouble here. Just want talk to owner. No trouble." Luciano stared first at Petrus, then at the guard. The increased pressure from Luciano's hand caused Petrus to take half a step back, though his eyes—still locked on the other man—betrayed his resentment.

The guard, still looking at Petrus, responded through his teeth: "Fine. Only you go inside, Verdan. Just you."

Luciano shot Petrus a look, warning him to stand down, then walked through the main gates.

The owner turned out to be much more obliging than his guard insinuated. Luciano learned the magus and her companions had stayed at the hospitia the night before and confirmed she headed north on the Via Borealis early that morning. Her goal had to be the forests of the Silva Aurea. Now there were less than two hours of daylight left, and Luciano cursed the time he had wasted in town.

After speaking with the owner, Luciano heard shouts from outside. He took in a deep breath. Digging in his pouch, he reluctantly laid a handful of coins in front of the owner and hurried out to the courtyard. As he neared the main gate, he heard more shouting. And something worse: cheers. Outside, he saw his men circling about, gawking and cheering at some spectacle as Raquin, seemingly disinterested, leaned against the hospitia walls. Luciano pushed past a couple of High and Mighty thugs, just in time to witness Petrus crouch over the fallen guard and plunge his sword into the man's chest.

The cheering stopped as one by one, the men turned their attention from Petrus to Luciano.

As Raquin casually approached him, Luciano ignored him. Instead, he watched Petrus murder the guard in utter silence.

Petrus, his chest still heaving with blood rage, pulled his sword free then spit on the dying man. Unaware of Luciano's presence, he wiped his blade on the man's leg and rose to his feet, towering triumphantly over the corpse.

"What does the philosopher say?" Raquin asked rhetorically. "Ah, yes. 'Barbarism. The true nature of humankind.'"

"And what is the nature of Elts, eh?"

Raquin spoke with an almost religious ecstasy. "Why, divine, of course!"

As if coming out of a stupor, Petrus caught sight of Luciano. Forcing an awkward smile, he sheathed his sword. "Hey, boss— er, Luciano. Get what you need? Where to now? What are your orders? I'll get the men back on the road."

Luciano offered no response.

Raquin did. "Indeed. What are your orders, Verdan?"

Fumbling for words, Petrus approached Luciano with hands extended wide. "I… he… he came at me… I had no choice… he… he pulled his blade on me, boss… I had to… he had it coming, Luciano."

Luciano stared bitterly at the fool, while Raquin looked on with gleeful anticipation.

"He had it coming, Luciano. He had it coming!" His voice descended into child-like tones. "What was I supposed to do? He had it coming. I… had to…"

Luciano stepped toward him, stopping at his side and placing a comforting hand on his shoulder.

Raquin followed close behind. "He had it coming, says the man."

Petrus froze, his eyes darting about, as if he were searching for help. His gaze settled on the Eltaran, who wore a subtle smile.

Luciano casually stepped around the giant, then stopped again, this time on his other flank, his hand gripping Petrus' collar bone.

Luciano never said a word.

The men watched in horror as Aguja emerged from Petrus' throat. It withdrew just as quickly, replaced by a crimson fountain that sprayed blood into the air with surprising force. Petrus fell to his knees, clutching his throat, gurgling and gasping as he died.

When he had finally drowned in his own blood, Petrus fell face first onto the road. Luciano bent down and wiped Aguja on his thigh, mocking the giant's earlier move.

I should have known better than to rely on brawn over brains. I won't make that mistake again.

He returned the slender blade to its hilt and spoke with his back turned to the men. "Decius. Lead men north on main road. Double time."

Decius emerged from the crowd. He looked around, then pointed at himself. "Me?"

"You lead men now."

Decius took a step towards Luciano. "Why me?"

"You lead men now, Decius. I know you not fool like Petrus. You lead men now, eh?"

Decius glanced back at the crowd of Imperaré soldiers, then stared straight at Luciano. "You know I'm a Portus Collegium man, right?" He pointed to the ink on his arm. A dark hexagon, with the numerals "XVII" floating in a nimbus above it. He puffed his chest before delivering the next line. "I work for Silo."

"I believe today…" Luciano searched for the Trumin words to finish. "Today we all work for Imperaré, eh?" He let his words settle in, then said, "Now go, Decius. North on Via Borealis." He gestured with his head. "Double time."

Decius said nothing. Did nothing. The two men maintained their locked gaze, while the others waited.

"Double time," Luciano repeated.

Decius nodded, then turned towards the men, shouting orders. As his new lieutenant corralled the men down the hill, Luciano shouted one last command: "Decius!" He didn't wait for an acknowledgment. "No more trouble."

Decius nodded again. He herded the men back toward the Via Borealis, leaving only Luciano and Raquin standing in front of the hospitia. Raquin knelt over the body splayed on the ground, then cocked his head in Luciano's direction.

"You certainly are a master of motivation."

Luciano clenched his jaw. The Elt wasn't worth a reply. He turned his back and started down the path toward the Via Borealis. As he walked, he took account of his current situation. A score of criminal scum, most of them dullards, none of them trustworthy. Decius, a man who served the same Imperaré prince as Darktalon. And this annoying Elt, whose presence had become more and more unnerving.

Luciano shook his head. *Brocchus should have just sent me. Alone.*

A Fair Burden

The small room in the House of Spineta had become unbearably hot. Ulric knew it wasn't his imagination. Magus Vipsania sat on a chair of ivory-inlaid wood, hastily draped in her collegium robe, her volcanic glare framed in a halo of wild hair like the famous Medusa. Her expression was just as welcoming. The dragon magus smoldered in silence as Ulric, Rexinda, and Julia struggled to explain their actions in the town of Corvaro.

Vipsania bolted from her chair, blue fire flashing behind her eyes. "The town was forbidden!"

For once, Ulric bit his tongue and remained silent, as did Julia and Rexinda. Behind them, Kehindé stood before the exit, stiff and stone-faced as a jailer. Nearby, Flaccus examined the shards of the strange mechanism the gladiators had used to communicate with Magus Modius Nero.

Vipsania approached Rexinda, looking like an aggrieved mother. "I'd have expected such brash impudence from the thief. What would your father or, Eltarus forbid, your *mother* think of such foolishness?"

"Would you prefer the gladiators alive, Theia?" Rexinda asked, sounding hurt. "Conspiring with your enemies? Planning your murder?"

"Planning *our* murders," said Ulric before Vipsania could reply. "That's what I said. Corvaro was my idea."

"Darktalon is a liar. I had to drag him into Corvaro!"

Kehindé broke his long silence. "So, you led an attack into unfamiliar territory against an enemy whose true numbers and capabilities were unknown. Have I not taught you better?" His voice was so deep and resonant with disappointment, even Ulric felt ashamed. Rexinda cast her eyes down and seemed to shrink inside her armor.

Magus Vipsania turned to Julia. "I thought one blessed by Queen-Mother Myrill would have been wiser. What do you have to say for yourself, hmm?"

"Forgive me, Magus Vipsania. I awoke from strange dreams and discovered Ulric was gone. Then I saw the two of them on the road to Corvaro. I had to follow."

"So you wanted to spy on us?" Rexinda asked. "Not help us?"

"Now, wait. I wouldn't call that spying," Ulric said.

"If intentions were honorable, Rexinda, why fear discovery?" Julia asked.

"My intentions?" Rexinda exclaimed. "We had hardly stepped foot in Corvaro before your man dragged me into a taberna." She gave Ulric a wink and said, "Wine and *Pleasure*, it was called."

"Oh, no, no, no... no!" Ulric protested. "More like wine and *information*."

Julia's dark eyes narrowed. "So you took her into a taberna?"

"We, uh, *entered* a taberna—"

"Enough," Vipsania said. "I see there's no hope for a reasonable answer." She then walked to Flaccus, who handed her one of the larger pieces he had been examining.

"It is—or, uh… I should say, it *was* an aetheric farcaster."

"Yes. I can see that." Vipsania rolled the oblong piece of crystal and glass in her hand as if she was trying to warm it up. "Little remains of its aura."

"True. But it feels like its last cast was from the south. At a distance approximate to the capital."

"We could have discovered so much more if it had been intact." Vipsania turned and asked, "Which of you three idiots destroyed it?"

"We told you already," Ulric said. "It destroyed itself."

"I heard it shatter behind me," Julia said. "Shortly before Aculeo fell."

Magus Vipsania only stared at the shard, saying nothing.

"So?" Ulric asked. "Are we getting flogged, crucified, or what?"

Before Vipsania could reply, Kehindé asked, "What about the magus? Who is this Modius Nero?"

"Magus Modius Nero, Herald of the Wrack and Tempest Rider." Vipsania sounded more than a little embarrassed. "A colleague. And a friend… or so I thought."

"I've tried to warn you," Flaccus said. "He's been far too interested in your research. He's always asking questions, but what help has he ever given you?"

"We've competed amicably in the same fields for years. It's hard to imagine he'd sink to treachery and violence."

Kehindé placed a gentle hand on Vipsania's shoulder. "And yet we have the testimony of three witnesses. And the remains of the magical device."

"Reason enough to doubt him," she replied. "When I return, I'll have Nero hauled before a tribunal to stand before the Light of Revelation. Eltarus will burn the truth out of him." To everyone else, she said, "No time for sleep or breakfast. We head north."

Ulric and Julia hurriedly packed their belongings, suspecting Vipsania would leave them behind if they delayed. Julia worked quietly, ignoring him whenever possible. During Vipsania's interrogation, she had heard everything he and Rexinda had said about their mad plan to hunt down the gladiators. Surely Julia had to know there was nothing sexual between him and the Gualdean mercenary, unless she thought murder and mayhem were particularly romantic. And what of Rexinda? Did she really want him? Or did she simply enjoy needling Julia?

By the time Ulric hoisted his pack onto his shoulders, Julia had left the stables. He flew down the loft steps and caught up with her on the path to the hospitia.

"Last night… I went to Corvaro seeking gladiators. That's all."

"That's all? Really?" She seemed disinterested.

"Well, maybe I also wanted to defy Vipsania."

"And Rexinda?"

"The same. And I think she just likes to fight."

"Why not wake me, then?"

Ulric hesitated because he feared the answer. Rexinda had shamed him into wanting to defy Julia, to prove his independence.

"I see," she said, then quickened her pace and joined the others at the hospitia gates.

Ulric stood and silently prayed to Neesis Amora for understanding.

They left the House of Spineta a couple hours before dawn, heading north along the Via Borealis. Already, a warm breeze from the south swept across the countryside, promising a long, hot day. The drier weather brought far more traffic on the road than the day before; drovers from Apuli, pilgrims from Enes, and a rich merchant caravan from Conric. There were no ex-gladiators, of course. Nor storm magi. Nor any signs of Imperaré.

Despite Ulric's best efforts, Julia wouldn't speak to him in anything more than brief, indifferent replies. By the fifth hour of the day, he had grown bored with brooding silently at her side. He wanted to be anywhere else. Magus Vipsania and Kehindé led the way, speaking with one another in hushed, private tones. He dared not approach Rexinda. He had tried speaking with Flaccus earlier, but he had been in his own peculiar mood.

Then he overheard the old slave Renier grumbling to himself in surprisingly well-educated Gualic. The language had a soft, lyrical quality that seemed strange to his Trumrician ears. His adopted mother, Tessa, would sing Gualdean songs and recite stories of her homeland's ill-fated heroes. Thanks to her, he could speak it well enough, although he could not write it. Sometimes he wished he could forget it. All of it.

As always, the thought of Tessa invited the one memory that obscured all others. The one memory he would exile from his waking mind. *I see Tessa curled on the bed, her blood-stained hands reaching toward me. The man's screaming as the brothel guards drag him from the room. I want to gag from the blood smell. Deep wounds. More blood. Tessa cries. The brothel owner shouts something about damaged goods.*

Gualic always reminded him of Tessa. He hated the sound of it.

Ulric stopped and waited for Renier to catch up. "*Saúdos,* Renier."

The old slave didn't seem at all surprised to be greeted in his native language. He adjusted the heavy pack on his shoulders and said, "Greetings, young master. How may I be of service?"

"If you're going to complain about your duties, do it in Trumin."

"Of course, young master. If foreign tongues offend you, I'll only bellyache in good, honest Trumin. Although, one might suspect you're trying to get me into trouble with Mistress Vipsania." He made a croaking sound that must have been laughter. "It won't work. Magus Vipsania speaks Gualic better than most of the lords of Gualdé."

The old slave's impertinence intrigued him. "Vipsania tolerates your complaining? I find that doubtful."

One of the young slaves listened to their exchange with a look of horror. He must have feared such talk could only end in a whipping.

"Shouldn't you be walking with your Myrill-Blessed priestess, young master?"

"I decide where I walk, old man," Ulric declared. "Besides, she's in a sulk. Better I keep my distance."

"Hmm, a clever stratagem… I think. I was young once, but I've nearly forgotten."

"I haven't forgotten my question. You expect me to believe Magus Vipsania puts up with such an insolent tongue?"

"Oh, she's gotten used to it. I've known her since she was a young girl. Her family bought me to be her tutor."

"Her tutor?"

"Yes, young master, I haven't always been a pack animal. I was a scholar in the great city of Url before the Harath rode in. The Harathi have no use for scholars, of course; only horses, women, and plunder. Those were hard years. I was quite relieved when they sold me to a Trumrician trader. It was good to be back in civilized lands."

Ulric spoke with Renier for hours, learning all he could about the sacking of Url and the ways of the Harathi nomads. Questions about Vipsania's youth or her current plans were deflected: the old slave's wits were as steadfast as his loyalty. Thanks to Renier, the afternoon passed quickly.

Drops of stinging sweat rolled into Ulric's eyes for what must have been the hundredth time. He flicked them away, cursing the heat with a lethargic mumble. By the afternoon, no one spoke; the still, hot air seemed to smother words. Everyone marched to the sound of their labored breath and the endless drone of locusts. He looked ahead, searching for signs of the next hospitia.

The Via Borealis cut a straight line between neglected pastures and wildlands, finally disappearing in a wavering haze that looked like a fabricator's poor imitation of a road. The sun sat low in the western sky, scorching the horizon in dull bands of fire. There were lodgings on every major republic road, each a day's march from the other, but he saw nothing. Ulric cursed again.

He walked alone for some time, until he noticed Renier had fallen behind. The old man was bent over, his face flushed and drenched in sweat. He plodded along slowly, struggling to keep his large pack from slipping. Ulric fell back and stopped alongside the exhausted slave.

"Why is your pack so heavy?" Ulric asked. Renier's only reply was a labored grunt. "It's all Vipsania's oils and cosmetics, isn't it?"

"Oh, young master," he croaked out, "you shouldn't say such things. I carry essential supplies, I assure you."

"Of course they're damned *essential*—I've seen the woman."

Renier chuckled again, causing the pack to slip from his back. Ulric snatched it away before he could secure it.

"No, no, young master," Renier protested. "It's not appropriate for a freeborn man to do a slave's work."

"Well, it's all right, then. I am rather *in*appropriate." He weighed the extra pack on his back while eyeing the other slaves' burden. Their loads looked no heavier than the one Renier had carried. Should young men bear the same burden as a man three times their age?

"Let me guess—one of the other slaves prepared these packs?"

He let Renier catch his breath, then they caught up to the three other slaves. "Stop a moment and drop your packs," he commanded. The slaves, so accustomed to following orders, did so without hesitation. Ulric set Renier's pack down and began transferring supplies from one to the other.

"Uh… should you be doing that?" one of the slaves asked. They looked for reassurance, first to Renier, then to Ulric. Renier shrugged, while Ulric ignored them.

As he worked, he glanced down the road, worried Vipsania might be watching, but everyone marched along, oblivious to the goings-on at the rear. Vipsania's robes must have been boiling hot and unbearable on such a day. Then again, could a hot day ever inconvenience a fire magus? Julia glanced back, looking surprised to see him working among the slaves. He gave her a wink, but she ignored him.

Once he had stuffed half of Renier's supplies into the other packs, a slave moaned, "But… the weight was fairly packed."

Ulric picked up the heavy pack and addressed the slave. "Let me tell you something the legendary Ghostwalker told me. 'Listen up, Darktalon!' … It always started like that. 'Don't let them lie to you—Life *is* fair. We all get what we deserve, some sooner, some later.'" He thrust the heavy pack into his hands and said, "Here's yours."

Ulric and Renier walked together as the sun dipped below the horizon and a welcome breeze blew across the fields and pastures. Soon after dusk, they reached a crossroads. A road stretching from the east crossed the Via Borealis, then quickly curved into the northwest. Nearby, a lone goatherd stood in a field, impassively watching the expedition while his two hounds rounded up his stray flock. Farther up the road, faint lights heralded the long-awaited hospitia, but to Ulric's dismay, Vipsania abandoned the Via Borealis for the smaller road heading northwest into wild country.

That night they made camp in a copse of thick-trunked trees, their branches heavy with pale yellow pods that curved like Aculeo's daggers. Julia said little, making her anger clear. When they lay down to sleep, she gave him a terse "goodnight" and turned away.

Neesis Amoris, spare me, he thought as he rolled over. From the far side of the campfire, Rexinda's glittering green eyes watched him from beneath a muss of blonde hair. Their eyes met, and she burst into a self-satisfied smile. Then she feigned a look of pity while pulling back her blanket to reveal slender curves beneath a short tunica. Ulric shot her a disapproving look and silently mouthed, "Stop it," but he didn't look away. Rexinda mouthed back, "Make me," and seductively stroked a spot next to her bedroll.

And why not? he thought. *Give Julia something to really be angry about.*

The idea was worse than madness: it was stupid. And wrong. He knew that the moment it had sprung unbidden into his mind. With a great effort, he screwed his eyes shut and fell asleep.

The next morning they followed the road northwest through a wild, hilly country. The first couple of days, they passed two obscure villages and little else. On the third day, the road ended at a long-abandoned stone quarry.

By that night, Ulric knew he hated sleeping in the country. It wasn't a matter of comfort; he had slept in many miserable places on the streets of Mist View and Trumric. No, it was a matter of exposure. How could you sleep on the ground where anyone—or anything—could just stumble upon you? And the nights were deceptively silent. When he listened closely, there was always the wind rushing through a field of grass, the drone of insects, noisome birdsong, and the distant cries of unseen beasts. To Ulric's city-bred ears, it was a portentous silence. He had trained to pick out the subtle sounds of danger in a bustling forum or rowdy taberna, but the sounds of the wilderness were indecipherable.

They saw no one after leaving the quarry; no fellow travelers, herdsmen, or hunters. Nor had there been any sign of habitation—no paths, pastures, or distant smoke. With no road to guide them, Vipsania led the way, occasionally consulting the Eltaran map. She spent her days with Kehindé or Rexinda, rarely speaking to anyone else unless it was to bark orders at her slaves or berate poor Flaccus.

Ulric felt bad for the magus' discipulus, who Vipsania treated worse than her slaves. He spoke to Flaccus when he could, even though his awkwardness was tiring. Luckily, he discovered they shared a love of chariot racing. Ulric was a fan of team Red, as was most of the Portus Collegium. Flaccus cheered for team Blue, as was his family tradition.

He did his best to avoid Rexinda, of course. Julia's anger had abated with each passing day, but her jealousy remained. She had never been jealous of the collegium women and hangers-on, all thieves, grifters, killers, and whores, but Rexinda was unique. She needled Julia at every opportunity and made a show of flirting with Ulric. What did she really want? To torment Julia or to steal him away? The scheme he ran was challenging enough; he didn't need the added distraction. For their part, the two ignored one another, although sometimes he caught one of them glaring at the other's back.

Three days after leaving the quarry behind, they came upon a ruin. An edifice of red stone and black columns stood atop a tall outcrop of rock, surrounded by a maze of crumbling walls. Ulric jogged ahead to the nearest line of stones, which reached no higher than his chest. He couldn't resist running his hands over the strange reddish-brown rock, which was rough, porous, and surprisingly cool, given how long it had been baking in the sun. It had to be Eltaran stone. It made him feel uneasy.

Magus Vipsania joined him, running her hand across the top of the low wall, her expression mirroring his own curiosity and trepidation. When their eyes met, she snatched her hand away, then reached into her robes to retrieve the Eltaran map. She unfurled the scroll and began surveying the area.

The ruins had to be one of the map landmarks. Ulric tried to recall an image from the scroll, but many days had passed since his brief look in the alley near the Quadrivium. He looked around. The ruin loomed high upon the rocky outcrop, at the base of a wedge-shaped clearing bordered by sparse woods to the north and a swift stream to the south. Tall, dry grass filled the clearing, its pale yellow tufts rippling in a warm breeze full of the smell of water and wildflowers. The stream ran quick and clear over several small waterfalls. To the west, a dark green expanse on the horizon could only be the Silva Aurea.

Ulric watched as Julia wandered near the stream, where a narrow black arch still stood among a field of shattered red stone. She raised her hand and took a few hesitant steps forward, then stood rooted to the spot as if paralyzed.

Ulric ran to her side. She was trembling. "Julia! What's wrong?"

She slowly pulled her hand away from the arch. "Cold Eltaran stone."

"That's right. Definitely an Eltaran ruin. Exciting, huh?" He tried to sound encouraging.

"Through black mists, I see walls of godless Eltaran stone."

"What in the Nine Hells does that mean?"

Julia turned to Ulric, and he saw eyes tormented by some terrible portent. "Impenetrable walls. Acid stained. The walls of a tomb. Something waits. No way out! No way out!"

She swooned and fell into Ulric's arms, saying no more.

A Game in Ruins

Julia lay unmoving before the black arch where Ulric had lowered her to the ground. She stared silently into the sky. Ulric knelt at her side trying to rouse her, all the while silently praying to Neesis, Myrill, and every god above, below, and beyond. It was no use.

He peeked over a nearby stone block. Vipsania put away the Eltaran map with a satisfied flourish and announced they would camp in the ruin. Flaccus asked if it was Eltaran and she snapped, "Obviously!"

No one had noticed Julia's outburst. And now they were hidden by a maze of walls and the waist-high grass that blanketed the field. He didn't want the questions that would come with Magus Vipsania's help, but what choice did he have? He stood, ready to call for Vipsania's aid, when he heard Julia come to with a great gasp of breath.

"Oh… Why am I lying in the grass?"

Ulric fell to his knees, relief evident on his face. "You don't remember?"

"I remember… speaking with Myrill. I was in the Empyrean realm. It was so peaceful."

"That's not what happened. You stood before that arch—" Ulric pointed at the black stone. "—then you went into some sort of trance. You said something about being trapped in Eltaran stone. Then you fainted."

Julia propped herself onto her elbows. "I don't remember any of that."

"No one saw it but me. Best keep it our secret."

Julia thought about it for a moment. "Agreed." Together, they rose from the grass and joined the others.

Kehindé decided they would camp on the peak of the outcrop, where the ruins of the central keep had once stood. A brief but arduous hike up the switchbacks created by the remains of the ruined walls and outbuildings made for an eminently defensible position.

Kehindé and Rexinda began clearing a space for a firepit while the slaves gathered firewood. Ulric eyed a particular corner of the ruins as the perfect sleeping spot. Finally, hard walls at his back! He threw his pack into the corner and tossed down his traveling cloak, but before he could join them in a much-desired rest, Julia grabbed his hand. She had volunteered to fill everyone's waterskins, which she had gathered and draped over her shoulder. There was no hint of her earlier mood. Mercifully, it was as if her vision before the dark gate had never happened.

As they walked, she confessed she really wanted to speak with the stream's naiad. She believed a water spirit was close by; the spot was idyllic and the old magic in the ruins would entice it. Julia explained the lore and history of water spirits, and Ulric followed as best he could. He was just happy she was speaking to him once again.

At the stream's northern bank, he filled the skins while Julia prayed and performed strange rites invoking Ulorin, Myrill, and even Fontus, the God of Deep, Hidden Waters. Ulric had his doubts, but Julia insisted she had a sense for such things.

No naiad appeared. Disappointed, Julia began the short trek back to camp. Ulric tossed the heavy waterskins over his shoulder and hurriedly stepped in front of her.

"Before we return, there's something I'd know."

Julia took a step back and to the side. "Oh? And what's that?"

"You said Myrill commands you to stay close. It's why you came along. Before, I thought the goddess sent you to help me, but now that we're here, I fear we're marching toward some terrible danger. What haven't you told me?"

"There's nothing, really." Julia looked away, first toward the stream, then the ruins, then the far-off forest—anywhere but his eyes. "You may know more than me. When I try to recall my visions, they seem like half-remembered dreams or fragments of a scroll."

Ulric knew she was lying. How much or how little, he didn't know. "So we're safe?"

"Myrill protects us." Julia stepped past him and walked toward the ruins. "We'll know more when we reach Tmia Culscva."

Once within the safety of the ruin, they sat down to a light meal of dried fruit, cheese, and flatbread, and watched the sun disappear behind the Silva Aurea. As the dark of a conquered moon descended over the campsite, everyone claimed their own spot among the ruins. Vipsania and Renier stayed near the campfire, poring over the Eltaran map and cipher while the slaves ferried things back and forth from her pack. Rexinda drilled with Trumrician gladius and Gualdean shield, expelling a shout with every thrust and cut. Flaccus preferred to brood at the dark edges of the ruin. Kehindé sat atop a tall wall, watching over the camp with a vaguely dissatisfied expression. Julia lay on the grass, hidden in the dark corner of two broad walls, softly singing to herself. Ulric lounged on a nearby wall, lulled by her melody and the sound of distant rushing water.

Julia looked up and smiled. She stretched and shifted her slender legs, causing her stola to slide past her knees and up her thighs at an excruciatingly slow pace. With widening eyes, Ulric leaned closer and almost fell off the wall. Julia silently mouthed, "I miss you," while one hand dragged the hem of her stola higher and higher. He rolled off the wall and fell into the darkness.

"Ulric Darktalon!" It was Kehindé.

Ulric popped his head over the wall. "What?"

Kehindé strode into the center of the camp. "Do you dice?"

"Of course! It would be impious not to."

He raised a wooden cup and gave it a rattle. "A game of Spoils?"

"Now?" he asked, trying not to sound annoyed. Below, Julia shook her head and clearly mouthed, "Not now!"

"Yes," Kehindé replied. "Now."

"What about later?" Ulric suggested.

"Best now, while it's early. And bring Julia. Let's make it a game of Allies."

"Okay, but... now?"

"Did I interrupt something?" Kehindé asked.

Ulric looked down at Julia, who was already rolling her eyes in resignation. "Fine… let's go," she said.

He waited while Julia straightened her stola and tossed her green palla over her shoulders, then they joined Kehindé near the campfire.

"Do you know the rules?" Kehindé asked.

She gave Ulric a sidelong glance and sighed. "How could I not?" Then she asked, "Who's your ally?"

"Ulric, of course."

"Wait… what?"

"Rexinda!" he called over his shoulder. "It's the men against the women."

"Well, that's hardly fair, Kehindé," Ulric said with exaggerated confidence.

"Hey!" Julia poked her elbow into his ribs.

Rexinda ran into the campsite and stood beside Kehindé, her face flushed and her body covered in a light sheen of sweat. She breathlessly asked, "Yes, Kehindé?" as if she was reporting for duty.

"A game of Spoils. Allies," he commanded. Then he broke into a wide grin. "You're with Julia."

The two women eyed each other warily. Julia sighed and Rexinda grunted a curse under her breath. Finally, they sat on the edge of a bare patch of ground, which would be their battlefield. Kehindé sat across from them and crossed his long legs, while Ulric stretched out on the grass as if he were on a dining couch.

"Before we set the stakes," he said, "I should warn you. My goddess is Neesis Fortuna. The spoils are already mine."

"Blood 'n battle!" Rexinda sneered. "My god is Cathus. This is a battlefield like any other, and Cathus grants victory." She looked hard into Ulric's eyes. "We both know you're afraid to seize what you desire."

Julia's eyes narrowed menacingly. She was about to say something when Kehindé asked, "And what says Myrill?"

Julia hesitated, embarrassed. "Honestly, the Temple of Myrill doesn't approve of gambling. In fact, we know She often chides Alakur and his brother Arakru for their own foolish wagers."

Rexinda rolled her eyes. "Oh, so you're going to be fucking useless?"

"Rexinda!" Vipsania looked up from her scroll. "Such language is inappropriate for a young woman! Where have you been raising her, Kehindé?"

"Barracks and battlefields, where else?"

Vipsania scowled, but Ulric saw the faintest hint of a smile cross her face before she returned to the cipher.

"We've heard from everyone but you, Kehindé," Ulric said. "What do your gods say about the game?"

"The tale of the dice has already been told."

"Uh… okay then. What about the wager?"

Kehindé thought for a moment. "What good is coin out here? The losers must carry the winners' packs for a whole day!"

Everyone agreed that was a worthy prize. Kehindé was first to cast the dice, shaking the cup with a loud clatter but throwing an unremarkable Legion combination. Next, Julia took the cup and gave the dice a brief shake, casting a high-scoring Dragons. Rexinda looked surprised, grudgingly admitting, "Not so useless after all." Then Ulric scooped up the dice and swirled the cup, creating a rhythmic, musical rattle. He invoked the name of Neesis Fortuna and cast the dice. They hit the hard packed earth and tumbled to a stop, displaying one of each possible number: a Neesis Throw! The round was over.

He teased Rexinda with mock sympathy, "Oooh… nooo… looks like someone never made it to the battlefield."

"Don't start gloating yet, Ulric!" Julia warned. She told Rexinda, "We'll beat the boys next round."

Rexinda snatched the cup out of his hand. "Be prepared to lose every battle but the last!"

"So wrote General Polyminius Trumerus in his Commentaries on the Prophecy War, regarding his campaign against the Demon King of Angrus."

Everyone looked up to see a very self-satisfied Flaccus.

"And?" Rexinda asked, annoyed.

"It's the quote's origin. Although, it's not applicable to a game of Spoils. Mathematically, if one loses all the rounds but—"

"Flaccus!" Ulric interrupted. "Speaking of maths, I need someone I trust to track the score. Could you do that?"

Flaccus nearly bounced out of his robes. "Oh, yes. Of course!"

The second round ended as Julia had predicted thanks to two high scoring Dragons. Flush with victory, the two women began mercilessly teasing Ulric. Flaccus tried to come to his aid, but that only made things worse.

Julia and Rexinda won the next round. *Why has Neesis abandoned me?* Ulric thought. Then Kehindé led them to a narrow victory in the fourth round when Rexinda rolled all ones—the dreaded Canine Cast. The bout of swearing that followed earned another shocked rebuke from Magus Vipsania.

The fifth and final round was about to begin. Julia and Rexinda laughed and swore together, telling the men how much they'd enjoy a day without their burdens. Ulric assured them Neesis wouldn't let him lose, and he hoped his pack wouldn't be too heavy for a girl to carry. He turned to Kehindé, eager for an ally against the two women. The Kekeksuan warrior sat in silence, watching Rexinda and Julia with a satisfied, almost proud, expression.

"Kehindé."

"Yes, Darktalon?"

"Thank you."

Kehindé nodded. He picked up the dice cup, ready to continue the game.

"Now for the final round of Spoils!" Flaccus announced. "Whichever team wins this fifth and final round wins the game."

Vipsania hurriedly put away the Eltaran scroll. Ulric knew she had only been pretending to study it for the last couple of rounds. She rose and advanced toward the game. "Come on, girls! Cast those dice and kick 'em in the balls!"

Rexinda burst out in shocked laughter. "Theia!"

There was a whooshing sound, and a streak of fire flashed near Vipsania. The sudden light set spots dancing in Ulric's eyes as the smell of charred wood filled his nostrils. An instant later, a second *whoosh* and burst of flame erupted near the magus. Why was she conjuring fire?

A few embers lingered in the air. One bright bit of debris drifted near Ulric; feathers, a bit of fletching, shriveling and burning. The streaks of fire had been arrows! Arrows that had burst into flames before they could reach their target—Vipsania!

"Kehindé! We're under attack," Vipsania shouted. "Bowmen! At the tree line!"

"Take cover!" Kehindé ordered. He drew his Bayjoni saber and crouched behind a wall, searching the darkness. Everyone scrambled, first for shelter, then for weapons.

"Myrill preserve us!" Julia cried. "Under attack? By who?"

Ulric grabbed her hand. They raced through the ruins, keeping their heads low. "I don't know. Nero? The Imperaré?" He shoved her into the corner of two low walls.

"Hey!"

"Stay down!" he shouted, vaulting over the wall and retrieving his weapons. He cautiously peered over the rough Eltaran stone.

Magus Vipsania had remained standing at the center of the ruin. The ebony dragon rod, embossed and capped in gold, was once again in her hand. Molten metal swirled in angry patterns across its surface, and the eyes of the dragon headpiece glared with white-hot flame. She pointed the rod at the campfire and the flames grew and twisted wildly. Then she traced a semicircle on the ground and the flames followed. They leaped from the campfire and formed a knee-high wall of fire between her and the tree line to the north.

What would such a short fire wall do against an arrow barrage?

Two more arrows descended from the darkness. Uncoiling dragon claws of flame sprung from the wall and snatched the arrows from the air.

Vipsania muttered to herself, "Imbeciles." She reached into her robes and retrieved a scroll of dull gray metal, likely lead. She knelt and rammed the scroll into the ground. A tremor ran through the ruins and a tear opened in the earth, unleashing a blast of heat and wavering red bands of light. Vipsania shouted a word—it sounded like Eltaran—and pointed her dragon rod toward the trees. The rift extended across down the hill and across the field quicker than the eye could follow. It breached the tree line and a column of flame blasted into the sky. A stand of chestnuts became a collection of blazing torches, and somewhere within, men screamed and died.

The firelight exposed a band of armed men skulking at the edge of the trees. What did such a small force hope to do against a fire magus?

"What are they waiting for?" Kehindé asked. He scanned the darkness around their camp.

"Their deaths!" Magus Vipsania's eyes shone with a blue flame as she raised the dragon rod. With her free hand, she traced strange glyphs into the air with delicate swirls of fire, chanting ancient words of devastation.

"Ow!" The chanting stopped, and the glyphs faded. Vipsania reached a hand to the back of her neck and pulled out a slender metal dart no longer than her index finger. "What… Oh no." She turned to Kehindé. "How absurd."

She collapsed. A moment later, she was writhing in pain and babbling nonsense.

A horde of men burst from the tree line and charged across the field.

Loyalty, Lies, and Betrayal

A couple of hours after leaving Corvaro, Luciano begrudgingly ordered the men to rest and eat as daylight waned. Decius began barking orders: stones for the firepit, wood and kindling, latrine, and small game to roast over the fire.

"Your men respect him," said Raquin. "They don't fear him. Not like they fear you. When they look at you, their faces betray their thoughts: 'Will I be his next victim?'"

Luciano chuckled at this, then leaned against a broad, gnarled olive tree. His face went blank, then he fixed his gaze on Raquin as he retrieved his sweet Aguja from his belt. The assassin turned the blade from one side to the other, examining it nonchalantly, then returned his attention to the Elt.

Raquin feigned surprise and pointed at himself with the exaggeration of a stage actor.

Luciano ignored him as he pulled a black pumice sharpening stone, a small vial of oil, and a well-worn polishing cloth from a pouch. As he glazed his blade, he studied the men.

They were already breaking up into factions, staking their various claims in the clearing or near the firepit. Brocchus had sent his "top men" to lead, but each collegium had sent additional soldiers, hand-picked by each prince. The other princes didn't trust Brocchus. Luciano had come to realize that *no one* trusted Brocchus.

Brocchus' men gathered near the road; a couple Night Legion men gathered stones for the firepit, while others stood around, no doubt griping about the heat. Ilus and the other Shrine Alley soldiers stood defiantly in front of a grove of trees while a small gang of shirtless men, Silo's heavies among them, wandered the area, glaring like a pack of wolves at any who dared look them in the eye. All the while, Decius stood in the middle of the clearing, doing his best to keep the peace.

Luciano watched them from the comfort of his olive tree. Two groups—a pair from Armis Crudelis, arms laden with cords of wood, and three Black Eels carrying dry brush—headed toward the firepit. The Armis Crudelis heavies arrived first and staked their claim. When the Black Eel thugs came near, one of the Crudelis men spoke up.

"Whaddya think you're doing, girls?"

"Making camp. The firepit's ours."

The other Crudelis man took a step forward. "Really? Seeing as we got here first, that don't add up."

Imbeciles.

Luciano kept polishing his needle-like blade. He briefly entertained the idea of intervening, but shook the notion off with a laugh.

The sound of Luciano's laughter brought the men's bickering to a halt. They stood glaring at each other, as if weighing their rivalries against their fear of the unpredictable Verdan. Decius walked between them and sat next to the firepit. He produced a small jug of wine.

"Liberated from the Vinum et Voluptas." He gave a knowing look to both groups. "I didn't think I'd be celebrating an unexpected promotion. Join me." When they hesitated, he added, "What I'm really grateful for is this: I'm Imperaré. It's good to remember. We're all Imperaré, and we have a job to do."

The Armis Crudelis man said, "Room enough for all, I guess." He sat down and took the offered jug from Decius.

The Black Eels dropped their brush in the firepit. "Always room for Imperaré."

The next morning Decius roused the men, and once again they set off north, the wiry Ilus scouting ahead. Luciano constantly scoured the road, looking for any sign that Magus Vipsania's expedition had abandoned the Via Borealis. One map he had studied in Brocchus' office showed a faint line branching from the road, pointing into the heart of Silva Aurea. Would they not prefer a good Trumin road over some makeshift trail pushing through rough hills and wild shrubs? He couldn't be certain, so he investigated all the same.

Near the end of the day, Ilus returned with news of the expected crossroads. Just as Luciano was about to order the men to pick up the pace, Ilus mentioned something which caught his interest: a lone goatherd in the western fields. Luciano brought the men to a halt. He instructed Decius to let the men rest for half an hour, then make for the crossroads at the double. Then he jogged north, taking his scout with him. Raquin followed close behind.

"What's the plan, boss?" Ilus asked.

Luciano hated being called *boss*. He resisted the urge to scold his dull-witted scout. Instead, through gritted teeth, he said, "I ask goatherd some questions."

"Oh." Ilus thought for a moment. "Just the two of us?"

Luciano turned to look at Raquin, who was noticeably eavesdropping on their conversation. "Three of us," he said with disdain.

Raquin responded with a smile.

Luciano looked at Ilus, who wore a befuddled look. "If twenty men march up on goatherd, goatherd disappears quicker than lightning. Miss our chance for information." He waited until a glimmer of understanding finally overtook the ferret-like face. "At least Imperaré give me one clever man," Luciano finished, rolling his eyes.

The Eltaran laughed. "I thought he was clever—for a man."

A short time later, they found the goatherd in the fields bordering the road, just as Ilus said. The goatherd eyed Luciano suspiciously as he left the road and started across the field. He called his dogs to his side and gripped the cudgel he carried a little tighter, standing his ground as Luciano drew closer. Why not? He was tall and robust, with two good sized beasts at his side.

Then something changed. Luciano guessed he had gotten close enough for the young man to get a good look at him. The goatherd broke and ran, making for a nearby tree lined ridge. As planned, he ran straight into Ilus, and Luciano calmly strode up to them.

He nearly lost his patience trying to convince the goatherd they were there to neither rob nor kill him. What could the peasant offer him? Only news of Vipsania and Darktalon, which the goatherd had an ample stock of. He told Luciano of all he had seen, even taking him to the grove of carob trees where Magus Vipsania and her companions had camped the night before.

They can't be much ahead of us now; we've made up some time. Good. Maybe Aguja can drink that boy's blood soon. Maybe I...

A slender, yellow-tainted spike pierced Luciano's brain.

Of course, first I will retrieve this map for that son of a bitch Brocchus. Yes, I will bring you your map. And then everything will be different.

The yellow spike retreated, and with it the pain.

When they had marched for a full day—well past sunset, well into Imperaré grumbling—they reached an area where granite boulders coughed up by the earth dotted the landscape, and a large grove of cypress trees provided a nice windbreak. Luciano gave Decius the order to make camp. "Let men sleep, not too much. We start chase at first light." He was confident he had further closed the gap between them and the magus. Soon their prey would be within striking distance, and he could hatch his plan at last.

After the campfire had dwindled into glowing coals and a cacophony of snores filled the air, Luciano sat with his back against a granite outcropping, isolating himself from the others as he often did. He cursed Brocchus for sending these dullards with him. However, this moment of self-indulgent bitterness was cut short by the sound of light footfalls upon crumpled grass. Luciano was a statue as his eyes darted, scanning the area. A half-moon hung in the cloudless sky, supplementing the assassin's keen sight. Movement. To the northeast. A solitary figure. From the flowing cape and dangling feathers, it was obviously Raquin, quietly making his way out of the camp towards that grove of trees.

What's the Elt bastard up to now?

As silent as the night itself, Luciano stepped past the slumbering men and into the copse of trees, following Raquin at a distance.

The Eltaran moved furtively, a pale shadow slipping between the gnarled trees, until he reached a large clearing. A gap in the treetop canopy allowed the gibbous moon's sickly glow to fall into the clearing, casting odd shadows onto the scene. In the center sat an immense chunk of granite, its top flattened as if sheared off by some enormous blade. Raquin stood in front of the boulder, whose girth was considerable but whose plateau barely eclipsed the Elt's height. He examined it—perhaps admiring it—for several seconds before prostrating himself at its base.

From behind a large cypress, Luciano watched Raquin with a growing curiosity.

Raquin extended an arm, placing his palm on the boulder. Were it not for the seconds it would take to cross the clearing, Luciano would have used the chance to end the Elt. But this was not the time. Sooner or later, that opportunity would come. Instead, Luciano watched as the Elt lifted his head towards the night sky, his hand still on the rock. He whispered something, though the words were undecipherable.

A stillness overtook the area.

Luciano could hear his own breathing and suddenly wondered if the Elt could, too. The assassin willed himself to take slow, measured breaths, but his racing heart fought against him.

Then, as if commanded to do so, every bird in every branch cried out, took flight, cawing, whistling, screaming into the distance. Raquin continued whispering into the darkness. A thousand bestial paws scurried off in every direction. A wind blew through the trees and a gloom overtook the clearing, as if clouds had suddenly obscured the moon. Luciano peered into the sky. The moon and stars were gone. The trees surrounding the clearing now arched overhead like skeletal appendages, growing towards one another and closing the gap in the cypress canopy.

Sorcery!

Raquin rose, scanning the clearing.

Luciano whipped his head behind the tree. He could hear Raquin moving about. Were the footsteps getting closer? Had he been torched? Soon, he heard other sounds. The clink of rocks? Was he wrecking something? Building something? The assassin dared to steal another look.

Raquin, a large sack in hand, walked about the clearing, gathering stones. When he had filled the sack, he ascended the boulder. Now kneeling on top of the great stone, he set down the sack with great care. One by one, he retrieved each stone. He hefted them with a ceremonial reverence, positioning each with purposeful precision upon the boulder. Slowly, the multitude of stones took form: an archway, each stone held to the next by some unseen force. The stillness returned.

Luciano exhaled a frosty breath as he shivered, more from the creeping sense of unease than the cold.

When Raquin placed the capstone, a palpable change suffused the clearing. The trees rustled, as if in dreaded anticipation. The arch, now complete, stood waist high. He knelt before it, gripping the sack tightly, head bowed, hands clasped.

But Luciano's attention was soon drawn away from the Eltaran. The arch's stones hummed, filling the area with an eerie resonance. The entire arch throbbed, and Luciano could hear the Elt muttering, not in any tongue of Man or Elt, but something… primordial. A cadence that froze Luciano's bones.

The Elt's words, the arch's thrums, Luciano's own heart, all melded into an accursed harmony. Raquin reached deep within the sack and produced a most grisly offering: a severed human hand, its pallor ghostly in the moonlight that trickled in through the tree limbs.

Luciano's gaze fixed on the hand, blood dried and cracked upon its lifeless fingers. With care, the Elt placed the appendage before the arch. He splayed its stiff fingers out, as if reaching out for him. A bronze bracer, still cuffed to the dead wrist, rested inches in front of the arch. The bracer seemed unsettlingly familiar. Luciano's eyes flashed wide.

Petrus?

The name had almost slipped through his lips, but Luciano managed to remain silent. Despite the cold that had overtaken the grove, his clothes were damp with sweat. His head pounded with the rhythm of the thrumming. That incessant thrumming. What accursed madness was unfolding before him? His anticipation turned to dread.

The Elt rose to his feet, stretching his arms wide. Luciano somehow knew he was staring at—or perhaps into—the arch as he spoke once more. He heard Raquin clearly this time. The Elt was making sounds unlike any the Verdan had heard before; primal, guttural sounds that resonated in the grove. The same phrase over and over and over. With each utterance, the arch throbbed with a growing energy. The air grew thick with the stench of a dankness beyond decay.

A wave of nausea washed over Luciano, bile creeping up his throat, nearly choking him. He swallowed it as he watched tenebrous shadows invade the clearing. The trees themselves seemed to recoil in response. Silence.

Darkness swirled inside the arch and dark tendrils unfurled from within, black as the void and writhing like serpents. These otherworldly tentacles moved with a sinister grace, undulating and coiling with sentient intent. An acrid, acidic odor assaulted Luciano's nostrils. He resisted the urge to cough.

In the eerie quiet, the hand began to crawl, each finger moving with a dreadful, insect-like precision, driven by a will of its own. Dragging its wrist behind, the fingers crawled away from the arch, desperate to escape the malevolent force emanating from it. But more snake-like tendrils emerged, teeming with a primal hunger for human flesh. One of them lashed out, wrapping around the wrist and pulling the cold, dead hand towards the arch. Towards that charnel gate.

The hand twitched violently, fingers clawing at the stone, trying desperately to resist the pull of the abyssal force. But more tendrils joined the first, their cold, slick surfaces gleaming in the faint light. They entwined the hand, each movement filled with a dire purpose. The hand writhed and twisted, its futile struggle only intensifying the horror of the scene. The darkness within the gate pulsed in rhythm with the surrounding stones. As the hand was pulled closer, the air grew even colder, the chill of the void penetrating Luciano's bones.

The tendrils coiled tighter, their grip unrelenting as they dragged the hand across the threshold. With a final, desperate twitch, the hand disappeared into the darkness, swallowed by the void beyond the gate. The tendrils lingered for a moment, writhing in a grotesque dance of triumph before retracting back into the shadowy depths.

The gate, the clearing, the grove, all stood silent once more. Raquin slumped back, exhausted.

There would be no sleep for Luciano when he returned to the camp. For the rest of the night, his mind was filled with what he had witnessed. He could make little sense of it, at times even wondering if what he had seen was real. Still, he came to one inevitable conclusion: the Eltaran was here for some dark purpose of his own.

For the next several days, Luciano tried to forget what he had seen in that accursed grove. Instead he focused on tracking Magus Vipsania's expedition into the wild, hilly country bordering the great forests of the Silva Aurea. He discovered that moving through the countryside, burdened by a score of men, was an arduous task. However, he felt confident they had nearly caught up with the wretched dragon magus.

As he watched the men from atop a small hill, he noted they weren't bickering and posturing like they had been a few days ago. Decius walked in and around them, taking inventory of them, sizing them up for their worth. He had adjusted to the role of centurion well. Raquin, who stood out from the rest in his colorful Eltaran clothes, kept his distance. The men had grown to despise his presence more and more the further they traveled. And the Imperaré men didn't even know what Luciano now knew.

Luciano leaned against a slender larch and searched through his belt pouch until he retrieved what he sought: a small, cork-topped red clay vial.

Perhaps I use you on that gods-damned Elt, eh, piquino?

He held the vial up to eye level, admiring it, caressing it between his thumb and finger.

No. No, he will have to wait. I purchased you, piquino, for a very specific target. You cost me one hundred coins, and I trust you will do your job. Seek her. And then… and then Aguja and I will do ours.

A lascivious smile overtook Luciano's lips as a vision of an impaled and helpless Ulric Darktalon danced through his head. A burst of laughter knocked him back against the tree. Consumed in his sadistic fantasy, he lost awareness of the men below, his mind dwelling on one singular thought: The magus' expedition was close, which meant the boy was close. Grinning, Luciano instructed Decius to await his return; he was going to scout ahead. He needed a lay of the land. He wanted to formulate his plan.

When he strode back into camp less than an hour later, Luciano bent Decius' ear. "Get men ready for battle! Bring me Spurius. And that Kreslan, Gregor. We march soon." He climbed back up the hill, where he watched Decius gather the two men.

As they made their way to Luciano, Raquin intercepted them. Decius attempted to continue up the hill, but the Eltaran placed his hands on Gregor and Spurius' shoulders, speaking to them and gesturing in that exaggerated Eltaran way of his.

What is that gods-damned Elt doing now? And why does he keep pointing at me while he talks to them?

Raquin finished with the two men, then nodded at Decius, who quickly escorted the pair to Luciano. The assassin stared at the duo from beneath a furrowed brow as he spoke.

"What Elt say to you?"

"Kept tellin' us to listen to you, Luciano," Gregor replied. "That you know what you're doin' and we should listen to you and stop with all the fightin'. Said it's gonna get us killed if we don't shut up and do what we're told."

Luciano looked at Decius, who said, "He's right. That's what he told them." Luciano narrowed his eyes menacingly, and Decius continued, "Hells if I know, Luciano. One minute he wants nothing to do with us, and the next he's handing out free advice. If you ask me, he's an odd one."

What's this Elt up to?

"Yes, odd one, Decius. You keep you eye on him, eh?" Decius nodded and Luciano returned his attention to Gregor and Spurius. "You two!"

The men stared sheepishly as though they were about to get dressed down.

"You will kill dragon magus."

The pair stared at each other with childlike confusion, then looked at Luciano.

"Decius tells me you men are best archers. This is true, eh?"

The two stood a little taller, but said nothing.

"I have plan for you two. You shoot arrows at dragon magus. I tip you arrows with poison. Very deadly. Surprise attack. Same time. No miss. Dragon magus dead."

The Verdan handed each man a small black leather pouch.

"This lemuroot powder. One dose. You no waste. Dip arrow before shot. I decide where you strike from. You men understand?" He clapped his hands. "Spurius! Gregor! You understand?"

The men nodded, and Luciano dismissed them.

"Decius."

"Yes, Luciano?"

"Bring me Elt."

Moments later, Raquin arrived at the top of the hill alone. "You wish to speak to me?"

"What you say to men?"

"To who?"

"Those two!" Luciano pointed down the hill.

"I simply told those buffoons that if they wanted to live, they should stop their childish bickering and listen to you. That they have a job to do. That's all."

"I think you lie."

"What you think is of no consequence. Now, is there anything else, *boss?*"

Luciano bristled at the word. "What's you angle?"

Raquin remained uninterested. "You're a paranoid one, aren't you?" He took a deep breath before speaking again. "Tell me, what is my role in this upcoming farce? I've heard the men talking. We are close to the magus and her party, are we not?"

"We are very close."

"And my role?"

"You role is…" Luciano looked the Eltaran straight in the eye. "You role is to watch."

Raquin laughed.

Luciano took a step closer. "Me and Imperaré men. We handle this dragon magus. And her group. You do nothing. You watch."

The Eltaran stared at Luciano for a long moment, then smirked as he shook his head. "Those men—your Imperaré men—they will *handle* the magus?"

"Yes. I have plan for that."

"And the Gualdean girl?"

"Yes."

"And will they handle the boy thief?"

Luciano's eyes flashed. "No! I handle boy! Boy is mine! Only I kill Darktalon!"

"I've touched an old wound with a needle, it seems. Fine. You'll handle the thief." They eyed one another while Luciano's chest heaved. Raquin continued. "Let me ask you, Luciano, while you do that, who handles the Kekeksuan warrior? Your men?" The Eltaran chortled as he pointed down the hill. "Those street thugs?"

Luciano looked at the Imperaré men below and chewed his lip.

"Cheap knife men and back-alley brawlers are no match for him. Not even in numbers. The nobility of Suloko are of the Old Blood, the mightiest of men. However, Luciano, I can assure you, the Kekeksuan has never faced—"

"No!" Luciano stepped towards Raquin. "You watch! That all. Understand, Elt? You watch!"

"None of those imbeciles stand a chance against a seasoned Kekeksuan. And with you handling the thief, that leaves only me. He will be a challenge, at least."

Luciano closed the distance between himself and the Eltaran. "What you plan on doing, Elt? Call on some dark power to aid you?"

Raquin's eyes flashed with surprise. "What exactly does that mean?"

Luciano leaned in even closer.

"Step. Back. Verdan."

"You. Watch. That is all."

"I said… step back, Luciano. This will not end any better for you than our last engagement. You don't want this."

Both adversaries reached for their sword hilts.

"I do want it. Whatever the outcome. Yes, Elt, I want very much." He took a step back and unsheathed his falcata.

Raquin responded in kind, and the two took their fighting stances.

Luciano's heart raced. *Fuck this Elt. Fuck Brocchus. Fuck it all. I want this.* His head throbbed as yellow pain crept in from his temples. He gripped his blade so tightly he lost feeling in his fingers.

A voice broke the tension. "Gods Below!" It was Decius.

"This is no concern for you," said Luciano.

Decius stepped in between the two, arms extended.

"Decius! Move!" yelled Luciano, a fire in his voice as he waved the falcata wildly.

"Whatever this is about, it sure ain't a good time for it!" Decius looked more frightened than confused as he stood between the two angry swordsmen. Raquin said nothing, but traded his normally condescending look for a grave one, not taking his eyes off Luciano.

Decius lowered his voice. "Luciano. The men, they want to know the plan. Gregor and Spurius couldn't keep their mouths shut, and now the men need to know. When do we move?"

Luciano gritted his teeth, as if to grind the yellow pain away. He glanced at Raquin, then stared at Decius through slitted eyes.

"Luciano?"

He took a deep breath. "Tell men to ready. Tell them I will share plan. We move soon." He turned away and walked down the hill.

Not long after, Luciano rejoined the men. "We attack soon."

A cheer rang out among the men as they celebrated the upcoming battle, no doubt anticipating their spoils, their coin back in Trumric. The one called Strabo punched a smaller dusty-haired man in the shoulder while two Armis Crudelis thugs bumped imaginary flagons in a mock toast. It took Decius some time to quiet down the raucous bunch. When he succeeded, Luciano spoke.

"Here is plan: Spurius and the Kreslan kill dragon magi from distance. Decius lead rest of you. Charge the gold hair Gualdean bitch and the rest. Overrun them. They cannot fight you all. Kill bitch quick. Kill others quick. Kill all but boy… boy Imperaré traitor… boy mine."

Luciano paused and looked each man in the eye.

"You know boy. Long black hair like girl. Lean. Gang ink on left arm. XVII. Called Darktalon. No one touch boy. Boy mine. Anybody touch boy and I let Aguja bleed you. Slow."

A voice rang out from the ranks of the Imperaré men. "What about the Keksu?"

Luciano realized he stood at another crossroads. His eyes fell upon Raquin. The Eltaran had revealed his true self. Whoever or whatever this Elt really was, he certainly could not be trusted. *But he can still be used.* So, Luciano played his gambit. Pointing at Raquin, he said, "He will handle the Keksu."

Raquin's stoic face broke into a wide smile. "It will be my pleasure. First real challenge I've had since entering the land of men."

Luciano glared, then returned the sentiment with a jackal's smile. *He can still be used.* He signaled to Decius, and his lieutenant ordered the men southwest.

Well after sundown, and just before they crested the hilltop that overlooked the ruin-inlaid clearing to the south, Luciano stopped the men. He and Decius snuck to the top of the hill, where the dense woods kept them hidden. With little moonlight for illumination, details were elusive. However, they could make out the ruins below, sprawled over a rocky outcropping at the center of a wedge-shaped field. The remains of a large building stood at the peak, surrounded by numerous columns in varying stages of collapse and decay. Further down the slope, an array of crumbling walls created a good defensible position. Near the center of the ruins, a campfire illuminated several figures. Four of them gathered about the fire as four others looked on from a distance.

Eight? Unexpected. But the plan remains the same.

Luciano informed Decius of the remaining tactical details, then they both returned to the men. Raquin, aloof as always, stood apart from the others. He wore no expression, but kept his gaze fixed on Luciano. Things would be forever different between the two of them now. He would soon have to rid himself of this dangerous Elt. Maybe the gods would smile on him and the Keksu would do the deed for him.

He wiped all thoughts of Raquin from his mind and came back to the present—back to the dragon magus and the map. Luciano gave the order, and his plan began to unfold.

Decius and seventeen of the Imperaré's thugs crouched low in the trees north and downhill of the ruins. There they waited, eyeing the campsite with anticipation. Luciano, who had already quietly retreated to the back of the group, worked his way unnoticed through the trees. It had taken some time to circumvent the hilltop ruins, and even longer to ascend the near-cliff to their east. It was now up to Spurius and Gregor, who had been sent to a suitable spot in a copse of trees closer to the hill.

When he had reached the plateau, Luciano worked his way through the tall grass, crouching, then crawling, stalking his prey like a masterful predator. When he reached an area of sufficient cover and angle of attack, he rose to a knee and retrieved a short cylindrical rod from his backpack.

He imagined at that moment Spurius and Gregor were stringing their bows. Luciano, holding the yellow-wood cylinder in one hand, pulled on its end with the other, revealing hidden concentric sections. When he felt as if each archer had retrieved an arrow from his quiver, Luciano placed one end of the now three-foot-long cylinder on the toe of his boot, resting the other end against his chest.

He could almost imagine the two bowmen smiling as the fools dipped their arrowheads into the pouches Luciano had given them, both unaware the powder was nothing more than black tea and dirt. From his own pouch he retrieved two items: the red clay vial and a tiny goose-feather tipped dart. Luciano flicked open the vial. He carefully dipped the dart into the thick, pungent liquid, then tossed the vial into the tall grass.

As the two bowmen were probably knocking their arrows, Luciano lifted the cylinder, then gently placed the dart into the narrow end. He held the cylinder with both hands and stared down the length of it. Beyond its tip, thirty paces away, stood a woman, full of self-importance, gesturing as she paced, obviously pontificating to the small group of dice players. Darktalon was among them. It took all of Luciano's discipline and professionalism to ignore him.

He imagined the archers taking a deep breath and pulling back their bowstrings, their eyes locked on their target—his target—and he inhaled a deep breath of his own. He placed the end of the wooden tube to his mouth, his cheeks bloated with air, and waited.

Two arrows streaked through the air and over the walls of the ruins. A flash of fire erupted around the dragon magus, instantly incinerating the arrows.

Vipsania's defensive magic was spent. It was time for Luciano to spring his trap.

Blood and Flame

Julia crawled from the corner where Ulric had shoved her and peered above a low wall of jagged stone. Magus Vipsania plucked a small dart from the back of her neck and stared at it in disbelief. She rolled it between her thumb and forefinger as if testing its solidity. Then a sudden look of understanding swept across her face and her familiar arrogance, so abrasive yet comforting, was gone. "Oh no," she mumbled. She looked at Kehindé, and in a voice tinged with bitter humor, she said, "How absurd." Then the firewall that had protected her from the bowmen faltered and burnt out. In a flash of flame, her dragon rod evaporated into the night air. The magus fell to the ground, writhing and screaming in agony.

The acrid smoke from the burning trees swept over the ruins. Julia coughed and tried to blink away the stinging in her eyes. A cold, sinking feeling settled over her heart, as if it had become a chunk of ice. From the north, a score of men charged from the tree line, their shouts and battle cries echoing across the field. Against the red glare of the fire, they appeared a horde of screaming black silhouettes; shades of the dead disgorged from the Underworld.

"Myrill preserve us," she whispered.

"Theia!" Rexinda ran to Vipsania's side and watched in horror as the magus' body twisted with convulsions, her feet kicking long furrows in the dirt while her arms thrashed in the air. Rexinda called to her again, but Vipsania only gibbered something that sounded like Kreslan. Whether it was a response to Rexinda or part of some delirium, Julia couldn't tell.

"Cathus shield us!" Rexinda cried. She peered into the surrounding darkness, her shield and gladius at the ready. "What the fuck happened?"

Renier pried the metal dart from Vipsania's hand and held it up in the campfire's light. "Poisoned!"

"Can't she cast a spell? Heal herself?" Rexinda asked.

Renier looked closer at the dart. Sniffed it. "No. The magi's healing arts are extremely limited. Besides, the poison—I think it's Mania's Embrace. It creates chaos in the mind, a sort of madness before death. It makes it impossible to concentrate. Some call it a Magus Bane."

"Ulric!" Julia extended a hand over the wall and made repeated grasping motions. "My pack! Pack! Pack!"

"I told you to stay down! There could be more bowmen!"

"Arakru take the bowmen! Vipsania needs my help." She grabbed Ulric's hand, leaned over the wall, and kissed him. "You know I'm not some helpless temple Initiate. Myrill—and Neesis—will protect us!"

"Julia!" Kehindé's voice boomed across the ruin. "Call upon your goddess; save Vipsania."

Ulric retrieved her pack and thrust it into her hands. "Do it."

Julia gave him one last reassuring look and ran to Vipsania's side.

Kehindé pulled Rexinda to her feet. "We're of no use here!"

She tried to protest, but he pointed below to the walls at the edge of the ruins. "Julia needs time to save Vipsania. We go to the wall; we make them fight for every step. Kill as many as we can! Do you understand?"

Rexinda straightened and turned her back to Vipsania's cries. "Yes. We kill the bastards!"

Kehindé pointed to a nearby spot where the hill was steep, but the walls were nothing more than crumbling rock. "Ulric! Guard our flank!" Then he glanced at the blackness toward the stream. "And the rear."

"Right! Right!" he said, nodding.

Julia thought he nodded a little too enthusiastically, trying to cover the same rising fear she felt as she watched him leap over a wall and disappear into the ruin.

"Flaccus… Flaccus!" Kehindé called.

Flaccus, who was crawling along the lee of a nearby wall, looked up and asked, "Those men can't intend to kill us all, surely? Perhaps we can parley?"

"Do your duty, discipulus; protect your mistress!"

"Of course," Flaccus squeaked with little enthusiasm. He broke from cover and crawled to Vipsania's side.

Kehindé and Rexinda left, racing down the maze of ruins to meet the oncoming horde of Imperaré soldiers. Julia did her best to ignore the impending battle and retrieved both a drawing salve and poison antidote from her pack.

"Blood! Her tears have turned to blood!" Renier cried.

"Renier! I'm unfamiliar with Mania's Embrace. Is it a venom-based poison? If so, I may have an antidote." Julia proudly held up a small but ornate silver bottle. "A theriac prepared by the temple with sixty-four ingredients, both common and rare."

"I couldn't say. I only know it by its dreadful reputation."

"We'll have to try. Hold her still, the both of you."

The old slave tightened his grip on Vipsania's arm and Flaccus took hold of the other. In an anguished voice, Renier begged Julia to save his mistress.

Vipsania tried to break free, twisting and bucking against her perceived captors. Her eyes wild, she looked at each of them with an expression of confusion and fear one moment, then contempt and rage the next. All the while, she babbled in Trumin, Kreslan, Gualic, and half a dozen other languages Julia didn't recognize. One unfamiliar word was often repeated: piré. It sounded like Eltaran.

Julia uncapped the silver bottle. With one hand she pressed Vipsania's head to the ground, and with the other she administered the theriac. Vipsania coughed and sputtered and cursed Julia in crude Kreslan and Gualic. Despite her best efforts, Julia feared she had spilled too much of the antidote.

"Now for the salve."

Julia examined the spot where the dart had struck; it was black and swollen like a rotten fig. She began applying the drawing salve. Vipsania grew still. Her babbling drifted off into silence. Was the theriac working?

A sudden burst of pain wracked Vipsania's body. She shouted nonsense in several languages and broke free of Flaccus' grasp. Vipsania lashed out, knocking Julia to the ground and sending her jar of salve flying into the darkness.

"I told you to hold her!" Julia exclaimed as she picked herself up off the ground. "The more she thrashes about, the faster the poison kills."

"It's not my fault," whined Flaccus. "She's stronger than you'd think! What's a salve going to do, anyway? She's dying!"

"You're right." Julia returned to her pack.

"Am I?"

"Yes, Flaccus. The salve isn't enough. We have little time left, but there is a prayer that can save her—Myrill willing." Julia pulled a battered scroll from her pack. "Here! I'll lead the prayer, but the Goddess demands a sacrifice of both blood and treasure. And it must come from someone who loves her."

Renier stroked Vipsania's cheek, pushing back strands of hair matted with sweat and blood. "I have little, but the Goddess can have it all." Vipsania jolted and looked up at Renier, wide-eyed and mumbling something in Gualic.

Julia took hold of his hands. "I know Myrill, Mother of Mercy, will accept your sacrifice." She pulled her sacrificial knife from her pack and set it next to the scroll. "What treasure do you offer?"

Renier reached into the neck of his tunic and tugged on a leather cord. He revealed a flat lens bound in a large bronze loop.

"A magical glass, to help tired, old eyes read. A gift from the magus."

"Perfect. I'll make the cut and begin reciting the prayer. There are some parts you must repeat. You must bleed for the duration. Understand?"

Renier held out his arm. "Yes. Hurry!"

"Wait!" Flaccus stepped forward and pushed Renier aside. "No slave can do this. And your 'magical' glass? Hardly worth a handful of sestertii."

Julia's eyes flashed with anger. "But Flaccus, don't you think—"

He tossed down a purse full of coins, dropped to his knees, thrust out his arm, and yanked back the sleeve of his robe. "As her discipulus, I insist!"

Julia grabbed her knife. "This will hurt."

He grimaced. "Of course it will. It's for Vipsania."

Julia made the first sacrificial cut. Flaccus hissed as the blade opened a long but shallow wound on the back of his forearm. His blood, crimson in the campfire's light, fell and puddled on the ground.

Shouts were heard in the distance, Kehindé and Rexinda—mostly Rexinda—trading insults with the Imperaré men. How long could two stand against so many? And what about Ulric? His orders were to guard the flank, whatever that really meant. Julia looked to the east, but all she saw was drifting smoke and shadowed stone. *Mother Myrill, please protect him. Whatever you would have me do. I need him.*

Renier drew a dagger from beneath his tunic and stood over Magus Vipsania. He had to know those Imperaré brutes would sweep him away in one sword stroke, but he looked determined to die defending his mistress all the same.

Julia unfurled the scroll and began reciting the prayer in a powerful, melodic chant.

> "Myrill Regina, shall deliver. Myrill am I! Myrill Regina Caelorum Triumphans! Seize and cast out all malignancy within Magus Vipsania Tertia, whether it is a venom—seize it! Whether a poison—seize it! Whether a spirit—seize it! Myrill Regina shall deliver. Myrill am I! Myrill Regina Caelorum Triumphans! Seize and cast out what torments Magus Vipsania Tertia this very day, whether it is a venom—cast it out! Whether a poison— cast it out! Whether a spirit—cast it out! Myrill Regina shall deliver."

Julia completed the prayer, then instructed Flaccus to repeat several key phrases before she began again. Once she had recited the prayer for a third time, she waited for Flaccus to speak his part, then she made a second sacrificial cut.

Julia continued the ritual even as the sounds of battle echoed through the ruins. The prayer needed the totality of her thought, her will, her power. Neither the clash of arms nor the screams of dying men could shake her. Not even the voice of the hated

Strabo, so close, so dangerously close, promising Ulric a swift and merciful end.

How? How did he get up here? Myrill preserve us!

The third and final sacrificial cut was made. Julia's chanting reached a crescendo and stopped. The ritual was complete. Exhausted, Julia slumped to the ground.

Vipsania was silent for a moment, then she let out a pitiful sounding moan.

"No… no! Myrill's Mercy!" Julia cried. "It should have worked."

Flaccus stood up and angrily wrapped a cloth around his forearm. "The ritual failed. I've bled for nothing!"

Renier ran back to Vipsania's side. "Alakur, help us!" He looked up at Flaccus with contemptuous, accusing eyes. "You! I should have made the sacrifice."

"What are you insinuating, slave? I'm Magus Vipsania's discipulus. I'm from an excellent family. She—" he made a dismissive gesture toward Julia "—is a thief's whore. Not a proper priestess and clearly tainted by Bayjoni blood. Why are we surprised Myrill abandoned her?"

"How dare you, Flaccus?" The betrayal struck deep, and Julia felt her eyes filling with tears despite her efforts. "I've only ever been kind to you."

Renier gathered Vipsania in his arms. "You make my case for me, Flaccus." He spoke as if he was schooling an idiot child in rhetoric. "You try to distract us from your guilt by lashing out at Julia, while you ignore your mistress dying at your very feet!"

Flaccus spoke a word and his hands burst into red-hot flames. "Silence, old man! Or I'll burn you! I'll burn you, slave!"

Vipsania reached for Renier and whispered, "Piré." Was it an Eltaran word?

"No, no, my sweet child." Renier rocked Vipsania gently in his arms and said, "Not yet. Please, Alakur? Not yet."

A shudder ran through Vipsania's body. She closed her eyes and said no more.

BLADE ECSTASY

Ulric reached the crumbling walls near the eastern cliffs of the hill, drew his spatha, and checked his knives and daggers. The terrain was uneven, covered by coarse grass and blocks of the strange, reddish-brown stone. Most of the walls barely reached his waist. How could he protect their flank, let alone stop an attack from the rear? He looked away from the burning trees toward the darkness in the south. With his Shadow Ways training, his eyes adjusted quickly. Low ridges and tall grass covered the fields between the ruins and the stream; enough hiding places for half a dozen killers.

Vipsania is dying, and her murderer is out there. I know it! She was facing the tree line when the dart struck the back of her neck. Kehindé knows this, so why am I the only one guarding the rear? Oh, and the flank! He looked below to the far walls where only Kehindé and Rexinda stood, ready to battle a score of men. The remains of the outer walls and outbuildings of the Eltaran outpost seemed to make for a defensible position. The ruins created a maze of switchbacks and chokepoints of which a small force could take advantage.

A small force? Ha! A force of two; not half enough to fill a legion tent. But what do I know? I'm no soldier. I've only read about the great battles. Not like Kehindé had a choice. What did General Rufius say? You go to battle with the army you have? Sounds like a pleasant way of saying, 'Soldier, you're dead!'

Ulric watched as the men slowed their chaotic charge thirty paces from the outer walls. One man ran through the horde, shouting commands and shoving fighters into place until they were in a loose line formation. "This ain't a back-alley brawl! We do this good and proper!" Ulric recognized the voice; it was Decius, the Portus Collegium enforcer who had shared his watch over the Collegium Draconis Aurei. The men were Imperaré.

Ulric had prayed the attackers would be anyone else, but he never really doubted their identity. He had gambled that the Imperaré wouldn't be willing, let alone capable, of tracking them into the wilderness. He lost. Now he had no choice but to fight his own. What if he had to face a friend like Igdir or Corvus? How much Imperaré blood could he spill before there was no return? Would the glory the gate-stone brought be enough to wash it all away?

"Kill the man! Take the girl," Decius bellowed. "For a bit of fun later." The men laughed, leering in anticipation.

Kehindé and Rexinda stood behind a stretch of chest-high wall atop a steep slope across from Decius and his horde. Rexinda held up her gladius. "If it's fun you want, how about I fuck you with this, you dickless catamite?"

The line trembled with suppressed laughter. "It's all right, men," replied Decius. "Let her joke while she can." Why did a score of men waste their time trading insults with a force of two?

Suddenly, Ulric needed to know if Julia was safe. He turned back to the center of the ruin and strained to see past the glare of the campfire. Julia was deep in prayer, her chanting clear and powerful despite the distance. She was safe, but even so, he fought a growing panic. He scanned the darkness toward the rear. Did a tuft of grass move against the wind?

"Cathus curse a coward!" shouted Rexinda.

Kehindé placed his elbows on the wall and casually leaned forward. "Are you imps going to bluster all night or charge this wall and start dying?"

"Strabo!" The Portus man at the end of the line looked at Decius with uncertainty. "Grab two shadow-walkers—good climbers. Go the long way round and finish the magus. I'm tired of her caterwauling."

Strabo called for two Shrine Alley men, and together they broke from the line and disappeared among the shadows and stone. Ulric glanced to where Julia prayed. The killers drew closer. Was there movement behind him? Did something lurk in the blackness between the ruin and the stream? What if Julia needed him? If Rexinda or Kehindé called for reinforcement? If the lurker in the dark struck again? How could he defeat three men?

Ulric spun around, choking down an urge to scream. Suddenly light-headed, he fell to one knee, gasping for air. He craved the calm and control of Shadow Mind. Such a trance granted peace and mastery over both mind and body. With it, he could control pain, accelerate healing, and refresh his mind. If he could only have that calm, that discipline in the waking world.

Sweet Neesis! Why not? Who says it can't be done? Ghostwalker knew how. If he had lived, who knows what secrets he would have shared? I've tried before, but I've never needed it until now.

Ulric crouched on his haunches and leaned back into the blackness of a crumbling wall. He closed his eyes and tried to slow his breathing. With great effort, he drifted into the still shadows of his mind, but instead of letting the light of his waking thoughts fade, he tried to embrace his senses, bringing on a Thieves' Glimmer. He heard Julia's chanting over Vipsania's cries and nonsense babbling, felt the strangely warm stone at his back, tasted the smoke from the burning forest. He tried to force the peace and discipline of the shadows onto the action and chaos of his luminous mind, but if he concentrated too much on shadow or light, on above or below, he felt the other slipping away.

Sweet Neesis! Glorious Goddess! What's the secret?

He was certain Strabo and the Shrine Alley men were climbing the cliffs. They were coming to finish Vipsania. They would kill Julia.

Fine! I'll figure this out on my own. For Julia!

Stuck halfway between shadow and light, his thoughts and senses formed a chaotic picture, like two mosaics whose tiles had been jumbled together. It was impossible for the images to keep their familiar shapes, but he had to transform two visions into one. He let his concentration go out of focus; he no longer sought the individual tiles of the competing mosaics. Instead he let them melt into new, astonishing patterns.

He heard the men reach his position. With a soft hissing sound, they drew their blades.

Ulric shuddered as a unique sensation washed over his body, both calming and thrilling. A new picture came into focus: a vision of shadow and light, memory and thought, control and chaos. The soft splatter of Flaccus' sacrificial blood now joined Julia's prayer with Vipsania's moans. The wall at his back and the earth beneath his feet now shook with every footfall of the approaching killers. A faint tingling in the stones behind him could only mean Eltaran magic. The air filled with the smell—even the taste—of blood and night-blooming wildflowers, mingled with smoke and ash. The men were breathing heavily, their stench pungent from their jog across the ruin. One man's sweat smelled different: sharp and metallic. Strabo was high on shadow-dust.

Ulric opened his eyes and calmly watched the killers walk by. They wore belted tunics and traveling cloaks. Two carried broad daggers, while Strabo the shadow-duster held a gladius with a nervous energy. The fear and panic that had threatened to overwhelm him were gone. Mastered by the discipline of Shadow Mind? No. Something new. The same way he could see every detail of the men's Shrine Alley ink in the dark. Not the heightened awareness of Thieves' Glimmer, but something different, something far more powerful. Somehow, he had brought shadow and light, discipline and chaos, together. How long could he maintain this new waking trance?

Sweet Neesis! No time to waste.

He silently slid to the top of the wall and readied a throwing knife. In one fluid motion, he launched the blade and fell back into the darkness behind the wall. The knife seemed to move sluggishly through the air, and he feared the throw had gone wrong. Then he heard a stifled cry and stumbling feet. He scurried along the length of the wall into the darkness of the ruin.

"Lurco!"

"Gods Below!" cried Strabo. "It's the traitor! Has to be!"

"Hold fast…"

"To the Nine Gates with him! Find Darktalon!"

Ulric crouched behind a large block of Eltaran stonework. He scanned the breadth of the ruin, watching, waiting.

The skirmish had been too loud and bloody to go unnoticed. He saw Renier standing over Magus Vipsania, dagger in hand. Brave, but pointless, he thought. Julia's prayer never wavered. She had remained perfectly calm when Ulric had nearly succumbed to panic. Was it solely her faith in the gods that gave her such peace? Or was it her faith in him? He didn't feel worthy.

Maybe victory will ultimately depend on Myrill's mercy for Vipsania, but right now I need Neesis' Luck to murder three men!

At the northern base of the hill, the Imperaré finally made their charge. They ran straight at Kehindé and Rexinda, trying to overwhelm their position. Instead of intimidating the two mercenaries, the mass of bodies only made breaching the wall more difficult. Kehindé and Rexinda became a whirlwind of shield, gladius, and saber, slamming, thrusting, and cutting their foes back down the slope.

The Shrine Alley man called Lurco leaned on a low wall, one red hand clutching his neck, the other hovering over the knife's hilt. It didn't matter if the blade stayed in or out; it was too late. His friend, a skinny, hirsute man brandishing a dagger, stood over him. He was trying to say something comforting. Then Lurco grabbed the hilt.

"No! Don't—"

A bright gout of blood erupted from his neck, drenching his friend and splattering Strabo. Lurco trembled, rolled off the wall, and fell face first onto the grass.

"Stones of Dis! I said leave him!" Strabo used the edge of his cloak to wipe the blood from his face. "He was dead already. Listen, Ilus, you can stand there weeping over Lurco if you want. I'm going to kill the bastard." He turned away, raised his gladius, and stalked into the ruins. Shadow-dust left a man with little patience.

"Strabo!" The man called Ilus remained at Lurco's side. "We're supposed to be finishing the magus, right?"

"If you think you can get to her without taking a knife in the back, go ahead!"

For a long moment, Ilus peered into the darkness, nervously brandishing his dagger. Then he lowered his blade and kneeled over his dead friend. As he stripped the body of coins and jewelry, he began mumbling to himself. "Damnable traitor. What's the point of hunting him, Strabo? Can't kill him, he says. To the Hells with that! I'll not let him get me." He flipped Lurco onto his back. "Lost a good Shrine brother, here."

Ulric crossed the distance swiftly, quietly, but Ilus must have heard something at the last moment. The Shrine Alley man stood, dagger in one hand, something shiny and valuable in the other. He was caught off-guard. For a critical instant, he couldn't decide between taking a defensive stance or breaking and running. Ulric closed in, and a terrible exaltation took hold of him. Since discovering his new waking trance, his enemies had been moving slowly, sluggishly, like they were drowning in deep water.

Ulric seized Ilus' wrist, pushing his dagger aside as he thrust the point of Ghostwalker's spatha up and under his sternum. Ilus released a short, uneven scream.

Strabo's dagger flew through the dark in a low arc aimed at Ulric's back. To his ears, it cut through the air like a hissing viper.

Strabo had left Ilus behind as bait. Ulric had spotted him lurking, waiting for this very moment. He took a step forward and to the side, twisting Ilus' body between himself and the dagger. The moment it struck, Ulric yanked his sword free and Ilus hit the ground next to Lurco.

Strabo charged. "You whoreson! To the Hells with orders!"

Ulric danced backward through the uneven terrain, narrowly avoiding several thrusts from Strabo's sword. Shadow-dust could make even a middling swordsman dangerous; it granted a strength born of madness and boundless, frenetic energy. And Strabo was no middling swordsman. He drove his gladius past Ulric's guard, but Ulric easily twisted away from the slow-moving blade. Avoiding Strabo's gladius was simple thanks to the strange ecstasy that threatened to overwhelm him.

Overextended, Strabo barely avoided Ulric's counterattack. "Come on! Best to end it now, traitor!" Strabo pointed to the tip of his gladius. "You'll find mercy here."

Ulric wanted to explain how wrong he was. He was no traitor. What could he say within earshot of Flaccus and Renier? What good would it do, anyway? He stood there looking guilty and readied himself for Strabo's inevitable attack.

Metal clanged and his hand throbbed as he blocked Strabo's first strike, then another, then a third, then he sidestepped a fourth. Finally, the fifth attack was a wild swing born of impatience. Ulric intercepted the blade with his own sword, one hand gripping the hilt of his spatha, the other palm supporting the end of his own blade. Twisting his sword and pushing Strabo's weapon aside, he lashed out in a backswing that turned Strabo's face into a red ruin to match the shattered Eltaran stone.

Strabo screamed. He dropped his gladius, stumbled back a few steps, and crashed to the ground. One hand groped his wounded face as the other struggled to draw a dagger. He forced himself to stand on shaking legs and searched for Ulric with his one remaining eye. He never saw him.

Ulric used Strabo's cloak to wipe the blood from Ghostwalker's spatha, and the Eltaran runes flared with a strange blue light. He stood and took a deep breath, immersing himself in the calm and the thrill of his new waking trance.

Waking trance? A poor name for such a fantastic discovery! What should I call it? It's like walking in both shadow and light; one foot in deep thought, one in waking awareness. It grants the discipline needed for battle, but… it also tempts one with the joy of killing. It's dangerous. It's a sort of ecstasy. A blade ecstasy.

Kehindé had ordered him to secure the flank, and it was secure. The three men who had come to finish Vipsania and kill Julia were dead. She was safe.

So why do I feel like such a bastard?

He turned away from Strabo's body and looked below for Kehindé and Rexinda. It looked like the Imperaré's charge was failing. Ulric watched them repel the attack, her speed and youthful aggression the perfect complement to his strength and technical mastery. Where Rexinda would crash shield first into her enemies, butchering them with thrust after thrust of her sword, Kehindé struck down his foes in a single move, usually a swift counter to the man's own clumsy attack. It was hard to keep track, but he guessed they had killed four or five of the Imperaré and wounded more.

Decius ordered a retreat.

"Cathus curse a coward!" Rexinda shouted. "Every one of you!"

The horde fell back, and Decius dispersed them into a long line. At his command, they surged forward again. This time, each man breached the hill at a point far from the other. Kehindé and Rexinda would rush to repel an attacker, but the man would fall back, offering no resistance, then run to some other spot. All the while, Imperaré men spilled over the edges, gathering on their flanks. Ulric was about to shout a warning, but Kehindé had seen the danger. He called to Rexinda, and they both retreated up the hill, toward the safety of the next cluster of stone.

Ulric wanted to help, but instead he looked into the darkness behind him. He suspected Vipsania's attacker still lurked there. What were they waiting for? Why didn't they strike while Strabo and the Shrine Alley men had distracted him?

Julia's chanting reached a crescendo and stopped. *Praying's over. That has to be a good sign, right? Sweet Neesis, we're due some good luck.* But instead of joyful praise, Ulric heard only angry recriminations. He ran back to the center of camp.

"How dare you, Flaccus? I've only ever been kind to you."

Even from across the ruin, Ulric saw the wet gleam of tears in Julia's eyes. He wasn't sure what Flaccus had said, but he marched straight for him, intending to smash his rat-face into pulp.

Flaccus' hands burst into red-hot flames and he shouted at Renier, "Silence, old man! Or I'll burn you! I'll burn you, slave!"

Ulric heard Rexinda cry out in pain. Flaccus' beating would have to wait. He leaped upon a nearby wall and looked down the north slope.

Kehindé and Rexinda hadn't reached safety; the Imperaré had caught them on a stretch of open ground. Rexinda was wounded, separated from Kehindé, and surrounded by half a dozen men. More men circled Kehindé, never engaging him directly, but harrying him like a pack of hyenas tormenting a lion. One strayed too close, and the lion's claws opened him from gullet to groin. He charged through the opening, trying to reach Rexinda but Decius intercepted him. Trumrician spatha and Bayjoni saber clashed. Decius was good. Good enough to stand his ground.

Good enough to distract him while the others closed in. Kehindé had no choice but to become the center of the circle once again. The lion waited for the next hyena to make a mistake.

Rexinda had fought her way to another wall further up the hill. Six men had trapped her against a stone ruin that rose to her mid-back. A long red line between her shoulder blades bled heavily. He imagined every sword thrust must have been a misery of pain. Still she fought on, slinging the foulest curses with every strike.

Vipsania is as good as dead, and now Rexinda's dying! How did it all go wrong? Neesis Fortuna, how have I offended you? Do you think I was taking all the credit for discovering my blade-ecstasy? No, no, no. Glorious goddess! No! Impossible without Ghostwalker's teachings. Impossible without you! Now, if it's madness and bold action you want, watch as I charge a score of men and rescue two veteran soldiers from certain defeat!

Ulric leaped off the wall and ran into the center of camp. "Flaccus, you rat-faced fool! You're burning no one! Save your fire for the enemy. I'm going to help Rexinda and Kehindé. Julia! If the men break through, follow the stream, flee into the forest."

Julia stood and wiped the tears from her eyes. She looked down at Vipsania, who lay unmoving in Renier's arms. "I'm sorry. I should have saved her." She hesitated, as if she wanted to say more, then she ran into Ulric's embrace.

She looked back toward Flaccus, who eyed them suspiciously. "You don't have to fight anymore, do you? I mean, if you wanted, you could just walk away. Can you admit this scheme has gone all wrong? We could take the map. Slip away into the darkness. Wouldn't that be enough for Silo?"

Julia was right: they could take the map and disappear into the night. Flaccus and Renier would be no obstacle. Would it be enough? Ulric doubted it. The Imperaré had already spent too much blood and coin for anything less than the gate-stone to balance the scales. Besides, ever since he had seen the map, his goal had been the Eltaran settlement of Tmia Culscva and the mystery of the Elts. But there was something even more powerful holding him there, something he loathed to admit to himself.

"No. I don't think the map is enough anymore. It will take the gate-stone to keep my oath. And do you really want to abandon Renier to these killers?"

"No."

"Or Kehindé?"

"No." She smiled. "Not even Rexinda."

"Flaccus?"

Julia scrunched up her face. "Uh…?" Her face smoothed and her eyes softened. "No, of course not, but I had to give you the choice." She kissed him. "Go. And… good fortune!"

Ulric started toward the far end of the ruin, but turned and opened his arms wide. "Don't worry." He grinned. "You're Myrill blessed, and I'm a lucky bastard! Everything will work out. It always does!"

Then he froze. The darkness filled with the sound of soft footfalls on grass; precise, measured, and professional. The wind shifted, replacing the acrid smells of smoke and ash with vile sweat and Verdan leather.

Luciano Porteles walked into the light, twirling his falcata in the air, its gently curving steel gleaming in the firelight.

"Why you lie to girl, boy? You such a damned liar!"

A Funeral Pyre

Julia watched Luciano rise out of the shadows like a spirit from the underworld. The sight of the Verdan assassin unearthed memories of her vision in Tubero's taberna: Ulric battered, bloodied, and beaten. Visions of Aguja, Luciano's dagger, protruding from his heart. The memory burst like a rotten corpse bloated with dread, unleashing fear like swarms of slithering maggots. They wormed their way into every thought, every limb. She couldn't move. She couldn't breathe. She could only stand mutely as the assassin stalked closer.

Ulric drew his sword, the Eltaran runes flickering in the faint light. He filled his offhand with a long dagger, then strode toward Luciano.

"Julia! Run for the forest. I'll find you."

She tried to shout a warning. She wanted him to flee, but no words would come.

"More lies, boy. Tell girl truth!" Luciano glanced at Julia and bared his yellowing teeth in a hateful grin. "Boy, die here tonight! Everyone die. You stay. Watch. You die quick. If I hunt you in forest, I skin you like deer."

It was a vile thing to say. And a foolish thing. Such hubris, to challenge the Ikon of Myrill within the sacred Silva Aurea. Decades of self-destructive hate had tainted Luciano's spirit. Julia thought she could almost see its stain, a sickly yellow patina about his soul. He was a thing to be pitied, not feared.

"You think you could harm me in the sacred forest? The gods see you and judge you. Myrill has no mercy for such sad, spiteful spirits such as yours! Turn aside. Seek Myrill's absolution or face Alakur's wrath."

His smile vanished. "You die first, bitch!"

Luciano raised his sword and the Verdan runes along its gently curving edge shifted and shimmered, as if they too were eager for blood. He charged. Julia stood unmoving as a statue. Myrill was her shield. She closed her eyes.

The sound of metal clashing; Luciano, snarling, rebuffed. Julia opened her eyes to see Ulric standing before her.

"You heard her, Luciano. The gods have judged you! Neesis awaits you in the Underworld."

"More lies, boy. You will see."

Thief and assassin circled one another, then Ulric unleashed a whirlwind of Eltaran steel. As blades clashed and sliced through the air, Julia had no choice but to leap clear. Ulric drove Luciano back into the shadows.

Julia gasped as he vanished into the night. She wanted to run after him. She wanted to unleash Myrill's dawning light. She needed to save him from Aguja! Instead, she hesitated, guilt gnawing and twisting her insides. The ritual had taken its toll, leaving her exhausted and fuzzy-headed. What if her weakness distracted Ulric at some crucial moment?

"Julia!" Flaccus and Renier called in unison.

She told herself Myrill and her daughter Neesis—the wild and unpredictable, the ever-fickle Neesis—would watch over

Ulric. Ignoring the sound of clashing blades in the darkness, she returned to the center of the ruins.

Flaccus and the slaves were frantically gathering their packs and supplies. Near the campfire, Renier still cradled the dying Vipsania in his arms.

Flaccus ran to her, a collection of supply packs haphazardly bouncing over his shoulder. "I heard. We do as he said: make for the forest. Right?"

"I'll not leave her," said Renier, gently rocking Vipsania in his arms. The dart wound had spread a web of dark veins across her neck and face, its malignancy a stark contrast to skin as pale as a winter's frost. "I promised I'd never leave. Though I'm sure she forgot." He looked up at Julia and said, "I made that promise long ago."

How she pitied the old slave in that moment. She had failed to save Vipsania, and now she saw the cost in an old man's eyes. It ate at her. It hollowed out a space big enough for all her failures and filled it with sorrow.

"Then stay here and die," Flaccus said, "Stupid old slave! We're leaving. We're—"

"Silence, little boy!" shouted Julia.

Stunned, Flaccus went quiet.

"Flee, if you want. I thought Collegium magi were no cowards, but abandon your mistress if you must. Spare us your pettiness. Your spite. Your hate. Our enemy provides an ample supply."

Flaccus appeared to shrink in the firelight. He let the packs slide off his shoulder and stammered, "I… I am… sorry."

"I'm staying with Renier," Julia said, collapsing to her knees next to Vipsania. She took her hand. It was ice cold. To Renier, she said, "A direct entreaty to Myrill? Dangerous, perhaps, but I'm certain the goddess wants Vipsania to succeed. She wants the magus to find Tmia Culscva!"

"What a happy coincidence. So do I!" The words were Trumin, but spoken in an unfamiliar accent. The voice had a strange melodic quality, almost ethereal.

Everyone searched for the speaker, peering into the dark corners of the ruins. As if produced by a fabricator, a white-haired, red-eyed figure appeared upon a high wall. Even in the campfire's faint light, the outlandish colors and foreign cut of the stranger's clothing were clear, as well as his golden-hued skin and pointed ears.

"By Alakur's light! An Eltaran!" Renier clutched Vipsania even closer. "Do you live? Or are you a phantom? An echo trapped in old Eltaran stone?"

"Oh, I live. I'm very much alive."

Julia thought the Eltaran smiled a most charming smile beneath his feral red eyes.

Flaccus took a brave step forward. "What do you want with us, Eltaran?" He raised his hands and they burst into familiar red flames.

The Eltaran looked offended. "You won't need any of that." He spoke an Eltaran word while making a slight motion with his hand, and Flaccus' flames were extinguished. "I've come to help you."

Shaken, Flaccus retreated next to Julia. She knew counter magics were rare and difficult to master. The Eltaran was dangerous. Weren't they all? But with so little hope for Vipsania, how could she refuse his help?

"You said you wanted Magus Vipsania to succeed. Why?"

The Eltaran came closer, leaping to the top of a lower wall with an acrobatic grace that reminded Julia of Ulric. "The magi are priests of Eltarus—May His Lamp Shine Eternal—and Magus Vipsania Tertia is a high priestess of their order. We Eltarans are His children. We are close to his heart, his mind. There are great things to be done at Urb-Altus Laetim. The place you call Tmia Culscva."

"If you can help, do it quickly," begged Renier. "There's little time left."

"Then waste no time. Throw her into the fire."

"Burn her?" Julia wondered if she had heard right. Eltarans had a reputation as mischievous tricksters and deceivers, but this? To provide hope, only to mock them. "What cruel trick is this? You'd have us hasten her death? Set her on her funeral pyre?"

"Piré," whispered Renier. Then louder, he said, "Piré. The Eltaran word for pyre. She's said it, over and over." He thought for a moment, then said, "I think we should do as he suggests."

"Even seven short decades is enough for some wisdom, I see. Place her in the fire, quickly."

Julia wasn't convinced. "No! She'll burn."

"You think a fire magus can burn?"

She looked to Flaccus for an answer.

"It might work," he said, "Maybe."

"You offend Eltarus with your lies. You know it will work," said the Eltaran. "The poison will burn away like impurities in a smelter. It will be but a shadow of the dragon flames she seeks, but it will save her life."

"Dragon flames?" Julia asked.

"It's rumored the greatest fire magi seek the remaining volcanic dragons so they may bathe in pure, elemental flame. It's all very secretive," Flaccus said. "It renews them. Or so it is rumored."

"It's true," said Renier.

"A mockery of Eltaran immortality born of jealousy," said the Eltaran, with no hint of his previous good humor. "Now, burn her!"

Renier lowered Vipsania to the ground and retrieved the Eltaran scroll from within her robes. He then grabbed her by the wrists and waited, with a look of resignation tinged with hope. Julia grabbed Vipsania's legs and together they hoisted her into the air. With her remaining strength she helped move Vipsania toward the campfire.

"Wait! What if he's wrong?" Flaccus looked at Renier, then Julia, his eyes filled with both a warning and an accusation. "You'll kill her. And why? On the advice of an unknown Elt?"

Julia hesitated.

"You failed to save the magus once," said the Eltaran. "Would you fail her again?"

Julia and Renier heaved and tossed Vipsania's limp body into the fire.

The campfire erupted into a searing blast of heat. Like a living thing, the flames danced out of the firepit and whirled toward the night sky. Magus Vipsania screamed. She tried to stand, but the flames greedily pulled her down to her knees. She screamed again. And burned. The conflagration had become Magus Vipsania's funeral pyre.

Julia turned away, shielding her eyes from the horror she had wrought. She looked to the Eltaran for answers, but he was gone. Only a lilting, maniacal laughter remained echoing across the ruins.

The Conflagration

Ulric had watched with mounting dread as Luciano emerged from the darkness south of the ruins. Of course, the Verdan assassin was here. Who else would Brocchus and the Imperaré send to torment him? In a moment of panic, he had felt his newfound blade-ecstasy slipping away.

No! He should be elated. He had made a vow to the goddess Neesis Fortuna: if She helped him escape the clutches of the widowed Aquila Secunda, he would kill Luciano Porteles, the man who had set him up. Neesis had done her part, but he had failed—twice. Now he could fulfill his vow. He could avenge himself on the man who had been Arrius Ghostwalker's enemy, who had played him the fool, who had threatened Julia and nearly killed him on the deck of the Neesis Insania.

Ulric plunged into the depths of his mind and seized his fear, dragging it squirming into the light. He let it burn there. He had saved Julia and drove Luciano back into the shadows where he belonged. Where they both belonged.

Eltaran spatha and Verdan falcata clashed in the darkness. When Ulric finally relented, Luciano bled from a shallow wound on his left shoulder.

Luciano looked down at the dark trickle of blood and let loose a howl of hyena-like laughter. "Boy been training, eh? Working hard, you not fail when meet Luciano again, eh? Is that it, boy?"

Ulric circled back to his left so he could see Rexinda and Kehindé across the ruin. He caught a brief glimpse of Rexinda just as the men surrounding her rushed in. Her sword snapped, broken by a heavy axe in the chaos of blows. She screamed defiance and threw the men back with a heave of her shield, then drew a broad infantry dagger and waited for the men to close in again. He had been on his way to save her, but now she would die because of Luciano.

Ulric had fought better than ever before thanks to the discipline he named blade-ecstasy. He felt no fear. His senses were unnaturally sharp, his reactions quicker than he thought possible. The discipline also gave him the clarity to realize what it couldn't bestow: twenty years of training and experience. Despite the advantage of his surprising speed, he had only slipped a quick thrust past Luciano's guard. If he were to have a chance at victory, he would need another angle of attack.

"Ha! I've hardly thought of you since that night at Capito's." It was some of Ulric's finest acting.

"More lies, boy! You not forget Luciano so easily, eh?"

Luciano's falcata lashed out in several quick, probing attacks. Ulric blocked each one with ease.

"Alright! You caught me. I admit, I have been wondering: if Brocchus took you into his service, why do I never see you on the river?"

Luciano's jaw clenched. He said nothing.

"You should be a big man in the Transnanpela Collegium," Ulric continued. "But you're not, are you?"

"Aguja will bleed you slow, boy. Then Aguja bleed you whore."

Luciano pressed the attack once more. Ulric retreated, using both sword and dagger to block the curved falcata. The clang of metal echoed through the ruin. Their swords clashed again, and he pressed his blades hard against Luciano's sword. He leaned in, eager to taunt the assassin.

"I think—Sweet Neesis!"

Luciano repositioned his falcata in an instant, giving him the leverage to drive Ulric's spatha aside and spin the curved blade around into a deadly cut aimed at his neck. Ulric darted backwards. If he hadn't been in blade-ecstasy, he would have lost his head.

"Bah! You talk too much. Like Ghostwalker."

Ulric would not be silenced. "Do you know I report directly to Silo? I do special jobs for him."

"Shut up."

"Trouble is—" Ulric grinned "—everyone's jealous I'm getting special treatment from the prince!"

"Shut up, damn you!"

Luciano's sword flashed like lightning, and a rain of strikes followed. Ulric retreated, letting the assassin's anger fall on the empty air. He led him away from the center of the ruin, away from Julia. If he couldn't defeat Luciano, he could at least give her time to flee into the forest. So why was she wasting it arguing with Flaccus and Renier?

Why in the Nine Gates aren't they running?

With Ulric's attention divided, Luciano closed in. Falcata and spatha crashed again. Ulric tried to entrap Luciano's wrist with his sword and dagger, but Luciano skillfully countered the move, stepping back and lashing out with a kick, sending Ulric tumbling over a waist-high stone block. He landed with exaggerated clumsiness, and Luciano eagerly leaped after him. Ulric rolled out of the fall and rose to one knee, his dagger aimed to disembowel the assassin.

At the last instant, Luciano spun awkwardly to the side, letting loose a backhanded slash to cover his retreat.

Almost! Could use a bit of luck here, Neesis! Hello?

"Clever. Another lie. You lie when talk. You lie when move."

He kept his eyes on Luciano while he circled behind the stone block. He shook his head back, tossing locks of dark, sweat-soaked hair from his eyes, and let out a long, shuddering breath. His chest heaved and his limbs ached. The assassin had almost made a fatal mistake. Although Ulric was nearly exhausted, he couldn't relent. He had to attack.

"How about some truth, then? I've been trying to get the whisper on you and Brocchus since the Concilium. My spies say you're no primus, no top enforcer, no gang leader, no… nothing."

"All you need know, boy," he said with a hate filled smile, "is Brocchus send me to kill you. For all Imperaré."

"Oh, you're his attack dog? That's fitting, because my spies said they didn't see a man standing next to Brocchus. They said you looked like his pet."

Luciano's body trembled with an uncontainable fury. It burst out in a guttural roar as he surged forward, falcata on point. Ulric calmly waited for the inevitable collision, spatha and dagger at the ready. He blocked Luciano's first rage-filled blow, which sent a numbing pain shooting from his hand to his shoulder. Hate and anger fueled a barrage of ever more brutal and wilder attacks.

Thank you, Neesis!

Ulric stopped a wild swing with his spatha, blocking the end of the falcata. Then he brought his dagger in low, catching the sword's pommel. Pushing his spatha down while bringing the dagger up, he spun Luciano's wrist and sword awkwardly across his body. He had done the move in the blink of an eye, and now his sword pressed against the assassin's gut.

For you, glorious Goddess! And you, Arrius!

He drove the sword forward.

Luciano screamed.

But then he did the unexpected. He let go of his sword, twisted his torso in time to turn a deadly thrust into a long slash, and caught Ulric between the eyes with an offhand jab. Both the assassin and thief stumbled away from one another and fell among the ruins. Ulric leaned against a wall, trying to clear his head and blink away his tears, while Luciano sat panting on a stone block, clutching the bloody wound beneath his chest.

The falcata! Luciano's sword was somewhere nearby. If he could retrieve it before Luciano…! Ulric pushed himself off the wall, but the ruins spun around him and he slumped back onto the stone. It took a moment to control the pain and stop the spinning. He thought his nose might be broken. He took a dizzying step forward, but an anguished cry from Kehindé stopped him. Ulric risked a glance to the edge of the ruins. An Imperaré soldier held a battered and broken Gualdean shield in the air. Rexinda Hamunds-Daughter had fallen. Ulric couldn't see her body; she would have been laying on the far side of a low wall. He didn't know if she was alive or dead.

Kehindé crashed through his circle of tormentors, swiftly killing two men but paying the inevitable price when Decius sunk a dagger into the back of his thigh. The wound barely slowed him down. He scattered the men who had felled Rexinda, brutally killing three of them before they were sure of what was happening. Decius shouted a command, and the remaining Imperaré regrouped and surrounded the Kekeksuan warrior. He was going to die beside his adopted daughter. And Ulric couldn't do a damned thing to save him.

"You want truth, boy?" Luciano called.

Ulric spun around, blades at the ready. Luciano stood, one red hand over the long slash beneath his chest, the other holding his sword.

Luciano slid his bloody hand across his body, indicating his wound. "This is truth. A truth I run from. What is it? I'm damned fool. So much hatred. Almost let boy end me."

"The night's still young!" Ulric joked with empty bravado.

"There is more truth, Ulric. I lie earlier. I here on mission from Brocchus, yes. But mission is to get map. Not kill you."

Luciano walked forward, his pace deliberate, his expression calm.

"I think I kill you for myself."

Ulric backed away, tightening the grip on his weapons. *Neesis forgive me; I can't kill the bastard! I tried. I came close. So damn close!*

"But why?" Luciano asked. "Kill you because…" He searched for the right Trumin word. "You echo of a bad memory? The shadow of a Ghost? Should I be stupid, like you?"

He slowly circled Ulric, his sword held out on point, his other hand protecting his bloody wound. His dark, stringy hair hung limply, and rivulets of sweat cleared trails down his filthy face and neck. He rushed forward, driving his sword into Ulric's guard.

"You escape from Secundus' home, eh?"

He attacked with a quick series of thrusts, ending in an unexpected slash. Ulric said nothing.

"You do smart thing? Thank your goddess? Move on?"

A brief exchange of blades; the clang of steel.

"No!" Luciano shouted, but there was no anger.

A swift slash of the falcata. Ulric blocked the attack, but the curved blade slid above and around his sword. He barely snapped his head back in time, only receiving a bloody cut above his right ear.

"Foolish boy, come to kill me. Come to die. But Imperaré take us."

Luciano struck again and again, driving him back toward the center of the ruin. He glimpsed Julia and Renier carrying Vipsania between them. Were they finally abandoning the ruin? Why did they burden themselves with her body? He had to give them more time.

"The Imperaré arriving when they did? That was thanks to Neesis Fortuna!" Ulric said proudly, more to reassure himself than to taunt Luciano. "Maybe I can't defeat you, but the goddess will never let you kill me."

He broke and ran, trying to lead him away from Julia. Luciano blocked his path. "Stupid boy! You not hear me? I don't need to kill you. I need map." Luciano paused, and when he spoke again Ulric thought the assassin sounded almost wistful. "Truth is, your foolishness make us both slaves of Imperaré."

Luciano's attacks resumed; measured, precise, steadily deconstructing his defense.

"You much better tonight, boy. Much better than back on boat. You move faster. Much smoother. But you technique… is still shit!"

A simple thrust became something intricate, something unexpected. Luciano's falcata cut a long gash on the inside of Ulric's forearm and sent his spatha tumbling through the air. An instant later, the sword's razor-sharp point was at his neck. He stepped back, but Luciano stepped with him, the blade at his throat never wavering. Ulric tried to make a fist with the hand of his wounded arm, but there was little strength in his fingers. He was beaten.

"I not kill you. Give me map. I return to Trumric. We never cross paths again."

Ulric was surprised Luciano would try such an obvious deception. The thought of the assassin abandoning his revenge was absurd.

"Gods Below! Shouldn't Mist View's best assassin be a better liar? I'll be dead the moment I hand it over."

"I gave you chance, boy! I did! Must have map. You first slave to die, Ulric." Luciano shifted his weight, readying the killing strike. "Maybe you lucky one, eh?"

Did you hear that, Neesis? I am the lucky one!

A bright flash of fire and a wall of blistering heat erupted from the center of the ruins. The campfire had become a conflagration, its flames spilling out of the firepit and twisting high and wild into the sky. Deep within the fire, Magus Vipsania lay unmoving, the flames of a funeral pyre ready to consume her body. With a piercing scream, she bolted upright, tried to stand, and fell to her knees. The flames whipped and curled about her, growing brighter with an unnatural intensity.

Luciano looked on with disbelief. "No… no!"

Vipsania's hair shriveled as her robes sloughed off in blazing strips. The flesh beneath bubbled, cracked, and blackened. Her screams reminded Ulric of his own torment under Aquila's hot irons, but this was so much worse. He grew sick with the thought of it.

Luciano's sword wavered and fell. "No! It was good plan! Damn you all!"

Ulric took a step back. What happened? Had Julia and Renier thrown Vipsania into the campfire? Why?

Luciano clawed at his forehead as if to drive off some sudden pain. He thrust his sword toward Vipsania. "No! Still good plan. Still time." He ran toward the flames, shouting, "Kill fire magus!"

There was no time to find his spatha, so Ulric tightened his grip on his dagger and ran after him. Vipsania was burning to death; why did Luciano fear her? He only knew Luciano wanted something, and he still had the strength to oppose him.

They both raced toward the blaze and the screaming figure at its center. Julia ran from the fire, a hand raised to shield her eyes from the light, or perhaps from the horror of Vipsania's torment. Flaccus backed away, mesmerized, while Renier herded the other slaves away from the spreading flames. When he spotted Ulric approaching, Renier frantically waved and shouted for him to turn back.

The air swirled with ash and sparks, scorching Ulric's throat. He could smell burning flesh and briefly something else— something pungent and rotten. Then it was gone.

At the center of the conflagration, Magus Vipsania rose like a weightless ember on a column of blue fire. The flames embraced her blackened legs and caressed her flesh. They healed her burns and danced across her body, leaving bright pink skin in their wake. When the flames reached the apex of their journey, Vipsania's screams became near-orgasmic cries of exultation. Then her hair blossomed into a shower of sparks and her eyes snapped open to reveal orbs of pure blue light. It was one of the most beautiful and frightening things Ulric had ever seen.

"No!" Luciano screamed.

"Vipsania! Help Kehindé. Help—"

The magus fell to the ground and her bare feet struck like a meteor. A wall of wind and fire hit Ulric and sent him tumbling into blackness.

Something sharp and cool pressed against Ulric's seared skin. It almost felt soothing. He opened his eyes and tried to focus his senses. Magus Vipsania stood nearby, her nakedness hidden by wreathes of flame, all that remained of the great inferno that had engulfed her. She brandished her dragon rod once more: it was a thing of ebony, molten gold, and pure wrath.

Luciano yanked Ulric to his feet, causing Aguja's edge to make a shallow cut along his neck. The assassin held him, using his body as a living shield against the threat of Magus Vipsania's fire. Panic washed over him, and the agony of every wound returned. His stomach soured, and he felt lightheaded. His legs weakened and his thoughts grew chaotic. The blade-ecstasy had ended.

"No, no, boy," Luciano hissed into his ear, "you with me. You lucky? You Luciano's lucky charm now." To Vipsania he called, "You give Eltaran map, I take men and go. Boy live."

The map! Surely Flaccus or Renier secured the map before they threw Vipsania into the campfire? Either way, Luciano had to know his offer was absurd.

Vipsania narrowed her eyes, causing blue flames to sputter and flare under her brow. She seemed to see them for the first time. Did she remember anything before the delirium of the poison and the torment of the fire? Her flames swooshed and crackled as they turned from red to white to blinding blue. The heat singed away the few remaining hairs left on Ulric's arms and legs.

"You think I would trade the Eltaran Mystery for the life of a thief? You think I would bargain with the Verdan filth that tried to murder me?" A gout of fire erupted from the mouth of the dragon-headed rod. "It would be so easy to burn the both of you and be done with it! And why not, hmm?"

"You're right," Ulric said, "don't waste time on us!" He pointed to the north, to where Decius and the Imperaré still surrounded Kehindé. "Do what I couldn't: Save Kehindé and Rexinda!"

"Quiet, boy!" Luciano tightened his hold on Ulric and began slowly backing away.

"Burn us! But keep Julia safe! Rexinda will need her help!"

"Shut up!" Luciano pressed the point of the blade into his neck and whispered, "You want us burn together, boy? No. Aguja bleed you first!"

The dagger didn't move. With a growl of pain and frustration, he said, "Damn them!"

"Who? Damn who?" Ulric didn't expect an answer.

Vipsania cast her fiery gaze over the ruins. "Kehindé? Rexinda!" She frantically searched the darkness. "Where… where is Rexinda?" She looked back to Ulric and Luciano, then thrust the dragon rod into the sky.

Ulric searched for Julia, but couldn't find her. He wanted one last look before the end, but Magus Vipsania's conflagration of blue flame was so bright all else had become a sea of black.

Sweet Neesis Umbra, protector of all thieves. Forgive me, I really thought that was going to work. Win trust and sympathy by offering to sacrifice yourself? It's a classic scheme! It even had the advantage of being true. Partly.

Magus Vipsania spoke. "Επιστροφή στη σφυρηλάτηση του Ούκορος."

Ulric awaited the blast of fire that would char him to his blackened bones. Instead, he felt a small point of searing heat under his chin. Luciano screamed and cast Aguja to the ground. The Verdan steel glowed red hot, as if fresh out of a forge. Aguja had burned an imprint of its hilt into Luciano's palm.

No longer under Aguja's threat, Ulric yanked himself free and drove an elbow into Luciano's face. It connected with a satisfying crack. He rolled clear as the assassin stumbled and cursed, throwing himself behind a block of stone an instant before Vipsania's dragon rod unleashed a blast of fire. Luciano grunted in pain as flame and hot rock scattered through the air.

"Vipsania!" Ulric called. "I'll deal with the Verdan. Help Kehindé!"

"Then be quick about it, Ulric," she said with an air of casual impatience. "By Eltarus, I'm going to enjoy incinerating this rabble!" She turned and walked to the edge of camp, where she could overlook the northern slope. She pointed the dragon rod toward Kehindé and the Imperaré soldiers. With swift, sweeping motions, she traced glyphs of fire in the air while chanting strange

Eltaran words. The glyphs crackled, flared, and vanished. The rod disgorged a slender bolt of living flame that took the form of a writhing, dragon-headed serpent as it flew across the ruins. Another fiery serpent followed. Then another, and another.

The Imperaré soldiers had watched the magus' fiery resurrection with awe and trepidation. Ulric didn't know what had kept them pressing the attack. Was it Decius' leadership? A desperate hope Luciano could still secure victory? Whatever it was, it withered before the heat of the oncoming fire serpents. The soldiers broke and ran, sprinting down the slope toward the far walls. The serpents flew high and wide, encircling the men before descending with a horrifying *whoosh* and a bright trail of flame. They chased their prey almost as if they were toying with them, flying just close enough to scorch skin and ignite clothing. Men panicked and burned, scattering in all directions, each desperately looking for cover, but the ruins provided no haven from Vipsania's wrath. Some men tried to fight back, but swords and axes passed harmlessly through the flames.

Ulric had never seen magic unleashed to such terrifying and deadly potential. It was difficult to tear his eyes away from the sheer spectacle of it. He stared into the darkness, trying to force his eyes to adjust to the night once more. Had Luciano fled? Where had his spatha fallen? He crept forward, looking for his sword, but instead of Ghostwalker's spatha, he found Aguja lying half buried in the blasted earth.

Ha, ha, sweet Neesis! Alright, you bastard. Maybe this boy bleeds you, eh?

Ulric reached the stone block, but Luciano was gone. He peered into the surrounding darkness, expecting to see the assassin spring from behind every edge and corner.

Nothing.

He bolted to the center of the ruin. The firepit was now a blasted crater, and their scorched packs and supplies were tossed across the campsite. He spotted Flaccus in the distance and ran to him.

"Did you see Luciano? Where is he?"

Flaccus stood perfectly still, transfixed by Vipsania's flame-shrouded form. One Imperaré soldier charged up the slope, screaming in mad desperation. He was instantly engulfed in a blast of fire from the mouth of her dragon-headed rod. When the flames passed, there was only a smoldering, blackened thing left to collapse onto the ground. "She's beautiful. So beautiful. So monstrous. Gods… I hate her."

Ulric saw Kehindé scrambling over the ruins, with Rexinda in his arms. She was limp and unmoving, but her father's haste gave Ulric hope she was alive. Behind him the fire serpents struck, coiling around their victims in an immolating embrace, filling the air with brief, horrified screams and plumes of oily black smoke.

Flaccus kept his eyes on Vipsania. They filled with tears and reflected fire. "Now the die is cast. That's something you'd say, isn't Ulric? 'The die is cast?'"

"What? Gods Below, never mind." Ulric could barely suppress his frustration. "The Verdan I was fighting. Did you see him?"

Flaccus finally focused his vision on Ulric. "Are you alright? You look terrible."

"No. No, I'm not. Now, did you see Luciano?"

"Yes. He ran south, toward the stream. The fool knew facing an angry fire magus meant certain death."

Ulric moved towards the stream, but stopped after a few paces. "Where's Julia? Rexinda needs her help."

Flaccus turned away to watch Magus Vipsania. "She ran from the flames, along with Renier."

Ulric ran on. He needed to find Julia, but he had promised Vipsania he would deal with the Verdan, and although he didn't feel up to it, he felt obliged to keep his word. And there was the minor matter of his vow to the goddess Neesis. If there was a chance to kill Luciano, he still had to try. He only hoped the broken nose he gave him and whatever wounds he suffered from Magus Vipsania's blast were enough to even the odds.

Oh, Sweet Neesis, but you do love me when the odds are against me, do you not?

Somewhere in the darkness, he heard Julia scream. He broke into a mad dash.

Neesis! You cheating bitch!

Ash and Water

Julia stumbled after Luciano as he pulled her into the darkness, the firelight fading along with the cries of the dying Imperaré. As they ran, smoke and ash swirled past them like a winter's storm before drifting into the blackness. Ahead, the rush and tumble of swift water grew louder.

"Let me go!" She tried to pull free, but Luciano only smiled and tightened his grip. The bones in her wrist felt like they were being ground into meal. Julia screamed. She didn't want to give him the satisfaction, but the sensation was agonizing. Her legs turned to straw, and she tumbled to the ground.

The assassin kept charging forward, dragging her through the tall grass.

"Myrill blight you! Alakur blast you! Arakru take you!"

Luciano howled like a hyena. "You waste curses on me, girl." He pulled her to her feet and gave her a bitter smile. "Cursed already."

Julia still hadn't recovered from the failed ritual to save Vipsania, but she gathered what power she could. A blast of divine radiance light erupted from her hand, causing Luciano to recoil and release her wrist.

"I said, Alakur blast you!"

"Gah! Damn bitch! Try to blind me?"

Julia ran. First for the safety of the camp, but then she abruptly turned south toward the stream.

Follow! Follow, fool! My strength may be spent, but the spirit of this land will aid one who Myrill blessed.

Coughing and wheezing through the swirling ash, Julia ran down the northern bank of the stream and splashed into the cool, shallow water. Pausing for a moment to catch her breath, she screamed when rough hands seized her from behind. It was Luciano, of course. Even though he must have run to catch up with her, he hadn't made a sound.

"Let me go!"

"No more running, girl. No more tricks."

"It will be worse for you if you don't let me go." Her dark eyes flashed with anger, but then she calmly said, "I'm blessed by Myrill."

"Don't lie. Magus can't hear. I see prayer fail. You no priestess."

Julia stiffened. "Ignorant barbarian!"

Luciano laid the end of his sword along her shoulder. "Scream again. I think boy lost."

"I'm right here, you filth." Ulric staggered from the tall grass with arms spread wide, hands empty. Blood ran from a slash on his forearm, dripping down his elbow and splattering on the ground.

Luciano snapped Julia against his chest, grunting in pain when she collided with the long gash on his abdomen. With a loud splash, he retreated a few paces into the stream. Julia stood calf deep in swift cool water—sacred water. She could sense it. The stream buffeted and caressed her legs with an animated purpose, while the gurgling waters spoke with a hidden voice. It called to her. All she had to do was answer.

Then the razor-sharp edge of Luciano's blade pressed beneath her chin.

"Ulric!"

"Quiet, girl," Luciano snarled. "Men talk now."

Ulric held up a hand, motioning her to keep silent.

Myrill have mercy! I think not!

He stepped closer and Luciano dragged her further into the stream.

"Let her go, Luciano. You've lost. Your men are on the run. Or dead." Ulric sounded confident, but was it just another performance?

Luciano looked down at Julia and forced her chin upward with the flat of his blade. She glared defiantly at the heavens and began chanting.

"I said quiet!" To Ulric he said, "Such a pretty girl. Half-blood Bayjoni? You pull her out of brothel or theater for scheme? Sell her as priestess to magus, eh? Good plan." He stared lasciviously down at Julia's heaving chest for a moment, then flashed Ulric a wolfish grin. "Ghostwalker and you always good schemers."

"What do you want?"

"I want map!" Luciano screamed. "I give girl when I get map. Go back, tell any lie you must, but steal map. Give me map. Then you get girl."

"As if I could trust you?"

"Bah! Trust. Don't trust. Take a chance, or watch girl die."

"Come now, sacred river spirit! An Ikon of Myrill needs your aid!"

Luciano turned the blade's edge against Julia's throat. "Quiet, girl. Or die now."

Ulric threw his hands forward in surrender. "No! No, wait! I'll do it!"

"What mortal threatens to spill blood in my sacred waters?"

It was a woman's voice, as light and ringing as trickling waters, yet there was an undercurrent as perilous as a crashing wave. It seemed to come from everywhere and nowhere.

"Eh?" Luciano whipped his head around frantically.

Julia's eyes gleamed with giddy anticipation. As she suspected, a naiad dwelled within the waters. A potameides; a nymph, a daughter of Ulorin. She looked at Ulric and smiled, despite the wickedly sharp blade at her throat. "I told you these waters were sacred! I knew it!"

"Shut up!" A quick sting and Julia felt a trickle of warm blood dripping down her neck. She said no more.

Ulric stared at her, first in confusion, then panic. Finally, understanding blossomed on his face. He dropped to his knees and spoke, imitating the language of her earlier prayers.

"O' daughter of Ulorin, divine flowing one, a blessed follower of Myrill needs your aid!"

The stream around Luciano's feet churned and a powerful spout of water shot up between him and Julia, throwing them apart. Free of Luciano's grasp, she splashed through the stream toward the shore and Luciano tried to follow, but wherever he stepped, the sandy mud of the streambed rose to envelop and trap his feet.

Julia reached the edge of the stream, and Ulric helped her up the embankment. She looked back and called to the unseen naiad. "Thank you! You are truly a queen of swift waters!"

She fell into Ulric's arms, and they embraced. She was soaked and he was bloody, but she didn't care. It felt like an eternity since he last held her. Into his ear she whispered, "Praise Myrill, you're safe!" Over his shoulder she called, "And thank the river goddess!"

"Yes. Thank Neesis I found you." He too looked at the steam and shouted, "And praise the river goddess!"

She gave Ulric a kiss, and a swift flood of words followed. "Oh, Ulric, you're hurt! Luciano? Maybe I was wrong when I preached mercy for that dreadful man. But I was right about the naiad. I told you there had to be a potameides here! And Renier was right about piré. Vipsania was saying the Eltaran word for pyre; she wanted us to toss her into the fire! We had no idea until… Ulric! An Eltaran! An Eltaran came to us in the ruins and told us to throw her into the fire. You should have seen him. So beautiful, yet strange. He knew the flames would burn the poison out. Now I only pray to Myrill there's still time to save Rexinda and Kehindé!"

When Julia finally took a breath, they both backed away from the stream. Luciano tried to follow, but he had to fight for each step. Ulric reached behind him and drew a slender dagger. It took her a moment to realize the dagger was Luciano's.

The assassin spat a cry of frustration. "Aguja! Give her back, boy!"

With great effort, he pulled his feet from the sucking mud at the cost of one lost boot. He charged for the shore.

Laughter echoed across the stream. **"Wicked, foolish mortal!"**

Slender columns of water lifted rocks from the streambed and launched them at Luciano with painful accuracy. Battered and bruised, he stumbled back to the center of the stream.

He stood knee deep in the rushing waters, stuck in the grasping streambed, brandishing his sword at the empty air. "No hiding, river spirit! Let me see you!"

From upstream came the roar of a great flood. Then a wall of water and white foam approached with terrifying speed. Julia and Ulric held each other tight, fearing it would sweep them away, but the wall of water slowed, sending a surge over the banks that nearly knocked them off their feet. Then the waters swirled together into the form of a stunning young woman. A wreath of water lilies floated in her chestnut hair, and a gossamer gown of palest blue clung wetly to her slender body. She held a large green frond high in one hand and cradled an ornate ceramic jug with the other. She stood with perfect poise as the wave deposited her upon a large, flat rock in the middle of the stream.

The naiad looked down upon Luciano and commanded, **"Look upon me now, mortal!"**

Luciano did. Humbled, he sheathed his sword.

"Am I not magnificent?"

His mouth gaped, then shut, and went through the motions of several abandoned replies. He looked like a fish tossed on dry land. Finally, he said, "Yes."

The naiad tossed her frond and jug aside, and they disappeared into the stream with a *plop*. **"Simply 'yes?' Where is your bluster and your threats? Will you not seize me? Place a sword at my throat and leer at me? Are only mortal maidens worthy of such attention?"**

"No, no, river spirit. They—" Luciano pointed to Julia and Ulric, who stood silently on the shore "—are thieves. They steal from my… master. I here to get stolen property. Do not listen to those two. They are liars! They are—"

"Boring!" The naiad waved a hand dismissively, and a gout of sandy mud shot from the streambed into Luciano's mouth. **"When the gods battle, the heavens roil and the foundations of the world tremble. Your squabbles, mortal, are felt to me less than a leaf falling into my swift waters."**

Luciano spat out a gob of mud and tried to speak, but another blast from the streambed left him choking and sputtering. Julia and Ulric, fearing to offend the naiad, tried to stifle their laughter, but their efforts only made their giggling and eventual outburst worse. Their laughter ended when the naiad's gaze fell upon them.

Julia dropped to her knees and pulled Ulric down next to her. "Forgive us, river goddess."

The naiad spoke in a much softer tone; one filled with longing and memory. **"Ah, but young love… fleeting, ephemeral, but so much more interesting. Each lover's tale is like a sudden spring storm: filling me with life and joy until I burst my banks."** She laughed and motioned for the two young lovers to rise. **"I see all that transpires near my sacred waters." Thana, daughter of great Ulorin, has made her judgment."**

Without looking back, the naiad waved her arm, and Luciano disappeared beneath the stream.

Julia gasped. Thana's verdict was both swift and terrible. Surely, a man as wicked as Luciano deserved an abrupt and ignoble end. So why did she turn away from the churning waters where he drowned? Should she not witness the god's justice?

"Mercy!" cried Ulric. "If our tale pleases you then don't end Luciano's now. I alone must defeat him. A vow to Neesis Fortuna binds me."

"I would not offend the Daughter of Shadows. Thana grants mercy."

Luciano rose a moment later, kicking and thrashing atop a cresting wave. He coughed and sputtered, yelling threats in both Trumin and Verdan, then the wave gathered speed and tumbled him downstream and out of sight.

Julia watched as Thana washed Luciano away like some foul stain. The power and wisdom of the river goddess was breathtaking to behold. She fell prostrate before Thana and heaped praise upon her and her mighty father, Ulorin.

A surge of water lifted Thana and gently deposited her on the shore. The naiad reached out and ran delicate, pale fingers through Julia's dark curls. **"Sweet Julia, there is still time to save your companions, but you must hurry. Only a faithful follower of Myrill can aid them now. Soak their bandages in my waters and you will see healing as swift as a spring flood. Now, be quick. Go!"**

"Thank you, Thana!" Without even a glance toward Ulric, Julia ran back toward the ruins. She called over her shoulder, "May your waters flow forever!"

Ulric called to her, but there was no time to answer. She had to return to the ruins and help Rexinda and Kehindé. Only she could save them. Thana had told her so. Julia ran on, despite the terrible feeling she had left something behind.

Ahead, the ruins stood stark and black against gray ash and red skies.

Traitor of the Imperarê

Ulric took a few halting steps, then called after Julia. She ran on, never looking back. How could he be so easily forgotten? And why wasn't he running after her? He turned, gazing into the eyes of the river goddess, and understood. Thana was beautiful. Perhaps the most beautiful creature he had ever seen. At that moment, he knew the stories of heroes falling under the spell of nymphs were not exaggerated. What if she wanted to steal him away to some hidden grotto, never to be seen again? What of Julia?

Summoning the last reserves of will from deep within the shadows of his mind, he took a single step back. "I best get after Julia. Uh… again… thank you."

Thana's laughter was like the sound of a crashing waterfall. "Brave Ulric, indomitable Ulric—to be so young and think love is eternal." The nymph reached out with the back of her hand and caressed his cheek. Her touch was cool, wet, and enticing. "Hold on to her as long as you can!"

He wasn't sure what she was getting at, but he didn't like the sound of it.

"Poor thing. Here's an easier task," she said, voice flowing with mock pity. "One of those foul mortals is skulking nearby. He's hiding in the shrubs further down the hillside. Warn him to stay far from my banks." She drew closer, so close he almost forgot why he wanted to leave. "Oh, Ulric, I'd kiss you goodbye, but then you'd be mine forever."

With a wry smile, Thana walked backwards into her stream, then fell into her swift running waters and disappeared without a splash or ripple.

Ulric tore a strip of cloth from his tunic and wrapped it around his bloody forearm, then peered into the darkness while he tested his makeshift bandage. Distant voices drifted across the hillside, along with the last waning clouds of smoke and ash. He hoped Julia had rejoined the others and Myrill's Mercy hadn't arrived too late for Rexinda. He began hobbling down the hillside.

Only eyes trained in the Shadow Ways could have seen the skulking figure moving under starlight and the dull glow of distant fires. A dark silhouette slid from under a tangle of shrubs and moved away. Ulric cast off the role of the wounded soldier and followed, moving swiftly and silently down the hillside, Aguja in hand. Despite his caution, his quarry broke and ran. The man moved awkwardly, favoring his left side with each desperate step. When he strayed too close to the stream, a sudden swell of water shot across his path, sending him tumbling down the slope. Then Ulric was upon him.

The man twisted onto his back and tossed Ulric off with surprising strength. It was Decius. His stocky frame displayed a fresh saber wound on his left bicep and all along the right side of his body, red, blistering burns were visible beneath the remnants of his scorched armor. His eyes caught the faint glimmer of steel in Ulric's hand.

"Ulric! You traitor!" He rose to his feet with a pained grunt. "Come closer with that cutter so I can—"

Decius fell silent and took a cautious step back. Had he recognized Aguja? Perhaps he believed Ulric had defeated the Verdan assassin? Even wounded, Ulric knew Decius was dangerous, but he'd take what advantage he could.

"You know, Aguja? No matter," he said, returning the dagger to his belt. "I only want to talk."

Caution turned into defiance. "I have no words for a traitor."

"No, Decius, you're wrong! I'm no traitor. This is all a scheme, and the magus is my mark."

"You watched her rat-faced pet, just like I did. Tell me, when did Silo's orders change?" The question was an accusation.

"Change is constant. All I can do is give you a message for Silo. Then perhaps you'll understand. Listen! The message is: The plan proceeds. *I will* bring him the gate-stone. Agree to that and you're free to go."

"A gate what?" Decius thought for a moment. "So that's what the map leads to."

"Yes. A gate-stone. That's the only reason it's valuable."

"And you think Silo will welcome you back as a brother? After all the trouble you caused? You've made him look the fool in the eyes of the other princes. He backed you at the Concilium, but now you're known as a traitor. His humiliation has only strengthened Brocchus. And now you stand with the victors on the site of a bloody Imperaré defeat."

Ulric began to feel the weight of his crimes. Even if Silo exonerated him upon his return, this job would make many enduring enemies among the Imperaré. "My scheme never intended the spilling of Imperaré blood."

"Tell that lie to the Shrine Alley men you slaughtered." A long moment of silence passed as Decius seemed to reevaluate the dark-haired young man from Mist View. "I'll deliver your message, for what it's worth. I still say returning to Trumric is a death sentence." He started down the hill, then stopped and turned. "You know, I thought you were just another sneak-thief from the provinces. But you're something worse, aren't you? You and the Verdan deserve each other."

Ulric trudged up the hill, Decius' words gnawing at him. How did things get so muddled that Decius, a man he admired, could compare him to an assassin like Luciano? They were nothing alike! Even after everything that had happened, how could Decius not see that? Had he played the role of traitor to the Imperaré too well? When he returned to the city, would there be anything left of Ulric Darktalon, the loyal Portus Collegium thief? What if no path led back to Silo? No path that honored the sacramentum he swore before Neesis Umbra?

He expelled a discouraged sigh, then choked on a lungful of acrid smoke drifting down the hillside. Ulric tried to recall a Ghostwalker homily about honest schemes gone wrong. For a long moment, there was nothing but a haze of memory. A terrible feeling of loss and guilt settled upon him like a shroud. Were memories of Arrius already fading? No! He needed the Ghostwalker's lessons more than ever. He pushed on through the haze until he saw Arrius leaning over a railing of the narrow bridge that spanned the Tiers District of Mist View. The air was muggy, and storms were gathering above the distant ocean. They were planning their first honest scheme together. Ulric was to be apprenticed to a wealthy jeweler, one with an unsavory reputation. Arrius had cried out, "Listen up, Darktalon!"

Ulric hadn't been paying attention. He had been hanging over the railing, dropping spit balls down upon the unfortunate citizens of the warrens. Embarrassed, he stood and wiped his mouth. Arrius continued, "Never think like a mark. They think they deserve something for nothing, but the gods know everything comes at a price. A good honest scheme is a divine education."

Ulric realized he had been thinking like a mark. Everything came at a price. Including success.

Especially success.

He continued plodding toward the ruins, sinking deeper into his own dark thoughts, when an unexpected voice made him forget his troubles.

"Ouch! Hells, I thought you proper Trumrician women could sew, at least?"

It was Rexinda. She sounded slow and sleepy, but she was alive.

"Hold still!" Julia said exasperatedly. "We'd be done by now if not for your squirming."

Ulric darted into the ruins and found Rexinda next to the hastily rebuilt firepit, stripped bare above the waist and lying face down on a blanket. Julia knelt over her, tending to her many wounds. The contents of her pack lay on the ground nearby: various herbs, salves, vials, needles, sutures, and bandages. With slow, deliberate movements, she closed the long cut between Rexinda's shoulder blades by the campfire light.

Kehindé sat on a nearby wall, his wounded leg elevated and wrapped in a makeshift bandage, his saber resting across his lap. He watched the surrounding darkness as if he expected another attack.

"Rexinda," he called, "listen to Julia. And obey."

Rexinda blew air past her lips in a dismissive display. She looked up and locked eyes with Ulric as he strode into the center of camp. Frowning, she slurred, "Curse you! You just lost me twenty denarii."

Ulric, his troubles forgotten, burst into laughter. "And I'm happy to see you're alive too, Rexinda!" He knelt beside her. He wanted to reach out, take her hand, reassure her, but thought better of it. Instead, he said, "By Neesis Fortuna, you should have known better by now than to bet against me."

Julia hurriedly draped a length of blanket across Rexinda's back, then returned to stitching the wound. As she worked, she unleashed a breathless torrent of words. "Oh, Ulric, I'm so glad you're here. Pay Rexinda no mind. I had to give her a physic for the pain, and it made her a bit silly. She wanted to bet twenty denarii Thana seduced you. She swore you weren't coming back. Can you believe it?! There's still a lot to do. I need to look at Kehindé's wounds next. You must return to the stream and soak all the bandages in Thana's waters. Take Renier with you. Oh, Vipsania? I told her we'd lose Myrill's blessing if she didn't do something about all those nasty fires. They're spreading across the whole hillside!"

Magus Vipsania had brought a conflagration to the hillside, beginning with her incineration of the bowmen and continuing with her relentless pursuit of the Imperaré. Now the hill was ablaze, and the fires continued to grow. Ulric could see Vipsania and Flaccus in the distance, small black figures silhouetted against the blazing tree line. Vipsania held her rod high, and flames leaped from nearby charred branches and blackened trunks to be gobbled up in the maw of her dragon-headed rod. He wasn't sure if the dragon's appetite could match the fire's hunger.

Ulric took all the bandages Julia offered. "Now, don't worry, I'll return." He gave her a wink. "Thana and I have an understanding. I think."

Julia made her last suture and looked up curiously. "What's that?"

"I'm indomitable, and our love is eternal."

Rexinda made another rude sound. "Ha!"

"Oh, is that all?" Julia laughed. "Still, take Renier with you. Just in case."

He tucked the bundle of bandages under his arm and left. As he passed Kehindé, the man spoke.

"Ulric?"

"Yes, Kehindé?"

"The flank?"

What could he say? "I… uh…"

Kehindé reached out and put a firm hand on his shoulder. "It held."

"It held."

Kehindé nodded and returned to his vigil.

Vipsania's explosive transformation had left the campsite a blasted wreck, and her slaves were trying to salvage the mess. Predictably, they grumbled about the unfairness of it all when he took Renier with him to Thana's stream. As they walked, Ulric asked endless questions about their struggle to save Vipsania: questions about poisons, failed prayers, and the Eltaran. Most of all, he wanted to know how throwing the magus into the fire would save her.

"In Mist View, they have a saying: No good plan begins with setting yourself on fire."

Renier thought for a moment as he laid the bandages next to the stream. "Has your city suffered an epidemic of self-immolation, young master?" he asked, with such scholarly curiosity Ulric wasn't sure if he was joking. "No? Still, sensible advice… unless you're a fire magus."

"I don't understand," Ulric said.

"I'll explain as best I can, if you tell me all about the naiad." A spark danced in his old eyes as he added, "Can you call her? I'd love to see such a sight. For scholarly purposes, of course."

Ulric and Renier shared their stories as they carefully soaked each bandage in Thana's clear waters. He pressed Renier over Flaccus' insistence on providing the blood sacrifice for Julia's failed prayer. Despite his earlier insinuations, the slave would not accuse his mistress' discipulus of anything beyond foolishness. After all, if Magus Vipsania had not recovered, Flaccus would now likely be dead along with everyone else. Ulric couldn't argue with Renier's logic, but something still tugged at his mind. Then he remembered what a fellow Low Street soldier always used to say when things went wrong: people don't make any gods-damned sense.

And he asked endless questions about the Eltaran, of course. The mysterious Eltaran had saved them all. Who was he? A helpful Elt who just so happened to lurk in the ruins, brooding over his people's past glory? *Not likely*, Ulric thought. Normally, such good fortune was a blessing from Neesis, but he wasn't sure. The Elt had said he wanted Vipsania to succeed. He said there were great things to be done at Tmia Culscva. Ulric thought the Elt was a liar.

But the Eltaran had told the truth about the magus. And Renier and Julia had the wisdom to listen. The Gualdean scholar who had spent over three decades at the side of a rising dragon magus knew fire magi did not burn. That was common knowledge. What was not commonly known, explained Renier, was that the greatest fire magi could rejuvenate themselves, purging disease, restoring youthful vigor, and extending their life. They did this by walking in dragon's fire. Only after years of study and many arduous and expensive rituals would the magi be ready.

Of course, the real difficulty was finding a cooperative dragon. In the past two centuries, they had become rarer than Eltarans, but if anyone knew where they still dwelled, it was the Collegium Draconis Aurei.

"And 'piré' means 'funeral pyre' in Eltaran, as you now know, young master. Vipsania must have thought that if dragon's fire could do so much, then maybe our little campfire would be enough to burn out the poison? The Eltaran knew. And thanks be to Eltarus, it worked!"

Ulric dipped another bandage in the stream and noted the few remaining singed hairs on his arms. "Oh, it did. Rather explosively."

"I tried to warn you, young master."

"There's still something I don't understand, Renier. I've heard fire can't kill a fire magus. Makes sense. And you just said, 'fire magi do not burn.' But I saw Vipsania burning in the campfire." Ulric suppressed a shudder at the memory. "I heard her screams, saw her skin blacken."

"I wish we could have spared her such suffering, but it was necessary. The foul poison in her blood was to blame. Magus Bane not only causes chaos in the mind and pain in the body, but it also suppresses magic in the spirit. And only because the poison had suppressed her magic could we burn it out."

Ulric thought for a moment. "Then why don't fire magi just jump in a bonfire when they get the odd gray hair?"

Renier chuckled. "There are many reasons. For one, the benefit of anything less than the pure elemental fire of dragon's breath is ephemeral."

"Efem-what?"

"Short lived," explained Renier. "Second, one must burn to be renewed. Quite horrible, as you saw."

Ulric nodded, recalling the horror of Aquila Secunda's hot irons.

"And finally, don't forget the magi are priests. They risk much if they abuse Eltarus' wisdom."

Ulric considered his words for a while, working on in silence. "Magic seems overly complicated. I think I prefer the life of a simple thief."

Renier gave a noncommittal grunt. "Now tell me about the naiad. I'd like to meet this Thana."

He told Renier the story of Julia's unexpected rescue at the hands of the naiad, pointing out the flat rock in the middle of the stream where she had first appeared. He answered all the scholar's questions, describing the nymph in great detail, but he was careful to stop before Decius entered the tale. As requested, Ulric called for Thana, hoping to give Renier a glimpse of the river goddess. When she did not appear, he walked into the stream and climbed upon the flat rock to call her again, but the only answer was the sound of swift waters.

Renier told Ulric not to worry. It was foolish of him to expect a beautiful naiad to show for an old man. Besides, she had likely had enough of mortal foolishness for one night. On that, Ulric agreed.

When they returned to camp, Julia gratefully took the bandages and began dressing Rexinda and Kehindé's wounds. As she finished wrapping the dagger puncture on the Kekeksuan's thick thigh, she glared at the makeshift wound dressing on Ulric's forearm with a look of disapproval, bordering on outright hostility.

"You're next! I need to redo that mess of a bandage."

"But O' Blessed Priestess, I only had one healing hand to work with."

Julia scrunched up her face and stuck out her tongue. "No excuses!"

"I've done all I can, Julia," Vipsania said as she burst into camp and threw herself down upon a low stone wall, falling into a posture that only feigned exhaustion. At some point she must have retrieved new clothes from her luggage, as she now wore a tight sapphire stola with fiery red trim, cinched high on her waist by a golden belt. A time-worn yellow palla rested loosely on her shoulders and the rest was gathered around her left arm.

"I'm afraid flames will spread through these dry hills a while longer," continued Vipsania, "but I've created a firebreak, so we're safe if the winds turn."

Ulric looked north. The hillside was dark. Only blackened trunks and scorched earth remained where Vipsania's wrath had been, but beyond it, a red haze was growing in the sky.

Flaccus stumbled into view and sat on the ground with a thud. He fell back and let his arms fall wide. "Nothing more can be done," he added breathlessly. He pulled a cloth from his tunic and wiped the sweat and soot from his face.

"Thank you, Magus Vipsania," Julia said. "Your efforts honor Myrill Regina."

"I do not wish to offend the gods, even in our defense. When I return to the city, I'll make a great sacrifice at Myrill's temple."

Kehindé stepped forward, testing his new bandages, and sat next to Vipsania. "Thanks to this goddess' teachings, Rexinda lives. I will join you."

He reached out and squeezed Vipsania's hand. Ulric noticed the slightest hesitation, but she did not pull back as she had done when Kehindé moved to embrace her that night at the Quadrivium. He recalled his first impressions of Magus Vipsania: fading beauty, pallid skin, graying hair, eyes heavily lined and weary with ambition. Now, new color graced her cheeks, her graying hair had darkened, and the deepest lines scarring her face had gone. The fire had done more than burn out the poison.

Vipsania left the wall and knelt over Rexinda, who had fallen into a physic-induced slumber. She gently pushed back a tangle of blond locks from her face. She was about to speak to Julia when Rexinda started from her touch, ready for another battle.

"Theia! Praise Cathus for victory." Rexinda put her head back down and drifted off. "Love my Theia… put 'em to fire and sword… we did… killed the bastards… right, Kehindé?"

"We did, Rexinda."

Vipsania placed her hand on Rexinda's cheek. "Sleep, child," she said, and Ulric saw a nearly imperceptible glow as a warm aura enveloped her body. Rexinda mumbled something incomprehensible and slept. The magus stood and asked Julia, "How soon can she travel?"

"Difficult to say. She lost a lot of blood. But I have faith in Myrill… and in Thana's promise of swift healing."

"Hmm… How soon?"

Julia hesitated, clearly not wanting to commit to a deadline. "Tomorrow. If we're careful and she carries no burden, of course."

Magus Vipsania returned to the wall and sat down, staring at Rexinda in silence. There was an odd expression on her face which Ulric could not interpret. When she looked up to address the group, he realized it was simple embarrassment. He had been so certain Magus Vipsania would never display such a common failing that his mind had refused to recognize it.

"I must apologize. I was a damned fool to let my guard down after we left Corvaro. I never—"

"No!" Kehindé's voice boomed. "I should have—"

Vipsania raised a hand, demanding silence.

"Do not forget, I'm the leader of this expedition. The responsibility is mine alone. I offer no excuses; there are none. By way of explanation, I can only say I didn't anticipate anyone would be so determined to stop my research."

In exasperation, Ulric blurted out, "No one cares about your research, Vipsania! It's the map to the gate-stone those killers were after."

The magus stiffened. "More fools, them! There's no gate-stone at Tmia Culscva."

Ulric stood, mouth slightly agape, blinking. Then Flaccus shot up, resting himself on his elbows.

In unison, they asked, "What?"

THE FOLLY OF THE GATES II

Taken from the Forbidden Histories by Achle Nesvah

Neither the Gods Above nor the Gods Below paid mind to the Gates' construction. However, they caught the eye of one: the Wyrm. As one of the Gods Beyond, the Wyrm was an eldritch being, predating Alakur and the Gods Above, predating Arakru and the Gods Below. But unlike our gods, rarely did the Gods Beyond—ever asunder in their cosmic sleep—concern themselves with the affairs of Eltarans or Men. Rarely. However, the Children of Eltarus, unaware of the Wyrm's gaze, built their Gates, one for every grand city.

And so the Children of Eltarus built, and the Wyrm waited.

One night, long into the construction of the Gates, the Wyrm visited Good King Cemthsta in his sleep, haunting his dreams and twisting his mind. Vague, shadowy visions tormented the king as he slept. Images of burnt forests and ruined Eltaran cities. The next morning, Cemthsta woke with a start, his bed sheets soaked in sweat. Through his will, the King plucked from his mind the incomprehensible thoughts The Wyrm had seeded. Good King Cemthsta prayed to Eltarus for wisdom and protection, but his prayers went unanswered. So, the King summoned his closest advisors and implored them to redouble their efforts on the Gates, though he mentioned not his dreams.

And so the Children of Eltarus built, and the Wyrm waited.

For many nights, the king was tormented by singularly hideous sights. In his dreams he felt the presence of the Wyrm, though he dared not look upon him. More visions: mountains of Eltaran corpses heaped upon a desolate kingdom. The King woke every morning, tormented and soaked in sweat. Cemthsta tried to cleanse his mind of the vile residue left by the Wyrm. Again, Good King Cemthsta prayed to Eltarus. And again, his prayers went unanswered. So the King summoned his advisory council, beseeching them to hasten the construction of the Gates.

And so the Children of Eltarus built, and the Wyrm waited.

Then one night, whence the Wyrm again crept into the Eltaran King's dreams, Cemthsta was ready. This time, the King confronted the Wyrm, and addressed the eldritch God:

> "I banish thee, Wyrm!
> I banish thee from my mind!
> I banish thee from my kingdom!
> I banish thee from this Earthly realm!
> Begone, Seed of Chaos! Begone!"

But the Wyrm could not be driven back so easily and taunted the King with the tormented voices of his own ancestors. And they said unto him:

"You have no power over the Wyrm,

Oh Cemthsta, last King of the Eltarans.

Your subjects will perish, your line will end,

You have no power."

A Dawn-Spirit

Ulric's heart skipped a beat. "No gate-stone?" He summoned all his actor's training to hide his panic, instead adopting the disinterested tone of a legal debate. "But I saw the map. It says: 'Eltaran gate-stone. Guarded? Trapped?'"

Magus Vipsania stretched out along a length of warm Eltaran stone and said, "No, Ulric, it does not. You don't know what the map says because you do not read Eltaran. However, you do read Trumin. You only read the ignorant speculation crudely scrawled across the scroll. Written by whom? We may never know; I've never been able to establish the map's chain of possession. I imagine another of your ignoble profession wrote it."

"Huh. That makes sense."

Ulric sat down against a nearby wall before he toppled over. Julia, who had been repacking her healing supplies, gave Ulric a look of confusion mixed with relief. He guessed she was thinking that if there was no gate-stone, there would be no reason to betray the people they now saw as friends.

"Magus, if no one has disturbed Tmia Culscva since the Ingothian Decline, why wouldn't there be a gate-stone present?" Flaccus asked.

Flaccus' question, though it came from a mere discipulus, gave Ulric hope Vipsania could be wrong.

"You know I've never been a believer in Vitellius' rapid diaspora or Costa's calamitous comet theories. Kingdoms don't fall overnight. When the Eltaran populations migrated to the

Cloud Wall Mountains, beyond the Wild Reaches, they would have never left behind something as valuable as a gate-stone."

"Some still linger," Ulric said. "What about the Elt who appeared tonight? Who is he?"

"And why was he so eager to help?" Julia asked.

Vipsania sat up and said, "An essential question, Julia. Flaccus told me the tale, but I wish I had seen this Eltaran for myself. Perhaps Eltarus—May His Lamp Shine Eternal—sent him? A blessing from the God of Magic?"

"Wait," interrupted Flaccus, "without a gate-stone, won't your research into Eltaran Gates, aetheric transversals, and multi-domain resonance suffer?"

"It will be enough to study the architecture of their temples and examine one of their infamous Gates. If a gate-stone was present, it would only complicate matters."

Julia grabbed her pack and settled next to Ulric. "Your turn. Give me that arm." She unwound the bloody strips of tunic that made up his bandage. "Well, I'll ask. What are these Gates, exactly?"

Flaccus sat up, eager to show off his knowledge. He glanced at Vipsania and she casually waved a hand, giving him permission to proceed.

"In plain Trumin," Ulric added. "I don't know a transversal from a dimension."

Flaccus brushed bits of blackened grass from his shoulders and adjusted his tunic. "I'll speak plainly. No one knows exactly what they are. Hence, the need for our expedition. The Eltarans have always been secretive and distrustful of outsiders, even those they considered allies. To this day, they deny the Gates exist. We know they built each of their cities around a temple to their creator, Eltarus, and we believe they added the Gates to the temples in the late Ingothian period."

"And when was that?" Julia directed her question at Vipsania. Her tone made it clear she hadn't forgotten Flaccus' earlier insults. Neither had Ulric.

"Sometime around the second Angruss Rebellion," Flaccus replied, oblivious.

Ulric searched his memory, struggling to work it out. Julia leaned over and said, "A little over three and a half centuries ago."

"The most popular theory," Flaccus continued, clearly pleased to be the center of attention, "is that the Gates allowed the Eltaran priests instantaneous travel from one temple to another. We believe they are a kind of permanent magical doorway or portal, the exact properties of which are unknown."

"How interesting! None of my tutors ever spoke of such things." Julia thought for a moment while she tied off Ulric's new bandage. "With these Gates, messages and administrative orders must have flown like lightning through their kingdoms. They could have sent grain and other commodities to blighted areas instantaneously. Could they have marched a legion through them? Sending soldiers wherever necessary in the blink of an eye?"

Julia's astute observations reminded Ulric he did not sit next to a common actress, but the daughter of one of the first families of the Republic. Her father was Gnaeus Trumerus Julius, former consul of Trumric and conqueror of Baladan; her mother, Karina, was a famous beauty and a princess of Bayjon. The best tutors had educated Julia, and she had spent over a year studying medicine at the Temple of Myrill. Ulric was an ignorant provincial by comparison, despite Ghostwalker's best efforts.

Flaccus lay back down, interlacing his fingers behind his head. He considered Julia's questions. "Unknown."

"All those advantages, and they didn't go to war with the Republic?" Ulric rolled his eyes. "Instead, they just abandoned their cities. It makes no sense!"

"I agree with Ulric," Kehindé said. "There's something else. Something the Eltarans have hidden."

Vipsania leaped off the wall and stepped into the center of camp. She clasped her hands together and stood erect, as if she was about to speak in a collegium hall.

"They were hiding their shame!" she said forcefully in a lecturer's voice. "The Eltarans had been superior to mankind for thousands of years in every endeavor: magic, philosophy, agriculture, rhetoric, medicine, architecture, and conquest. That changed with the rise of the Trumin people. The Eltarans, in their hubris, had grown unbending, unchanging. Although their leaders long denied it, eventually they had to admit they had fallen behind the Republic. They wisely retreated behind their ancient borders instead of waging a war they would have lost."

Ulric raised his hand. "Will there be a test?"

Flaccus erupted in laughter, but it quickly turned into a coughing fit at a glance from Vipsania. Julia jabbed an elbow into Ulric's ribs. Hard.

Magus Vipsania glowered at Ulric, though a hint of a smile tugged at the corners of her lips. "When we reach Tmia Culscva, there very well may be."

She strode through the camp and faced Thana's stream. "Now we need to sleep," she said. Ulric heard her whispering indistinct words; perhaps Kreslan. Then she reached out with one hand, her fingers peculiarly curled, and made a beckoning motion. Curious, Ulric and Julia stood. They looked at one another, wondering what was supposed to happen. Vipsania kept repeating the chant, filling the darkness with a soft droning.

The sound changed pitch and grew louder. A swarm of green insects emerged from the darkness, shimmering like stolen emeralds on black cloth. They descended on Vipsania and surrounded her in a churning cloud of color. The insects had two sets of large, flat wings and long, narrow bodies—dragonflies.

"Oh, how beautiful!" Julia ran forward, her hands outstretched. A large dragonfly came to rest on her palm. It buzzed its wings once and was still.

She turned to Ulric. "Look!"

He had always liked dragonflies. They were never buzzing around the filth, decay, and corpses of Mist View's alleyways, the playgrounds of his youth. Instead, he recalled chasing blue-black dragonflies along the banks of the Ricmor River while Tessa toiled over the brothel's laundry. She would watch, laughing, scolding him if he became too reckless. He tried to hang on to the memory, but her hands smeared the linens with blood and the river ran red. He had to let it go.

"Don't be afraid," Julia said. "Dragonflies are harmless… mostly."

"I know what a dragonfly is," he replied dryly.

He cradled Julia's arm and looked at the insect. It was big, as long as his thumb. Its segmented body was emerald green, with faint blue highlights and a metallic sheen. Were they metallic? Maybe the green ones had copper in their bodies? The dragonfly left Julia's hand and rejoined the swarm, which now circled Vipsania in a distinct and unnatural halo.

"How are they going to help us rest?" he asked.

"They'll help me do what I should have done these past few nights." She reached out with both hands and slowly moved them through the halo of dragonflies.

"μεταμορφώνω!"

One by one, the insects were consumed by a flash of blue fire, leaving behind a body of swirling flame and wings of shimmering, translucent smoke.

"τρομάζω!"

At Vipsania's command, the swarm beat their smokey wings in unison, creating a loud buzzing that sat Ulric's teeth on edge. Julia and Flaccus plugged their ears, and even Rexinda stirred in her sleep.

"Enough!" Kehindé shouted.

Magus Vipsania made a brief gesture, and all was silent. "If any danger draws near, we will awaken to that sound." She gave the fiery swarm another command, and the dragonflies flew in all directions, becoming distant points of blue light.

Julia watched them disperse with disapproval. "Are they dead? Did your spell kill them?" she asked.

"As dead as any sacrificial animal in the temple of Myrill. They'll act as our pickets, patrolling our borders, keeping us safe. Now stop being so sentimental, child. Get some rest."

Vipsania ordered one of the slaves to prepare her bedroll, then checked on Rexinda one last time. Kehindé unfurled a blanket on the ground nearby.

"You'll stay close?" Vipsania asked him.

"Always."

With a mere glance from Vipsania, the campfire doubled in size. Finally she summoned Renier to confer with the scholar about Eltaran matters before retiring for the night.

Ulric took Julia by the hand and led her back to the secluded corner where their evening had begun. Their belongings were where they had left them, the relatively high walls of the ruin having protected them from Vipsania's explosive resurrection. He lay down on their bedroll and pulled Julia close.

"I guess we can sleep. The dragonflies will look out for us. You think Luciano drowned?"

"Ulric," Julia whispered. "What about the gate-stone? If there isn't one. Then what?"

"Don't know," he mumbled sleepily. "Too tired to think. Plunge ahead… see this Eltaran city for myself. Trust Neesis… always trust the goddess."

"Ulric, I—"

Blackness. Then dreams of black mists and terror before a dark gate.

Ulric jolted awake. He was alone. The black mists faded, replaced by Magus Vipsania's voice booming across the ruins—giving orders, as usual. He fell back into his bedroll and tried to remember the nightmare, but it was gone.

He lay there a moment, watching the stars fade out as the eastern horizon brightened. In the north, a wall of smoke and ash hung in the sky, bathed in a faint red glow: somewhere below, the forest still burned. The air was cool and still, and he could feel a dew settling. The first songs of eager robins and thrushes overwhelmed the fading drone of night insects. He loved mornings.

I love staying up for mornings, he thought, *not waking up for them!*

Sleep beckoned. He felt his mind sinking, pulled back down by Somnus, God of Sleep, Sender of Dreams. Had He sent the nightmare?

Why was he so tired? He had slept through the night like everyone else. Was it the aftermath of blade-ecstasy? Would this strange exhaustion be the price of his new combat trance? Perhaps the time needed to recover would improve with practice.

Ulric reluctantly sat up and peeked over the nearest wall. Renier and the other slaves hustled through the ruins, hastily packing up the camp under Vipsania's watchful eye. Kehindé had finished combining Rexinda's pack with his own, and he was now inspecting their weapons.

Where was everyone else? Where was Julia?

He knew she greeted every sunrise with prayers to Alakur and Myrill. What better place to pray than the banks of Thana's divine waters?

He stood and carefully stretched. His entire body hurt, the exposed skin on his front still tender from straying too close to Vipsania's flames. His nose, while thankfully not broken by Luciano's fist, was swollen, causing his entire face to ache. The gash on the side of his head still throbbed. Yet the worst wound he received had been when Luciano had disarmed him. The assassin's spatha had left a long gash on the inside of his forearm, robbing his fingers of nearly all their strength. He ran his hand over the white linen bandage: smooth, taut, with a ragged red line staining the middle. It was still damp from Thana's waters. He tried to make a fist and found surprising strength there. It appeared the naiad's promise of swift healing was true.

Ulric left the ruins and headed for the stream.

He hadn't gone far when he spotted Flaccus bounding toward him. Vipsania's discipulus cut through the high grass with the enthusiasm of someone who possessed what the Ghostwalker had called a "dawn-spirit."

Arrius and Ulric hated dawn-spirits.

Flaccus had washed away the dirt and soot of the previous night, and his reddish-brown hair hung flat and wet, exposing his prominent ears. Ulric noticed a fresh bandage on his left arm where he had made the sacrificial cut that had failed to save Magus Vipsania. The sight filled him with anger.

"Ulric!" Flaccus shouted, waving his bandaged arm. "There's something I need to say. Last night I said some… inappropriate things to Julia. Some things I regret."

He had not forgotten. Flaccus had called her a thief's whore, insulted her Bayjoni blood, and said Myrill had abandoned her. He remembered her tears.

"I apologized!" Flaccus called.

Ulric said nothing.

"She forgave me. See!"

Flaccus slowed his pace, unnerved by the silence. Ulric closed the distance.

Flaccus held up his fresh bandage. "She wouldn't have done this if—"

Ulric's fist snapped out, striking Flaccus square on the nose. He fell back and disappeared into the tall grass. When he came back up, his hands covered his face, coming away bloody. He rose to his elbows and cried, "I apologized! You didn't have to hit me!" The way his voice wavered and cracked, Ulric thought he must have hurt his feelings worse than his face.

"Of course I had to hit you." Ulric stared down at Flaccus and tried to look dangerous. "I'm Portus Collegium. Insult me or mine, and you're lucky if a beating is all you get."

"I'm sorry! I told Julia I was sorry!" Tears filled his eyes. "I thought we could be friends."

Ulric relaxed and extended a hand. "Maybe now we can."

Flaccus grasped Ulric's hand and pulled himself out of the grass. He began walking in small circles, head tilted back, nose pinched between his thumb and forefinger.

"We need to talk about the gate-stone." With his pinched nose, Flaccus' voice sounded ridiculous.

"Do you think Vipsania is wrong?" Ulric asked. "Could there be one at Tmia Culscva?"

"I think so," Flaccus replied. "But… why do you care? I thought it was the Eltaran mystery that interested you."

"It does. It always has. When so many are willing to kill for something, my professional curiosity can't help but be roused." He held his hands flat, palms inward, then slowly pulled them apart. "I'm imagining this gate-stone is a pear-sized emerald. No, maybe a melon-sized sapphire?"

Flaccus, his nose still pinched, stared at Ulric with one dubious eye. "No one knows its size; records are unclear. It's not valuable because it's a precious stone."

"Then what makes a gate-stone valuable? Vipsania thinks the Eltarans would never leave one behind."

Flaccus' brow furrowed. "The gate-stone gives a Gate its impetus, like a river gives a grain mill's water wheel power. If you had to abandon a city, I guess you'd want to take the mill with you, but that would be impossible. What if you could take the river with you instead? In your pocket?"

"Oh, I see. You can't move the Gates, but you can rebuild them. It's the gate-stones that—"

Ulric grew quiet when he saw Rexinda approaching. She walked slowly, with a straight back, arms stiff, clearly still burdened by the wound on her back. He warned Flaccus of her approach, and Flaccus hurriedly wiped away his blood and tears.

Rexinda's blonde hair, loose and unbraided, was still damp from a morning bath. She already wore her feathered cuirass and apron of bronze-weighted leather strips, despite how the heavy armor would exacerbate the pain from her wound. Considering how the Imperaré had ambushed her without armor, Ulric imagined it seemed a slight inconvenience. A new gladius with a simple black pommel hung from her belt, along with a Gualdean-style hand axe. All taken from the fallen Imperaré, no doubt.

As she walked by, she glanced at Flaccus' red-rimmed eyes, then at the Flaccus-shaped impression in the grass, then back at Flaccus. "I told you."

She stopped before Ulric.

"Darktalon."

"Rexinda. Damn good to see you up and about."

"I hear you killed three men," she remarked matter-of-factly. "And fought the assassin."

Despite her flat tone, there was something challenging in her green eyes, something alluring in the determined set of her mouth. He wanted to boast, tell her about his battles, about his blade-ecstasy, but what had he done that could compare to her accomplishments?

"True, but what choice did I have? You and Kehindé did the real fighting. You faced twenty men, and killed how many? Six? Eight? Ten?"

"None of us had a choice. We gave Julia time to save Vipsania. And she did."

"Yes, but not exactly how we expected."

"She has my thanks regardless." Rexinda drew closer. She leaned forward and whispered, "I was wrong about you, Ulric. I want to… I…"

She abruptly stepped back and slammed her palm down on the pommel of her sword. "I know you can fight now, so I expect you on the front lines in our next battle."

"Maybe there won't be a next battle."

"There's always a next battle." She turned toward camp, calling over her shoulder, "Julia's waiting for you by the stream. There's a pool under the tall oak. Hurry! We're leaving at first light."

Flaccus jogged by in a panic. "We'll finish our talk later. I haven't packed. Magus Vipsania will be furious."

Ulric found the tree far upstream from where Thana had revealed herself the night before. It was an ancient evergreen oak, whose canopy could have easily brushed his fourth story balcony back at Portus Towers. Under its thick boughs, night still lingered, and Julia knelt beside a shallow pool nestled between the roots of the massive oak. Together, the stream, the pool, the roots, and the oak formed a secluded grotto. She faced the horizon, hands held before her, palms upturned in supplication, her chanting mingling with the soft trickle of flowing water. It was a song of welcoming; a morning prayer for Alakur Brightest and Greatest.

Ulric stripped and slipped into the pool, careful not to disturb her. A gasp escaped his lips, his body tensing; the water was colder than he'd expected. He sank into the stream and leaned back on the shore. His mind sank into the shadow of his thoughts, falling deep into a Shadow Mind trance. It was a place of calm, a place of order. A place where thoughts were forged into commands the body had to obey. He took stock of his wounds, suppressing his pain and redirecting vital energy toward recovery.

He no longer felt the cold. Thana's waters embraced him like a perfect bath, the kind you never wanted to leave. All he could hear were the sounds of tumbling water and the soft breeze sighing through the boughs of the great oak.

When he opened his eyes, Julia was gone. He called out, but there was no reply. He twisted his neck and peered into the darkness beyond the grove, but there was nothing.

When he looked back, Thana stood in the middle of the pool, her chestnut curls heavy and dripping, dappled with white water lilies. The naiad reached up and pushed the straps of her gown off her silvery-white shoulders. She shrugged off the blue fabric and it fell into the pool, floating about her slender waist.

"Am I not magnificent?"

"Oh, yes. Very," was all Ulric could say.

Thana lowered herself into the pool and swam out of her gown toward Ulric. "I shall not kiss you goodbye. Unless…" She thrust out her arms on either side of Ulric's shoulders and caught herself on the bank. Her naked body floated in the water less than a hand's breadth above him. "You'd like to stay with me a little longer, mortal?" She drifted closer. Her eyes were the palest blue, almost white; beautiful, mesmerizing, but also unnaturally large, almost frightening.

He wanted to look away, but her strange beauty held him. She was magnificent! He made himself think of Julia's dark eyes, always so expressive, always filled with love. Thana's bright gaze burned through them, and Julia's face vanished. He felt himself falling into pale blue pools.

"Stay with me. Love me. I will save you such heartache," she said.

Ulric saw another pair of eyes, those of a dying man betrayed by the Dark Assembly and crucified by the Empire. He remembered the promise he made to his mentor when he fled Mist View: that he would travel to the capital to steal a fortune and become a legend.

"There's too much to do, Thana."

The naiad gave a small, disappointed sigh. "A goodbye kiss then, Ulric?"

She plunged toward him, but Ulric remembered what she had said at their last parting: a single kiss and he'd never leave the grove. He tried to slip away but Thana's bright eyes pinned him against the bank. Those pale orbs grew and grew until they filled his vision and Thana's will flowed into his mind with the irresistible weight of a waterfall, drowning all resistance. Held fast, he awaited the naiad's kiss.

Murus umbrae!

Ulric came to with a jolt, the strange command echoing in his mind. Had it been his voice, or his mentor's? He wasn't sure.

Rebuked, Thana retreated to the center of the pool, her delicate hands clutching her head.

"Who dares deny me, daughter of Ulorin? Who is this… Ghostwalker?"

Ulric tried to scramble out of the pool, but he fell beneath the water, sinking deeper and deeper into the darkness.

"Ulric!"

He awoke with a frantic splashing and sputtering. The morning sun had cleared the horizon, illuminating the pool with stark bands of golden light. Julia stood on the bank, looking more amused than concerned. She wore a long golden tunic cinched at the waist by a broad leather belt, and her green palla hung loosely on her shoulders. She held several small wreaths of fig and oak leaves, which she toyed with as she spoke.

"Are you okay?" she asked. "You started mumbling, then slipped under the water. Did you fall asleep? You've been in there far too long—you must be chilled to the bone."

He flipped onto his back and pushed himself out into the middle of the pool. "I did fall asleep. And I had a very odd dream." He tried remembering the dream and realized that, unlike his previous nightmare, he recalled every detail.

Julia watched him float, arms spread wide, naked except for his bandaged arm. "Oh! Not so chilled, I see. You had better have been dreaming of me!"

Ulric gave her a wink. "Always."

"Uh huh." Julia's eyes lingered. "Gods above! I'd join you, but I've already bathed. Now, get dressed. They're calling for us."

After a hasty bath, Ulric dressed, and they ran across the field toward the sound of Vipsania and Kehindé's impatient calls. When they arrived, everyone was eager to leave—except for Rexinda, who still fought a losing battle over her backpack. Nothing she said could convince Kehindé to let her carry a burden so soon after her wounding. While they argued, Ulric hastily gathered his own bedroll and supplies. By the time Rexinda admitted defeat, he was tightening the straps on his backpack. Then he snatched Julia's pack out of her hands and tossed it over his shoulder.

"Hey! What are you doing?"

Ulric ignored her and said to Kehindé, "We never finished our game of Spoils."

The giant Kekeksuan tugged at his short-cropped beard. "True."

"We agreed the losers would carry the victors' burdens, right? And now you carry Rexinda's pack. That means Neesis would have bestowed victory on the girls. So, I'll carry Julia's pack today."

"Unnecessary," was all Kehindé said.

Julia crossed her arms, looking lost without her pack. "Ha! We won!"

Rexinda's eyes widened with mockery. "Admitting Neesis abandoned you? After you went on and on about Her favor!"

"Neesis has never abandoned me!" He caressed the hilt of Aguja at his side. "Her divine luck doesn't come when wanted, but when needed."

"Now that we have the luggage sorted," Vipsania called from the edge of the ruins, flanked by Renier and the other slaves, "shall we proceed with our journey before we're ambushed by a second band of idiots?"

"Oh, no!" Julia cried. "Not yet."

"No more delays, child!" Vipsania said with mounting exasperation.

"But Magus Vipsania," she said, spinning Ulric about and retrieving something from her pack. "I've prayed to Myrill, and She has answered." Julia held up the small wreaths Ulric had seen her holding earlier. "I twisted these wreaths of fig and oak, and Myrill blessed each one this very dawn. While we wear them, we'll leave no trace; no footprints, no crushed blades of grass, no broken branches. Nothing for the assassin to track, assuming he's still dumb enough to come after us."

Vipsania's scowl softened. "All right. I commend your initiative. Now, distribute the wreaths and let us be off."

Flaccus stepped forward to receive his wreath and asked, "Do we have to wear it like a laurel crown?"

Rexinda shoved past Flaccus and grabbed a wreath of her own. With a sidelong glance, she said, "Think you deserve a triumphal parade for your self-inflicted wound?"

"You can wear it like a crown if you want, Flaccus. Or it could be shortened and worn on your arm like a bracer. Maybe I could make it into a necklace. Or we could wear them from our belts…" As Julia listed the possibilities, she displayed the wreaths across her body with the enthusiasm of a Night Market hawker.

"I'm sold!" Ulric took the green tangle of oak and fig leaves and placed it securely on his own tangle of black curls. "I'm feeling victorious this morning."

Flaccus turned to Ulric, and with a look of defiance likely aimed at the world as much as Rexinda, he shoved the wreath down on his head to rest upon his oversized ears.

Kehindé took a wreath and smiled. "Thank you once again, Persius Julia. And thanks to your goddess Myrill. The gods of your lands are always a wonder."

Julia studied him as he attached the wreath to his broad, bronze-plated belt. "But Myrill and Alakur are the gods of every land, Kehindé. It is only that the people of Suloko do not know them."

"Such knowledge always spreads with the march of Trumrician legions. We prefer our ignorance."

Ulric cast his eyes about their empty camp, looking for a suitable spot to test Myrill's blessing. The area around the firepit was blasted and scorched, the earth soot-covered, the grass blackened. There was no way he could cross it without leaving footprints. He grabbed the straps of his two packs and ran through the middle of the scorched ground. He looked back and saw—nothing! No. There were plenty of tracks from the morning and the night before, but had he made any now? He stepped forward and slammed his foot into a soft, sooty patch of dirt.

When he pulled it back, it disappointed him to see the imprint of his sandal.

An instant later, the tiny mounds of soot at the edge of the print swept inward as the ground rose and smoothed the footprint out of existence. Delighted, he turned and performed an absurd backwards jig across the firepit, torso forward, knees high, feet stomping. He laughed as his footprints vanished one by one.

Nearby, Flaccus repeatedly smashed his foot into a tuft of tall grass, watching the blades spring up perfectly straight and unharmed each time.

Sweet Neesis Umbra, patron of all thieves! I wonder if Julia can make these whenever she wants? Could be particularly useful for some burglaries.

Julia gave a wreath to Renier and each of the three slaves, then Magus Vipsania took the last. Rexinda, who had twisted her wreath into an arm bracer, insisted on weaving Vipsania's wreath into her hair. The magus protested the absurdity, the vanity, and the waste of time, but she relented when Kehindé reminded her it had been a fashion in the days of her youth.

Finally, they left the ruins and headed west toward the wild expanse known as the Silva Aurea. Ulric wasn't sure where the forest really began or ended. It seemed to him they were already there. The wooded hills, glades, strange ruins, and even Thana were all a part of the forest. They were the land's outer pickets; sentries standing guard between Trumrician civilization and old Eltaran secrets.

A Broken World

Luciano's eyes fluttered open to rustling leaves and the gentle babble of flowing water. His senses, dulled by the fog of unconsciousness, gradually sharpened as he took in the world around him. The sun had just begun to crest the horizon, casting a golden hue over the land.

His damp clothes clung to his skin, and his hands were cold and wet; he realized he was lying on the bank of a stream, the crisp, cool water lapping at his fingertips. His body ached, though he couldn't remember how he had ended up there. And why was he wearing only one boot?

Then the memories came flooding back: the magus, the girl, Darktalon, the naiad, and then… darkness.

Approaching footsteps pulled him back to the present. Luciano's hand instinctively moved to his waist, but his precious Aguja was no longer there. *Darktalon!*

He looked up at the pitiful figure hunched beside him. It was a wiry young man with hollow eyes and a nervous twitch, one of the many Imperaré thugs who had been sent with him on this gods-damned mission. Luciano thought Vico was his name, though he couldn't quite remember. The thug clutched his side, a dark stain spreading across his tattered shirt.

"You're awake," the man croaked, his voice trembling. "I thought… By the looks of you, I thought you were already floating down the River Nyx."

Luciano sat up slowly, his movements calculated despite the pain that lanced through him. He scanned his surroundings but saw no sign of Darktalon or the girl. "Where everyone else?" His voice was low, commanding, though edged with a weariness he couldn't mask.

The thug winced as he shifted closer, his hand still pressed to his wound. "Most are dead. Seen a couple make it out, I think. Who knows? The dragon magus, that big Keksu, all the others—they just disappeared." He swallowed hard, his eyes fading into blank globes. "And that fire… All that dragon fire!"

Luciano's expression remained inscrutable, though a cold rage simmered inside. One thing was clear: Raquin had betrayed him. And betrayal had a bitter taste sensation Luciano knew all too well. His plan had failed, and that Elt had had a hand in its undoing, leaving him with nothing but the taste of defeat and his own blood.

"And you?" Luciano asked, his tone sharp. "How you survive?"

The man hesitated, his eyes flickering with something that looked like guilt. "I fled," he admitted, his voice barely above a whisper. "When the dragon fire started, I… I couldn't… They screamed. They all screamed as the flames ate their flesh." Vico trailed off, his shoulders sagging.

For a moment, Luciano said nothing. The surrounding land was alive with the sounds of morning, birds chirping in the trees, the stream flowing steadily past. It was a stark contrast to the violence that had taken place mere hours ago. He stood, his decision made.

Revenge.

Yellow tendrils infiltrated his head.

But first… of course… resume the hunt for the dragon magus and the map.

With that, the pain subsided. Luciano was weaker than he would have liked, but there was no time to waste. Best place to start would be the ruins. From there he could pick up the Eltaran's trail.

"Cowardice should be punished," he said, his voice as cold and sharp as the blade he unsheathed. "Or I can forgive, eh?"

Vico nodded vigorously, relief flooding his features. "I'll do whatever you need, boss. I swear it."

"We go." The assassin had been bested but not defeated, and he didn't need a yellow spike of pain to remind him the chase was not over.

He needed to pick up the trail once more, so he headed upstream, albeit at a respectful distance in case the naiad took offense. He had to catch up to the magus and complete his mission. Kill her, perhaps? And Raquin would die, too—if he could find him.

Eager for Eltaran blood, the assassin marched back toward the ruins.

But the trail had gone cold.

No footprints, nor broken branches, nor errant belongings. Nothing. Not even a bent blade of grass. The field north of the ruins was littered with bodies, and Luciano took the opportunity to liberate a decent pair of boots from its dead owner. However, the magus and her expedition were gone, and there was no telling in what direction.

Luciano slumped against a granite outcropping and tried to think. There had to be an answer. Everything left a trace. As he scanned the crumbling walls and broken columns to the south, something caught his attention: a wisp of long white hair behind a pillar of red stone. His eyes narrowed into predatorial slits. There—a brightly colored frock revealing a slender, sun-kissed arm. Luciano grinned, pointing, and the Imperaré heavy nodded.

Luciano whispered, "Make you way through grass to west. I go east. Wait for my signal. We attack together. He cannot defend against both of us."

Vico did as he was told and disappeared under waves of grass.

Luciano slithered through the tall grass, moving in the opposite direction until he reached a crumbling wall of fire-blackened Eltaran stone. From his hidden vantage point, he watched Raquin move like a blur from pillar to pillar, on a collision course with Vico.

With the Elt's attention diverted, Luciano closed the distance, using the occasional ruined wall or column for cover. The foolish Imperaré thug had obviously lost track of the Eltaran, who now stalked him. All the while, Luciano closed in on his own unsuspecting quarry. Raquin quietly unsheathed his blade; the golden, wing-hilted sword reminded Luciano of his first encounter with the Elt back in Mist View. That had not ended in his favor, but it would not happen a second time.

The Elt flattened himself against a large column and waited, affording Luciano the opportunity to sneak even closer to his prey. The morning sunlight bounced off a sliver of Trumin steel in the grass. There was a blur of hair and feathers, followed by a single stroke of an Eltaran sword.

Luciano couldn't see Vico, but the blood-choked gurgle and crimson spray told him enough.

Raquin returned sword to sheath and stood triumphantly over his victim, nudging the body with his boot.

Luciano leaped at the Elt from behind, sticking a dagger at his back and placing his falcata along his throat.

"You betray me, Elt." He put pressure on the dagger, allowing it to penetrate clothing and Eltaran skin. Raquin did not move.

"Now we see if Elts bleed blue like they say. Eh?"

Raquin dropped his sword.

"I kill you," Luciano said, his voice low, almost a growl. He stared into the heart of the nearby Silva Aurea forest. "Then I finish this... gods-damned mission," he said, returning his attention to the Eltaran. He pushed the dagger in a little further.

Raquin flinched. "A mission, yes, but an unwelcome one."

Luciano grunted.

"Brocchus truly is your master, is he not?"

Luciano tapped Raquin's chin with his blade, a not-so-subtle reminder of his precarious predicament. "Shut up! You betrayed me. Talk to girl. Help her save magus life. Help Darktalon! You betrayed me, you fucking Elt! Almost get me killed!"

Raquin winced as the assassin's sword pressed against his throat. "You have it wrong! It's not a betrayal, Luciano. It's merely part of a bigger plan! We are allies, remember? You and I have been sent together on this mission. By Brocchus."

"You shut you mouth, Elt. We not allies."

"Brocchus… He has cast some sort of compulsion upon you, hasn't he? A compulsion is powerful magic. Not the deep magic known to the Children of Eltarus, of course, but powerful nonetheless. Yes, a compulsion forces you to act against your own interests. I see that."

Luciano felt his heart thumping hard against his chest as it heaved. "You know nothing, Elt. You are liar. And betrayer."

"I know this: Brocchus has enslaved you. And your mission to find—no, steal—" Raquin's body trembled with barely suppressed rage "—your mission to steal… our map!" He took a deep breath and lowered his voice before continuing. "This mission is not your own, but you cannot defy him, can you? Not without pain. Or worse."

"Your words mean nothing, Elt. Nothing! Now I—"

"I know people that can help you, Luciano. Priests of Eltarus that know the deep magic. Eltaran enchantments. They alone know the spells that can release you from such bondage. From that pain which torments you. With their aid,

I can…" Raquin chose his words carefully. "I can offer you freedom."

Luciano winced just hearing the word. "You gods-forsaken Elt! You trying to scheme me? I kill—"

"Wait!" shouted Raquin, his voice hinting at panic. "I will help you. I'll help you find the magus and retrieve the map. Together, we can complete the mission! Once you're free, you can do as you will."

Luciano grunted, then smiled sarcastically. "What you angle, Elt? You bargain for you life now, but you make no sense. Why help me?"

"Because you know the truth, as I do." Raquin paused as if waiting for a response. When the assassin offered none, he continued. "This world is broken, taken over by corrupt men—imbecilic men—who enslave the rest. You've seen this firsthand. Look at your own life. You've become nothing more than a slave, a puppet whose strings are pulled by Brocchus and his kind."

The name made Luciano's blood boil, causing him to grit his teeth. Then came the yellow shards of agony once again. He closed his eyes tightly, holding back a gasp.

"You see? You have no free will. Truly, none of us do. The world has been upended. Broken. By weak men who worship even weaker gods."

Luciano spoke through labored breaths. "What you get at, Elt?"

"It wasn't always this way. At the dawning of our world, things were right and just. I intend to peel back the layers of time and usher in a new era. A golden age of freedom and might to replace this age of servitude and weakness."

Luciano allowed the Elt's last few words to bloom in his mind. "Get on you knees, Elt."

"What?"

"Get. On. You. Knees. Now!"

Raquin complied.

With his blade still at Raquin's throat, Luciano sheathed his dagger and retrieved the Elt's weapon from the ground. He removed his blade from Raquin's throat, pushed him prone, then took a few steps backward. "Nice sword. Eltaran steel. Light but deadly."

Raquin, now crouched on all fours, said nothing.

"Maybe when I kill you, I take this, eh?" Luciano taunted.

Raquin turned to face Luciano and glared at him with intense red eyes.

Luciano released a hyena's laugh, then approached, a sword in each hand. "I let you choose, Elt. Which one slice you neck? Heh."

Raquin's eyes flashed in response, though he made no attempt to flee. "Tell me, Verdan. How do you plan on tracking the magus now that she has concealed her trail?"

Luciano gritted his teeth, but offered only a grunt in response.

"What if I told you I know exactly where they went?"

He furrowed his brow, but still said nothing.

"The Trumins call it 'Tmia Culscva,' but its true name is hidden from men. It was one of the great Eltaran cities of old. That is their destination. And I know how to get there."

"How you know this, Elt?"

"Because I was born there."

The two stared blankly at each other, saying nothing.

Raquin was the first to speak. "There, in the heart of my birthplace, lies the key to welcoming back the old gods. Together with our true king, they will usher in a new age. At last, I will break the chains the Children of Alakur have forged, and free my people. Along with you." The Eltaran licked his lips before continuing. "But I need the dragon magus' aid. Long ago, the Gates were sealed behind powerful Eltaran wards, preventing any Child of Eltarus from reaching them. No Eltaran shall ever possess the power to break them. Fools! They had no vision of the future. Of what could be!"

There was something in Raquin's blood-red eyes. Something familiar and strange at the same time—clarity mixed with madness.

"So I need the dragon magus to break the wards."

"More lies, Elt?"

"Why do you think we arranged for the map to fall into the hands of men?"

Luciano studied Raquin closer than ever. *If he leads me to the magus, I won't have to return to Brocchus in failure. So I can still use him. And the rest? We shall see, Elt.*

He lifted Raquin to his feet.

"My sword?"

Luciano looked guardedly at Raquin before inspecting the Eltaran's blade once again. He laughed, taunting the Elt with a sound filled with more malice than mirth. In one hand he held the golden-hilted blade, and in the other his new falcata. Glancing at Raquin with indifference, he dropped the sword at the Eltaran's feet.

"We go."

The Light of Revelation

With the Eltaran map as her guide, Vipsania led the expedition deeper into the Silva Aurea. At the end of each march, they made camp in a defensible spot chosen by Kehindé. Then Vipsania would summon a swarm of flying creatures to stand guard throughout the night.

In the evenings, many games of spoils were played. Everyone agreed Ulric had uncanny luck with the dice—everyone but Rexinda, who promised to give him a proper thrashing when she proved he was cheating.

On the morning of the third day, Magus Vipsania called for a halt, stopping the expedition on the side of a gentle slope covered in a thick carpet of broad-leafed shrubs. Rows of slender beech trees, their gray trunks straight and smooth, formed an endless colonnade like some impossibly vast temple.

Vipsania and Kehindé strode to an outcropping of rock rising from the hillside. It stood as tall as a three-story insula, sharp and angular, thrusting into the sky as if Arakru had thrown a spear into the roof of the Underworld. The entire structure looked as if giants had broken apart blocks of red stone and haphazardly re-stacked them. Vipsania pressed her back against the cliff face and walked a precise number of steps forward, then unfurled the Eltaran map.

Ulric watched her with growing anticipation, but Vipsania only stared at the map.

With groans of relief, the slaves walked up and dropped their burdens on the ground. One young slave joined Ulric, fear and worry creeping across his face. He turned to Flaccus and asked, "Master Flaccus, what is the mistress doing, if I may ask?"

"You may not," Flaccus replied.

The slave shrunk back and turned to Renier. "I have decided I dislike forests," he said. "There's something evil about them."

Renier looked at him as if he had discovered a new species of idiot. "Bah! Nonsense. Well… it depends, really. Master Ulric! Remind me to share the tale of the Harathi chieftain Trostheri, who pursued the malefica Willelda into the Tangled Forest."

"I will. When we're safe on the streets of Trumric." He stepped closer to Flaccus and leaned in conspiratorially. "She's doing something with the cipher, isn't she?"

"Yes. It's time."

"What do you mean?"

"Why do we need a map at all?" Flaccus asked, in the tone he might use on a collegium student he had caught copying his notes. "Why haven't looters or some woodsmen stumbled across the Eltaran city in the last few hundred years? Think about it. We're not *that* far from civilized lands."

"Okay," Ulric said, suddenly feeling stupid. "It's hidden. I get it."

"No, you don't. More than distance, memory, and centuries of forest encroachment hide the Eltaran city. The Eltarans were first in magic, and they perfected the art of fabrication. It's said their illusions even impressed Eltarus."

"So the cipher opens the illusions like a key opens a lock?"

Flaccus broke into a wide, goofy grin. "Now you get it." Then he looked back to Vipsania and he pressed his lips together. "She's ready. This might feel a bit… weird."

Vipsania stood before the cliff face with her back toward the rocks, taking one last look at the cipher. Then she unleashed a staccato series of Eltaran words, her powerful voice echoing through the beechwood colonnade.

Ulric felt the strange tingling he had sensed in the stones of the Eltaran ruin—the sensation he now knew meant deep magic. Then everything became a blur. His stomach lurched, and the whole world shifted around him. With great effort, he kept his balance. To Flaccus, who was only swaying a little, he said, "Right. Weird."

Julia, who had been chatting with Rexinda nearby, clung to a slender beech tree, looking nauseous. "Ooh, whatever that was, let's not do it again."

Rexinda had fallen to one knee. She drew her new gladius and shouted, "Battle 'n blood! What the fuck was that?"

"The shattering of a fabrication, I believe," Renier said over the sound of one of the slaves vomiting his midday rations.

Ulric looked around and realized the cliff face, the hillside, the trees, were not as they had been. Vipsania and Kehindé now stood on the other side of the rocks, and everyone faced the crest of the hill instead of standing along its slope. Ulric peered through the forest canopy, trying to catch a glimpse of the sun or the wall of gray smoke in the north—anything to get his bearings.

Kehindé stepped onto a path of half-buried Eltaran stone that hadn't been there before. "Now that we're marching in the right direction—double time!" He charged down the path, devouring the hill with his impossibly long strides.

With a flourish, Magus Vipsania slid the Eltaran map back into its scroll case. "The cipher works!" She ran after Kehindé, shouting, "No time to dawdle! Come along, now!"

Julia grabbed Ulric's arm and leaned on his shoulder. "Ugh. That felt terrible... wrong."

"We were heading the wrong way? How in the Nine Gates?" Rexinda asked.

Flaccus rolled his eyes. "I've explained it already." He turned to Ulric. "Ulric?"

"Uh... it's a key that's not a key..."

"Master Flaccus, with your permission?" Renier asked.

"Yes. But explain as we march."

"Of course, Master Flaccus." Renier hoisted his pack and everyone hurried after Vipsania. "You see, three walls of fabrication protect the city of Tmia Culscva. Not walls of wood or stone, of course, but of illusion. Any who stray too close are turned away. They become like rocks skipping across the surface of a pond; they bounce off the water but never sink beneath. Fortunately, we have the Eltaran map. We can find the weak point in each wall where the cipher—the key Ulric mentioned—can shatter the fabrication."

The expedition followed the remnants of the Eltaran road into a ravine of steep paths and deep shadow. It eventually spilled into a broad valley of immense ash and oak, where the next landmark was located.

At first, it appeared to be nothing more than a fallen tree caught between two great oaks. Then Ulric saw past the blanket of moss and entwining vines to the dark stone beneath. An obelisk of black stone. A monument of some sort? Did he stand on the site of a great Eltaran victory? Or was the obelisk just an overly elaborate sign post?

Whatever it was, everyone was better prepared when Vipsania read the second cipher. Once again, the world shifted as she destroyed the Eltaran illusion.

It was nearing the eleventh hour of the day when they reached the third landmark and thus the innermost wall of illusion. With little daylight left, a premature dusk settled under the thick canopy of the Silva Aurea. The occasional bit of Eltaran stone underfoot was the only reminder that the tangled path they walked upon may have once been a broad thoroughfare.

Ulric had never felt claustrophobic navigating the warrens of Mist View or forcing his way through the capital's surging crowds, but there was something about the closeness of the forest that unnerved him. Here the trees towered taller than any monument, with trunks thicker than the columns of the greatest temples. No sea breeze disturbed the heavy air. There was no market chatter to drown out the call of strange beasts. Ulric knew what dangers hid in a Mist View alley or a River Market taberna, but he didn't know what lurked in this forest, where a blood-red glow oozed through the tangle of trunks and branches like a seeping wound.

Everyone fell silent; they needed no command. Kehindé drew his Bayjoni saber and crept toward the red light. Rexinda joined him, her new gladius at the ready. Magus Vipsania waited a moment, then followed, dragging Flaccus in her wake, who chanted the Kreslan words for fire, flame, and pain in hushed, nervous tones. Finally, Ulric drew Ghostwalker's spatha and led Julia into the undergrowth.

"Is that who I think it is?" Kehindé asked, his booming voice shattering the silence.

"It is," Vipsania replied.

Ulric and Julia slipped from the tangled greenery and walked into the strange red light. Together, they exclaimed:

"Sweet Neesis!"

"Mother Myrill!"

It was neither. A statue of Eltarus, God of Magic, stood in the center of a small clearing, rising to a height that rivaled the surrounding oaks. The god wore a long, cloak-like garment over a tunic that flared into a short skirt. It was a decidedly un-Trumin style, and Ulric had seen none of the gods depicted with such odd clothing. He wondered what colors the strange garments had been; any paint had chipped and faded away long ago, leaving only stark white marble under a layer of dirt and moss. In his right hand, Eltarus held his Rod of Magic tight against his chest. In the other, the Lamp of Revelation hung from an adamant chain, bathing the surrounding woods in a dull red glow rather than the golden light of a traditional Eltaran lamp.

Vipsania consulted the map once more. "This is the next landmark." She looked down at the scroll, then said in an uncertain tone, "The final landmark... but the penultimate cipher."

Ulric searched his memory for the meaning of the word "penultimate." His struggle must have been evident, for Flaccus began to speak, a self-satisfied look on his face.

"Next to last," Ulric said, cutting him off.

"Correct." Flaccus looked surprised and a bit disappointed.

"Remember what I said back at the Quadrivium? I'm an educated thief."

"And a very boastful one!" Julia added.

"It's not boasting if it's true."

Rexinda rolled her eyes. "Ugh. Gods save us!"

Julia looked up at Eltarus' Lamp. "Why is it emitting that terrible red glare? Shouldn't it be golden?"

Flaccus followed her gaze. "Simple. Magic lamps don't last forever, but they do last for a *very* long time. Assuming this one began with traditional golden light, then its magic hasn't been replenished for... hmm... roughly three hundred and ninety years. Give or take."

"Excellent, Flaccus," Vipsania called from beneath the towering shrine. "So you *were* paying attention to my lecture on chromatics." She positioned herself under Eltarus' lamp, then faced the woods, imitating the posture of the shrine. Ulric thought the god's stony gaze looked over the forest with just the right mixture of serenity and divine smugness.

Kehindé's powerful voice called for quiet. "Vipsania is ready to read the cipher. Prepare yourself."

She began reciting the Eltaran cipher, each word echoing through the clearing, building to a crescendo that would shatter the final fabrication.

Everyone stepped back and prepared for the now-familiar stomach-churning sensation.

When it was over, it surprised no one to learn they had been facing the wrong direction; the clearing had changed and shifted around them. Now, Eltarus' Lamp pointed down a previously unseen road of well-preserved Eltaran stone.

Kehindé suggested the clearing would be a good place to take a brief rest, and Vipsania agreed. She approached the massive stone plinth and reverently knelt at the statue's feet. Ulric tossed his sandals aside and leaped upon the base. He began scaling the shrine, using the straps of Eltarus' sandals as handholds.

Vipsania sprang to her feet. "What are you doing? Get down!"

Ulric had already reached Eltarus' calf, so he continued climbing. "Don't you want to know how close we are?" he asked. "Maybe I can see the ruins from up here!"

"From down here," Vipsania shouted, "it looks like sacrilege!"

Ulric was at the hardest part; there was too much smooth marble from knee to thigh. He relished the difficulty of the climb, despite the transition from thigh to flared skirt leaving him hanging far above the forest floor, his feet dangling in the air.

Julia gasped and cried out for him to be careful.

I'm always careful, woman! He thought. *...Okay, we both know that's not true.*

He pulled himself higher, resting his chest on the hard, cool stone, then stretched and felt for another handhold. He seized a fold in the marble and scrambled onto the skirt. The strength in his grip was a testament to Julia's skill and Thana's promise of swift healing.

The folds in Eltarus' strange clothing made the rest of the climb much easier. In no time, Ulric stood on the shoulder of the god. He had risen above the gloom beneath the Silva Aurea, but he still couldn't see over the forest canopy. The Lamp of Revelation still beckoned, held high in the statue's left hand.

"I still can't see over the treetops!" he yelled. "I can get the best view from atop the lamp!"

He took a few tentative steps forward, then looked back to see the god watching him with barrel-sized marble eyes. Eltarus did not look pleased. Ulric knew the god had a reputation for impulsiveness, mischief, cruelty, even. It was where the Elts got their most charming traits. He decided a quick prayer to the God of Magic was best. Unsure of the proper form, he kept it simple and assured the god he meant no disrespect. He turned back to the lamp, drew a "∞" in the air for luck, and walked out onto the arm. The limb was broad, his balance excellent, and the red glow of the lamp didn't look so ominous mingled with the late afternoon light.

The sound of cracking marble echoed across the treetops, causing a nearby flock of blackbirds to take to the sky.

Ulric froze. His heart skipped a beat. Had Eltarus not heard his prayer?

He stood motionless, a few steps past the statue's huge elbow. Looking over the arm, he spotted several hairline cracks he hadn't noticed before. But he could almost see above the treetops! So close! The arm had held for centuries. Surely it could handle his paltry weight. He took a single step forward, concentrating on the vibrations from the marble underfoot. Everything else became distant and muted, like the sound of Julia's fretting and Vipsania chastising him for his foolishness. Ever so slowly, ever so carefully, he ascended the arm toward the Lamp of Revelation.

What do the priests and magi say of the Lamp of Revelation? That it guides men toward the truth. And a man finds either wisdom or their doom. Hmm. I can't say the truth and I have been on good terms.

Ulric reached the statue's highest point: the fist that grasped the adamant chain suspending the Lamp. He ignored the small fortune of metal beneath his feet and scanned the horizon.

The Silva Aurea stretched endlessly in all directions. After the gloom of the forest, the glare and heat of the setting sun were overwhelming. The way sunlight highlighted the tallest trees in stark greens and yellows while casting other regions in deep shadow reminded Ulric of a vast, undulating ocean. Instead of a sea breeze, there was a pleasant, earthy scent, the smell of countless growing and blooming things.

And there was something else in the air. He looked to the northeast; the clouds of gray smoke from Vipsania's fires were still there. They had risen so high their tops were being sheared off by impossibly distant winds. He couldn't be sure, but he hoped the forest fires were finally ending.

He turned to the east. The sky was hazy and growing dark. Somewhere in the capital, Silo waited. Ulric wondered if Decius would deliver his message as promised. Did he hear the marble groan?

He turned his gaze southward, shielding his eyes from the setting sun. There appeared to be an island rising out of the ocean that was the Silva Aurea canopy. He glimpsed a dark mound the size of a mountain, with stepped, symmetrical sides, surrounded by a forest aglow with thousands of red Eltaran lights.

Ulric felt a tremor underfoot.

Race back to the shoulder, or leap for a nearby branch?

Before he could finish his thought, there was a cracking, grinding sound like thunder, and the statue's arm snapped below the elbow. The hand of Eltarus and the Lamp of Revelation plunged toward the forest floor. Ulric followed to his doom.

"Sweet Neesis!"

He kicked off the god's knuckles and tried to reach the nearest tree. He now fell to his death with a handful of useless twigs and oak leaves.

Below, Julia shouted something about "Daughter Caris and Mother Myrill." Then the closest ash tree miraculously sprouted a new branch. Long, slender, and supple, it grew into Ulric's path.

He caught it with both hands and swung around it, his shoulders straining and his palms chafing on the young bark. The branch, green and flexible, bent to its limit. Marble arm and adamant lamp continued toward the ground, impacting with a terrific crash that echoed throughout the forest.

Ulric looked down, desperate to know if Julia and the others were safe. Fortunately, everyone had scrambled out of the way.

"I'm alright!" he cried as the last echoes of the fallen marble died. "I—"

The branch snapped. It was a short fall onto the springy turf of the forest floor, and he hit the ground and rolled. He planned to spring up in triumph, ready to share what he had seen. Instead, his feet got tangled in the shattered lamp's chain and he hit the ground in an embarrassed jumble of limbs. He rolled onto his back and took a moment to catch his breath. Overhead, a one-armed Eltarus gazed off into the distance.

Julia rushed to his side, her dark eyes filled with worry. "Are you hurt?"

Ulric held up his scraped hands and shrugged.

She crossed her arms and said, "I warned you to be careful."

Magus Vipsania and Kehindé came into view. "Desecrator!" she said. "I don't have to be an auger to know this is an ill omen."

Kehindé looked unconcerned. "This story was told long ago," he said. "Why worry about it now?"

"Do you even try to understand the Trumin way?" Vipsania's tone spoke of an old, well-worn argument.

"Hrmph," was all Kehindé said.

Vipsania turned away in exasperation and looked down at Ulric. "And you! So you're going to keep us safe from the 'guards' and 'traps' at Tmia Culscva, huh? And how do you propose to do that, hmm?" She stared at him impatiently. "Well?"

Ulric considered the question.

"Hrmph."

Vipsania ignored him and busied herself by performing rites of purification upon the statue's remains, then praying to Eltarus for forgiveness. When she had done all that she could, the expedition followed the well-preserved Eltaran road.

A few miles south of the now-armless shrine, the forest air was filled with the unmistakable scents of civilization. First, there was the sting of smoke from hundreds of cooking fires, mixed with the aroma of herbs both familiar and strange. Next came the inevitable reek of thousands of people and livestock packed inside high city walls. Then the trees began to vibrate with the faint drone of distant crowds.

It seemed the Eltarans had not abandoned their city, after all.

Tmia Culscva

Vipsania and Kehindé sprinted down the remnants of the old Eltaran road, impatient to stand before the walls of an inhabited Eltaran city. As Vipsania ran, she shouted out several questions to no one in particular: Why lie about abandoning the Silva Aurea? Would the Eltarans honor the old treaties? Would they welcome her? Or turn her away?

Or worse? Ulric thought. *There's a third option, Vipsania. How do we know these Elts won't be furious that you broke their illusions? If they want to keep their secrets, maybe they'll just kill us all.*

The buzz of faraway throngs grew into the din and racket of a bustling city. Far ahead, through the thinning trees, Ulric glimpsed impossibly tall walls of red stone. He feared running headlong into Tmia Culscva's front gates. What thief used the front door? One with a great scheme, he thought, but Vipsania had none. He tried to catch up, desperate to warn her, but the extra burden of Julia's pack slowed him down. Just as he reached the magus, they burst out of the forest's edge.

A massive rectangular gatehouse of pale Eltaran stone stood before them, its roof crenelated and rimmed by dragon-headed sculptures. The city walls, so smooth they appeared to have been conjured from a single, vast block of stone, stretched into the distance. A wide blood-red stripe ran the length of the walls, bordered by narrow yellow bands filled with strange geometric patterns. Ulric's eyes ached when he stared at them for too long. The gates of the city stood wide open.

The rest of the expedition followed Ulric out of the forest and gathered around Magus Vipsania, where they stood speechless, marveling at the walls of Tmia Culscva.

Julia stared at the walls as if she might see through them with great effort. "The Eltarans built things far grander than I ever imagined," she said, then shuddered as if she had glimpsed something horrifying hiding behind the red stone. "But there's something wrong… something missing."

"Magus Vipsania," Ulric said, "maybe we should—"

A bell rang from somewhere high within the gatehouse, and a score of Eltaran spearmen marched out. Each soldier wore a short, brightly colored sleeveless tunic and a conical helmet with a tall crest of red and green feathers. A fierce Eltaran armored in a golden breastplate and helmet took the lead as the roof of the gatehouse swarmed with archers.

"No one says a word!" Vipsania commanded. "I alone speak to the Eltarans."

Kehindé chuckled. "Not like I speak Eltaran."

Vipsania gave him a playful, if somewhat exasperated, look. "You know as well as I that one does not always need to know a word to understand its meaning." She turned and addressed everyone. "I didn't come this far to end up fleeing for my life over an errant phrase or gesture." Her eyes lingered over Rexinda. "Keep your hands off your weapons."

Rexinda threw her hands into the air and pouted, an expression she reserved exclusively for Kehindé and her theia.

Then Vipsania's gaze struck Ulric. "And you! You keep your mouth shut."

Ulric pointed at his chest with an exaggerated look of confusion and silently mouthed, "Me?"

Magus Vipsania spun and boldly marched to meet the Eltaran spearmen. Everyone else followed with decidedly less enthusiasm.

Julia grabbed Ulric's arm and leaned close. She spoke in a whisper, so rapidly her words seemed to smash into one another. "There's something about this city I don't like. It seems hollow. Godless, somehow. Still, it's exciting. I haven't seen an Eltaran since I was little, and even then only at a distance. And you? Ulric! You're finally going to meet the Eltarans. Remember, don't call them Elts; they don't like that. Do you think they'll let us in? Or turn us away? I almost wish they'd send us away…"

"I don't know. What I'd like to know…" Ulric had wanted to ask Julia why the Elts were guarding a road from nowhere. He wanted to know why they allowed the forest to grow wild within a few dozen paces of the city walls. Growing up in Mist View, he had overheard enough arguments between army veterans to know a city typically cleared the surrounding countryside to provide an unobstructed view of approaching enemies.

But the question died on his lips, his doubts shoved aside by a new, uninvited idea: It all made sense, and he would understand once he passed through the gates.

The lead guard shouted *"Mur!"* in a deep, resonant voice, and the Eltarans stopped within two spear lengths of Vipsania. At the command of *"Thina!"* the guards swiftly surrounded the expedition, lowering their spears with a snap. The guard then spoke to Vipsania in what sounded like a mishmash of Eltaran sounds. Unfazed by the martial display, she responded in kind.

Ulric glanced at Flaccus and waved him over. "What are they saying?"

"Yes, I'd like to know too," Julia whispered, huddling close.

"Me too!" Rexinda said, too loudly. Ulric grinned upon seeing her arms crossed, fingers fidgeting; anything to keep her hands away from her weapons.

"Uh, he said something like, 'Uninvited guests are often most welcome when they leave.' Then the magus introduced herself, emphasizing her position as a high priestess of Eltarus and reminding them of their alliance with the Trumin people and their treaty obligations. Now he's saying…"

While Flaccus translated, Ulric took a moment to get a good look at the mysterious Elts.

Eltarans were tall. Taller than the average Trumin, though not as tall or as powerfully built as the men north of Gualdé. Their skin ranged from deeply tanned to golden brown, with hair of darkest black, brightest gold, or silvery white. Their ears were pointed, but it was their eyes that were most extraordinary; they were narrow and slightly upturned with creaseless eyelids, like the people from the far east beyond Bayjon. Their color was at once alluring and frightening, ranging from unnatural pale blues to a terrifying red.

It all conspired together to give the Elts a mischievous, if not outright sinister, look. Ulric didn't trust them.

No. All will be fine, he thought.

Negotiations between Vipsania and the guard ended abruptly, and Flaccus finished his translation.

"The guard has agreed to take us before their *Ervi*, or lord. He'll decide our fate."

The Eltaran spearman marched everyone toward the open gates while the bowmen on the battlements watched with arrows at the ready.

Ulric slipped beside Renier and asked, "What do you think of all this?" He spoke in Gualdean—just in case.

"Well, young master," he replied in Gualdean, "I think… there's something very wrong." The old scholar hesitated and seemed to reconsider. "But I'm sure Mistress Vipsania knows best." With a forced smile, he added, "She'll sort things out once she's spoken to the *Ervi*."

Ulric forgot why he was so worried. "Yeah, of course."

Wasn't there something else he wanted to ask Renier? He tried to think, but his thoughts grew muddled as they drew closer to the black maw of the gatehouse. He took one last glance toward the forest. The sky was darkening with approaching dusk, and only a few wispy clouds lingered in the east. Where was the gray wall of smoke from Vipsania's wildfires?

The question was lost when they plunged into the deep shade beneath the gatehouse, the boom of marching feet echoing around them. Strange Eltaran eyes watched them from behind several arrow-slits in the stone passageway, and an overwhelming panic seized him.

Grab Julia and run! Flee into the forest!

But the Eltaran guards kept them surrounded and hemmed in with a wall of spears. The lead guard shouted a command and the spearheads at the rear closed in, driving them around a sharp bend in the passageway and through several more open gates. He had to go on. The *Ervi* awaited.

The passage took another sharp turn, then straightened for the final run toward the exit. Ahead, the inner gates stood wide open, granting a tantalizing view of the marvelous city beyond.

A bustling plaza flanked by enormous buildings of whitewashed stone stretched down the center of the city. No two seemed alike. There were tall, square buildings, with huge stone columns and archways under crenelated roofs decorated with strange beasts. Some were only a couple of storeys high, but broad and big as a palace. Others were a series of diminishing concentric platforms stacked one upon another, topped by a small building or tower with luxurious rooftop gardens, where artificial streams fell in glittering waterfalls to fill canals and public pools. And color was everywhere: blood-red, pale blue, and bright yellow paint highlighted every surface.

Despite the late hour, the plaza was abuzz with merchants and shoppers. Magic and fabrications were commonplace. Fish leaped playfully from a fabricated river above a fishmonger's shop; giant flatbread spun in the air, slowly turning a crispy golden brown high above a bakery; jugs and bottles with Eltaran faces danced a drunken jig above a wine seller. Wooden platforms laden with goods floated in the air, pulled by chained men—carts without wheels! Human slaves were everywhere, driven by the lash or by strange pain-giving wands. Eltaran lamps hung from every building, filling the city with a soft golden light.

At the far end of the plaza rose the mountainous structure Ulric had glimpsed from atop the Lamp of Revelation. It was a massive edifice of five stone platforms with sloping sides, all stacked one on another, each taller than a typical insula. Each tier was slightly smaller than the one beneath it, and each roof was trimmed in red and gold. Two sets of broad steps ascended the front of the structure, flanked by a stone platform that magically rose and fell along the length of the stairs. At the summit were two square buildings with tall, tapering roofs. Between the buildings stood a large black ring, wide enough to drive a cart through. A flame of white light shone at the ring's apex—a gatestone?

Not a wasted trip, after all. But now the job's gone from nearly to completely impossible! How can I steal something in broad daylight atop the highest building in the city? A city full of Elts, no less! A city that was supposed to be empty. A city that didn't look like this from atop the Lamp. How did I miss that blazing beacon?

Eltaran lamps hung from every building and signpost, each a bright point of golden light. Where was the dull red glow of fading magic he had seen from atop the Lamp of Revelation?

Ulric hesitated and a guard spat something in Eltaran, thrusting his spear point dangerously close. He instinctively went for the hilt of his spatha, but Renier gave him an alarmed look. He ignored the guard and marched toward the gate.

Wait, he thought, *why do I even have my spatha? Why didn't they disarm us?*

There were too many questions. Something was wrong. He knew it, and he knew the others had their doubts, too. But every time he tried to think about it, *really* think about it, a voice came uninvited into his head—

It will all make sense once we speak with the Ervi.

That was a lie.

Ulric was on intimate terms with deception, and he was a jealous lover.

Don't try to scheme a schemer!

He froze, fearing what doom the Elts were really marching them toward. He shouted, "Julia! Vipsania! Everyone, stop!"

The guards closed in, their spears raised. The lead guard turned and issued a series of angry commands.

Julia, who had joined Vipsania in her eagerness to see the city, called back, "Ulric? Careful, don't anger them!"

Vipsania looked so furious Ulric thought she'd burst into flames. "What are you doing? You're risking our lives! And worse—you're embarrassing me!"

Behind Vipsania, Julia took a step forward and silently dropped out of sight as if she had been swallowed by the Underworld.

"Vipsania, this isn't real! This is the final fabrication. Julia's vanished." He pointed to the unseen sky. "There was no wildfire smoke. And this isn't what I saw from atop the Eltaran shrine. I saw a dead city. Glowing with dying Eltaran light!"

The spearman shook their spears and yelled commands, but otherwise did nothing.

Realization kindled on Vipsania's face as she cast out her own uninvited liar.

"Three walls of illusion in the forest, but four ciphers?" Vipsania unfurled the Eltaran scroll. "Eltarus, damn me for a fool! I wanted this too much."

Kehindé gave Vipsania a wide smile.

"And why are you so happy?" Vipsania asked.

"It isn't real now, but I've seen an Eltaran city in its full glory. I may be the only man from Suloko who can say that."

Vipsania returned the smile. Then she winked and said, "Stay with me and who knows what sights you'll see, hm?"

The words of the Eltaran cipher rang out over the protests of the fabricated spearman, echoing across vast, unseen empty spaces.

There was a nauseating lurch and the city of wonders vanished, replaced by a forlorn expanse of crumbling stone and encroaching greenery, bathed in the dull red glow of fading Eltaran glory.

The stone passageway remained much as it was, a narrow hall flanked by arrow-slits under a high ceiling peppered with murder holes but now there was a wide pit between the expedition and the inner gate. Its sharp edge yawned beneath Vipsania feet like a long-starving beast.

Vipsania stumbled, swayed, then cursed as she fell. Kehindé, quick as a tiger, grabbed her stola and pulled her into his arms.

No far from Vipsania, Julia clung to the edge of the pit screaming for help.

"Can anyone hear me," Julia cried. "I'm slipping!"

Sweet Neesis! No, no, no!

Ulric ran and skidded to a stop at the brink. Flaccus already laid sprawled out over the edge, clutching Julia's palla. Ulric thanked both Neesis and Myrill when he saw her dangling below, her left arm tangled in the green fabric.

He tossed his packs aside and knelt over the pit. "Hold on!"

"Myrill have mercy!" Julia stared at Ulric, her always expressive eyes wide with dread. "Don't drop me!"

Ulric peered into the gloom past her dangling feet. The bottom of the pit was filled with stagnant rainwater and the twisted remains of several beasts impaled on rusted spikes.

"Ulric!" Flaccus called, "Help…"

Julia released a panicked squeal as Flaccus slid toward the pit's edge. Rexinda dashed forward and caught him by his tunic. Ulric fell flat against the stone and grabbed a handful of Julia's palla, and she slowly turned to face the pit wall and carefully gripped the palla with her right hand.

Ulric pulled.

The sound of ripping cloth sent a chill down his back. A treacherous tear formed, fabric frayed, and Julia slipped farther into the pit, a prelude to the final plunge.

Ulric stretched, desperate to save her. She was out of reach. She had fallen too far. Was there time to retrieve his rope? Should he climb down the pit wall alongside her?

Too late. The palla tore, and Julia screamed.

Kehindé's long arm shot past Ulric and seized Julia by the wrist. He raised her out of the pit. Then Ulric grabbed her other hand, and they both hauled her to safety.

Julia threw herself into Ulric's arms. "Praise Mother Myrill! And thank you, Kehindé! But most of all, thank you, Flaccus. If you hadn't caught my palla…"

Flaccus picked himself up off the ground, massaging a strained shoulder. "I… I was just lucky to be nearby. That's all."

Julia wrapped the lifesaving garment around her shoulders. "Still, I thank you."

Ulric gazed into the pit, then scanned the ruined city beyond. Dusk had settled over the remains of Eltaran glory. The sigh of winds eroding crumbling stone and the muted sounds of the Silva Aurea were all they could hear.

"What was the point?" Kehinde asked. "A single pit would hardly keep out a determined invader."

"To punish looters, I guess?" Rexinda offered.

"The Eltarans' cruel and unpredictable nature is well documented," Vipsania said. "A fabrication leading into a pit: typical spiteful Eltaran thinking."

Flaccus glanced back into the pit. "More like… spike-ful!"

Everyone groaned.

"That was terrible, Flaccus," Ulric said. "Well done!"

Julia rolled her eyes and looked to the heavens. "Forgive me if I don't laugh."

"Oh, and Vipsania—" Ulric waited until he had the magus' attention "—that's trap number one I've saved you from." He gave her a slight bow. "I'll waive my usual fee per our previous agreement at the Quadrivium."

"Yes, it was at the Quadrivium you introduced yourself as a part-time actor. I assume comedy was your specialty, hm?"

"When I'm not cast as the heroic lead, conniving scoundrel, or doomed lover." Ulric bowed again.

"Well, if you're done boasting, why don't you lead us safely across the plaza to the Temple of Eltarus? True, I didn't expect to find a gate-stone, but I did at least expect a Gate. I want to know why this one has vanished."

Ulric looked to the summit of the mountainous temple at the far end of the plaza, where the fabrication had shown a black ring and blazing gate-stone. Now there was nothing but empty air and broken stone.

Vipsania insisted on reaching the summit of the temple immediately, despite the waning light. Since no one relished a climb of hundreds of steps, she tried to activate one of the stone platforms that sat at the base of the temple. She called it a "riser." An ancient magic, rare but not impossible to reproduce. The block of pale red Eltaran stone was huge; it could have easily held three wagons abreast, with room to spare. Everyone stepped onto the platform and waited while Vipsania, with the occasional suggestion from Renier, spoke a series of Eltaran words. After a time, calm commands became frustrated shouts and finally, Ulric guessed, Eltaran curses. Still, no matter the words spoken or the spells cast, the stone sat stubbornly on the ground, like a riser should not.

Eleven hundred steps! Ulric, Julia, Rexinda, and Flaccus had agreed to count—loudly—each step as they climbed. When they reached the summit, they were all in agreement: risers were a great idea, and their time had come again!

The summit of the Temple of Eltarus, the roof of the fifth and final tier, was a broad expanse occupied by the remains of two stone buildings. In the fabrication, they had been whitewashed and painted with colorful designs under magnificent sloping roofs. Now they were only walls of pale red stone, choked with their collapsed remains. Everywhere else, the seasonal rains and constant winds that buffeted the summit had swept the stones clean. There was no sign of the massive black ring they had glimpsed in the fabrication.

While Vipsania and Renier theorized on temple architecture and the nature of Eltaran Gates, Ulric and Julia stood on the eleven hundredth step, overlooking the ruins of Tmia Culscva. A cool, damp breeze blew in from the east, tearing at Julia's palla and sending her dark curls fluttering around her face. On the far horizon, lightning flashed. Ulric pulled her close.

Below, a deep darkness had descended over the ruins, and the abandoned city was aglow with hundreds of fading Eltaran lights. It was as if he stood atop a mountain at the center of a still lake, its waters reflecting the stars above. Except these waters took starlight and twisted it into an angry, red mockery of divine radiance.

"The city looks beautiful at night," Ulric said. "But… dangerous."

Julia leaned in closer. "I don't like this place. Something's wrong. If this truly was a temple of Eltarus, then He abandoned it long ago. The gods are not here. That scares me."

Ulric wasn't sure what to say. He knew better than to admit she had just sent a chill down his spine. "Don't worry." He pulled the Tesserae out from underneath his tunic. The two small wooden cubes inlaid with silver dots dangled on their chain, shimmering in the starlight. "I carry Neesis' divine luck everywhere I go."

Julia forced a half-hearted smile. "Oh, is that how it works?"

"You're the priestess. You should—"

There was a bright flare of light behind them, followed by excited voices. Ulric and Julia ran to join the others, who stood near the center of the summit under a small but exceedingly bright ball of orange flame. Vipsania used the light to show everyone what she and Renier had discovered on the temple roof.

She believed the Eltaran priests had lowered the Gate into the temple. There were seams in the roof, of adequate proportions to allow for the passage of such a large structure. The wear on some sections of stone hinted at movement, possibly a hinged action. And, she asked, where else could the damned thing have gone?

Vipsania decided they would camp at the base of the temple, then explore the interior in the morning.

So, for some reason, the Elts dropped their Gate inside a mountain of stone? Now that scares me.

Meetings Under Moonlight

Ulric knew it would be hellishly dark in the bowels of the Eltaran temple, and he couldn't rely on Vipsania's flares. What if they got separated?

Ghostwalker had taught him that a little preparation now meant no aggravation later. And Arrius had provided just the thing—the only magical trinket he possessed. Once camp was set up, all he needed was an excuse to slink away.

When Vipsania announced she was going to walk the perimeter of the temple to get a rough idea of its measurements, he knew his time had come. Renier eagerly volunteered to help, but she gave him other duties. Instead, Kehindé would accompany her. She conjured another picket alarm—this time an army of moths answered the call—and told everyone to stay in camp.

Ulric slipped away moments later.

Not long after, he found himself sidetracked, looking for loot in a long-dead Eltaran city. A city already proven to be filled with traps.

Ulric crouched in the cracked and slightly askew doorway of a ruin. It was like the buildings he had just explored: several spacious chambers built around a central courtyard. They had all been the same, with sagging and collapsed roofs, sinking foundations, and overgrown courtyards. Their rooms were empty except for a thick layer of dirt and moldering leaves. Rarely, he would find a bit of rusted iron or tarnished and pitted bronze, once a hinge or handle to a piece of decayed furniture.

He guessed these structures had once been the dwellings of noble Eltarans. The lure of their wealth had drawn him, and he finally found what he had been searching for.

Ulric had previously adopted a Thieves' Glimmer, so the dull red glow from the city lights was enough to help him see a small metal box a few paces inside the doorway. The box was embossed with intricate designs of interlocking triangles and maze-like patterns. Its hinged lid was open, and its contents spilled across the floor: Eltaran jewelry worth a small fortune in the markets of Trumric. Time had ruined the copper, bronze, and silver pieces, but that still left gold, adamant, and gemstones.

It was all too simple, too obvious.

He extended a long branch of oak and prodded at the stone around the scattered jewelry. The tiled floor was solid. He looked up. The ceiling was intact—mostly.

He crept inside, snatching a pair of adamant earrings off the floor, and rolled back to the doorway, quick as lightning. There was no pit, no falling blocks, no trap of any kind. Just the darkness and the smell of dirt and damp stone.

"Listen up, Darktalon," he heard Ghostwalker's familiar voice say, "always go with your instincts. If something feels wrong, then you can be damn certain something is very, very wrong. But never be indecisive! Neesis Umbra admires daring and swift action."

Ulric pushed the Myrill-blessed wreath back down on his head—it had nearly fallen off during his maneuver—and took a moment to admire the earrings. They were simply three triangles dangling one beneath another, each composed of precious adamant, a rare crystal that could be worked like metal and made stronger than steel. Ulric guessed the earrings were worth more than the combined wealth of all the families in the Portus Towers. He wanted to give them to Julia, but he'd be a fool to let her wear them.

He gathered the rest of the jewelry, then picked up the metal box and weighed it in his hands. It would make an excellent treasure box for Julia, but it was simply too heavy to take with him. He set it back down and headed for the center of the building.

Greenery choked the inner courtyard, and the incessant pulse of insects infected the air. Thanks to Julia's wreath, he walked easily through a mass of thick shrubs and tangled grass toward a grove of oak and chestnut trees at the center of the ruin. Their roots had long ago burrowed into the foundations and cracked the inner walls. Ulric looked past the towering treetops to admire Seranon's slender crescent of pale moonlight. In an endless cycle of corruption and revelation, Alakur's daughter cast off the baleful influence of Nyx, Goddess Beyond Night, and once again became worthy of Her father's divine radiance.

Ulric planned to steal a little piece of divine light for himself. He pulled out a palm-sized piece of clear quartz and thrust it into the sky, shouting the Kreslan words, "Κλέψτε όλο το φως, δώστε μου θέα!" In Trumin, the words roughly translated as "Steal all the light, to grant me sight."

A sudden screech from a nearby oak answered. A little owl with huge round yellow eyes stared at him from its nook.

Beams of light shimmered and bent, twisting and falling into the quartz and causing the crystal to glow. In a moment, it was as bright as a candle. Not enough for the depths of an Eltaran ruin.

He repeated the Kreslan words.

The stone continued to gobble greedily at the moonlight. Now it was as bright as a torch. But how vast were those chambers?

He shouted the command phrase again. The owl screeched another protest and retreated inside its hole.

The quartz seemed to tear at the moon itself, demanding every last bit of radiance from her slender crescent. Now the crystal shone like a star.

With a single word, the light vanished in an instant. Ulric placed the quartz back in his pouch, a blazing moonstone at his command.

Then he heard voices beyond the ruin.

He bolted out of the courtyard, pushing through the tall grass and tangled shrubs. He glanced back as he stepped into the building. There was no sign of his passage; the Myrill-blessed wreath had worked as expected.

The voices grew closer. He exited the ruin and crept into the blackness outside the faint, red glow of the nearby streetlights. Vipsania charged into view, Kehindé close behind.

"There was a light. A white glow; not red. Somewhere—" Vipsania made a wide sweeping gesture "—here."

"Hmph."

Vipsania stopped in front of the dwelling next to the one Ulric had just explored, then turned to Kehindé. "Don't tell me you didn't see it."

"I say you're chasing lights instead of answering my question."

"Nonsense!"

"Then answer me." He stepped closer. "When this is over, do you want me to stay in Trumric?"

She stepped back, peering into the ruined dwelling. "It would be excellent for Rexinda's development," she said, then plunged into the ruin. "Perhaps the light came from here!"

"The question needs only a simple yes or no," Kehindé said, then followed her inside.

Ulric swiftly crossed the shadows between his hiding place and the ruin. It was like all the other noble dwellings he had explored before, albeit more broken by time. He leaped upon a fallen stone and watched the bickering pair through a crack in the wall.

The fading Eltaran street lamps cast a long stripe of red light through the empty doorway. Vipsania stood at the edge, staring into the gloom. "What do you want me to say?"

Kehindé put his hand on her shoulder. "I want you to say yes." He gently turned her around to face him. "Or say no. I will stay in joy or go in peace."

"I don't want to disappoint you." She tugged on a long lock of her hair and held it out between them. "Look. The gray is already returning. Along with the lines on my face. And my bitter moods, perhaps, if we don't find a Gate."

Kehindé took the lock of hair gently between his fingers. "Bah! How much gray is in my beard? I said you were beautiful when I saw you at the Quadrivium, and you called me a liar. You know better. I've considered settling in Trumric since I received your letter. It has nothing to do with your fiery rejuvenation—I know that won't last. You explained how it all works, long ago."

"Kehindé, what we discover here should be enough to give me a position with the Oculi Quaeritis." She clasped her hands over his. "I would have far more independence. I would travel often. I would be free to come and go from the collegium and associate with whomever I wanted."

"Then let us travel together for whatever time I have left. When I'm gone, and Rexinda has grown and is too busy for her theia, you can find your dragon and be reborn."

"My answer is yes. Stay in Trumric."

Kehindé ran a hand through Vipsania's graying hair, pulled her close, and kissed her. She eagerly returned his kiss, wrapping her arms around his neck.

Vipsania pulled back and said, "Oh, it's been too long!"

"Since we last kissed?" Kehindé asked. "It was goodbye, on Pharos Island, I think."

"Since anyone kissed me, to be honest."

Kehindé gathered her into his arms and kissed her again, running his hands over the curves hidden beneath her sapphire stola. She began tearing at his red tunic and fumbling with his bronze-plated belt.

Vipsania mumbled something about a "double damned buckle" and Ulric decided it was time to withdraw. He leaped down from the stone and scurried away into the darkness, retracing his steps back through the block of noble dwellings.

To his surprise, he saw Flaccus creeping down the middle of a weed-infested avenue. As he drew closer, he heard Flaccus calling his name in a loud, hoarse whisper, too quiet to do any good and too loud to be stealthy. He entertained the idea of letting Flaccus pass by, only to sneak behind him and give him a terrible fright, but he decided the prank wouldn't be worth the risk of a face full of fire.

"Flaccus! Over here!" Ulric called in his own whisper-shout.

Flaccus looked around. "Ulric! Where are you?"

Ulric stepped into the dull red glare and beckoned him into the shadows. Flaccus joined him in a rubble-strewn alley between two stone dwellings.

"Finally!" Flaccus said, relieved. "I've been looking for you."

Ulric sat on a conveniently shaped bit of rubble. "Clearly. Why?"

"We never finished speaking about the gate-stone."

"True, but… Wait. Why, of all the places in this vast city, were you looking for me here?"

Flaccus spun around, looking for a comfortable place to sit. Finding none, he remained standing. "I noted this place from the top of the temple. The structures' uniformity, quality of stone, proximity to the central market—this was a patrician district. I reasoned you couldn't resist a bit of late-night looting."

"Have I become so predictable?"

"I hope so," Flaccus replied.

Ulric ran his hands through his dark curls and shouted at the ground beneath his feet. "Neesis Insania, send me a madness that I might confound my enemies!"

"Ulric!" Flaccus shrunk back in fear. "Don't say such things."

"Calm yourself. The Goddess and I are on excellent terms. She knows I'm only joking."

"Don't tempt Her. Neesis is a subject of Arakru's court—a goddess of the Underworld."

"Less lecturing. More Gate talk." It was time to discover what Flaccus was up to.

"Of course. I believe Magus Vipsania is correct: The Eltarans secured the Gate inside the temple. This makes the presence of a gate-stone likely."

"Good news, then," Ulric said flatly.

"Is it? I thought you were only interested in the Eltaran mystery?"

"So I've said."

"Forgive me, but I don't believe you." Flaccus began pacing before Ulric, occasionally stumbling over jagged pieces of rubble.

"You're a thief from south of the river—no offense. You've made enemies of your fellow Imperaré. Now, you need coin to either buy your way back in, or help you flee the city."

"You have it exactly," Ulric said with a smirk that made it plain he didn't mean a word of it.

"Not just me. Vipsania knows. When you move on the gate-stone—" for emphasis, Flaccus thrust a bright, burning fist into the air "—she'll burn you to ash. Or she'll order Kehindé to kill you. Perhaps she'll spare Julia because she's a woman... and favored by Myrill."

"Things aren't looking good for the hero of this play you're writing."

"There's a way he survives."

"I'd love to hear the big twist."

"The hero doesn't get the gate-stone," Flaccus said. "Instead, he gets a great deal of coin. All he has to do is make the right decision when the... *other* hero claims the stone."

"There's another hero?"

"And why not?" Flaccus snapped. "Is no one else worthy of the role? Have they not suffered? Do they not deserve freedom?"

Ulric let those bitter words echo in the dark alley for a long moment before asking, "You think the gate-stone can buy us both freedom? Then your buyer must have great wealth... and power. I fear I already know his name."

"Would it matter if you did?"

"Flaccus, your play is light on details. And I can't tell if it's a comedy or a tragedy. What I need to know is—"

Ulric stopped, jumping to his feet so fast that Flaccus yelped. He pointed back toward the weedy avenue and whispered, "Shh. Someone's very close, and drawing closer."

"We shouldn't be seen together. I'll slip out the other end. Think about what I said." Flaccus fled down the alley.

Ulric smelled Julia's perfume before she came into view. He stepped out of the alleyway and nearly ran into her.

"Ulric! There you are! I thought I heard voices. Were you talking with someone?"

"I was just speaking with Flaccus. When we heard someone approaching, he ran off. Probably thought you were the angry shade of some long dead Elt."

Julia inspected the alleyway. "What were you talking about?"

"Temple architecture. Then he tried to lecture me about Neesis, of all things. Can you believe it?"

"No, I can't. I was getting worried, and now I'm tired." She took him by the arm. "Take me back to camp."

As they walked, Ulric asked, "Julia, why were you looking for me here, exactly?"

"Well, this was some sort of noble district, right? So, I figured—"

"Say no more!"

"What?"

"Yes, these were noble dwellings. And yes, my looting was successful!" Ulric produced the Eltaran earrings before her, as if out of thin air.

"Ulric! Are those... adamant?"

"They are indeed. So they're only safe to wear among your wealthier friends. Anywhere else, and my fellow thieves will descend like flies."

"Or—" she plucked the earrings out of Ulric's hand "—the Silva Aurea should be safe from thieves. Mostly." She carefully placed each earring in her lobes and asked, "How do they look?"

"As I thought," Ulric said too seriously. "Even adamant pales next to your beauty."

"Oh, spare me!" she said, but gave him a kiss, anyway.

When they approached the unseen border of Vipsania's alarm spell, a swarm of blue lights raced out of the darkness and resolved into a dozen moths of flame and wispy smoke. They swirled around the pair, as if inspecting them. Ulric thought they lingered over him too long, their smokey wings fluttering and faintly humming. Could they sense thoughts of treachery?

What did Flaccus have planned? Nothing he had seen of the discipulus gave him much confidence in his schemes. But if the timing was right, the chaos of a bungled plan could be used to his own advantage. Could Flaccus' failure gain him the gate-stone?

The fiery moths finally dispersed and disappeared into the night.

He resolved to keep Flaccus' betrayal a secret. He would remain silent and wait.

Before a Dark Gate

Ulric woke up with a start. Next to him, Julia whimpered, lost in a dream. Nearby, Magus Vipsania prayed at the southern end of the grand plaza, a stone's throw from the temple steps. Her voice was hushed, rhythmic, insistent. Kehindé watched over her, adjusting his belt and saber over and over, filling the predawn darkness with the creak and clunk of leather and bronze. Somewhere, Renier snored.

The rest of the city was utterly silent. Ulric brought on a Thieves' Glimmer to sharpen his senses, but he heard nothing beyond their camp. The air, still and heavy with the scent of distant rain, seemed to devour sound. Then Vipsania's prayer reached a crescendo and ended, plunging the area into a deeper silence.

Kehindé stalked through the camp, rousing the others. Julia made a terse comment about bad dreams, then went alone to the eastern edge of the plaza to greet the coming dawn with morning prayers. Everyone else prepared for their journey into the temple interior. They moved about the gloom, focused on their tasks, speaking little. The dread descending over the expedition was palpable.

Ulric craned his neck to get a better view of the temple summit. The mountainous ziggurat towered above him, a monument to Eltaran secrecy. It stood at the center of an abandoned city, which great effort and subtle magic had purposely hidden away from Men. Now Magus Vipsania had shattered the

Elt's illusions; their fabrications were exposed, their secrets ready to be plundered. Even the magus seemed to fear what they might uncover.

Such a day demanded a full thieves' kit. Ulric left camp and slipped behind a nearby building, where he changed into a night black tunic and dark wool pants tucked into a pair of dark leather boots. Tightening a braided leather belt around his waist, he secured a small pouch and his spatha at his side. A throwing dagger was secured in each boot and another slid into a sheath on the inside of his left wrist. Aguja remained hidden underneath his tunic, strapped against his chest. He placed the enchanted quartz within a secure pocket inside his cloak. Next, he made a quick inspection of his tools: lock picks, oils, solutions, a small pry bar, and a coil of rope with a whisper-enchanted grapnel. Everything was in order. Carefully, almost reverently, he returned each tool to a small backpack. A fine cloak of mottled blacks and grays completed his kit.

As he crept back to camp—when so outfitted, he found it difficult not to creep, sneak, prowl, or stalk—he slipped on a pair of dark gloves. He clenched his right hand into a fist. There was full strength in his grip and no pain. He pulled back the sleeve of his tunic, cut open the bandage covering his forearm, and tossed it aside. There was only the faintest scar where Luciano's sword had cut him. Upon prodding the side of his head, he found no wound. Thanks to Julia's skill and Thana's waters, he had healed in only a couple of days.

By the time he returned to camp, the sun had risen, a pale orb obscured behind distant rain clouds. Fortunately, the feeble light was enough to expel the dread that had infected the camp. Everyone was more talkative, going about their business with renewed vigor. Julia examined Rexinda's bandages as they whispered and laughed at some private joke, while Flaccus lectured the slaves about what they should bring or leave behind. Magus Vipsania and Kehindé stood together, smiling, talking, and sneaking little touches when they thought no one was looking.

Ulric couldn't resist. "You two look very satisfied. Any particular reason?"

Vipsania turned and looked him over, noting his thieves' kit. "And you look like you're planning to mug someone."

"I might!"

Magus Vipsania led the expedition to the second tier of the temple, where, after three hundred and twenty steps, the stairs split and narrowed to make room for a deep gallery. At the rear of that shadow-haunted space, two massive stone doors barred the way. Fierce dragons and the enigmatic Sphinx—the two beasts most favored by the God of Magic—were carved into their surface. Dirt and debris had long ago blown into the corners of the gallery and settled against the doors in thick heaps. It looked as if they hadn't moved in centuries.

Kehindé grabbed one of the door handles, a curved dragon tongue. Before Ulric could protest, he pulled with all his might, his muscles knotting and bulging. The door shuddered and expelled a brief shower of dust. Kehindé released the handle with a frustrated grunt.

They were locked, of course. Moments before, Ulric had noted a keyhole underneath one of the handles. Not surprising, as the Elts had abandoned and sealed the temple long ago. He imagined no key had turned the lock since the Eltaran diaspora over three hundred years ago. He knelt and examined the keyhole as best he could in the shadowed gallery.

Hello there! So you've been rusting and getting dirtier for centuries? And they expect me to get you open. Good thing I'm a professional.

"Well?" Vipsania asked.

Ulric poked at the keyhole with a hooked pick. "A simple 'mechanical inconvenience,' as you once said. I'll need to deal with the rusted mechanism first. A little light, please."

"Bring a torch!"

One of the young slaves hurried to fulfill his mistress' command and ran to stand beside Ulric. At a word from Vipsania, the torch blossomed into a pillar of bright flame.

Ulric laid out his tools. First, he used a flat pick to scrape as much loose dirt from the lock as possible. Then he blew into the keyhole and flushed out the remaining debris with a squirt from his waterskin. The mechanism remained unmovable. Next, he unsealed a small bladder and squeezed a stream of white liquid into the keyhole, causing an unpleasant vinegar-like smell to fill the air. The slave coughed and shrank back, taking the torchlight with him.

Ulric had no choice but to wait while his solution dissolved the rust. The rest of the expedition, who had previously watched with curiosity, now looked on with growing impatience. He flushed the lock out once more, then waited for it to dry.

The rising sun did little to illuminate the northward facing gallery. Everyone fidgeted and paced, except for Flaccus, who stood unmoving, staring at the doors, lost in his own dark thoughts.

Magus Vipsania walked over and put a hand on his shoulder. Flaccus recoiled, as if from a sudden blow.

"Forgive me, Magus."

"No, forgive me, Flaccus, for startling you."

Her discipulus stood with arms hovering before him, shoulders slumped, head slightly bowed. He blinked at her, unsure of what to say. Ulric watched them at the edge of his vision while he feigned organizing his tools.

"Everything changes today," Vipsania said. "I'm confident there's a Gate inside. Maybe more."

"A gate-stone?" Flaccus asked.

"Perhaps. The discovery will be enough to propel me into the Oculi Quaeritis. That means more freedom and privileges… for both of us."

"Of course, Magus." His voice was flat. His posture remained nervous, guarded.

Vipsania gave a small, exasperated sigh and stepped away. Then she spun around and said, "Flaccus, I have not always treated you well. My career at the collegium had met with certain frustrations, and you were a convenient scapegoat. A priestess of Eltarus should not let her passions control her."

"I… uh… I'm sorry. I…" Flaccus spluttered.

"No, I'm sorry. Things will be different once we return to the collegium. I pray to Eltarus you can forgive my past cruelty." She stood awkwardly for a moment before her discipulus then hurried to join Kehindé and Rexinda in the sunlight at the edge of the gallery.

Flaccus shuffled to the wall and slumped against the hard stone. He stared at the ceiling for a long time until he slid to the ground and his head fell against his knees. He checked to see if anyone was watching him, then wiped the tears from his eyes.

What did those tears mean? Did Flaccus still intend to betray his mistress? Or had Vipsania's surprising confession made his job harder? The one thing Ulric knew was that uncertainty was nemesis to a good plan.

And Ulric's plan began with getting inside the temple. Now that the lock was dry, he blew in a small pinch of powdered black lead for lubrication and attacked the mechanism with his picks.

The lock was surprisingly simple. It may have guarded the Eltarans' most precious secrets, but lockcraft had advanced in the centuries since its construction. It unlocked with a satisfying click-thunk a few moments later.

The slave jumped at the sound and scurried back, brandishing his torch before him as if all the shades of the Underworld would burst out of the temple.

Ulric announced that the doors were unlocked and the temple awaited plundering.

"Oh, finally!" Julia stood and hoisted her satchel of healing supplies across her shoulder. "I was getting terribly bored."

"Mind your sacrilegious tongue, Ulric," Vipsania chided. "We plunder nothing. We're here to study an Eltaran Gate. And if I take some religious artifacts back to the collegium—"

"Then they're simply being taken from one temple dedicated to Eltarus… to another! Right, Theia?" Rexinda asked.

"Exactly, child."

Kehindé grabbed the dragon tongue handle once more and pulled. The door defied his efforts with a cry of grating stone and stressed metal. The Kekeksuan warrior bellowed a cry of his own, and the door lurched open. A blast of stale air erupted from the gap, causing their torch to flutter. Ulric and Rexinda rushed into the widening breach and shoved against the door.

Ulric summoned a Thieves' Glimmer and peered into the darkness. The entrance chamber was large, with a floor of well-worn flagstones and walls covered in carvings of Eltaran warriors and priests, surrounded by sweeping geometric designs. A wide hall at the center of the far wall led deeper into the temple interior. Two dark, narrow passages exited to the left and right.

Vipsania approached, practically dragging a reluctant slave and his torch along with her. Everyone stood in the gap of the half-opened door and surveyed the chamber for hidden danger.

"A simple reception area, I suppose," Vipsania mused.

"Empty," Renier said, looking over Ulric's shoulder. "A pity. It looks like the Eltarans took anything interesting." He grabbed the young slave's arm and pulled the torch closer, showering Ulric in flakes of hot ash.

Ulric hissed at the sudden pain and jumped toward the interior. "Get off!"

He spun around and wondered why everyone was staring at him. Waiting.

Oh. Right.

He cursed himself for leaving his oak branch in the noble district and gingerly stepped into the temple. The flagstones were smooth and solid. He slowly made his way across the chamber, checking the floor and ceiling for irregularities, though the black depths of the two side tunnels constantly drew his gaze. They angled deeper into the structure and expelled the faintest breath of air, along with a soft droning sound that he felt more than heard.

Someone had scrawled the word "Guarded?" across the Eltaran map. What had they feared?

Ulric ignored his growing unease and pressed on until he stood under the arch of the main exit, beyond the edge of torchlight. Here the air was still and silent. More stairs waited somewhere in the darkness ahead. He took a few cautious steps forward. He was about to pull out his quartz stone for a little light when Julia called out, begging him not to go too far. Her voice echoed through the reception chamber and into the hall.

Kehindé's booming voice joined hers, asking Ulric how he could even see.

He froze. Their voices echoed in the darkness, and an absurd notion overcame him that those voices would awaken something. Fear raced up his spine and threatened to freeze his heart. He told himself he wasn't afraid of the dark. It was true. He was a creature of midnight streets and shadowed corners, of moonless rooftops and pitch-black alleys. Yet here was a place of pure abyssal black, untouched by Alakur's light for centuries.

"Guarded?" A warning. It was right there on the map!

Ulric took three slow, deep breaths. His panic faded, and he forced the notions out of his mind. Was he not the protégé of Arrius Ghostwalker? Was he not favored by Neesis Fortuna? Besides, he told himself, the "Guarded?" on the map no doubt referred to the illusionary Eltarans they had faced at the city gates.

He strode confidently back to Vipsania and told her the room and the hall beyond were free of Eltaran traps and fabrications.

Everyone filed in and Kehindé took a second torch from the slave's pack. Vipsania lit it in an instant with the same simple spell as before. Renier wanted a closer look at the wall carvings, but she gave them a cursory glance and told him there would be time later once they found the Gate. She led the expedition deeper into the temple, with Kehindé and Ulric at her side, giving Ulric authority to call a halt if he saw any sign of danger. Julia, Flaccus, and Renier followed close behind. Rexinda, with her sword at the ready, brought up the rear along with the slaves.

Ulric could sense the enveloping darkness pressing upon the expedition. It lurked all around, teasing with its malignant possibilities. Everyone grew quiet, peering into the blackness at every echo or imagined sound. Often, someone would jerk and look behind them, perhaps remembering the two unexplored side tunnels.

Despite their caution, Ulric felt exposed at the center of an amateur racket he feared had been heard in every corner of the temple. Yet there was no choice but to continue down the hall with his blundering companions and clumsily ascend the steps.

The stairs led to a broad landing, where steel gates stood closed at the end of a short hall. Once again, two narrow tunnels gaped from either side of the landing. Kehindé stepped forward and raised his torch higher. A slender bar of adamant rested across the gates.

"Barred? But from our side," Rexinda said. "Easy, then."

Julia grabbed Ulric by the arm. She stretched up to whisper, "I hope we find it soon. I want out of here. I need to stand in Alakur's light, breathe Myrill's air."

"You will. I think it's close."

Kehindé beckoned Ulric forward, and he reluctantly pulled away from Julia's grasp.

The landing was the same simple flagstone as before, and the walls were smooth, unadorned Eltaran stone. It was the gate that had been built to intimidate. They were embossed with the images of the God of Magic and his consort Kura—the great dragon of the Underworld who taught him the art of shape-shifting, thus freeing him from his imprisonment in the Dragon's Breath Mountains. Eltarus raised His lamp high overhead, its Light of Revelation shining forth as a focused beam to meet a blast of Kura's fiery breath. At their feet, the adamant bar rested on several thick hooks.

Ulric took a closer look. As far as he could tell, there were no spiteful Eltaran tricks, so he grasped one end and gave Kehindé a nod. They easily lifted the bar, set it aside, then returned to grab the handles; iron rings inset within the gate.

The doors swung open, accompanied by an unnerving metallic screech from the long-neglected hinges. A few steps beyond, a thick iron portcullis blocked the way.

Everyone released a cry of frustration.

"Gods below!" Ulric grabbed the portcullis and pointlessly shook it.

He and Kehindé gazed through the iron slats. There was a long hall with a floor of colorful tiles. The ceiling was high and contained rows of holes, both small and large. Thin, evenly spaced vertical openings lined the walls.

And then, what looked like a dead end. Ulric doubted Kehindé could see that far into the dark, so he decided to say nothing until he could get a better look.

"Iron?" Vipsania stared at the portcullis as if the Eltarans had placed it there as a personal insult. "I can melt iron. Given enough time."

"You won't have to." Kehindé retreated to the rear of the landing and called to Rexinda, "Come with me. And be on your guard."

"Finally!"

Kehindé plunged down one of the side tunnels, and Rexinda eagerly followed.

Some time later, the slave brought out a fresh torch. He handed the old one to Renier, which sputtered and went out just as the portcullis rose with a terrible screech. Everyone jumped at the noise.

They faced the opening gate with suspicion, fearing what it might unleash, but it only rose with a clamor until it disappeared into the ceiling. Ulric wedged the adamant bar into the groove beneath the portcullis, just in case.

When Kehindé and Rexinda returned, they emerged from the tunnel opposite from the one they left.

"It seems you found the simplest and most direct solution," Vipsania said. "Well done."

"This part of the temple is like a gatehouse," Kehindé said. "So we looked for the winch and found a series of guardrooms."

"They run along the sides of the hall," Rexinda said, pointing through the now-open gate. "Each has arrow loops, and a room above the hall for dropping stuff down on the enemy!" She grinned at the thought of such carnage.

"Sweet Neesis! So the hall is one gigantic trap?"

"Not much of one, without Elts to defend it," Kehindé said.

"Still, if the Elts were going to hide more hazards, I imagine they'd put them in the Murder-Hall. I'll go first." Ulric grabbed the torch, leaving the slave scrambling to light another.

"Of course, Ulric." Vipsania stood aside and pointed the way with a flourish. "As per our agreement at the Quadrivium." As he walked by, she said under her breath, "But do be careful. I'd hate to lose you now, so close to the end."

A moment after Ulric passed under the portcullis, a dull red light filled the space. The smaller holes in the ceiling held Eltaran lamps behind small iron grates, their magic having long ago faded from a healthy golden glow to a sickly red.

A few steps ahead, the simple flagstones became a dizzying field of fiery red volcanic dragons and pale blue storm dragons. The beasts were nearly as long as a man was tall, and each looked to be identical except for their coloring. Their shapes interconnected seamlessly, stretching the entire width of the wide hall. The pattern was dazzling to the eye. In one moment, the floor appeared to be covered by volcanic dragons against a blue sky. In the next moment, there were only storm dragons flying over a fiery land.

It seemed an overly elaborate floor for what was essentially a gatehouse "murder-hall," as he had dubbed it.

"Listen up, Darktalon!" He recalled the voice of Arrius Ghostwalker once again. "Never trust overly elaborate flooring. Trap makers can't resist it! I know it's obvious, but the bastards think they're being clever. Tread carefully."

Ghostwalker had said a great deal more on the subject, but it all added up to fear of the dragons.

He approached the edge and held his torch low over the floor, trying to shine as much light as possible on the tiles. Then he carefully walked the length of the border between the flagstones and the dragon tiles. The dragons had only a few gouges and scuff marks, which would be typical of an infrequently trafficked area, and they were surprisingly clean; no dust, no debris, only ashes from his torch.

Wait!

Ulric retraced his steps. No ashes lay on the storm dragons! Why?

Julia must have noticed the change in his posture, the quickness of his gait. She called out, "I can tell you've found something. Be careful!"

He recalled the last time she had told him to be careful. Soon afterward he had been plunging to the forest floor, with only Julia to save him.

He stepped onto a red volcanic dragon where a few ashes lingered. The floor was solid and smooth. Then he took a couple more steps and placed a foot on a clean storm dragon.

His foot sunk into the floor. Into nothingness!

He pulled his foot back, grateful for the hours of balance drills Arrius had forced him to endure.

The blue storm dragon tiles were a fabrication, hiding a pit. So the red dragons were safe; the blue dragons were deadly. Ulric looked down the length of the hall. *Or,* he thought, *a clever trap-maker—a spiteful Eltaran trap-maker—would mix it up unexpectedly.*

Ulric announced his discovery and explained his concerns. He began weaving a safe path down the center of the murder-hall, marking each tile with soot from his torch. Despite his worry, every blue dragon tile he tested was an illusion, and every red dragon tile was solid. At the end of the hall there was another brief section of plain flagstone, and a wall with a wide arch in its center. Beneath the arch, a single massive stone blocked the passage.

He sat his torch down and ran his hands across the barrier. It had a pale red tint and was slightly porous, with a faint tingle of magic; typical Eltaran stone. It was no fabrication. A dead end?

Ulric doubted it. So far, other than the outer doors, they had designed nothing to keep people out. A way to raise the stone had to be nearby. He checked the walls on either side of the archway.

When he found what he wanted, he put on a show of casually skipping back across the dragon-tiled floor.

"I've marked a safe path across the dragons. Step only on *red* dragons, and only on ones marked with a lemnis—just in case."

"Excellent, Ulric," Vipsania said. Almost as an afterthought, she added, "But I could have told you storm dragons are a bad omen."

She crossed the hall, following the red dragons. Kehindé was close behind, giving Ulric a satisfied nod as he passed. Rexinda went next, gracefully leaping from dragon to dragon. Then Renier took a deep breath, hoisted his pack tight, and slowly crossed. The slaves begged to remain behind, but Vipsania denied them. Ulric gave the torch back and did his best to help them with the crossing. They went so slowly Renier had to return to help.

"These storm dragon pits," said Flaccus, "how deep are they? Is there anything down there?"

"I have no idea. I'm not putting my head through a fabrication! You can, if you want."

"Just asking!" Flaccus made his way across the hall, wobbly and unsure.

Ulric held out his hand to Julia and smiled. "Shall we?"

She took his hand. "If we must."

Once Ulric and Julia had joined everyone at the far end of the hall, Magus Vipsania turned to them. "Any ideas?" she asked. "I can't melt stone."

Ulric grinned mischievously and leaned against the wall. "I have one: Let's open it!"

"Is that a joke?" Rexinda asked. "You're usually funnier."

In response, Ulric pushed on a section of wall where he had earlier noted the faint outline of a hidden panel. As hoped for, it swung open on a concealed pivot to reveal a small mechanism. He grinned even wider and reached inside. It was the stone raising switch; all that was missing was the lever!

"Wait! Wait." Julia stepped before the archway and threw her hands wide. "Gates barred on the outside, and then we open the portcullis just as easily? And now a simple mechanism to raise the stone?" She paused, examining her companions' faces for a reaction.

"Uh… about the lever…" Ulric prompted.

"Don't you see? The Eltarans didn't build this place to keep looters out. They trapped something here. Can't you feel it? The… wrongness? Magus Vipsania, I don't know what lies beyond. I only know that if you raise this stone, all our fates will be irrevocably changed."

There was a moment of stunned silence, then several reactions at once.

"Calm yourself, child," Vipsania said, sounding equal parts irritated and concerned.

"Ridiculous!" Flaccus sneered.

"Battle 'n blood, Julia! It's these weird red lights! They've nearly driven me to madness, too."

Ulric didn't know what to say. Did he feel a "wrongness" in the temple? He couldn't be sure. Neesis Fortuna was his goddess, and She'd never reveal such a thing—why ruin the surprise? But Julia's connection to Myrill was extraordinary. He knew he should heed her warning, but the path to honoring his sacramentum with Silo—and thus pleasing Neesis—lay deeper inside the temple.

Julia looked at Ulric, her eyes pleading for support. He said nothing.

"If you will not listen to me, Magus, listen to the silence. Eltarus is not here. Such a grand temple, yet no gods are present."

"Julia, no one has worshiped here for over three centuries. Silence is not unexpected." Vipsania spoke softly, obviously trying to allay her fears. "I have not forgotten the miracle Myrill performed the day we met. Breaking the storm was a sign the goddess wanted you to accompany me. You said so yourself."

"I did."

"Then you are meant to be here. If the queen of the gods has shared some forewarning that Eltarus has not, I would hear it!"

"Myrill spoke to me… words of portent… words of doom. Yet now her warning is no better than a half-remembered dream. I do know Myrill guides me toward some great purpose. Perhaps it is to warn you? To save everyone from some terrible doom?

"Julia." Kehindé stepped forward. "You once asked if a legion could march through an Eltaran Gate. Perhaps they could. Now imagine a city falling to an invader. If they controlled the Gate, other cities would fear invasion. The Elts would have built a way to secure their Gates, trapping the invaders behind stone walls, portcullises, and barred doors. They would have killed them with pits and arrows and murder holes like any well-designed fortress."

"Kehindé is right," Ulric said. "This is simply the gatehouse of a fortress. We must go on."

Julia lowered her arms and looked at her companions with pity. "Then onward. Together, we'll face what doom may come." She retreated and stood next to Ulric.

"Ulric!" Vipsania called. "Get this stone out of my way!"

"Sorry," Ulric whispered, "but right or wrong, I have to raise that block."

Julia peered into the mechanism. "Good luck. The lever is missing. Speaking of luck, I thought Neesis always provided?"

Ulric pulled his pry bar out of his backpack, then wiggled it into the lever housing. It was a near perfect fit. "*Luckily* I had this."

He gave Julia a playful smirk and gripped the bar with both hands. "Get ready, everyone!"

He pulled with all his might, and the makeshift lever triggered the switch. There was a sudden rumbling beneath his feet, deep in the stone. He put his ear against the wall and imagined he heard the moving of great counterweights. Was magic, similar to what had powered the ancient risers, part of the mechanism?

There was a terrible grating sound. Ulric stepped back and watched the stone rise into the ceiling. The block was massive, filling the entire hall for several paces.

Julia gasped.

On the floor underneath the rising stone were flat, crumpled sheets of gold and gray metal, radiating odd lines of dull white rock chips and dust. It took Ulric a moment to realize he was looking at the remains of armored Elts who had been crushed to a pulp.

The thought sickened him. Had their deaths been quick? Or had they been trapped, the descending stone an inevitable doom, its image inescapable in their last horror-filled moments? Was its descent excruciatingly slow? Was there growing dread and panic until a terrible weight slammed into their bodies? Until the pressure built on their skulls, until they were ready to crack, eyes popping?

He remembered a spring long ago, tax collecting with the Low Street gang in Mist View. A crane helping to build a statue of Polyminius Maximus collapsed. Marble blocks bigger than the hovel he had been camping in rained from the sky. When the dust cleared, Ulric met eyes with a slave who had been caught under the crashing marble. He was both horrified and amazed that a man could still live, with so much of his body a smeared ruin upon the cobblestones.

Ulric shook his head to cast out his macabre thoughts.

The stone block settled into the ceiling with a loud thunk. It looked secure, but Ulric still planned to run when passing beneath it.

Renier fearlessly stepped under the stone block and examined the crushed remains. "Some of Kehindé's theoretical invaders, perhaps?"

Vipsania joined him. "Hard to say from the bodies, but I think the armor was Eltaran."

"Had Eltaran ever warred against Eltaran?" Kehindé asked.

Flaccus, peering at the remains from a safe distance, added, "The last recorded civil conflict was centuries before the time of the Gates."

"Hmph. Maybe a destructive civil war was the shame they'd been hiding?"

"Kehindé, hold up your torch!"

He did as Vipsania asked. Then she ran down the hall, shouting excitedly for everyone to follow. Kehindé ran after her.

"No! Wait!" Ulric shouted.

No one listened, so Ulric ran swiftly under the stone block and followed. Soon everyone was racing headlong down a pitch-black hall, with only a bit of torchlight to show the way. Then the hallway spilled into an immense chamber.

And the expedition finally stood before an Eltaran Gate.

Magus Vipsania looked up and said, "Children of Eltarus… what blasphemy have you sired?"

The structure towered above Ulric, a ring of rusted metal fused with desiccated flesh. Julia gasped, and Rexinda cursed at the sight of it. At that moment, Ulric wished he stood anywhere else. But at its apex, a palm-sized jewel glowed with a faint white light.

As time passed, Ulric's dread turned to merciful boredom. He never imagined finding an Eltaran Gate could be so boring, but Magus Vipsania managed to make it so. First, she commanded everyone to touch nothing. Then she ushered everyone, except for Flaccus and Renier, back into the hallway. While her discipulus and slave emptied their packs of scrolls, wax tablets, inks, styluses, and measuring tools, the magus walked the perimeter of the gate-well, as she called it. She often stopped to cast a spell; a brief chant or prayer accompanied by the tracing of fiery glyphs.

Once she had completed a circuit of the chamber, she launched a small orb of orange flame into the air. It hovered high overhead, illuminating all corners of the gate-well. The ceiling, if there was one, remained lost in darkness.

A full hour of ritualistic measuring and note taking followed. Ulric watched and listened from the edge of the hallway. He learned the Gate was a perfectly circular ring, one gradus wide, half as thick. It was composed partially of a flaky, mottled gray material that looked uncannily like mummified flesh. Sections of a strange, rusted red metal, which Vipsania thought was an alloy of adamant, bound the ring. The Gate was set into the floor at a depth of two gradus to facilitate passage through the portal, and the diameter of the ring was seven gradus.

A mass of unsettling, perfect blackness filled the Gate. Vipsania dared to touch it, and she announced it was cold, smooth, and solid as marble. The gate-stone rested in a small setting at the very apex of the ring, which Ulric thought looked like a mass of writhing snakes. On the floor before the Gate, large Eltaran runes read, "Oh, glorious Father Eltarus, may your lamp shine the way home."

Vipsania pronounced the Gate "currently inert."

So it's big, Ulric thought. *And ugly. I don't like this place; not one bit. I say we grab the stone and get the hells out of here.*

When Vipsania began debating domain resonance theory with Flaccus and Renier, he gave up trying to follow their research. He went back into the hall, where Kehindé stood alert, ever on guard. The slaves huddled close by, whispering nervously. Julia and Rexinda sat together, making plans for their triumphant return to the capital. He dropped next to Julia and took her hand. "See? No doom. Just a big room with a surprisingly hideous and boring Gate."

Julia withdrew her hand. "I'll agree when we're all back under the open sky. In here, we're under too much stone. It's... suffocating."

"When we get back to Trumric, we'll drink under the stars for a month!" Rexinda said. "I promise."

"Excellent idea!" Ulric said. "And I agree about all this stone." He reached up and ran a hand over the wall behind him. "These walls here are different. I didn't notice these faint patterns before."

Julia looked around. "Yes. I can see them now, thanks to Vipsania's flame. The stone's discolored. It's all very haphazard. Not Eltaran-like at all."

"Ulric!" Vipsania called from the gate-well. "It's time we have a good look at that gate-stone."

Ulric leaped to his feet and trotted over to Vipsania. "And…?"

"I need a thief. Fetch it for me."

He smiled and gave her a slight bow. "Of course, Magus. I am here to do the dangerous work, after all."

In unison, magi and thief said, "As per our agreement at the Quadrivium."

Ulric approached the Gate. The ring would be an easy climb, thanks to the strange metallic sections that wrapped part of it like armor. Still, some parts looked jagged and razor sharp. And he didn't relish the thought of touching the red metal or the crumbling flesh. He was confident he could secure his grapnel near the summit, close to the gate-stone housing. Then he could simply climb up the rope, supporting himself against the black nothingness of the Gate.

"I'll have to climb up. Is this blackness safe to touch?"

"I've touched it," Vipsania said.

"I find that answer evasive and unhelpful."

As he retrieved his rope and grapnel, Flaccus marched up to the Gate. He stretched out his hand, and with the slightest hesitancy, he placed his palm against the inky black surface.

"Safe," he said. Then he snatched his hand back as if he didn't trust it to remain so. He cast a furtive glance toward Vipsania and drew closer to Ulric. Speaking quickly and in hushed tones, he said, "You'll soon have the gate-stone in hand. Remember our deal."

"What deal? We had a deal?"

"I have to do it soon. Here, in the temple."

"Do what? Don't be a fool. Now's not the time."

"It is. Remember what Julia said: The gods aren't here. They'll be no witnesses to what I must do. What *we* must do."

Ulric grabbed Flaccus by the arm. "Listen, you idiot! Do nothing until we've had a chance to talk later, back in the ruins."

"Flaccus!" Vipsania called. "Stop bothering Ulric."

Flaccus kept his eyes locked with Ulric's and jerked his arm free. "Yes, Magus!"

"Do nothing!" Ulric hissed under his breath.

Flaccus retreated to join the others, who had gathered nearby to watch the theft of the gate-stone.

Ulric cast the grapnel, and it silently caught on the red metal. He pulled on the rope, testing the strength of the hold, then cautiously placed one foot against the perfect blackness of the

Gate. He expected to sink into limitless depths, but it was solid as stone.

Once he climbed to the top, he gingerly straddled the ring next to the gate-stone.

"How difficult does it look?" Kehindé asked.

The gate-stone was a palm-sized, oval-shaped jewel of golden crystal. A soft white light emanated from deep within. Ulric leaned over and took a closer look. The stone was simply hovering within its setting, suspended between several fleshy, finger-like prongs.

"It *looks* easy."

"Praise Eltarus!" Vipsania moved closer. "Be careful, but… do what you must."

Ulric imagined several methods of retrieving the gate-stone without touching it, but then he thought, *Neesis favors madness and bold action!*

With one swift motion, he seized the gate-stone.

And the gate-stone seized him. He felt it in his mind. It sang to him. The song imparted two overwhelming passions: deception, and a hatred of Elts. The emotions passed through him and were gone in an instant.

Deception? he thought. *That's my kind of magic. Hating Elts? Why would an Eltaran gate-stone hate Elts?*

He yanked the stone free and triumphantly held up the glowing jewel. "Got it!"

From atop the Gate, Ulric saw Flaccus lurking behind Vipsania. He raised his arm and pointed a small metal pyramid toward her back.

"Vipsania!" Ulric shouted.

There was a deafening crack, and a blinding flash lit up all corners of the gate-well. Ulric had the vague impression of a line of white light leaping from the tip of the pyramid, blasting through Vipsania, then arcing across the chamber into the stone in his hand, where it plunged into the empty gate-stone setting. Then there was the sensation of flying, followed by blackness.

The Emissary

Julia looked down at Ulric with tear-filled eyes. "Our doom approaches."

Ulric lay on the hard stone, having been thrown from the Gate by Flaccus' lightning bolt. He shook his head and tried to focus, though the ringing in his ears made it difficult. As did the knot rising on the back of his head and the sharp pain in his side that could only mean a bruised rib or two. In his hand, the gate-stone blazed with a brilliant white light.

"Are you alright?" he asked.

"Vipsania.... I couldn't save her."

"It's not your fault. You warned us." Ulric tried to rise, but he fell back to the hard floor. "Help me up?"

With Julia's help, he stood.

Magus Vipsania lay still, a faintly smoking heap of contorted limbs. An ugly scorch mark marred her beautiful sapphire stola. Kehindé stood over her body, unmoving, his face a blank mask with dead eyes. Rexinda knelt beside her, sobbing for her theia. The slaves looked on in shock; Renier stared at Vipsania with the look of a man who thought it all to be a cruel fabricator's trick.

Ulric felt ill. None of his plans had included murder. Not of Vipsania, not of anyone. The deaths of fellow Imperaré had been bad enough. Now he had underestimated Flaccus, leading to the death of an innocent woman.

Kehindé turned and faced Vipsania's murderer. He walked toward Flaccus, drawing his saber. To Ulric's surprise, Rexinda remained crying over Vipsania's body.

Flaccus took a step back, brandishing the small but deadly metallic pyramid. "Aren't you going to ask why?"

"No."

"I would have done anything to get away from her." His voice broke and squeaked. "She was cruel. Hateful. She was a monster!"

"No." Kehindé advanced.

"So I made a deal: The stone for my freedom." As Kehindé drew closer, Flaccus failed to hide his rising panic. "He can't be denied! Modius Nero must have the gate-stone! I had no choice!"

"No." Kehindé raised his sword.

Flaccus raised the metal pyramid. "Stay back! Don't you fear death?"

"Now I fear life."

Flaccus unleashed another blast, filling the gate-well with blinding light and thunder. The bolt went wild. Only a small portion struck Kehindé, sparking down his saber and sending him tumbling to the ground. The rest flew across the chamber, passing harmlessly through the stone in Ulric's hand, then arcing across the air to strike the Gate. Crackles of light danced across the metal ring.

Rexinda stood, wiped her eyes, and drew her gladius.

As if awakening from a nightmare, Renier tore his gaze away from Vipsania's body. He pointed at Flaccus and shouted, "He's a murderer! The penalty is death!"

Ulric tried to speak, but the Gate emitted a sudden drone that pierced skulls and shook bones. It shuddered once, then pulsed with a mockery of organic life. Its desiccated flesh appeared to heal, transforming from dead gray skin into raw pink meat. With a screech of tortured metal, the rusted plates protecting the ring began to spin and shift, rearranging themselves into a new, sinister configuration.

Everyone froze, staring at the Gate in horror. The perfect blackness at the center rippled like the surface of a pond.

Julia pulled Ulric close. "It comes."

Then the surface became sea-tossed and chaotic, as if an unseen tempest drove it.

"What? What's coming?"

The Gate screamed. Ulric covered his ears, but nothing could block out that soul-piercing sound. Then there was a sudden, deafening silence.

The churning nothingness receded to the edges of the ring, and for an instant, Ulric glimpsed strange vistas of a dim, twisted landscape under mist-filled skies. The clouds briefly parted, revealing strange stars and… something else. Something that made Flaccus clutch his head and trace a protective sign in the air. That made Rexinda stumble and hesitate. A thing that made Renier gasp and turn away. Something that made even Kehindé falter. A dagger of pain shot through Ulric's mind and sent his eyes fleeing to the far corners of the gate-well.

The slaves fell to their knees, screaming.

"It deceived the Eltarans!" Julia said.

"How do you know—"

An unrelenting torrent of cold, fetid mists blew from the Gate. The gale turned everyone's breath to frost, the acrid air stinging their eyes and throat.

Something moved inside the mist.

The gate-stone in Ulric's hand pulsed coolly as the thing's hatred of Elts passed through him. Then it became a lump of ice as it imparted a new emotion: terror. He secured the jewel inside his pouch and braced himself.

A figure, tall and impossibly thin, emerged from the billowing clouds. The golden breastplate, bracers, and greaves of an Eltaran warrior hung loosely upon a spindly frame draped in a tattered cloak. An adamant crown rested upon its head of long, night-black hair. It carried a long spear of dark metal.

"Our doom."

Ulric dared to look the creature in the eyes and trembled. Its face was gaunt, its flesh pale and tight, and things seemed to slither and squirm just beneath the surface of its skin. Worse, it had no eyes; only two pools of nothingness, like the Eltaran Gate.

"**Thou art no Children of Eltarus.**" it said in archaic Trumin. "**Nay, thou art the spawn of the accursed Alakur.**" The creature's voice sounded hollow, as if it had traveled from a vast and desolate space. "**Good. My master will be pleased.**"

It smiled.

Ulric recoiled, pushing Julia behind him and drawing his spatha. The Eltaran runes upon the blade burst to life with an intense blue light. "What in the Nine Gates are you?"

It turned its eyeless gaze toward Ulric, and his blood froze. Julia looked away, burying her face in Ulric's tunic.

"Yes. Beyond the Ninth Gate my master, the Wyrm, lies gnawing at the root of Creation." It considered Ulric for a moment. **"Who art thou? There is a shroud about thou."**

While Rexinda yanked Kehindé to his feet, Flaccus ran for the exit, skidding to a halt near Ulric.

"We have the gate-stone!" he said, just loud enough for Ulric to hear over the freezing wind. "Remember our deal. We run!"

"Deal? What is he talking about?" Julia asked.

Ulric pointed his sword at Flaccus. "You rat-faced murderer, there was no deal! I'm making sure Kehindé gets out of here so he can gut you."

Flaccus took one last greedy look at the glowing stone in Ulric's hand, then sprinted down the hallway.

"I am an emissary of the Wyrm. My master commands thee to travel through the Nine Gates. Thou shalt know pain. Thou shalt know suffering. In the end, thou shalt kneel before the Wyrm and know emptiness."

The mists behind the Emissary twisted and solidified into a mass of dark, writhing tendrils. With an intricate flourish, the creature thrust its spear toward the exit, its metal blade smoking and dripping darkness. A steaming, hissing slug broke off from the dark mass and raced across the floor, leaving a trail of acid-stained stone. It reached the hallway an instant after Flaccus escaped, then exploded into a glistening web of acidic blackness stretching across the archway.

They were trapped.

Kehindé stood unsteadily, still dazed from the lightning bolt. He leveled his bejeweled Bayjoni saber at the creature. "Let us go, devil. Or you will know death."

"I belong to the Wyrm; death has no meaning for me. Thou belongs to the Wyrm now."

"Fuck you!" Rexinda screamed. "I belong to no one!"

"I shall begin with these pathetic specimens." The Emissary pointed its spear at the young slaves, who were on their knees in a state of shock, muttering and praying. **"If only to end their mewling."**

A dark cloud surrounded the spearhead and a portion of the roiling darkness before the Gate lashed out like vipers, enveloping the slaves. They fell to the floor, thrashing and screaming hideously as the acidic tendrils scorched their bodies. Between hacking sobs, they begged Alakur and Myrill for mercy. Their cries were cut short when the clutching mass poured itself down their throats, burrowed into their eyes, and tore into their flesh. As one, their bodies convulsed and rose into the air, supported by a pillar of mist. Their heads hung limply, black eyes staring as things crawled beneath their acid burnt skin. The slaves receded into the mists and disappeared through the Gate.

Kehindé and Rexinda charged. The Emissary's spear snapped down and shot out in a one-handed thrust that nearly pierced Kehindé's chest. He deflected the spearhead at the last possible moment, keeping his forward momentum to slash at the creature's throat. Blindingly fast, the Emissary pulled the spear back into a two-handed grip, blocking the saber while simultaneously spinning the butt end forward to slam into Rexinda's gut. With a grunt of pain, she stumbled away.

Kehindé unleashed an onslaught of blindingly fast saber strikes, driving the creature back. Rexinda caught her breath, cursed, and charged again, her blonde hair flying wildly in the icy wind. She tried to flank the Emissary with a series of thrusts and slashes, but it twisted and spun, dodging and blocking every blow in an impossibly swift acrobatic dance.

Ulric approached the glistening black web that blocked the way out. It trembled as he drew close, then sprouted several acid-dripping tentacles. Recalling the horror of the slave's fate, he scurried back to Julia's side.

There had to be a way out! Was their only chance of escape defeating the creature? This self-proclaimed Emissary?

Sweet Neesis! Can you hear me from this accursed place? I need your divine luck! Help me kill it, or just knock it senseless. Then maybe that wall of black shit will vanish. He commands it with the spear, I think. Can I break it? Steal it?

"Renier!" he called. "Watch over Julia."

The terrified old scholar dutifully hurried over and placed a protective arm around Julia. Of course, he knew there was nothing the old man could do to protect her if he failed.

"We can't escape our doom," Julia said.

"We'll see."

Ulric tried to sink into the ordered shadows of his mind while holding onto the energy and chaos of his waking thoughts. To face the Emissary, he needed to enter a blade-ecstasy trance. He tried to take a deep, calming breath.

Then he coughed as acidic air filled his lungs, causing sharp pains to shoot through his chest.

It was no use. His ribs made breathing difficult, and even if a deep breath was possible, it only invited cold, stinging air into his lungs. There were just too many distractions.

Ulric secured the brightly glowing gate-stone in the pouch at his side; they would have to make do with the dim light emanating from beyond the Gate. Then he ran as best he could into the fray.

He tried to plunge his sword between the Emissary's shoulder blades, but he was too slow. With a deadly hissing sound, its spear cut through the air in a wide arc, forcing everyone back. Ulric ducked and rolled under the attack, popping up with one of his boot daggers in hand. He launched it at the Emissary's black eyes.

The blade missed its mark by a hair's breadth. He cursed.

The Emissary looked upon its opponents. **"Such spirit. Such pointless bravery. The Children of Alakur always made for unruly slaves."**

Kehindé and Rexinda closed in, and the sound of clashing swords and spear drowned out the otherworldly wind.

Ulric drew his long dagger with his off hand but hung back, engaging only to distract or take advantage of a perceived opening. He feared he was of little help; his ribs ached and the acidic fumes, or perhaps the blow to his head, had left the room spinning and his stomach churning.

The Emissary's spear shot between Kehindé and Rexinda, then whipped back and forth, knocking them apart. The creature leaped high through the gap, knocking Rexinda's sword aside and thrusting down into her chest. Bronze plates crumpled and the padding beneath tore, but the spearhead did not penetrate her armor. The force of the blow knocked her to the floor and sent her gladius clattering into the darkness.

The Emissary landed and twisted away from Kehindé's saber to snap its spear toward Rexinda, leaving a trail of black mist in its wake. From the writhing mass before the Gate, a column of seething blackness launched itself toward her.

Rexinda desperately clawed the floor for her fallen sword, but found nothing. The head of the black column split into a mass of seeking tendrils and fell upon her. With a scream, she rolled out of the way at the last moment. The blackness splattered against the floor, hissing and steaming more of its acidic stench into the air.

Kehindé tried to reach her, but the Emissary pressed its attack, using its long spear to hold him at bay.

Rexinda struggled to stand, wincing as she clutched at the dent in her armor. She went for the Gualdean axe at her belt, but the blackness reformed and shot forward before she was ready.

Ulric struck, swinging wildly at the thing's flank. A foul mist erupted from its body, and the blackness recoiled like a living thing. The head of the column pivoted toward Ulric and prepared to strike, but Rexinda's axe struck first. There was another eruption of fetid mist and the thing deflated like a punctured bladder.

Rexinda laughed, expelling her terror and frustration. "By the Red Blade! We *can* kill these things!"

"Maybe together we can—"

Rexinda's sandaled foot slammed into Ulric, pushing him out of the path of the Emissary's spear. The creature crashed between them, and Kehindé followed close behind. Ulric backpedaled furiously, blocking the blows with his sword and long dagger.

Ulric was grateful to draw the creature's attention away from Rexinda. At least it ignored Julia. He didn't understand why, but he'd take what miracles he could get.

Rexinda retreated, clumsily defending herself with her axe. Ulric could tell that despite her Gualdean heritage, she preferred the Trumin gladius.

The three of them circled the Emissary, each breathing heavily and struggling with the pain of their wounds. Ulric wasn't sure if the creature felt fatigue; he wasn't sure if it even breathed.

The spear snapped forward, tracing a line of black mist in the air, then pointed at Kehindé. A tentacle of acidic darkness burst from the roiling mist and shot toward his back. The spear swept around, still trailing mist, and thrust straight at Ulric. In an instant, his own slithering horror was snaking across the floor with the singular purpose of delivering a fate worse than death.

We're trapped in a nightmare play. This is the sort of fate reserved for the worst offenders of the gods! Did I damn us all? Neesis, forgive me! Ulric marveled that a thought could occur to him so swiftly, in the fractured moments between heartbeats.

The thing pursuing Ulric reared back, and its end split into a mass of flailing black whips. Kehindé threw himself to the side, slashing at the dark tentacle as it soared past.

With the two of them distracted, the Emissary descended upon Rexinda. Its spear lashed out with blinding speed. She screamed as it punched through the leather strips of her armor and pierced her thigh.

"No!" Kehindé cried. Another saber slash, and the tentacle attacking him evaporated into a cloud of foul mist. He ran to his adopted daughter.

Rexinda staggered, choking back tears, and grabbed the spear. "Cathus damn you!" She raised her axe, intending to hack at the shaft out of pure spite.

Before the blow could fall, the Emissary raised the spear—and Rexinda—into the air. She unleashed a terrible scream, and the axe fell from her hand. The Emissary whipped its spear to the side and tossed Rexinda across the gate-well, where she crashed into the far wall. It spun around just in time to meet Kehindé's maddened onslaught.

Julia and Renier ran to Rexinda's side. The Emissary pointed its spear, and the flailing tentacle before Ulric shot past him—heading straight for Julia. Ignoring the pain in his ribs, he ran after it, spatha raised, hoping to cut the thing in half with one stroke. But before the blow fell, it reached Julia. She screamed.

"No, no… no!"

To Ulric's amazement, the thing soared past her and descended upon Renier. The old man skidded to a halt and cried, "Sweet, merciful gods!"

His stroke fell and the Eltaran blade cut the thing in half—almost. It writhed on the ground, connected by a few slender tendrils of black mist. In an instant, the two halves rejoined and the dark horror snaked toward Ulric.

Julia and Renier pulled Rexinda away from the battle, leaving a long trail of blood across the stone floor. Julia examined Rexinda's wound, then upended her satchel of healing supplies and anxiously searched through the pile. "Myrill, have mercy!" she said, loud enough for everyone to hear. "It's bad! Very bad!"

Ulric swung again but missed the slithering black mass. He was tired, and the pain in his ribs had only gotten worse. He needed this thing, this nightmare *dark-seeker*, gone, or he would suffer the slaves' fate.

The dark-seeker exploded from the floor like a viper. He tried to roll to the side, hoping to strike at its flank, but he was too slow. With a whip-crack, several tendrils struck his back. Ulric felt a line of fire run down his left shoulder, as bad as any of Aquila's hot irons. His cloak was in smoldering tatters, but it had saved him from the worst.

He came out of the roll unsteadily, grimacing. Supported by its snake-like body, the mass of thrashing tendrils rose into the air. It surged forward and Ulric once again found himself in retreat, desperately fleeing from a nightmare. Something caught underfoot, tripping Ulric and sending him down to the hard floor.

The thing skidded away with a metallic clang. He had found Rexinda's gladius.

The dark-seeker dove toward him, and Ulric knew he couldn't escape.

It suddenly lurched and twisted as Kehindé's saber slashed through it, then shriveled and evaporated into a cloud of black mist.

Kehindé spun around to meet the Emissary's attack, but saving Ulric's life had cost him valuable time. He deflected the spear thrust too late and the dark blade cut a red line along his left bicep. Kehindé countered with a dizzying series of saber strikes that set the Emissary back on its heels.

The creature gazed at Kehindé with something approaching respect. **"Thou art a mighty warrior, for a Child of Alakur. Art thy people of the old blood?"**

Kehindé reached down and yanked Ulric to his feet, nearly launching him into the air. "Get the girls out! Only Julia can help her now. Don't let Rexinda die here. Unless…" He grabbed Ulric by the shoulder and stared down into his eyes. "Do not let this thing take her. Understand?"

"Yes! But how—"

"Swear it!"

"I swear!"

The Emissary attacked, and its spear clashed against both saber and spatha. Its spear sliced through the air again and Ulric felt a warm gush of blood running down his left side. He glanced down and saw a long, bloody cut in his tunic. Then the pain hit, and he fell back with a cry.

"Enough!" Kehindé shouted. His saber whistled through the air as he drove the Emissary back.

"**Thou art defeated. The first Gate awaits.**" With its distant, hollow voice, the words didn't sound like a taunt, only a recitation of cold fact.

"Our story was told long ago. That is true. But it is not for you, demon, to know how it ends."

The Emissary's spear shot through a hole in Kehindé's defense and plunged into his gut, emerging from the other side. The Kekeksuan warrior staggered, but never made a sound. When the Emissary tried to retrieve its weapon, Kehindé yanked the spear forward, pushing it through his body and pulling the Emissary off balance.

As Kehindé's saber strike punctured its armor and plunged into its heart, the first real emotion appeared on the Emissary's death mask-like face: surprise. It made a horrible gurgling noise that was neither the scream of Eltaran or man. The creature quivered, and a mass of squirming black things welled up in its gaping mouth. With a mighty kick, Kehindé sent the thing flying off his saber and tumbling back into the roiling blackness.

The black mists before the Gate seemed to retreat, and the cold fetid winds lost much of their force. Kehindé of Suloko, warrior of the Old Blood, fell to his knees, his saber steaming and hissing with black goo.

Ulric rushed to Kehindé's side. With gritted teeth and a remarkable will, Kehindé pulled the spear through his body and cast it aside.

Behind them, Renier shouted, "The way is clear! Thank the gods, the way is clear!"

"We get everyone out," Kehindé said. "Then we drop the stone. Seal this place forever."

"Yes! Then we find Flaccus and kill him?" Ulric asked.

Kehindé looked over at Vipsania's body, his eyes revealing a pain greater than any spear wound. "Yes."

Ulric followed his gaze. "Wait a moment. Rexinda's sword and axe! She'd never forgive me." With a groan of pain, he crossed the chamber and retrieved Rexinda's sword, slipping it into his belt. Then he hobbled over to where the axe had fallen, near Vipsania's body. He bent to grab it and fell to one knee with a cry of pain. His tunic and pant leg were now soaked with blood. With gritted teeth, he tucked the axe into his belt while simultaneously lifting the Eltaran map from Vipsania's body.

Forgive me, Magus Vipsania Tertia. Neesis Umbra! Look here! I honor the sacramentum.

Ulric returned and helped Kehindé to his feet, and they slowly made their way to the exit where Julia and Renier waited. Rexinda lay still, her thigh tightly bandaged. Even Ulric could tell too much blood was seeping through. She looked at Kehindé through heavy-lidded eyes and weakly raised a hand.

"Father?"

"Rest. It's over. You fought well." Turning to Renier, he said, "I can carry no one, barely myself. Do your mistress one last service and carry her out of this damned hell."

Ulric could see on Renier's face that every moment in the gate-well was sheer terror, but he swallowed his fear and dutifully said, "Yes, of course. It's not proper to leave so great a lady in such a place."

Julia hoisted her satchel onto her shoulder. "I need to look at your wounds. And quickly."

"Once we're out of here and have sealed this place," Kehindé said. "Then we'll see what miracles you and your goddess can perform."

Ulric and Julia carried Rexinda down the hall. Kehindé leaned against the archway, in sight of Renier, to give him courage as he retrieved Magus Vipsania's body. Kehindé would likely be dead by the time they left the hall.

The Gate unleashed a blast of howling, stinking wind that tore through the hallway. The black mass before it seethed and churned, and a long, misty claw crawled across the floor and pulled the Emissary's spear into the blackness.

Renier stumbled into the hallway, screaming for everyone to flee. Ulric and Julia ran as best they could, carrying Rexinda between them. The Emissary's spear emerged from the mists, cutting through the air in an intricate pattern, commanding something hissing and dangerous to emerge from the blackness. It raced past them and burst into thick, dark strands that stretched across the hall, blocking their escape.

"No, no, no!" Having hope snatched away so soon seemed to drive Renier mad. He kept running, and the web of blackness extended a long tentacle that lashed out and knocked him back down the hall. He fell to the floor, screaming as acid dissolved the flesh along a narrow line from one side of his face to his knee. Half blinded, he lay there moaning and babbling. Then he fell silent.

The Emissary emerged from the roiling clouds. **I am of the Wyrm. Death holds no power over me."**

Kehindé staggered forward to meet the Emissary. He tightened the grip on his saber, but he didn't have the strength to lift it.

The mists behind the Emissary billowed and rose, obscuring the Gate and plunging everyone into darkness.

Exhausted, defeated, Ulric and Julia collapsed to the floor. Rexinda released a plaintive moan, alive but barely conscious. Ulric pulled Julia close.

"I'm scared," Julia said. "The gods are not here. I am beyond Myrill's sight under these accursed stones. I have no power, no aid to call upon. Is there no way out? No hope?"

"Maybe." *You're a damned liar*, he thought. "No. Only the oath I made to Kehindé: that I wouldn't let that thing take Rexinda."

In the darkness, only his eyes trained in the Shadow Ways saw Kehindé clumsily swing his saber and fall to his knees before the Emissary. He alone saw the undying abomination step back as a column of blackness rose behind it, blossoming into a writhing mass of horror.

With a trembling voice, Julia pleaded, "Don't let it take me." She kissed him, and he felt her hot tears brush against his cheeks. "I love you." She reached out to rest a hand upon his heart, but it fell on Aguja instead. "Send our spirits to Myrill and Neesis."

"Yes." He drew Aguja from her hidden sheath. "You belong to Myrill. Never this Wyrm."

"I hear Her! I can hear Her at last, Ulric! She's calling me. I belong to Mother Myrill now, totally and completely."

Ulric screwed his eyes shut and looked away as the black mass seized Kehindé. He screamed.

Julia slammed her hands against her ears, and Rexinda stirred in her oblivion.

"Merciful gods!" Julia cried. "Remember your oath! Rexinda should never hear such a thing!"

Ulric rose and stretched over Rexinda's body. He raised Aguja and plunged the needle-like dagger toward her heart.

Her body spasmed and slid across the floor. Aguja struck empty stone.

"Ulric!"

A dark-seeker had hold of Rexinda's legs, pulling her across the floor toward the Gate. Ulric slashed frantically at the blackness, but it only oozed farther up her body. He and Julia tried to pull her free, but it jerked her high into the air and out of their grasp.

Rexinda disappeared into the mist.

"No. No!" Ulric screamed. "Godsdamn me! Godsdamn this world!"

Julia reached out for him in the darkness and pulled the neck of her tunic down, exposing her breast. "Ulric! Ulric! There's not much time."

He turned and grabbed her, kissing her deeply, passionately. He placed Aguja's point next to her heart.

"Ulric? If you serve at Neesis' side, you'll be at Arakru's court in the Underworld. When will we ever see each other?"

It seemed such an absurd thing to ask. Ulric tried to laugh, but it came out as a choking sob. He could no longer hold back his own tears. "Silly. Neesis is also a goddess of love. Everything will work out."

He thrust Aguja into her heart.

THE FOLLY OF THE GATES III

Taken from the Forbidden Histories by Achle Nesvah

With a chorus of ancestral voices, the Wyrm painted horrific visions upon the king's mind: the death of the Eltaran people and the end of his kingdom. He laughed as the visions tormented the king, mocking him, filling him with weakness, and futility. But still the king was unwavering. Then the Wyrm showed Cemthsta a new nightmare: his brothers fallen in battle, his children enslaved, his beloved queen slain.

Unable to endure such horrors, Good King Cemthsta summoned his remaining will, and turned to face the eldritch God. For the first time, a mortal being looked upon the indescribable horror of the Wyrm.

The Wyrm ripped through Cemstha's mind, scorching his sanity, leaving only madness in its wake. The Wyrm promised to spare the king's family in exchange for his servitude.

"What must I do?" asked the king.

And so, the Wyrm shared the secret lore needed to build the Gates in days instead of decades: powerful arcane gate-stones, one each to be placed at the apex of every archway.

This knowledge came at a heavy price. The Wyrm demanded an offer. An offering of blood. And so the next morning, Mad King Cemthsta summoned his advisors and unto them he said:

"Bring me the eyes of Men,
Dripping with their Mortal blood.
And for each and every one so done,
A day's Gate labor shall be won.

Bring me the tongues of Women,
Ripped from their Human mouths.
And for each and every one so done,
A month's Gate labor shall be won.

And bring me the hearts of Children,
Spawn of Alakur must they be.
And for each and every one so done,
A year's Gate labor shall be won,
And the Gates to Heaven shall be done.
And the Gates to Heaven shall be done."

And so did the Eltarans slaughter thousands of Men, discerning not for innocence nor age. Thirty-three years of bloodshed passed, and the Gates were done. Mad King Cemthsta gathered his most skilled magi and bade them enchant the Gates, awakening their great power. But unknown to Cemthsta, the Wyrm had corrupted the Gates with his own malignant will.

When the Mad King directed his people through, rather than transporting them to the promised land of Empyrea, the Gates brought them before the Wyrm, the chaos that gnaws at the root of Creation. There, the Eltarans would live for eternity in a state of perpetual pain and madness, as twisted servants of the Wyrm.

By the time the tragic truth was known and the Gates closed, a hundred thousand Eltarans had vanished into the Void. We scant few survivors call ourselves the Shamed. And so it was that the great kingdom of Eltareah faded into ruin. And so it was that the Shamed went into hiding. Never again to speak of Mad King Cemthsta, emissary of doom. Never again to recall the folly of the Gates.

Myrill's Sacrifice

Ulric felt the warmth of Julia's last, shuddering breath against his cheek, then lowered her body to the cold stone and closed her dark, expressionless eyes. As he pulled Aguja from her heart, blood soaked her tunic. The dark stain spread across her like the black corruption flowing from the Gate.

He knelt in the hallway, shivering in a chaos of freezing winds and stinking mists while the screams of his friends echoed all around him. There was nothing left, no hope of escape. There was only the Emissary and his promises of unthinkable pain and horror.

Ulric placed Aguja's sharp point against his own chest, pricking the skin. "Divine Neesis, O' glorious goddess! Forgive my offenses and pardon my vows unfulfilled." He raised the dagger and scrunched his eyes shut. "Embrace my spirit to your ample bosom."

He plunged the dagger toward his heart.

A grip as strong as oak grabbed his hands. He opened his eyes and saw Julia standing over him, her delicate fingers wrapped around his fists. A boundless, uncomprehending joy filled him. He burst out in triumphant laughter and fresh tears. He wanted to leap up, embrace her, but he was too weak; the spear wound had cost him too much blood.

"Julia! I don't understand!"

"I do." When she spoke, the swirling chaos was silent. "I know now why I became an outcast, why we met at the theater, why I found you in the alley off Dyer's Street. It led me here so I might let Queen-Mother Myrill into this godless place."

Julia's caramel skin glowed with a light as golden as the first spring dawn after a dark, desolate winter. Pale green vines grew from her fingertips and raced across Ulric's body. Wherever they found a wound, they took root, sinking their slender shoots beneath the surrounding skin. The sensation was strange, unsettling, but there was no more cold, no more pain. The vines changed from the pale colors of spring into summer's deep greens. Then, their vitality sacrificed, they faded to autumn shades and crumbled away in the wind. Myrill's divine power had healed every ache, every wound.

When Julia next spoke, the change was so astonishing he fell back onto his hands. Her voice resonated with the sound of wisdom earned through long ages, and the echo of immeasurable sadness. And there was power. Power befitting a goddess, the Queen of Heaven. Julia spoke with the voice of Myrill Regina. "**I will not abandon the faithful to face the gaze of the Wyrm.**"

Ulric had heard the voice before, in a half-remembered dream while dying in an alley off Dyer's Street. He fell to his knees and raised his hands in supplication.

"Thanks and praise to Myrill!"

Julia—no, the goddess Myrill—marched toward the Emissary. As she stepped into the gate-well, her body erupted with holy light. The black web blocking the exit hall burnt away into a foul mist. The dark, squirming nightmares enveloping

Kehindé and Rexinda recoiled, steaming and evaporating in the light. The scorching tendrils retreated from their limp bodies, leaving behind terrible wounds. The dark-seekers retreated into the writhing mass before the Gate. Then they, too, boiled away.

"I, Myrill Regina, command you to leave this place. This is not your world. Your corruption does not belong here."

The Emissary stepped back, an arm raised to shield its inky black eyes from Myrill's light. **"No! This cannot be! Thou should not be here! I was told thy kind could not interfere!"**

Where the goddess stepped, young vines, shrubs, and saplings sprouted from the bare stone. They grew and entwined, covering the surrounding floor in a thick carpet of greenery. Behind Ulric, a low rumbling sound rose like the rush of storm winds through city streets. A gale of warm, fragrant air blew down the hallway and into the gate-well, driving the stinking mists through the Gate. Then Myrill raised her hands, and every vine, shrub, and tree burst into an array of colorful blossoms.

Ulric breathed deeply for the first time in what seemed like forever. The air smelled sweet, somehow familiar. Then he remembered.

He walked along a winding, wooded road in the hills outside Mist View. His adopted mother, Tessa, held his hand, smiling down at him through a halo of red curls. He looked up and returned her smile.

The memory had been lost, sunk beneath a sea of regret. *I was so little*, he thought. *I never could have saved you, Tessa. But you saved me, and I love you for that. Goodbye.*

Two long bundles of vines reached out for Kehindé and Rexinda and gently lifted them from the floor.

"**My master cannot be denied!**" The Emissary charged, spear raised. "**Shall not be denied!**"

Ulric ran to meet the Emissary, but there was no need. Julia—no, Myrill—had caught the spear. She held it in one hand as the Emissary, towering over Julia's small frame, tried desperately to ram it through her chest. A subtle twist of her wrist bent the spear down, inexorably forcing the Emissary to its knees. With a contemptuous gesture, she cast the spear and the Emissary aside.

"You dare raise your hand against a goddess? At your noblest, you were unworthy, King Cemthsta. Now, you are a corrupted, pathetic... thing."

The vines lay Kehindé and Rexinda in the hall on a bed of ivy next to Renier's body. With his sharpened senses, Ulric heard their shallow breathing, even Renier's, who he had thought dead. He watched as the vines covered them, seeking their wounds. Their breathing grew stronger as the plants gave their vitality, withering and dying as they healed them.

Kehindé sat up, tearing himself loose from the crumbling vines. Squinting against the sudden brightness, he spotted Rexinda stirring nearby and gathered her into his arms.

She clung to him, clutching his torn and bloody tunic. Shuddering at the memory, she said, "I dreamt of the Wyrm."

Renier rose to his knees and stared into the blinding glare. "Are we dead?"

Ulric stepped out of the light and handed Rexinda her gladius and axe. She leaped out of her adopted father's arms and said, "Ah, my blades. Cathus bless you in blood!"

"Well, Kehindé, you wanted to see what miracles Julia and her goddess could perform. What do you think?"

Kehindé retrieved his saber from the bed of ivy and stood. "I think the way is clear. Tell Julia we should leave. Now!"

Ulric took offense that the practical minded warrior wasted no time on awe or praise. Myrill was moments away from closing the Gate. What was there to fear? Still, a part of him couldn't deny the wisdom behind his words.

"Begone, Cemthsta, betrayer and thrall of corruption!" Myrill's voice echoed unnaturally throughout the gate-well. **"Crawl back through the Gate. You chose your path and now a maelstrom of nothingness awaits you."**

Everyone stepped forward to watch the Emissary crawl. It pulled itself along the last patch of bare stone, dragging its once deadly spear. Blinded by Myrill's divine light and choking on fresh air, the creature seemed utterly defeated. It knelt at the edge of the Gate, where some mist still gathered in defiance of the cleansing wind.

The Emissary dared to glance back over its shoulder. "**And what choice was there? Where was thou mercy when the armies of Men put my kingdom to the torch? Where were the gods? Where was Eltarus when my kinsmen were slain?**"

"**Enough! You lacked the courage to choose a better path and doomed your subjects.**" The wind intensified, threatening to knock everyone off their feet. It blew the remaining mists through the Gate and across the twisted landscape on the other side. Myrill's divine light flared like the sun and focused upon the Emissary. Its pale flesh burned.

"**Master!**" It prostrated itself before the Gate and shouted into the mists. "**Do not let this mere echo of creation stand against thy eternal glory! Can the lords of one world measure against infinity?**"

Beyond the Gate, above a bent and desolate world, the mists cleared to reveal strange stars dancing in the sky. Ulric watched as that which should have been immovable and eternal spiraled into new configurations. Somehow, he knew the stars themselves were like a lock being picked to open a pathway across creation. He felt a terrible will approaching; a fraction of the Wyrm's gaze.

Kehindé ran to Myrill's side. "Julia! Let's go! Now!"

"**Leave this place, brave Kehindé. Seal the chamber. I will face the Wyrm.**"

It took a moment for Ulric to understand. "I'm not leaving without Julia!"

The goddess turned to Ulric and said, **"Do not be foolish, young Ulric. Stay here, and you will almost certainly perish. Julia does not want that."**

"Please—"

"Go now. The Wyrm is nearly here!"

Dark mists oozed across the border of the Gate, wrapping themselves around the Emissary. The raging torrent of fetid, freezing winds returned, pushing back against Myrill's cleansing air.

Ulric caught the faintest glimpse of something in the Gate, an indescribable thing filling the sky at the center of strange stars. The sight of it sent a terrible pain tearing through his skull, and he fell to his knees. Though its gaze was fixed firmly on Myrill—on Julia—he wanted nothing more than to go unnoticed. He knew the fear a tiny insect should feel, if only it could, when it fell under the gaze of a cruel child.

The Emissary rose from the mists, darkness writhing and solidifying around it.

"I know what thou art. Thou and thy fellow 'gods.'"

"What you believe, betrayer, is of no interest to us."

The Emissary approached Myrill, its cloak of glistening blackness protecting it from her divine light. **"Thou art wayward children, fled across creation to this miserable rock, masquerading as gods!"**

"Sad, tortured thing. Your mind is as corrupted as your body and spirit. I have no pity for what you've become."

Myrill raised her arms and the greenery lashed out toward the Emissary. A writhing mass of black tendrils rose to greet it. For a time, wholesome life fought against otherworldly corruption while fresh air strove against the dark miasma. At last, the black filth burnt away, and the foul mists were blown back through the Gate.

The Emissary lay humbled before the Gate, huddling within the remaining blackness. With a desperate cry he announced, **"Behold, the power of a true god from beyond this petty world!"**

Ulric felt something cross the Gate. Despite his fear, he ordered his thoughts, calmed his mind, and risked a glance. From the depths of the stars, something stretched out toward Myrill—toward Julia. Was it the Wyrm's gaze? A thought? A color? A touch?

Myrill screamed.

The scream of a goddess filled Ulric with equal parts awe, terror, and sadness. The temple, with its untold thousands of pounds of stone, trembled to hear it. Myrill's divine light flickered, then tendrils of darkness pulled her through the Gate.

THE QUEEN OF HEAVEN

Aguja's ice-cold point grazed Julia's breast, causing her to gasp. With a strange detachment, she wondered how the freezing steel would feel when Ulric pierced her heart. She pulled him closer, kissing him harder, desperately, hoping it would never end. *And why should it?* Julia thought. Soon, they would both be dead and reunited in the Empyrean Realm. Then a fresh fear seized her, more dreadful than Aguja. More dreadful than death.

"Ulric? If you serve at Neesis' side, you'll be at Arakru's court in the Underworld. When will we ever see each other?"

Through tears, he told her everything would work out. Was it another lie? A foolish hope? No. It was faith. Ulric's devotion to the goddess Neesis Fortuna was unbreakable. As was her faith in Myrill.

Ulric slid the dagger into her heart, and she was unafraid.

Julia awoke with the certainty that someone had been calling her name. She opened her eyes and blinked against the glare of a perfect summer day. The sun shone brilliantly in the center of a deep blue sky, caressing her in a warm embrace. Had she been cold? She couldn't remember. A cool breeze blew down the mountainside and swirled through the paths of a lush garden, shifting her tunic and stirring her dark curls. She reached for a nearby balustrade of marble and gold and pulled herself to her feet. Far beneath her, a sea of billowing white clouds stretched into the distance above a land of green fields and rolling hills.

Julia had visited the garden once before; it was the Empyrean Realm, home of the gods. The revelation struck her like a landslide, sending long forgotten memories tumbling through her mind. It had been Myrill's mercy. A perfect moment. The goddess had spoken words of comfort, words of portent, words of doom. Myrill had prophesied she'd die at Ulric's hand, a dagger thrust to the heart. She had warned Julia that she'd do the same.

Her heart froze like a lump of cold steel as tears stained her cheeks. Nothing made sense. It shouldn't be possible to feel sorrow in the Empyrean Realm. Julia gripped the balustrade and cried to the heavens.

"Ulric!"

"Fear not, my Ikon. You will be reunited with the thief—for a time."

Julia turned and fell prostrate before the goddess. Myrill Regina looked resplendent in cloth of purest white and spun gold. Upon her head, a crown of silver and adamant shone like the dawning sun. And as before, there was something else, something hidden, something *other*. Julia could almost peer beneath the veil, but she feared what it might reveal.

"Forgive me, Mother Myrill. I don't understand. Have I… have I failed you?"

"No. You have not failed me, child." Myrill smiled and Julia's tears, along with her sorrows, evaporated. **"You have done as I asked. You have held close to the thief, opening a path for me into the Eltaran temple. We are**

shrouded, you and I; invisible to the Wyrm and its Emissary King Cemthsta."

"That would be thanks to me, Julia."

With those words, Julia realized she was no longer in the garden. Instead, she knelt before a deep grotto at the base of the mountain. A dark silhouette stood in the cave's gloom, all voluptuous curves under a glint of blonde hair. Her wild eyes shone with madness and desire.

"I know it pains you to share a bit of the glory, Mother, but this plan would be nothing without my Shadow Cloak."

"A cloak you stole!" Myrill's tone was all too familiar, one Julia had often heard from her own mother, Karânî. "Perhaps now that you see its true worth, you'll return it to your sister?"

"Nyxos never deserved it. The cloak has been mine since this world was molten fire. What is ownership, after all, but the possession of a thing?"

The top of the mountain erupted in a deafening rain of thunderbolts. In answer, the earth quaked. Myrill looked to the summit and said, "Pardon our ill reunion. A meeting of mother and daughter should be one of love—and forgiveness."

Neesis bowed her head and shrunk into the shadows. "Arakru is wise to command the loan of the Shadow Cloak. It will be done." She smiled, beautiful, alluring, feral. "Now, we spring our trap!"

Julia stood and asked, "What are we to do?"

"Long has the Wyrm pursued us. It has chased us across creation, ever covetous of the worlds we create. It thinks its victory is near, but we are so much more than we were. Together, we will meet the Wyrm and blast it back through the Nine Gates."

Julia watched in awe as the gods girded Myrill Regina, Queen of Heaven, for battle. Alakur, Bright and Greatest, gave Her power. His brother Arakru, King of the Underworld, gave Her guile. Cathus, God of War and Herald of Justice, placed the Red Sword in Her hand, its blade both beautiful and terrible. Ulorin, God of the Seas, granted Her strength. Ukorus, God of the Earth, gifted Her a goatskin hood with fierce horns, and a shield of sacred oak bound in shining adamant. Morbus, God of Death, imbued Her with His relentless savagery. Then Eltarus whispered to Her secret lore and bade Her avenge His children. Finally, Neesis wished Her luck and reluctantly loaned Her the Shadow Cloak.

Myrill Regina was now Myrill the Saviour. She turned to Julia and said, **"Trumerus Julia Minor, faithful servant and Ikon, take my hand."**

Julia approached and grasped the hand of a goddess.

All masks were stripped away, and the *other* beneath revealed. The light of revelation was brighter than the dawning sun, hotter than a dying star. It consumed her. It showed her a creation more wondrous and terrifying than she could have ever known, a knowledge alien and unfit for mortal minds. Julia wept.

Julia returned to the temple just as Ulric plunged Aguja toward his heart. Quicker than she thought possible, she caught his hand. She wanted to explain, to share her revelation, but mortal words were inadequate. Instead, she said what she could, offering words of comfort as she healed him with the tiniest fraction of her divine vitality.

Julia entered the gate-well and cast back her Shadow Cloak, unleashing Alakur's light. Its holy radiance burned away the Wyrm's filth, freeing Kehindé and Rexinda. With a thought, new life burst forth from barren Eltaran stone, healing all it touched. King Cemthsta, the Wyrm's emissary, was a mere afterthought, unworthy of mercy. Defeated, the king called to its master. And the Wyrm answered. From across the stars, it came, the primordial chaos that gnaws at the center of creation.

The Wyrm's mind fell upon her with the weight and impact of colliding worlds. Its thoughts were pure malignancy wrapped in chaos, the very seed of evil. Julia felt unclean in its presence, violated by its merest touch. The Wyrm's attack threatened to disorder her thoughts, her flesh, her spirit.

Julia—and Myrill—screamed. She fell to her knees, crushed under the weight of the Wyrm's gaze. How could a mortal, even one with the power of a goddess, stand against a god from Beyond? Despair gutted her like a sacrificial knife. The wound ran deep, spilling her spirit into the maelstrom of chaos that was the Wyrm. Then she recalled the words of Eltarus:

"Remember, you are the goddess Myrill Regina. Within your essence is the order that gives birth to life. And that order is an abhorrence for the Wyrm."

Now Julia understood why Alakur had chosen Myrill as His champion. And Myrill had chosen Julia as Her Ikon. With a guile worthy of Arakru, she feigned weakness, and the Wyrm took the bait. Dark tendrils caught her and dragged her into the realm of the First Gate.

With a cry of defiance, Julia erupted with divine light, burning the black tendrils entwined around her. The Wyrm blinked. Girding her thoughts within the Shadow Cloak, she fixed her shield before her and summoned the Red Sword to her hand. As she rose, she looked upon a benighted world neglected beneath a dying star. The dark mists were poison, and so cold wholesome air fell from the sky like rain onto a landscape cruelly carved by rivers of yellow sludge. On the horizon she glimpsed mountains and the remnants of ancient cities, their metal towers twisted and crumbling. Somewhere, the Eltarans lurked, tormented guardians of the First Gate.

Far above the world, the Wyrm filled the sky, gazing upon Julia with limitless hate. It said it would not destroy her. Instead, it would bend her to its will, forging her into a weapon against her fellow gods. It reached out to seize her, but Julia sensed hesitation. Doubt.

She looked into the sky, facing the Wyrm. And she laughed; a laugh born of joyful anticipation. She would bring life to a dead world. Concealed within Neesis' Shadow Cloak, her thoughts slipped past the Wyrm, crossed the void, and plunged deep into the heart of a dead star. With the power of Alakur, Bright and Greatest, Julia reignited the fires of creation. The sun was reborn!

Yet the world remained shrouded in deadly cold and darkness.

Why wasn't the star blazing in the sky? It should have worked. She had witnessed the star's rebirth.

The Wyrm's malice descended from the sky like a falling mountain, a grasp vast and inescapable. Julia threw herself aside, an act of pointless defiance. Instead of being crushed, she flew across the plain, cutting through the dark mists like lightning. The feeling was overwhelming; the weightlessness, the rushing landscape, the exaltation of power. It should have taken her breath away, but she realized she hadn't breathed since passing through the Gate.

A moment later, she stood miles away upon a blighted mountainside. Far behind her, the Wyrm's malice struck. The world cracked and a deafening boom shook the mountain range. Untold tons of rock and boiling yellow sludge scoured the landscape, flying across the plains. A terrible fear came with it and Julia cowered behind her shield, her screams lost in the storm of debris. The shield of Ukorus held fast, its sacred oak and adamant enduring where mountains could not. The ground beneath her feet crumbled and gave way. Julia plunged into the abyss and the mountain fell upon her.

Julia's mind and heart raced, her thoughts lost in a chaos of terror. The weight of the mountain crushed her, pushing her divine vitality to its limit. Had they failed? Was there no hope against the Wyrm? The rocks shifted and Julia sank deeper into the abyss. Somewhere above, the Wyrm's gaze approached, eager to remold and corrupt her very spirit.

"Despair not, Julia," Myrill said. **"Soon we will witness the first dawning of Alakur's light upon this world. You must fight on for a little while longer. Together, we will see the Wyrm humbled."**

Chaos and death were the essence of the Wyrm. It was her enemy. Myrill the Saviour brought life and order. Her words gave peace, turning Julia's fears into a fierce hope for victory. With the strength of crashing oceans, the Ikon of Myrill shrugged off the ruined mountain and thrust the Red Sword into the foul air. Its blade grew red-hot, nearly molten, then flared with blinding white light. Julia streaked across the sky like a fiery comet and the Wyrm descended through the black clouds to meet her.

The Wyrm gathered the dark mists as it fell, transforming the foul air into writhing, seeking tendrils. But the memory of the dark-seekers could not intimidate her. Julia shrouded herself in the Shadow Cloak, and the Wyrm grasped empty air. The Red Sword struck home. The Wyrm recoiled.

In vain it sought her, and again and again she evaded its grasp. The Red Sword of Cathus burned through the dark-seekers with ease. Seven times she smote the Wyrm; seven grievous wounds. But what was pain to a god from Beyond? What good were wounds against chaos and death?

No more, cried the Wyrm. The dark mists thickened, stretching across the sky, the very air an extension of its will. With nowhere to hide, nowhere to flee, Julia became trapped in the Wyrm's embrace. Its touch disrupted flesh, disordered thought, transmuted spirit.

Julia became lost in a world of searing, blinding agony. She wanted to scream, but there was only silence; a scream could have been some small release, and the Wyrm allowed no escape from its torment. All she could do was try to keep her thoughts ordered, try to remain Julia—and Myrill. To save Ulric and the others, she had to endure the unendurable. As its thoughts corrupted her mind, the Wyrm violated her flesh brutally, deeply. Julia felt herself slipping away, changing into something unrecognizable.

Then the light of a reborn star lit the sky. The black mist evaporated, and the seas of yellow sludge boiled. Freed from the Wyrm's grasp, Julia plummeted toward the ground. As she fell, she reached across the sky and cast the poisonous clouds into the void. With a thought, she covered the world in clean, wholesome air. As her feet touched the ground, a peal of thunder rolled across the shattered plain. A torrent of warm rain followed.

The Wyrm's anger was palpable, its retaliation swift. The rains became an uncontrollable tempest, battering Julia with scouring winds and blasts of lightning as the Wyrm reached for her once again. But she relished the storm's ferocity and rode its winds into the sky, forcing the Wyrm to suffer her gaze, endure her touch. Wherever Julia's reach extended, she transformed the Wyrm's swirling chaos into life-giving order. It grew upon it like a tumor, inflicting wounds deeper than the Red Sword, more terrible than any it had felt before. The Wyrm's cry echoed across the stars.

One tumor burst and spilled life into the newly formed oceans. Another sowed seeds across the world, giving rise to verdant plains and towering forests. Yet another erupted into an endless stream of insect life. More tumors grew, birthing creatures both strange and beautiful to populate a once desolate world.

For the first time in eons, the Wyrm knew pain; the Wyrm knew fear. It offered parley, but Julia knew it only sought a new means to corrupt her. In return, she offered no quarter, no mercy. Only the unbearable, relentless savagery of new life.

The Wyrm fled into the void, faster than light, faster than thought. Behind it, the stars reeled and locked into their rightful configuration, sealing the path across creation.

Julia looked upon the world she had helped birth and shed joyous tears. Together, she and Myrill blessed the infant realm, and then they reluctantly stepped back through the Gate.

An Oath Fulfilled

Ulric stared at the Gate. Julia and the goddess Myrill were gone. The Wyrm's victory had been swift and decisive. A part of him couldn't believe it, refused to believe it. All around him, the greenery that had held back the black mass of corruption withered and fell inert to the floor. With newfound power, the freezing winds returned, driving out the remaining fresh air. He rose to his feet in stunned silence and took one hesitant step toward the Gate, hoping to find the courage to follow—but he knew somewhere, on the other side, the Wyrm waited. And he was afraid.

The Emissary turned its black-eyed gaze upon Ulric.

"That was but a small taste of my master's power." It pointed its dark metal spear toward Ulric. It pointed its dark metal spear toward Ulric. **"Now do you understand?"**

Bereft of hope, he wanted nothing more than to die upon the Emissary's spear. With a little luck, he would impale himself through the heart and die before he could be taken. He raised his spatha and charged.

Then the gate-well filled with the dawning light of a new star, and Ulric slid to a halt. He raised a hand against the blinding glare and watched the desolate world he had glimpsed through the Gate transform into a verdant paradise. And somehow, he knew the Wyrm had been defeated.

Kehindé and Rexinda moved to join him, peering through the Gate in amazement.

"She did it!" cried Rexinda. "Praise the Queen of Heaven! And praise Cathus, who grants victory. But…" Turning to Ulric, she asked, "What of Julia?"

Kehindé placed a comforting hand on Ulric's shoulder. "I'm sure—"

"No! Impossible!" The Emissary screwed its eyes shut against the sunlight and gathered the last of the dark mist about it. **"This is some foul trick. A fabrication!"**

Julia stepped through the Gate, her dark curls wild, her green palla missing, and her blood-stained tunic in tatters. Ulric thought she had never looked more beautiful.

"Your master is defeated," Julia said. She sounded weary, exhausted beyond her limits, but she was herself again. "Humbled, he fled back across the stars."

"A lie! You lie!"

"With no dark will to hold it, the power of the Gate wanes without its stone." Julia stumbled forward and collapsed into Ulric's arms. She reached up and caressed his cheek, saying, "Oh, Ulric, Myrill promised we'd be reunited, but I didn't understand. But I do now… Forgive me."

"There's nothing to forgive."

The Gate closed, plunging the chamber into darkness. Only the blue glow from his spatha and the pale red lights of the distant murder-hall lit the chamber. The interior of the ring was once again utterly black, perfectly smooth, like marble. Its raw flesh faded to gray, and its metal plates lethargically shifted back to their original configuration.

"If I am to be an agent of the Wyrm's vengeance, so be it!" The Emissary wove its spear through an intricate set of movements to summon another acidic web of blackness. **"There will be no escape."**

As one, Ulric, Kehindé, and Rexinda charged forward. Kehindé leaped ahead, smashing his saber into the Emissary's spear with such force the creature spun off balance. Ulric fell into a blade-ecstasy trance as he ran, blocked the sweeping spear, made a feint of a quick sword thrust, then threw his last boot dagger as he retreated. The blade sank deep into the creature's left eye, sending it into a rage. Rexinda slammed into its blindside, shouting several insults as she drove her gladius underneath its breastplate. Finally, Kehindé smashed his fist into its face. There was a sound like a stonemason cracking a slab of marble, and the Emissary tumbled across the floor.

Rexinda started forward, eager to hack the creature into pieces with axe and sword, but Kehindé held out a hand to stop her. "Don't get too close! There's no killing the thing. I've tried. Look!"

The black, squirming things inside the Emissary were healing it.

"Renier!"cried Ulric. "Get Julia out of here!"

"Yes. We must flee while the way is open!" With a groan, the old slave helped Julia to her feet.

"Renier's right. We should go," Ulric said. "But the thing that blocked our way before? It's too fast. We can't outrun it. We need to get that damned spear!"

The Emissary rose from the billowing mists and looked upon them with empty eyes, coils of darkness rising from the spearhead. It snapped the weapon forward, pointing toward Rexinda, then swept it to the side to point at Ulric.

Two sinewy columns of acidic blackness erupted out of the dark mass at its feet. One snaked toward Rexinda, but Kehindé cut it out of the air. He immediately spun about and his saber caught the Emissary as it tried to summon a web to block their escape. As Ulric waited to intercept his own dark-seeker, he thought he saw a bit of smugness drain from the Emissary's face.

The black mass flew toward him. He rolled out of the way with ease, but his strike was off the mark. The thing veered away at the last moment and slithered past him. He wasn't its prey! The end of the column tore itself open into a mass of slender tendrils and plunged after Julia and Renier.

"Renier! Run!"

The old scholar ran as best he could, dragging along an exhausted Julia. It wouldn't be enough.

"Rexinda!"

The two of them descended on the snake-like body, hacking it to pieces until it deflated in a cloud of foul mist. Once Renier and Julia were safe, they rushed back to Kehindé's side and rejoined the battle. Between the ring and clash of blades, a desperate debate began.

"If we can't kill it?" Rexinda asked.

"Then we have to take its spear," Ulric said. "Maybe we—"

"No! You two get out of here!" Something in Kehindé's voice made the command immovable as a mountain.

But it didn't matter, because Rexinda would upend a range of mountains for her father. "Hells, no! The three of us can—"

"We can die, child. I've lost you once today! I'll not lose you again."

"By the Red Sword, I'll—"

"Ulric, remember your promise," said Kehindé. "It's rare for a man to get a second chance at an oath once failed."

Ulric had hoped Kehindé didn't know he had failed to save his daughter. Now the shame was overwhelming. There was nothing he could say, so he fought on in silence. He would not fail again.

The three of them retreated from the Emissary's onslaught, trying to lure it away from the Gate. They had hoped to draw the fight closer to the exit, where a mad dash to seal the chamber would be possible, but the Emissary would not follow. If they fell back too far, if they gave it any respite, it tried to summon another black web to block their escape.

If they ran, the Emissary would most certainly trap them. If they fought, they would exhaust themselves against an undying foe, falling one by one.

Rexinda caught the Emissary's spear with the downward curve of her axe and yanked it aside, clearing a path for her sword. She scored a shallow thrust through a previous tear in the thing's armor before it stepped back, pulling its weapon free of her axe. It drove its spear forward, shattering the bronze plates of her armor. Rexinda's scream was cut short as she stumbled away, bruised and breathless.

The Emissary looked down. A wiggling mass of black things were already closing the cut. **"Wounding me is pointless. Fighting me is—"**

Ulric cut the Emissary's taunt short as plunged his long dagger into its throat. It angrily gurgled something unintelligible and lashed out, overextending itself with a wide, sweeping attack. Ulric released the dagger and leaped over its spear, retreating to Rexinda.

Kehindé struck before it could regain its balance, nearly chopping the creature's arm off. It made a wet hacking sound as its scream caught on the dagger stuck in its throat. Black sludge oozed from the deep wound, stretching across the gap to pull the limb back together. Kehindé tried to wrest the spear from the Emissary's weakened grasp, but the mists swirling at its feet solidified into a dark, angry mass. Glistening black ropes shot up from the floor and whipped around the spear, casting off drops of acid that sizzled and smoked on Kehindé's clothing and bare arms. With gritted teeth and a cry of frustration, Kehindé released the spear.

The Emissary emerged from the mists, all its wounds healed. **"Run, and I will trap thee. Fight, and I will exhaust thee. Surrender to my embrace."** With a flourish of its spear, it fell into a low stance, ready to begin another onslaught.

Kehindé stepped back, his saber extended on point. Never taking his eyes off the Emissary, he said, "Ulric! Fulfill your oath."

"Ulric? What the fuck does that mean?" Rexinda asked between gasping breaths.

Ulric shrank away from the Emissary in exaggerated fright, slipping behind Rexinda.

"It means I made a promise."

He slammed a gloved fist into the back of her head. A shock of pain hit his knuckles and flew up his arm. Rexinda's knees wobbled, and she crumpled to the floor.

"Easy!" Kehindé called.

"What else was I to do? You know how stubborn she is!"

"Have Julia tend to that blow. And… farewell, Ulric!"

Ulric didn't know what to say. How could he just abandon Kehindé? Somehow, it felt as bad as anything Flaccus had done. He never thought himself a coward, even when he ran away from larger boys on the streets of Mist View. The only certainty was that Rexinda would never forgive him.

The Emissary fell upon Kehindé in a dark whirlwind of spinning slashes and explosive thrusts. Kehindé countered each attack with a perfect economy of motion. A simple sidestep, a small twist of the body, a perfect block and counterattack.

Ulric secured Rexinda's weapons and hoisted her over his shoulders. She stirred and struggled weakly in his grip, slurring her way through a tirade of profanity.

"Goodbye, Kehindé!"

He turned and dashed for the exit. Behind him he heard the clash of saber and spear, and the Emissary's calm, echoing voice once again remarking on the futility of escape. As he ran through the now-withered tangle of vines and shrubbery, Ulric thought, *Sweet Neesis, I'd give good coin if he would just shut the hells up!*

The sound of battle had become a constant ringing of metal. Kehindé wasn't giving the Emissary the slightest moment to summon an entrapping web, or even to send a column of grasping tendrils to seize them. As Ulric neared the end of the hall—neared freedom—the Emissary's calm proclamations exploded into a desperate rage.

"Stop this pointless struggle! The Children of Alakur shall kneel before me!"

Ulric heard a cry from the Emissary that could have been pain or rage. Then Kehindé shouted a warning. An instant later, he heard something crashing and sizzling its way through the faded greenery, though he didn't dare look behind him for fear of losing speed or tripping over a tangle of vines. The acidic stench of a dark-seeker drew closer. He tried to run faster, but Rexinda, with her bronze breastplate and leather armor, was growing heavier with each step. With the heightened senses of his blade-ecstasy, the thing's reek became overwhelming, and he heard a sloppy tearing sound that meant the dark-seeker had torn itself into a mass of acidic tendrils.

He had to be faster! With one last burst of will, Ulric shot under the huge sealing stone at the end of the hall and tumbled to the floor.

The dark-seeker flew over them, grasping the empty air.

Ulric rolled out of the fall, gripping Rexinda's axe in his off hand. His eyes were already adjusting to the murder-hall's dull red light. He launched himself at the impossibly long body trailing behind the thing's writhing head.

Julia released a panicked scream. He feared it was at the sight of another dark-seeker, but then he saw Rexinda had partially fallen on a storm dragon tile. Her legs disappeared through the fabrication as she slowly slid toward the pit underneath.

The head of the tentacle seemed to hesitate, unsure who to pursue. It folded on itself and shot for Ulric, but it was too late. He was already stabbing and hacking at it with his sword and the unfamiliar axe. It deflated, leaving behind nothing but a foul stench and acid-etched stone.

Julia and Renier pulled Rexinda away from the storm dragon tile and fell back onto the floor.

"Merciful gods! Will this ever end? This is too much for an old man."

Julia looked down at Rexinda, who was probing a lump on the back of her head, and asked, "Is she alright? Where's Kehindé?"

Ulric said nothing. He dropped the axe and ran to the mechanism that would seal the gate-well forever. He risked a quick glance back at Julia, ignoring the questioning look in her eyes. *I'm going to save you! I'm going to get everyone out of this accursed temple—everyone but Kehindé. Forgive me, Rexinda!*

He pushed up on the makeshift lever with all his remaining might. With a loud thunk, the switch locked into position. The floor beneath his feet trembled and the great stone began its descent. Slowly. *Too damn slow*, he thought. He could feel, almost hear, a rhythmic banging from deep within the walls. Was the mechanism damaged after centuries of neglect?

Rexinda stood on wobbly legs and asked, "Where's Kehindé?"

Ulric tossed the pry bar across the murder-hall, where it was soon swallowed by a storm dragon tile. A moment later, a bolt of lightning erupted from the hidden pit beneath. Rexinda watched the pry bar get blasted into molten slag, coming to a dreadful realization.

"No! Cathus curse you!" Without hesitation, she ran beneath the descending stone. "Kehindé!"

Ulric raced after her. "Rexinda! It was the only way!"

He overtook her, but she drew her sword and spun around, swinging it in an overhead arc designed to intimidate rather than harm. At the apex of her swing, the gladius awkwardly stuck on the descending stone. Ulric slammed into her, taking them both to the floor.

"Let go! I'm not leaving him, you coward! Kehindé!"

He used one arm to apply pressure to her neck while keeping one of her limbs twisted. She flailed impotently. With his other hand, he seized her sword arm and did his best to stop her from stabbing him.

The grinding of thousands of pounds of approaching death grew louder. Despite the calming clarity of blade-ecstasy, a rising panic grew within him. He staggered to his feet, dragging Rexinda with him. As he took a step, his head struck rough stone.

"I promised Kehindé I wouldn't let that thing take you!"

"Then… then let me go to him. I'll kill him! Then fall on my sword!"

With no trick or technique, only pure strength born of love and desperation, Rexinda broke free. Crouching low under the falling stone, she ran.

I will not fail again!

With a speed born of blade-ecstasy and pure will, Ulric grabbed her, spun her around, and jumped into the air to slam both booted feet into her chest. The two of them flew apart.

Rexinda spilled back into the murder-hall, clutching her twice-bruised chest.

Ulric hit the cold floor and skidded farther under the descending block. Looking up, he saw only approaching doom. Was it gaining speed as it descended? He was certain it was. He tried to sit up, but struck his head on hard stone. Panic shattered the calm of blade-ecstasy; no well-timed sword stroke or clever deception could save him. He was too far from the exit. Could he make it without getting caught and ground to a pulp? Was he that lucky?

In an instant, his fear-addled mind decided for him. He rolled out from beneath the stone block and back into the gate-well.

The Gate-Stone

Ulric looked back across the rapidly shrinking space beneath the descending stone block and locked eyes with Rexinda, who lay on the floor sobbing. She gathered what breath she could and exhaled a pitiful wail.

"Father! Don't leave me! Don't—"

The air flowing from the gate-well whistled loudly through the narrowing gap, drowning out Rexinda's cries. Then it crashed into the floor with an echoing boom. But all he could hear was the echo of Rexinda's voice. It was the hopeless voice of a child losing their only parent. Ulric recognized the sound.

He'd feel like a real bastard if he only had the time.

Once again, he was trapped, left to choose between facing the terrors of the Emissary or death at Aguja's point. It was an easy decision; he had made it before. And this time, Julia and Renier were safe, and Rexinda lived, his vow fulfilled.

Flaccus was also alive, but that was one regret he would have to die with.

Ahead, the sounds of battle still raged. How long could Kehindé fight on? Myrill's touch had not only healed their wounds, but also infused each of them with an excess of divine vitality. Yet now he felt a terrible exhaustion creeping into his limbs.

Still, it'd be a pity not to gloat to this thing's face.

Summoning a blade-ecstasy trance, Ulric ran down the hall, repeating to himself a popular litany of the goddess Neesis Fortuna: madness and bold action!

The Emissary pressed its attacks with the same vigor as before, but Kehindé was clearly tiring. It drove him back with a quick series of thrusts and immediately summoned a thick spire of blackness out of the surrounding mist. The spire towered behind the Emissary, then split in two, each half slithering through a wide arc to strike from both flanks.

Kehindé shifted his stance and raised his saber, keeping his eyes on the Emissary. In unison, the ends of the twin spires burst into a mass of writhing tendrils. At the last moment, he leaped back, slashing through the head of one dark-seeker. It deflated and fell to the floor, oozing a stinking mist. He pivoted to strike the other.

Seeking tendrils quivered in anticipation of tearing into Kehindé's flesh until they, too, deflated and fell to the floor. Kehindé turned and saw Ulric standing over the thing's evaporating remains.

"Rexinda is safe! It's just us now," Ulric said.

Kehindé rushed to his side, a calm, contented look upon his sweat-strewn face. Ulric thought it was very out of place in a hell of swirling mists and death.

"Why are you here, Ulric?" Kehindé asked.

Madness and bold action, he thought. "I wasn't leaving until I told this ugly bastard—" he pointed his sword at the Emissary "—that it's lost. And it's going to keep on losing. It's hit a run of bad luck, you see; it just doesn't know it yet. You and your master get nothing more!"

There was a moment of silence as the thing that called itself the Emissary stared at him with two ink-black pools. Ulric wasn't sure why he had said those things. It felt as if he was reading from someone else's script, but he liked where the scene was going.

Kehindé burst into laughter, and the Emissary charged.

"I will not be mocked!"

Kehindé blocked a spear thrust, then Ulric ducked under the spinning shaft. Backpedaling away from its attacks, he taunted the Emissary again.

"Do you even hear yourself? I've heard better dialogue in *The Tyrant, Unbound*, and we booed it off the stage."

The Emissary screamed in rage and unleashed a barrage of blindingly fast strikes. Without the heightened awareness and speed of blade-ecstasy, he would have been skewered several times over. Instead, the creature's rage only gained it a couple of humiliating wounds from Kehindé's saber.

It retreated, shrouding itself in a veil of darkness until it healed.

Kehindé let out a long, exhausted breath. "An undying, never tiring foe? This only ends one way. I'll not let it take me."

"You'll make a liar of me if you do," Ulric said.

They faced one another, placing the tips of their weapons against the other's heart.

"Do not worry," Kehindé said. "Rexinda and Julia will take care of each other."

They grasped each other firmly by the shoulder and prepared to end it.

The Emissary's spear shot out of the mists, flying between them with such force it seemed to have been launched by a ballista. It knocked Kehindé's saber from his hand and sent the two of them stumbling back. With the sound of cracking stone and a metallic twang, the spear embedded itself in the far wall.

Before they could regain their balance, the Emissary leaped from the mists. It thrust its empty hand forward and tendrils of darkness raced across the chamber, wrapping themselves around its spear and yanking it free. As the Emissary soared through the air, the mists delivered its weapon back into its hands. It landed and spun its spear in a deadly arc. Kehindé pushed Ulric out of its path, but unarmed and off balance, he caught the spear shaft against his temple.

Dazed and bleeding, the giant Kekeksuan warrior staggered and fell. Ulric tried to reach Kehindé, but the Emissary beat him back time and time again.

"**This**—" the Emissary looked down upon Kehindé "—**is proper and good. Men should crawl at my feet.**"

It drew a line of darkness in the air with the tip of its spear, and a dark-seeker slithered out of the mists. Ulric charged, hoping to hack the thing to pieces before it reached Kehindé, but the Emissary intercepted him. He leaped back at the last moment, its spear having carved a shallow cut on his thigh.

The seeker blossomed into dozens of writhing tendrils and seized Kehindé's legs. It lifted him into the air and held him before the triumphant Emissary.

Acidic tendrils crept up his body, burning and burrowing into his flesh. Kehindé didn't scream. With supreme effort, between halting breaths, he looked at Ulric and said, "My story… was told… long ago!"

Ulric retrieved Kehindé's saber and swung it with all his might.

"I said… you get *nothing!*"

Kehindé's head flew from his shoulders. His torment was over. The dark-seeker released his body and retreated into the mists.

"But I have thee," it said in a distant voice, empty of emotion. **"And thou hath angered me. Such a terrible rage thou hath inspired."**

Ulric ignored the Emissary. Saying nothing, he stared at Kehindé's severed head, trying to feel nothing. Kehindé had saved his life, and now Ulric had done the same for him. So why did it feel like a betrayal? Was his own story already written? Did it end in death unwitnessed, entombed forever in Eltaran stone? Or worse? Did he deserve it?

Whatever the end of his story, his role was to fight on, so he secured Kehindé's saber and drew his spatha once more.

The Emissary advanced, unleashing a barrage of potentially crippling strikes, intending to render him vulnerable to the dark-seekers. He blocked and dodged each blow, wasting no thought on attack, and retreated across the dying remains of Myrill's improbable meadow. The Emissary followed.

"You have nothing! Oh, you took some frightened, defenseless slaves. Thou art *so* mighty, O' king of wiggling slime! You stand before the Wyrm empty-handed! But fear not," Ulric taunted, "he seems a forgiving sort of master."

The Emissary pressed its attack, driving him back into the hallway, which now led to a dead end blocked by thousands of pounds of stone. **"Babble to the end, fool. Thou art mine."**

Why was he taunting the Emissary? The faint voice of despair, a constant whisper, told him to fall on his sword. It said, "Do it now, before the Emissary takes you like those poor slaves." Another voice, one of hope and madness, demanded he fight on. It said, "You never know what fortune might bring. Perhaps it holds the impossible, the wild luck that could lead to escape."

The Emissary's onslaught lost momentum thanks to the thick greenery choking the hall. Vines tangled about its feet, shrubs hindered every thrust, and dead saplings snapped and crashed in its path. As the creature struggled, Ulric scored infuriating hit after hit, causing the Emissary's calm facade to shatter. With a cry of frustration, it retreated several paces, its wounds healing swiftly.

"Why art thou still fighting? I have thee! Thou art trapped!"

The Emissary's spearhead bled darkness as it made two quick thrusts into the air. Two dark-seekers invaded the hallway, slithering down the length of each wall. Ulric felt a rising panic trying to break the calm surface of blade-ecstasy. Even Kehindé had not been swift enough to defeat two of those black nightmares. What was he to do?

Now! Despair whispered. It was time to fall on his sword. His luck had run out. Time to follow Kehindé. Time to join Arrius in the Underworld.

No! I'll fight on, hoping for the impossible. Neesis demands madness and bold action till the end!

Ulric stared into the empty eyes of the Emissary. He pulled his last dagger from his wrist sheath and tightened the grip on his sword. The dark-seekers drew closer, their glistening black bodies staining the walls with acid. They flanked Ulric, coiling like serpents ready to strike.

Ulric lowered his stance, leaned forward, and prepared to charge.

The Emissary lowered its spear, the hint of a smile on its death mask-like face.

Ulric dashed down the hall. "Your luck's run out, Emissary! You get—"

The dark-seekers shot from the walls, blossoming into twisted flowers with acidic petals.

And Ulric fell flat on his face.

What? Thrice-damned vines!

Above him, the dark-seekers crashed into each other with such force their heads exploded into a cloud of acid and foul mist. Ulric threw the tattered remains of his cloak over his head and rolled out from underneath the burning shower.

The Emissary was on him in an instant, driving its spear down, hoping to pin him to the floor. He tumbled away, barely avoiding impalement. Every strike was so close, he felt the spearhead tear through clothing or deliver a shallow cut.

A sudden light illuminated the hallway, casting stark shadows through the decaying greenery and stunning both Ulric and the Emissary. Ulric recovered first, rolling beneath a poorly aimed spear thrust. He drove his last dagger into the side of its knee, then twisted the blade so hard it snapped at the hilt. The Emissary screamed and fell, leaning on its spear.

Ulric sprang to his feet and ran toward the unexpected light. It was the gate-stone! It lay on the ground, atop a tangle of vines. Glancing down, he saw that the Emissary, by chance, had cut the leather cord securing his pouch. It must have been thrown free when he was frantically avoiding getting impaled. He snatched it from the floor, and a new passion seized him. He felt an overwhelming desire to run; to flee; to escape. A chorus of voices sang to him from inside the jewel, a triumphant song of strange motion and impossible escapes.

Ulric stared at the stone in his hand, blazing like a star. He tried to understand its song. He gripped the gate-stone, tried to capture its light, but it only turned his hand into a fist of molten fire and shadowy bones.

The squirming things inside the Emissary's body spat the broken blade out of its leg. It stood and extended its hand. "**The gate-stone is not for mortals. Give it to me!**"

The chorus inside the stone reached a crescendo. They asked the impossible, but promised the impossible in return. It was the wild luck he had waited for!

"I don't think so," he said. "I'm leaving now. And, as promised, I'm leaving you with nothing!"

Ulric ran down the hallway, laughing maniacally. He had given into madness long ago, and now this was the final insane act: dashing headlong into a wall of solid stone. He could hear the Emissary crashing after him, smell the stench of two newly summoned seekers in pursuit.

"Stop! Thou shalt—"

Ulric didn't know what would happen, but in his manic state he knew he wouldn't hit hard stone. He had Neesis Insania's blessing. So he didn't even flinch as he passed into the stone as a rock might pass through still water.

For an instant, he was inside the block, like a swimmer beneath the surface of a pool. He had a definite sense of space and direction, but he knew it would be wrong to call it sight. Swifter than an arrow, he flew. Then he was running headlong through what he had dubbed the murder-hall.

Unable to stop himself, he stumbled across one volcanic dragon, leaped over a storm dragon, then finally skidded onto the safety of a red dragon tile. With a quick prayer to Neesis, he secured his pouch and placed the gate-stone inside.

With Renier's help, Julia rose to her feet. "Ulric! Thank the gods!" Fresh tears streamed down her face as she ran, arms wide, toward Ulric.

Rexinda turned away from the broken sealing mechanism and grabbed her axe.

"Ulric! How?" She ran toward him, fury and hope battling across her face. "Where's Kehindé?"

Ulric stepped back on the flagstone landing and, unsure of what to say, simply shook his head.

Rexinda reached him first. She threw him against the sealing stone and pressed close, pushing her axe blade under his chin. "Did you run? Leave him behind? Cathus damn you! How are you even here? How are you alive?"

"Rexinda! Please!" Julia cried. "Give him a chance to speak."

"Kehindé died to save us. He died to save *you*. He would have faced the Emissary's hell for you!" Ulric pushed her away and drew Kehindé's saber, which had been hidden beneath his tattered cloak.

Rexinda gripped her axe, ready for battle.

"This is all I can give you." He held the saber toward Rexinda, hilt first. Kehindé's blood still stained the exquisite blade. "He was not taken."

Rexinda's axe slipped from her fingers and clattered on the floor. She took her father's saber and held it before her, mouthing a silent prayer. The blade shone a fiery red in the dull Eltaran light. Finally, she heaved a great, shuddering sigh and said, "By Cathus, I'll cry no more. All worthy of tears are now gone."

Ulric grabbed Julia, pulling her into a tight embrace. Her hair was a mess of sweat-soaked curls, and her tunic was torn and stiff with drying blood, but he didn't care. He kissed her, and for a moment she made him forget the horrors of the gate-well.

Renier took Ulric's hand and shook it vigorously, interrupting their kiss. "So glad to have you back, young master!"

Ulric looked past Renier, and his face hardened.

He put a hand on the old man's shoulder. "Stay here. Watch over Julia." He walked past Rexinda and said, "Give me time to draw him out, then do whatever you want."

Ulric hobbled onto the dragon tiles, carefully crossing from one red dragon to another. He favored his right leg, feigning a wound to his left side, where his tunic showed a long cut and his pant leg had been soaked black with blood. He slowed, then stumbled perilously close to a storm dragon before falling to his knees. In a hoarse whisper, he called out into the darkness beyond the raised portcullis at the far end of the murder-hall. "Flaccus! Flaccus!"

Silence.

Ulric hopped from one tile to another, wincing in pain with each jump, until he reached the center of the chamber. "Sweet Neesis! I know you're cowering there, Flaccus!"

Still nothing.

"What are you doing? Skulking about in the dark? Like a thief!" Ulric laughed, then pretended to fall into a painful coughing fit.

Magus Vipsania's former discipulus emerged from the shadows beneath the portcullis, stopping on the safety of the flagstone landing. He looked weary—no, not weary, beaten. The purple bruises under his eyes and blood at the corners of his mouth told the tale. Another voice sounded.

"No one's skulking, Darktalon."

Ulric scrunched his eyes shut, shaking his head in disbelief. "Gods be damned. Is that you, Luciano?"

"Yes." Luciano strode under the portcullis and grabbed Flaccus by the arm. "Try nothing, Darktalon. No tricks this time! Or you friend here gets gutted."

Ulric spread his hands wide. "I promise he'll not die by your blade today."

Luciano loosened his grip but did not let go. "Where is map?" Shaking his head, he continued. "All I want is map."

Ulric searched for a clever response, but a fresh voice from the shadows interrupted his thoughts.

"And I will take the gate-stone."

Ulric's eyes widened with astonishment as a third figure with long white hair, blood-red eyes, and angular ears walked out of the shadows to stand beside Flaccus.

An Eltaran! This has to be the one Julia mentioned.

Despite his heart pounding out of his chest, Ulric couldn't resist another jab. "You're keeping strange company, Flaccus. An Eltaran? Luciano I can understand—an assassin and a murderer have much in common."

"Enough prattle." The Eltaran surged forward, wild-eyed and eager. "You may address me as Raquin Velthar Usil, son of Aptrui Velthar Isil, follower of the true king of Eltareah. Now… the Gate. Is it open?" His voice was oddly melodic, but assertive.

"It was…" Ulric grinned. "Until we closed it."

"What? You imbecile! What happened? Did he come? Did you see them? As we approached, I saw something. No… felt something."

Even shouting, the Eltaran's voice carried an unmistakable persuasive lilt, though Ulric sensed within it the desperate tones of a madman. Out of the corner of his eye, he saw Rexinda glaring at Flaccus, Kehindé's saber gripped tightly in her hands.

From behind Ulric, Julia said, "The Gate stays closed."

Raquin unsheathed his sword and took another step forward. Flaccus grabbed his cape. "Stop. It's trapped."

Raquin froze, intently scanning the floor of the murder-hall. When he had finished, he nodded his head and murmured something under his breath. Staring down the length of his blade at Ulric, he said, "What have you done?"

"Battle 'n blood!" Rexinda stepped to the edge of the dragon tiles and said, "I'm in no mood for this. I don't care who you are; take another step and I'll plant this blood-honored saber between those pointy ears."

Ulric flung his arm out at Rexinda, waving her back.

"Give me map, Darktalon. I get map, we all go our separate ways."

"It's not that simple, you Imperaré cretin!" screamed Raquin. "Now that the Gate is closed, I must have the gate-stone itself." He yanked his cape from Flaccus' hands and turned to Ulric. "Give it to me!"

With a feeble voice, Julia said, "That Gate… must never be… reopened."

Ulric saw her pleading eyes.

"I've seen what's on… the other side…" Her gaze lingered in the distance before returning to Raquin. "By the power of all the gods, it will not be allowed…" She took another breath and continued, "It will never be allowed to come here."

Ulric could never forget her look of desperation. He had seen that expression only once before, on Tessa, what seemed like a lifetime ago. Seeing it carved on Julia's face wilted his heart. He had to think. And fast.

Act on your instincts, you fool! Were those his words? Or Ghostwalker's? Either way, they rang true.

Ulric reached into his tunic and retrieved the Eltaran scroll case. "Is this what you want, Luciano?"

"Yes. Give to me, and you never see me again."

He reached into his pouch and whispered a faint prayer before pulling out the stone. Its pale radiance pierced through the cracks of his tightly clenched fingers. "And this, Elt… Is this your prize?"

Raquin's red eyes were wild with madness. Not the madness of Neesis, Ulric thought. No. This was Infernal madness. Madness with no purpose, no end in mind. Madness which leads only to death.

"Yes! Give it to me!"

"Send Flaccus. I'll exchange these for his life."

"Ulric, no!" cried Julia.

He hardened his gaze. "That's the deal. Flaccus for the map and the gate-stone."

Luciano shoved Flaccus forward. Narrowly avoiding a storm dragon tile, the shaken discipulus landed on the snout of a fiery volcanic dragon instead. With one last glance at his captors, he took a deep breath, then carefully leaped from one red dragon tile to the next until he stood over Ulric. He bent down and extended his hand.

"Give it!" Flaccus looked past Ulric, staring at Rexinda, who he seemed to fear more than his captors. "Hurry!"

"What are you going to do?" Ulric asked in a conspiratorial whisper.

"What? If those two don't kill me, I'm going to run!" whispered Flaccus. "I'll bar the gates. Drop the portcullis, too!"

"You'd trap Rexinda? Julia and Renier? Kill us all?"

"Are you insane?" Flaccus clawed at Ulric's fist, trying to tear his prize loose. "I'd never make it out of the ruins with Rexinda after me!"

With a cry of pure hate, Rexinda leaped across the dragon tiles.

Flaccus screamed. "Give it to me! Or I'll burn you!"

Ulric grabbed Flaccus' arm and shot to his feet, slamming his knee hard into his gut. He twisted his wrist behind his back until he heard something pop. Flaccus squeaked.

"You're not hurt! You tricked me! It's not fair!"

"Well, I am a thief and a damned liar, Flaccus. I told you that in the Quadrivium."

Flaccus' eyes locked on Rexinda. Her features were contorted with rage and stained by blood and sorrow. He saw an avenging goddess. He saw his nemesis with a red sword.

"Let me go!" His voice became barely a whisper. "Please."

Ulric dragged him a few steps over to the edge of a storm dragon tile. "I will. Once Rexinda has said her goodbyes."

With a word, Flaccus' free hand erupted in fire. He reached back across his shoulder, and Ulric felt the terrible heat. He leaned away as far as he could, but the flames seemed to leap toward him, singeing his hair and blistering his skin.

Rexinda pounced with the strength and precision of a lioness. "This is for Magus Vipsania Tertia! My theia!" She ran Kehindé's saber through Flaccus' stomach with such force Ulric barely held on. Flaccus made a pitiful sound, and his fire was extinguished. Then Rexinda twisted the saber cruelly and tore it across his belly. Flaccus screamed. "And that's for Kehindé of Suloko! My father!" She withdrew her saber, and Flaccus kept screaming as he tried to hold in his guts.

"You wanted the gate-stone, Flaccus?" Ulric shoved the glowing stone inside his robes. "Here, take the thrice-damned thing!"

He stopped screaming long enough to look surprised before Ulric threw him onto the storm dragon tile. Flaccus fell through the nothingness of the fabrication and disappeared into the pit beneath, his screams ending when a torrent of lightning shot from below. Silence, as well as the stench of burnt flesh, permeated the murder-hall.

"You fools! What have you done?!" Raquin screamed with Infernal madness, launching himself across the chamber toward Ulric. With an echoing clash of steel, Rexinda intercepted the Eltaran blade inches from Ulric's neck. Raquin, possessed with a strength born of rage and madness, knocked her blade aside and tossed her onto a storm dragon tile.

"Cathus curse your cock!"

As she plummeted through the fabrication, Rexinda grabbed the lip of a red dragon tile with one hand, her white-knuckled fingers clutching the slick marble with all her might. "Ulric!"

An Eltaran curse echoed through the room. Raquin clutched his arm, wincing in pain. He glared at Luciano, whose falcata dripped red.

"Your curse will never be broken now, Luciano! The Gate is impotent without the jewel, and those Beyond cannot return without a Gate. We're left with nothing but our doom. But I will see you dead first." Raquin looked down at his arm and screamed, "You are not worthy of Eltaran blood!"

With each combatant balanced precariously atop his own fire dragon, feet danced and swords clashed. The sounds of steel filled the Murder-Hall.

Ulric leaped to the red dragon tile and dropped to his knees. "Hang on, Rexinda!"

"What do you think I'm doing?"

Ulric couldn't believe that even in her dire predicament, this mouthy and unruly girl insisted on being— well, mouthy and unruly. It reminded him of himself. *Sweet Neesis! If there's any luck left, I'll take it.*

Raquin snarled. His breath came in ragged bursts, but his red eyes burned with flames fueled by madness. He moved swiftly, his Eltaran boots effortlessly finding the safety of the red dragon tiles. Luciano smirked, dancing from red tile to red tile with equal ease, his falcata at the ready. With a sudden burst of speed, he lunged, his blade slicing toward Raquin's ribs. The Eltaran parried and a terrific clang echoed across the murder-hall. Raquin stumbled back, the impact clearly sending shockwaves of pain up his injured arm.

Ulric grabbed Rexinda's wrist with both hands and heaved. "Damn, you're heavier than I thought!"

"It's the armor!" Rexinda retorted.

"Give me some leverage—use your feet. Now, on the count of three, pull!"

"Pull? Are you crazy?"

"You heard me! Do you want to get saved or not? Ready? One… two… three! Pull!"

Luciano's boot slipped on a smear of Eltaran blood, sending him teetering on the edge of the destruction. The blue storm dragon gaped below him like a hungry maw, but with a desperate leap, he flung himself onto the safety of a red dragon tile. He landed off balance and gasping for air, beads of sweat trickling into his stinging eyes. Raquin wasted no time pressing his attack, moving like a hungry predator. He slashed his sleek Eltaran blade down in wide, powerful arcs. Luciano blocked each blow, but he was growing tired. As exhaustion set in, resistance became more and more arduous, and the storm dragon tiles circled all around him like a pack of stalking predators.

Ulric yanked on Rexinda's arms with everything he had. Perhaps he found a new reservoir of strength, or maybe it was simply the divine luck of Neesis Fortuna. Regardless of the reason, Rexinda shot out of the pit and fell heavily atop Ulric. The two of them lay together on the red dragon tile, gasping and clutching each other like spent lovers. He pulled her close, trying to keep her from falling into an adjacent fabrication, hoping Julia didn't get the wrong idea. He needed to catch his breath, but seeing Luciano struggle nearby, he realized there was no time. Lying prone under Rexinda, Ulric drew Aguja and whispered a prayer to Neesis.

Yet he hesitated, watching Raquin rain down blow after blow, trying to break Luciano's defense with pure rage. *Wait*, he thought. *Wait and watch the Verdan bastard die. Why not? Avenge Ghostwalker. Fulfill my vow to Neesis.*

Aguja flew and sank deep into the Elt's thigh. Raquin screamed and reached for the needle-like dagger, but Luciano grabbed it first. The assassin pulled Aguja loose and plunged it into Raquin's chest. He looked down in disbelief as Luciano used the dagger to pull himself off the floor before reclaiming his blade. Raquin, still in shock, did nothing.

With his precious Aguja in hand, Luciano kicked Raquin into a storm dragon tile. He plummeted through the illusion and a moment later, an array of lightning bolts erupted from the pit beneath. Then the murder-hall returned to its silent, lethal stillness.

Rexinda stood and helped Ulric to his feet. They both eyed Luciano warily.

Thief and assassin faced one another in the center of the murder-hall. For a long, tension-filled moment, neither said a word, neither made a move. Then Luciano sheathed his weapons and extended a hand.

Ulric moved toward Luciano, hopping over one blue dragon tile before stepping perilously close to the edge. In the palm of his outstretched hand lay the map to Tmia Culscva.

"You take the map, Luciano. Then we go our separate ways. That was the deal, right?"

"Yes, Darktalon. That is deal."

Luciano took the map and headed toward the exit. Once he reached the flagstone landing, he turned, standing half in shadow, half illuminated in the vapid red of dying Eltaran light. "Of course, our separate ways lead us both back to Trumric."

Ulric considered Luciano's words for a moment, then said, "Fair enough."

THE SPOILS

Ulric leaned on the ship's prow, squinting against the glare of the midday sun. He searched the city for signs of danger as they crossed the slow-moving waters of the Nanpela River. The rhythmic slap of waves on the hull, mixed with the distant drone of the city, lulled him deeper into his own dark thoughts. He never moved as the barge, heavy with cargo from the interior of the republic, navigated its way from the river, through the canals, and into the inner harbor of the Portus complex.

He knew the Imperaré watched the city gates, so that morning they had abandoned the Via Borealis and traveled southwest until they arrived at one of the many fishing villages that dotted the banks of the Nanpela. The plan was to board a ship bound for Trumric and the Portus complex using one of the jewelry pieces he had taken from the Eltaran ruins as payment. First, he had needed to convince a fisherman to take them onto the river so they could petition a passing ship. Ulric thought it would take his last few coins, but a kind word from Julia and a smile from Rexinda had several young men competing for the job.

Every ship they approached greeted them with raised oars or bowmen until they finally met the agreeable captain of a barge laden with lumber from Astia and marble from Umbric. The cargo was due to be transferred to a ship bound for the Kreslan Isles, so they would sail past the river docks—past Brocchus and his Gutter-Fish—and into the relative safety of the Portus complex. Once on board, he had reluctantly handed over an Eltaran silver band inlaid with diamonds and amethysts—a heavy price for such a short voyage.

As the barge slipped into her berth at the inner harbor, Ulric knew something was wrong. The docks were as busy as ever, but there was the unfamiliar taint of chaos in the air. The dockworkers seemed to be distracted, on edge, while the clerks were nervous and abrupt. More alarming still, there were strange faces mixed among the Harbor Men. Men who watched from the shadows.

"You look worried, young master."

Ulric slid from the prow and sat on the deck, looking up at the old man from under the shade of his flat palm. Renier had been at the stern with Julia and Rexinda, who had been chatting with the captain for most of the voyage. Now the slave stood behind him, wringing his weathered hands. Ulric was worried. He had to dodge whatever trouble was brewing on the docks and deliver the gate-stone to Silo. Which meant he would have to confess to Julia how he had palmed the stone while slipping his enchanted quartz inside Flaccus' robes.

"A bit. Nothing I can't sort out." Ulric pulled his hood over his head, grateful for a little shade. "And you?"

Renier's hands froze. "Yes. I worry. How could I not?" he said, straightening and folding his hands behind his back. "After all that we have endured? And now, my final duty draws near: I must report Magus Vipsania's fate to the Collegium Draconis Aurei."

"About that…" Ulric smiled from the shadows beneath his hood. "Perhaps certain details could be—"

"No! Do not ask such a thing, Marcus Octavius Ulric!"

"Okay!" He held up a hand in surrender. "I just don't want any collegium trouble, you understand?"

"Why fear the truth? I don't judge you for paths not taken. You were true to my mistress till the end."

Ulric stood and let his gaze drift back to the sun-drenched city.

The barge was swiftly moored and the gangplank extended; it was time to disembark. They all gave their final thanks to the captain, except Ulric. He considered the Eltaran ring thanks enough for several voyages. Everyone hurried off the docks through a gauntlet of overburdened slaves, careless cart drivers, and shouting dockworkers. Finally, breathless and sweating, they took refuge in the scant shade provided by a small popina.

"I fear this is where we must part," Renier announced. "I'll make my own way to the collegium."

Julia rushed forward and embraced him. The old slave stiffened, his arms hanging awkwardly at his side. "I'm going to miss you!" Julia said. "May the blessings of Alakur and the Mercy of Myrill be upon you."

"And you too, child." Renier raised his arms and returned her embrace. "Blessed of Myrill!" When he withdrew, his tear-filled eyes glinted in the sun. "I will not forget what you did for us."

Julia smiled and wiped away a tear of her own.

"No need for tears," Ulric said. "Once I've sorted things, there's no reason we can't meet again, right? Vipsania's will might even hold your manumission. Imagine, Julia, the next time we see Renier, he'll be a free man!"

Julia said nothing, only gave a flat smile.

Renier put a hand on Ulric's shoulder. "I've seen you endure many blows since I've met you, young master. I fear the hardest is yet to come. Later, if you would hear the words of a foolish old man, find me." He moved toward the busy street and turned to Rexinda. "Farewell, young warrior. May Ulorin watch over your voyage. And take good care of Julia."

"Goodbye, old man. I will."

Renier stepped into the street and disappeared into the fast-moving traffic.

"It's time I find the captain of the Galatea." Rexinda shot a parting glance at Julia and jogged back toward the docks.

Ulric waited until Rexinda was out of sight then pulled Julia into a nearby alley, away from the prying eyes of the crowded popina. "Julia, there's something I have to confess."

"Ulric, I—"

"I have the gate-stone."

"What? But... I saw..." Julia stammered.

"You saw what I wanted everyone to see, but Flaccus died with an old, enchanted piece of quartz tucked into his robes."

"You lied?"

"Forgive me. It was a necessary deception. I can't risk the Imperaré or the collegium knowing I have it."

Tears welled up in her dark eyes. "What else have you been lying about?

"Silo. He knows everything. I chose the role of traitor to shield him from the other princes."

"Were Vipsania, Kehindé, Flaccus, Strabo, and all the rest mere props in your play?"

"No! What else could I have done? What choice did I have?"

Julia turned her back to him. Her body trembled beneath her green palla.

"There's always a choice," she said. "A path to a nobler end." When Julia turned around her face was tear-streaked and heavy with pity and regret. "I must return to Myrill's service. She calls me to Her temple—in Kos. I'm so sorry."

Ulric stumbled deeper into the alley as if struck by a blow. He heard the words, but they made no damn sense. They felt like a dagger piercing his heart.

"I'm sailing to the Kreslan Isles with Rexinda. Myrill's most magnificent temple awaits."

"I can't believe this. You're leaving today? Over a few lies? Is that where Rexinda went? To secure a ship?

"Were you not listening?" Julia cried. "The Goddess calls. I cannot refuse."

"Why not, Julia? Why not?" Ulric paused, but she remained silent. "Is there no mercy for us? Why would Myrill tear us apart after all we've been through? After we've faced so much horror and death together?"

"Horror and death? Do you hear yourself, Ulric? The goddess Myrill Regina is *life*. Myrill is healing and rebirth. You follow the path of Neesis, a goddess of uncertainty and danger.

It's a sort of madness. A madness I can no longer endure." Julia turned away, hot tears staining her face. "I'd never seen so much death, so much horror and pain, than what I saw in the long months since my exile from the temple."

"Exile?" Ulric lashed out, desperate to turn sorrow into something more familiar. "So the pampered daughter of a consul dabbled in the theater and Father made sure 'swift and ignoble exile followed,' but now that you've seen how nasty life can be for us plebes, you're running back to the temple."

"Damn you!" Julia's expressive eyes flashed with anger. "You're twisting my words. On purpose!"

"Remember—" Ulric jabbed a finger in the air "—I wanted you to stay in the city. I tried to keep you far from danger. *You* insisted on joining Vipsania's expedition!"

"Perhaps I would have chosen differently if I was not lied to. And if I had remained in Trumric, what sort of deal would you have made with Flaccus?"

For a long moment, he said nothing. "What?"

"I overheard you and Flaccus talking in the ruins. And then, as he fled the temple, he spoke of a deal."

"And I said there was no deal. You heard me promise revenge. A promise I kept!" He pointed toward the harbor. "Ask Rexinda!"

"I know," Julia said. "Why didn't you warn Vipsania?"

"Why didn't *you*?"

"I didn't know if there was a deal or not." Julia's lips quivered, and a torrent of tears broke free with an anguished cry.

"If I had warned her, I could have condemned you! Instead, I tried to convince her to abandon the temple! My love for you, my silence, doomed the innocent to torment and death!"

Julia turned her back, sobbing into her hands and trembling. Ulric tried to embrace her, but she pushed him away with a cry. He threw himself back against the alley and knocked his head against the wall, again and again. Pushing his hands back through his night-black hair, he groaned, "Gods above, gods below, woman! Forgive me!"

Julia wiped away her tears with her palla. "Gods above. Gods below. Exactly. Myrill and Neesis. Fortune and Mercy. We were always on different paths. We should thank the two goddesses for letting ours cross, if only for a little while." She smiled, a sad, forgiving smile.

Ulric took Julia into his arms and kissed her for the last time. He looked into her dark eyes and told her, "You were goddess sent."

He stepped back, and his voice and heart hardened. "Tell Rexinda goodbye. Tell her fighting alongside her and her father was an honor."

"I will."

"Goodbye, Julia."

Before she could reply, Ulric fled the alley and vanished into the crowd.

The Transnanpela Collegium had come for blood. They hit the Street of Hidden Pleasures like a red wave, flooding every twisting path and blind alley with Gutter-Fish, Sons of Mania, and Shrine Alley Soldiers. What began as a search for Portus men soon turned into a deluge of indiscriminate killing. As predictable as the incoming tide, the gangs had given in to their bloodlust.

None of this surprised Luciano. The rivalry between Brocchus and Silo had been simmering for years, and the Eltaran map had provided the heat needed to bring it to a boil. Now the roiling pot spilled over, unleashing a torrent of blood. Luciano didn't care. He had returned to the city yearning for nothing more than a proper bed and a very large jug of wine, but the yellow spike in his head had driven him onward. *Of course there's no hope of sleep or wine-induced oblivion*, he thought. *A slave has every choice made for him.* He would report to Cornelius Brocchus and, with any luck, his news would drive the collegium prince to murder. It was a ridiculous hope—he'd never be that lucky. Luck was the domain of Neesis Fortuna; Darktalon's goddess, not his. Dreaded Nyx, Goddess of Night, Goddess Beyond, was his goddess, and She had been as silent as a midnight alley.

So he marched straight to Brocchus' office, only to find Evander, the collegium primus, drinking in the prince's chair. He looked dour despite his colorful tunic and garish jewelry. An impressive collection of wine bottles cluttered the marble tabletop before him.

"Ah, Porteles!" Evander beckoned Luciano forward with his wine cup. "This day is full of surprises. You're supposed to be dead." He took a quick sip, then continued. "I imagined you rotting in a ditch in some miserable interior province. Yet here you are."

"Here I am." Luciano had no time for his drunken blather. "Where is Brocchus?"

Evander leaned across the table, knocking over an empty jug with a loud clatter. He took a long, hard look at Luciano. "You look thirsty, Porteles. Here," he said, pouring wine from a slender blue bottle, "have a cup of Feyolo. I think it was a gift from the Wine Sellers Collegium."

Luciano drank the wine in one long gulp, then slammed the cup down. "Brocchus?"

"Seems we've both been left behind." Evander leaned back in his chair and took another drink. "You? Inconveniently dead. Me?" He arranged the empty cups and bottles into a makeshift wall. "Well, someone has to lead the defense."

"Against what?"

"Counter attack!" With a wave of his hand, he scattered the bottles. "As we speak, our glorious prince is raiding across the border into Portus territory. Revenge for poor Tubero, we say, but one excuse is as good as another, is it not?"

Luciano found it difficult to imagine the obese Brocchus raiding anything. "This I must see. I find him, make report." Luciano turned and headed for the exit.

"Good news, no doubt?"

Evander burst into drunken laughter as Luciano walked on.

A short time later, Luciano picked up the trail of blood in the winding streets west of the Calidius Amphitheater. Having had no desire to join the raid—he'd already dealt enough death in Brocchus' name—he moved from shadow to shadow, from rooftop to rooftop, until he saw Brocchus, along with several bodyguards, enter Tubero's taberna. The Portus Collegium had long since restored the old sign, with its big blue lettering reading TUBERO'S. He had heard Silo liked it when patrons asked after Tubero. His fate made for a good story—and a warning.

Luciano descended onto the Street of Hidden Pleasures and headed for the taberna, stepping over several bodies along the way. It looked as if Silo's men had put up a fearsome defense, but had been surprised and overwhelmed by numbers. Even now, the sounds of a battle drifted from the open doors.

Could Brocchus be in danger? Would the portly prince get himself killed? Luciano tried to relish the thought, but a part of himself, the part the Dominator had twisted into a nagging yellow spike, urged him to action. It screamed: Do your duty! Protect your master!

He ran. With supreme effort, he stopped himself and stood motionless in the middle of the taberna. The yellow spike protested, causing him to nearly pass out from the pain, but he leaned against the bar and told himself a hasty entrance could distract Brocchus at a critical moment. The pain receded a little, and he pressed onward.

Luciano peered into the back hallway just as the last of Brocchus' bodyguards fell, struck down by a club-wielding Harbor Man. He thought Brocchus looked absurd in an ill-fitting cuirass and leather cap, but then he noted the bloody fileting knives in his hands and the smile on his face.

With surprising speed, Brocchus charged, using his bulk and flashing knives to drive the Harbor Man back down the hall.

I guess he won't need my help, after all. I underestimated the fat bastard. Foolish. I should know better.

The Harbor Man was forced into a frantic retreat, desperately swinging his club to fend off the razor-sharp fileting knives. It was a clumsy defense, and Brocchus scored several bloody but shallow cuts.

Of course the fat sadist would toy with him.

Behind Brocchus, a woman emerged silently from a hallway door. She was beautiful. Something about her wild mane of dark hair and fierce eyes reminded him of a woman he knew a lifetime ago, a woman he had forced himself to forget. A woman whose memory the Dominator had used to enslave him. When he saw the dagger in her hand, the resemblance became uncanny. He saw Rhoswen, the only woman he ever loved. She raised her dagger, preparing to stab Brocchus in the back.

Luciano wanted to do nothing. He tried to do nothing. The spike in his head threatened to split his skull, boil his brains, and he prayed to Nyx for the strength to let it kill him. The warm trickle of blood from his nose and ears was a promise of freedom. He cried tears of joy, bloody tears. The Dominator had underestimated his will. He would stand and do nothing, and Brocchus would die.

Luciano flew down the hall, swift and silent as death. Aguja was already in his hand. He wanted to scream, but he had no mouth, no will of his own. The woman who was not Rhoswen shuddered and gasped as Aguja's slender blade pierced her heart.

Brocchus, who had dispatched his foe moments before, spun around with his knives at the ready.

"Porteles! Gods, you look like hell." He glanced at the dying woman at Luciano's feet. "Sweet Neesis, what luck! A moment later, and I'd be dead." He pulled a cloth from beneath his cuirass and began cleaning his blades.

Luciano kept his eyes on the dying woman. "Yes. Dead."

"Forget the whore, Luciano. What news?" He looked around conspiratorially, making sure they were alone. "Do you have it?"

"Who was she?" Luciano asked, now staring at a dead woman.

"The woman? Diantha, I think. We tried to recruit her." Brocchus looked down at the woman and laughed. "Made the wrong choice, I'd say."

Luciano tore his eyes away from Diantha's corpse. "I have the map."

"Thank the gods!" Brocchus heaved a great sigh of relief. "And the Elt?"

"Swallowed by a storm dragon."

"What?"

"As you said, such expeditions can be dangerous and unpredictable."

"The magus?" Brocchus asked.

"Dead."

"Good, good." Brocchus nodded along absently, Raquin and Vipsania already forgotten. He sheathed his knives and extended a pudgy, bloodstained hand. "Now, the map."

Without hesitation, Luciano handed over the Eltaran scroll case.

Brocchus seized it and carefully removed the map. He stared at it, wide-eyed, in an ecstasy of greed. "I'll be wealthy beyond all measure!"

Luciano simply shook his head and said, "No."

"No? No! What are you babbling about, Porteles?"

"Map worthless. A trinket now. How you say… a curiosity?"

Brocchus returned the map to its case. "Make sense or I'll have you flayed, damn you!"

"What use is treasure map when prize already taken, eh?" Luciano allowed himself a little smile before continuing. "All this trouble over map? No. All about a jewel. Called a gate-stone. Elts only want gate-stone."

"And where is this gate-stone?" Brocchus demanded.

"With Darktalon."

"And you let him take it?" Brocchus screamed.

"My orders were kill magus, kill Elt, get map."

Brocchus seemed to lose the capacity for speech. He just stood there gaping, his face twisting into a mask of rage and frustration.

Luciano burst into hyena-like laughter, then left to find the bar.

He needed something to scald his throat and fire his belly. Anything from Verdith would do, but there was only Trumin swill. He finally settled on a golden liquor imported from far Cearalon and downed half the jug in one long gulp. Luciano slumped against the bar and thought of the gate-stone.

It pleased him to think of the jewel in Ulric's hands, if only to spite the Imperaré prince. What he didn't understand was why the Dominator's curse had failed to compel him. The ever watchful spikes of torment should have driven him to steal it. True, his orders never included the stone. Brocchus didn't even know it existed. Yet Luciano never doubted he desired it.

Brocchus stormed out of the back hall, knocking over tables and chairs as he headed for the street. He paused and glared at Luciano as if he was considering new orders. Luciano stared back, then took another swig from his jug. The voices of approaching collegium soldiers interrupted the silence. Without saying a word, Brocchus left the taberna.

Luciano finished the jug, then tossed it aside. A half decent wine was needed now—the moment called for a celebratory drink. He had found the flaw in the Dominator's curse. It was Cornelius Brocchus.

The Imperaré prince had wanted Mist View's best assassin, not some mewling slave. Brocchus had said so himself. So the Dominator had left Luciano with his mind—and his hate. A hate that drove him to push the limits of the punishing yellow spikes. As with any poison, he had, by sheer will and a masochistic disregard for his own comfort, developed a tolerance for the Dominator's power.

It was a small victory, but it gave him room to maneuver. If he could be patient and subtle, he would steer Brocchus toward disaster.

Luciano uncorked a bottle of wine—an excellent vintage from southern Gauldé—and took a long drink. It tasted good. It tasted like freedom.

Julia had no idea how long she stood in the alley. She knew only that it was long enough for one last cry, long enough for the sea breeze to dry her tears. Why couldn't Ulric understand? It wasn't about his lies or whether she loved him. *I still do!* she thought. *Myrill Regina, Queen of the Gods, has summoned me. What would he have me do? Defy Her? The fate of those who defy the gods is quite clear.* She thought of the current high priestess, Pompilius Gemella, who narrowly avoided Myrill's wrath—and her predecessor, Octavia the Elder, who did not. And there was poor Medusa, of course. Julia shuddered.

Suddenly, the cool shade of the alley became gloomy and oppressive. Julia hurried back to the street and took a moment to relish the warmth of Alakur's light on her face. She took a deep breath, inhaling the scents wafting from the nearby popina. There was a soup heavy with tomato and basil that made her stomach grumble. It seemed like forever since she'd had a decent meal. Perhaps there was time for a quick bowl?

With a jolt, she realized she needed to catch up with Rexinda. Where was the Galatea docked? As she struggled to remember, she noticed a couple of rough-looking men loitering at the popina, watching her.

Perhaps a lone woman shouldn't wander the docks. But what have I to fear? I, who have faced the Wyrm?

Then another thought occurred to her: Did they overhear her breakup with Ulric? Was that why they were staring? Having battled gods from Beyond was no defense against embarrassment, so she hid herself within the folds of her palla and headed deeper into the Portus complex, where the bustling crowds seemed to fight against her at every turn.

How did Ulric move with such ease? I should have asked, but now it's too late.

Julia came to an abrupt halt, nearly causing a collision between a grain wagon and a parade of heavily laden dock workers. *Not even a hundred steps*, she thought, *and I'm thinking of him.* She tried to fight back her tears, but it was no use. Her guilt strangled her spirit like rank weeds choking a once beautiful garden, smothering all beauty, all joy, all life. She rushed out of the street, gasping for air. Her heart raced, pounding to a rhythm of regret, a drumbeat of shame.

Ulric had the gate-stone. He'd be a fool to give it to a man like Horatius Silo. And he'd be a fool to keep it. She feared the gate-stone was cursed: it could only bring disaster. He needed her now more than ever, and she had abandoned him.

Why couldn't Myrill give them more time? Julia had asked that very question, beseeching the goddess for answers that never came. Upon leaving the Eltaran temple, Myrill had given Julia one last command: to travel to the Kreslan Isles. Since then, silence. All that was left was a powerful longing to seek Myrill's temple in the great city of Kos. Julia could only surmise the goddess was still recovering from their battle with the Wyrm.

Where was Rexinda? Was she already aboard the Galatea? The thought made the tightness in her chest worse. She had been so nervous about speaking to Ulric that she had paid no attention when the barge captain had told them where to find the ship. She'd have to ask around and hope she didn't attract the notice of Silo's Harbor Men.

She pushed onward until she came across an enormous stack of crates piled high against the side of a warehouse. *They're arranged like steps,* she thought. *An easy climb. Maybe a better view will jog my memory?* The warehouse workers were busy elsewhere, so she climbed the stack and surveyed the port.

Julia stood on the south side of the hexagon-shaped harbor amidst a small city of docks, granaries, warehouses. A series of winding canals connected the inner harbor to the outer harbor, a vast basin carved from the coast and protected by two massive stone breakwaters. She felt dizzy just trying to take it all in. Through the morning glare, she could just make out the towering lighthouse at the harbor entrance.

It was no use. Julia had no idea where to find Rexinda or the Galatea. Overwhelmed, she clumsily descended the crates—

And fell right into the arms of her former bodyguard, Corvus.

With a look of astonishment, the giant Harbor Man caught her and sat her on her feet. "Praise Neesis, you're back!"

Julia rearranged her palla, nervously tugging at the green fabric. "Salve, Corvus. I am back, but for only a little while." She hesitated, fearing to divulge too much, but then decided—who better to help find the Galatea than a Harbor Man? "I'm leaving today, in fact."

"Now? But Ide's been worried sick. It'll break her heart."

Julia tried not to think of the friends she was leaving behind. "Have you heard of a ship called Galatea? Do you know where it's berthed?"

Corvus' eyes widened as a new thought occurred to him. "Where's Ulric?"

"Ulric? I… uh… he…" Julia stammered, unsure what to say.

Corvus' usually jovial face turned as dark and serious as a funeral procession. "He's not dead, is he?"

"Oh, no! No, he's alive and… well."

"Sweet Neesis, of course." Corvus relaxed and returned to his jovial self. "He's always been a lucky bastard."

"About the ship…"

"But where is he? Silo needs to talk to him, and I'm sure he wants to set things right with Silo."

"I'm sorry, Corvus. I don't know."

"Ah, that's too bad."

Something in his tone made her nervous. "If you can't help me, I'll have to move on. I need to find the Galatea."

As she turned to leave, Corvus put a huge paw-like hand on her shoulder. "Silo wants to talk to you, too."

Julia's dark eyes narrowed. "Unhand me. Now."

"Sorry, Julia." Corvus snatched his hand back, then motioned toward several Harbor Men emerging from the warehouse. "Silo's orders."

From behind the crates, Rexinda walked into view, her hand resting on the hilt of her Bayjoni saber. "To the hells with your orders!"

"Where have you been?" Julia asked.

"Securing our ship. And looking for you."

Corvus looked confused. To Rexinda, he said, "Whoever you are, walk on. You don't need to be a part of this."

Rexinda gripped the hilt of her saber. "Oh, but I am a part of this."

"Wrong, Corvus," said one of the Harbor Men. "Orders are we take in anyone who left with the magus. That includes the blonde."

In a flash, Rexinda drew her saber. She gave Corvus a feral smile. "See? I told you!"

"Rexinda, please." Julia hated the thought of more violence. Besides, she liked Corvus, and some of the Harbor Men were once Ulric's friends. "I don't want to hurt them."

"Hurt us?" The lead Harbor Man burst into deep, guttural laughter, which ended as abruptly as it began. "Take them!"

Julia stepped in front of Rexinda and called upon Myrill, fearful she'd be met with a dreadful silence. An instant passed like an eternity.

Then the goddess answered, divine power channeled from the Empyrean realm. It came in sparse, weak bursts, but it would be enough.

Golden, blinding light erupted from Julia's outstretched hand with such force it scattered the nearest crates and knocked the Harbor Men off their feet.

"Run!" Julia grabbed Rexinda's hand and pulled her into the street, where an astonished crowd was already gathering. "The ship?"

"Not that way!" Rexinda sheathed her sword and led Julia through the crowd. "This way."

They ran, quickly outpacing the few blinking, disoriented Harbor Men who gave chase. A short time later, they raced onto the deck of the Galatea, their hurried steps beating a desperate staccato on the wooden gangplank. Julia and Rexinda took a moment to catch their breath as the crew eyed them curiously.

Rexinda approached a man Julia assumed to be the captain and asked, "How soon do we sail? The sooner, the better."

The captain, a stocky Kreslan man with a kindly, sun-worn face, held out his hand. "As soon as you like, if what you promised is true."

Julia placed one of the Eltaran earrings Ulric had given her into the captain's hand. It felt like another betrayal.

The captain held the earring aloft, and the adamant flashed in the sunlight. "You were true to your word, girl." He secured the earring and stepped back. "Sorry. I can't do the same."

"What? What do you mean?" Julia asked.

The door of the sterncastle flew open and Gwynedd, Silo's primus, strode onto the deck, followed by a dozen or more men displaying the Imperaré scarlet. With a snarl, Rexinda drew her saber. Julia's heart fell. *Mother Myrill, have mercy! Is a fight inevitable?*

Gwynedd stepped forward, hefting his twin axes. His fire-scarred face was cruel.

"Where's Ulric?"

Ulric dashed through the crowds of the Portus complex, his hood pulled low to hide the shame of his tear-stained eyes. Finally, hungry and exhausted, he dropped on the bench of yet another dockside popina. Leaning on the counter, he looked at the painted menu on the wall with little enthusiasm. After a moment, he asked for a bowl of porridge and a bottle of posca—a poor, diluted wine infused with herbs and spices that wouldn't get him drunk nearly fast enough. He needed barrels of strong wine and bundles of red leaf. Or better yet, bags of shadow-dust and ice wind. Anything to make him forget. All he could do was cram down his meal and try not to think of Julia.

As he scraped up the last of his porridge, a burly dockworker sat at the bench and called for a bowl of crab stew. Ulric thought he was likely a warehouse foreman, given his thick frame, powerful voice, and air of authority.

Ulric raised a hand in greeting. "Salve, friend."

"Salve, traveler." The foreman took note of Ulric's small pack, acid-burnt cloak, tattered tunic, and unfashionable, bloodstained pants. "Looks like you've traveled through the Nine Hells."

"That's about right. Been away since the fifth day before the kalends of Sextilis." Ulric motioned across the Portus complex. "Feels like I missed something."

The man considered the implied request. "You dress strange, but there's an air of honest Trumin about you."

"I'm as true a Trumin as any man here. So tell me, why is everyone on a knife's edge?"

"You could say the city's on edge, after such a day of blood and foul omens."

Ulric sat up straighter.

"It was ten days ago, eight days before the ides. The night before had been hot, wet, and miserable. I remember, 'cause it was like trying to sleep in soup. The next morning, I awoke to rumors of murder, and then the gangs were slicing up each other in the streets, filling the gutters with blood. Before I could make any sense of it, the very gods themselves joined in!"

"You shouldn't speak of such things, Pontius," said the proprietor, fearfully shrinking back from the counter.

Pontius took the interruption as an opportunity to down two hasty mouthfuls of stew. He gestured toward the proprietor with his spoon, flinging bits of crab everywhere. "Bah! This young traveler needs to know." Turning back to Ulric, he continued,

"The skies filled with Alakur's rage. Thunderbolts blasted the city. Arakru and Ukorus shook the ground. Ulorin drove the very sea against us; parts of the outer harbor are still under repair. Odd thing is, the temples called for a celebration, saying the gods had won a great battle." He shoved another bite of stew into his mouth and mumbled, "Very odd."

"What of the gang troubles?" Ulric kept his voice steady, acting the part of the disinterested traveler.

"Soon settled, I think. And maybe not for the best."

"Careful, Pontius!" said the proprietor. "What if one of those thugs hears you? Don't bring trouble to my door."

"You complain like a woman! I'll say what I like. Those river rats will make a mess of Portus security. Silo was a right hard bastard, but he knew what he was doing. This Brocchus? Bah!"

"Wait!" Ulric leaped from the bench. "What's happened to Silo?"

"Some say dead, some say fled. Others say a prisoner. Hey! Wait! Where you run'n off to?"

Ulric ran, his heart hammering an incessant drumbeat of warning, his breath catching in his throat. He had returned to the city a traitor and enemy of the Imperaré, but he could change all that by presenting the gate-stone to Horatius Silo. Now he didn't know if the man to whom he had given his sacred oath was dead or alive. And if he was alive, where was he? A prisoner of the Transnanpela Collegium? Or long gone from the city? Finally, he stumbled to a halt, the crowds swirling about him in a blur of danger.

On the far side of the street, four blood-red scarves burst from the crowd like a sudden wound. The crimson meant Imperaré, and their tattoos marked them as members of enemy collegia. He had left the city a traitor. If he was searched, and the gate-stone taken…

He hunched down and kept pace with a train of carts loaded with amphorae, watching the men draw near through gaps in the tightly packed jars.

His heart slowed to the rhythm of shadows, his breathing quiet as whispers of smoke.

The men were arguing among themselves, waving their hands and stabbing the air. He tried to make out what they were saying, but he could hear nothing over the noisy crowd and trundling carts. Then they unexpectedly crossed the street and headed straight toward him.

Ulric froze. A simple hood was no disguise at all, and his tattered and bloody clothing would only arouse suspicion. Now that they were closer, he saw they were openly carrying arms in the Portum Mare district. A very bad sign. He needed to cross the street, but the endless parade of ox-drawn carts that had earlier shielded him now blocked his escape.

He turned and headed down the street, hoping to cross behind the last cart before the Imperaré men spotted him.

"You there! In the dark cloak! Hold!"

He walked on, as if the call had been for some other dark-cloaked stranger. Behind him, the crowd protested as the four men barreled through in pursuit. Ulric casually pivoted into a side alley, then burst forward at full speed.

It all seemed so terribly familiar. He was once again utterly alone in the city, a criminal among criminals.

Acknowledgments

Our heartfelt gratitude goes out to our spouses, whose unwavering support kept us motivated. We're grateful they tolerated our shared dream of writing a second fantasy novel instead of showing us the door. We could not have done this without you.

A special note of thanks to Derrick Cummings, as our developmental editor, for his keen insights on character arcs and the delicate interplay of relationships. A true professional and an invaluable second set of narrative eyes.

We are also indebted to Michael Hanna, who generously guided us through the nuances of Latin grammar and phrasing for both the text and the accompanying illustrations. Rest assured, any lingering Latin slip-ups stem solely from our own insistence on certain choices, in spite of his well-informed advice.

Lastly, we want to acknowledge the talents of Moreno Paissan & Angela Gubert for mapping the city of Trumric, as well as BMR Williams for charting the wider realm. Witnessing our setting come to life through their precise and beautiful renderings has been both humbling and inspiring.

Dennis is a 6th grade English teacher. He has dabbled in writing his whole life, but the *Fortune & Mercy* series is his first foray into novel writing. Dennis has previously written a children's book series titled "Azarah and Baldur." He lives in Texas where he is happily married and has three grown children.

Riley has created scores of characters and hundreds of scenarios as a roleplaying game enthusiast. *Fortune's Shadow, Mercy's Light* is his first foray into novel writing. Riley is happily married and lives in Texas with their cats, Cleopawtra and Clawdius.

Dennis and Riley have been friends since 1979. Their shared interests over the decades include comic books, cats, video games, roleplaying games, world history, and the literary works of Howard and Lovecraft. They watched *Return of the Jedi* together at the theater in 1983. They stood in line together at the mall for the release of the original Playstation in 1994. Notably, Riley has been the game master in an ongoing tabletop roleplaying campaign in which Dennis and their other friends have played since the early 1980's. The setting of that TTRPG was the inspiration for the backdrop of this book series.

FORTUNE'S TRIUMPH
MERCY'S REGRET

Ulric fled under darkening skies, and the storm followed. All signs of the pursuing men were soon lost in the rising gale and rattle of stinging rain. Ahead, Lucomo Square loomed. Should he cross it and enter the First Stones District? Or take the next canal bridge deeper into the Portum Mare? Was he looking for an escape route or a battlefield? Fight or flight? Did it matter when you were the quarry of a storm magus? The only thing he knew was that he had to face Modius Nero alone. He had to lure the magus as far from his friends and allies as possible.

A jagged white line split the sky, followed by a deafening crack that rattled the senses. In the corner of his eye, Ulric caught movement in the low swirling clouds, but when he looked there were only fading phantoms of light. Blinking furiously, he wiped the rain from his face and scanned the sky. There were only black clouds and hard rain. Ulric ran for Lucomo Square.

By the time he reached the square, the rain fell in thick sheets, and the thunder seemed to never cease. The sudden storm had driven nearly everyone indoors, and only a few stragglers remained. A man ran by, looking undignified holding his unfurled toga above his head to ward off the rain.

"Get indoors, you fool," he shouted. "This is no proper storm. The gods punish us!"

Ulric looked around, frantic. Behind him, down Canal Street, Brocchus' men were closing fast. To his right, a tightly packed row of buildings bordered the square, offering no clear way out. Far to his left, another high arched bridge led deeper into the Porta Mare District. Directly ahead stood the great Lucomo Column, a towering obelisk of granite, a gift to one of the last Trumin kings from a long dead Suhtean ruler. Beyond lay the way to the First Stones District with its well-ordered streets and great houses.

"Across the square into First Stones," Ulric muttered to no one in particular.

He reached the base of the obelisk and slumped to the ground, breathing hard against the wet marble.

Hunted by a storm? Absurd. I've run far enough in this damn rain.

Ulric stood and drew his sword. "Sweet Neesis, I've decided I'd rather fight." Ulric looked up into the rain drenched heavens. "If this madness pleases you, I'll need you to do your part."

A flash of lightning lit the square and shook the very air.

Brocchus' men ran into the square, looking soaked, angry, and ready for vengeance.

"Is that him?" one of them asked, pointing at Ulric.

"Yes," replied Igdir. "That's him." He approached Ulric, daggers drawn and raised. "Sorry. I've always had to go where the coin leads me."

He ignored Igdir and tried to calm his thoughts, seeking a blade-ecstasy. Instead of the clarity of the battle trance, all he found was the chaos of anger and loss.

The Imperaré men closed in, following Igdir's lead. Ulric tightened the grip on his sword and awaited the inevitable.

It came with a sudden tingling dancing along his limbs and the odd taste of iron filling his mouth. He had felt the sensation before! A comical look of surprise crossed Igdir's face as his dark hair stood on end.

"Run." Ulric warned. "Scatter, you idiots!"

He threw himself at Igdir and they hit the ground hard as a thunderbolt struck with shattering force.

The storm, the square—everything—vanished into hot light and noise. The cries of the dying melted into a single piercing tone. Ulric rolled off Igdir and tried to stand, but his legs were useless. He fell onto his back, staring into the sky. The sound of the storm returned, distant and hollow, barely a whisper above the ringing in his ears. All around him the Imperaré men had fallen, the nearest only crumpled smoking corpses but for him and Igdir. Ulric reached into his pouch and touched the gate-stone: it had the unnatural coldness that meant it had stolen much of the thunderbolt's power.

Ulric lay there, gathering his strength while cool rain pummeled his face. His gaze climbed the length of the towering obelisk, its granite surface thick with Suhtean writing. It was all nonsense bugs, birds, eyes, and squiggly lines.

Is bird-bug-bump-squiggly supposed to be a word? He wondered.

Something fell out of the sky and alighted atop the obelisk as lightning blasted the column.

Magus Modius Nero had found him.

A few Imperaré stirred and struggled to pick themselves off the ground. Ulric stood and helped Igdir sit up.

"You have to go. Now!"

"Trying," Igdir replied. He stood, massaging and thumping his numb legs. "Thought you wanted a fight?"

"You don't want to fight what's coming!"

Ulric watched Modius Nero step from the obelisk, a height twice that of a four story insula and plummet toward the ground and certain death. At the last moment, a whirlwind swirled out of nowhere and rose to meet him. At the center of a torrent of wind and rain, the man's sandaled feet lighted onto the paving stones as gently as if he had stepped out of a litter.

Ulric ducked behind the obelisk, hoping to stay out of sight until he could think of a plan, but he couldn't resist taking a closer look at the man that had nearly killed him. He crept to the edge and peaked around the obelisk base.

The magus was tall and slender, draped in a simple but expensive looking sleeveless blue tunic adorned with jagged silver trim and cinched by a wide golden belt. He had a handsome face marred by what Ulric guessed was a permanent sardonic scowl. His head of thick brown hair hung straight and heavy with dripping rain and the Lamp of Eltarus hung around his neck. A slender rod rested gently between the thumb and forefinger of each hand.

The magus surveyed the square, giving no more heed to the fleeing Imperaré men than he did to the raging storm. As he turned, the rods moved closer together until they touched in a shower of sparks. They pointed straight at Ulric.

The winds calmed, and the rain fell straight and steady.

"Ah, there you are!" Nero gestured with the two rods, then slipped them into the satchel at his side. "And the gate-stone? You have it with you?" Nero's voice was oddly lyrical, somehow compelling. He broke into a wide grin and lightning flashed in the distance.

Ulric readied his lies and began to speak, only to gag on a wave of nausea. Before he could understand what had happened, he said, "The gate-stone is here. In my pouch." He stared at Nero, astonished.

"Yes, that's right. There's no point trying to lie to me. I came prepared."

"So it's real? A spell that can unmask any lie." Such a spell had been long feared among the criminal elements of the republic.

"Oh, yes. In magica veritas! Cheaper than a bottle of wine, once you know the trick."

Brocchus' surviving men had slowly backed away, relieved to discover the magus had no interest in them. Only a few remained watching at the edge of the square.

Magus Nero thrust out his hand. "Now, hand over the gate-stone and you won't be harmed."

"I don't need a spell to know you're lying, Nero." Ulric reached into his pouch and grasped the stone. "I'd never give the stone to Vipsania's murderer!"

"Oh, don't look at me that way, thief! I didn't kill her. Well, not technically. Besides, you were there to rob her. You would have killed if needed."

"No! Not her."

"And yet… you have the gate-stone."

"She was dead when I took it. Killed by Flaccus—following your orders!"

"Oh, you would have robbed her anyway."

"No, I… I mean…" Ulric choked on his lies. He lowered his gaze, unable to look the magus in the eyes. "Yes."

"Did you kill in pursuit of the stone?"

"Yes."

"Did the gate-stone cost you something precious?" Nero asked.

Ulric wanted to lie, most of all, to himself, but a wave of nausea drove him to his knees. "Yes! Julia."

Modius Nero's triumphant grin melted into a look of pity. "Now you begin to understand. So don't you dare lecture me on the cost of power."

Ulric stood and revealed the brightly glowing gate-stone within his clenched fist. "You'll never have it."

"Do you know how easy it would be to blast you and collect the stone from your corpse? I don't think you do."

A long rod of shimmering blue metal, embossed and capped in silver, appeared in Nero's hand. The headpiece was solid adamant and sculpted in the visage of a fierce storm dragon with blinding white eyes. Lightning arced from its gaping maw and arcane symbols sparked across its surface. The wind howled and driving rain swept through Lucomo Square.

"It won't be as easy as you think," Ulric said. When he saw Magus Nero hesitate, he continued with a newfound confidence. "That's right! If I can say that, despite your spell, then you know it has to be true. Which means I know something you ought to know but don't. And that means—"

"Oh, by Eltarus' Lamp, I get it! Shut up!"

The dragon-headed rod spat death, filling the space between them with a thick bolt of white light.

DENNIS RILEY

FORTUNE'S
CLOAK
MERCY'S
BLADE

FROM THE SECRET SCROLLS
OF THE IMPERARE